Dark Winds

Dark Winds

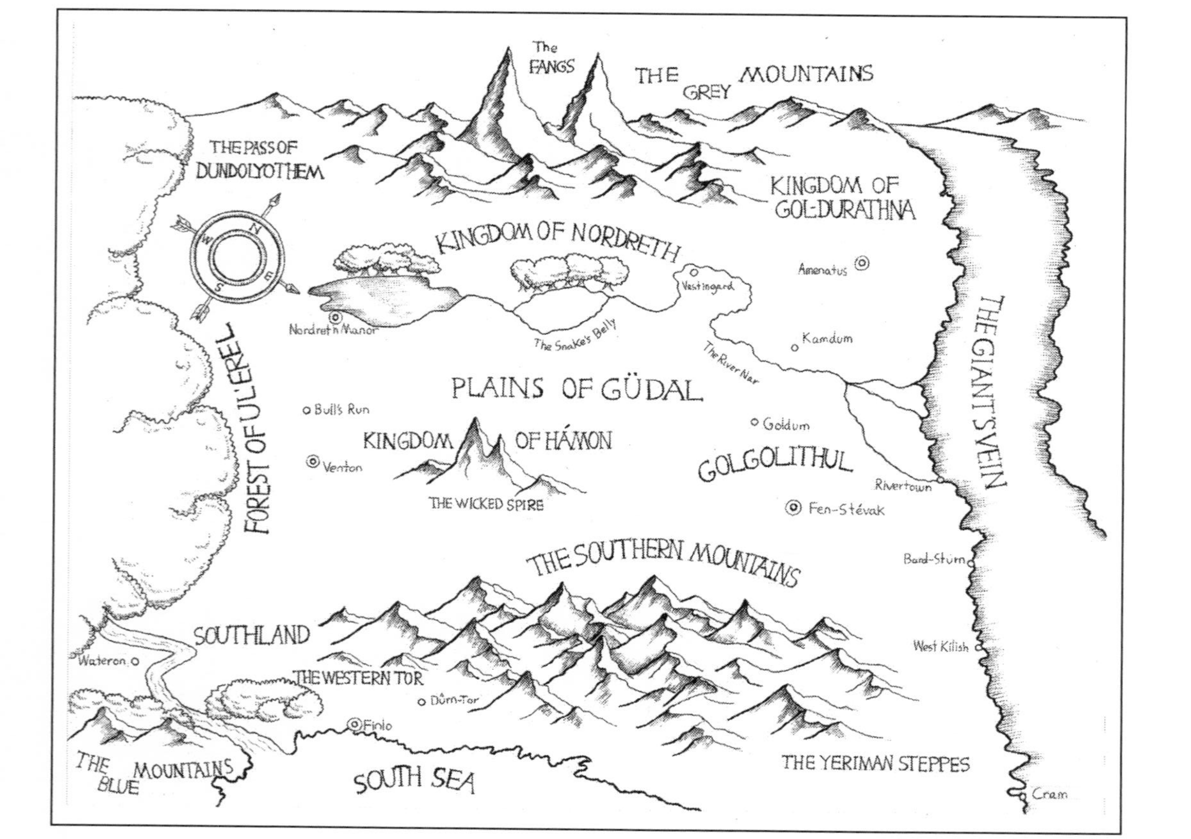

The FANGS
THE GREY MOUNTAINS
THE PASS OF DUNDOLYOTHEM
KINGDOM OF GOL-DURATHNA
KINGDOM OF NORDRETH
N
E
S
W
Vastingard
Amenatus
Nordreth Manor
The Snake's Belly
Kamdum
The River Nar
FOREST OF UL'EREL
PLAINS OF GÜDAL
THE GIANT'S VEIN
Bull's Run
Goldum
KINGDOM OF HÁMON
Venton
GOLGOLITHUL
Rivertown
THE WICKED SPIRE
Fen-Stévak
THE SOUTHERN MOUNTAINS
Bard-Stûrn
SOUTHLAND
West Kilish
Wateron
THE WESTERN TOR
Dûrn-Tor
Finlo
THE BLUE MOUNTAINS
SOUTH SEA
THE YERIMAN STEPPES
Cram

Chapter 1

ERIK HEARD THEIR BREATHING; DEEP and heavy. He knew they were there, standing over him, but he wouldn't open his eyes. Finally, he stared out, and there they were, just standing, swaying. They stared back, with white, lifeless eyes. They were beaten and twisted and burnt…and eaten.

What's happening? Erik felt his mouth move, but there was no sound, only thought.

They inched closer to him. He could feel cold toes touch his legs and arms, and he shuddered.

It's just another dream. Another stupid dream.

Their mouths began to move.

Why? Why? Why?

He could hear their thoughts, voices that screamed through his head like pigs going to slaughter. So many different voices with so much pain. He shook his head to rid it of the sound, but to no avail.

Why? Why? Why?

What are you talking about? replied Erik in his mind.

Why? Why didn't you save us?

Who are you? How was I supposed to save you?

He felt a tear at the corner of his eye, and as he wiped it away, he saw her standing before him, an accusing finger outstretched. He was the one. The guilty one suggested this little girl, her skin and hair as pale as her white, blank eyes. Tia? Was it Tia?

Why, Erik?

Another voice was whispering next to him. Deeper and the sound was much closer.

He looked to his right, and a gypsy man lay next to him. A gaping wound on his forehead seeped blood; he could see the bone beneath.

Why, Erik?

When the man spoke, his breath—hot and putrid—hit Erik's face. He wretched and felt vomit rise in his throat, but he could only swallow, and acid burned in his chest.

Why did you let me die?

The gypsy man's words crashed through Erik's head.

What was I supposed to do? he replied.

He continued to gag at the man's breath but then realized the gypsy's flesh was rotting, adding to the stench. Maggots crawled across the man's face, in and out of his flesh, his eye sockets were a squirming mass.

You let me die, the gypsy said.

Erik shook his head. He tried screaming, but the sound caught in his throat.

You let me die! This time, it wasn't just the gypsy, but a whole chorus of voices, echoing through his head and getting louder and louder.

You let me die! You let me die! You let me die! Why? Why? Why?

Erik felt something touch his foot followed by a strong tug at his pants. He felt strong claws dig into the skin of his leg and tried to lift his head, but it was too heavy. Finally, he looked down and saw him, his pale skin even lighter, his red hair a sickly pallid pinkish-white. Fox. The dead slaver's neck was twisted, all purple and blue.

Fox crawled up Erik's legs, his fingers digging deeper into the flesh and drawing blood where his pants had been ripped. He reached for Erik's belt, grabbed it, and pulled himself closer. The slaver's cheeks were gone, exposing bone, but still, Erik could see a smile that revealed black, rotten teeth. Fox was a slight man, but as he pulled himself onto Erik, he felt like a pallet full of stone. The dead slaver's skin was cold, sending a freezing chill through Erik's body.

The others—the ones standing—moved in, shuffling closer, and their presence suffocated him. He couldn't move. He felt Fox's head resting on his chest, then the bony, sharp fingers grasped at his neck, burning his skin like hot irons as Fox moaned low.

Then, suddenly, the fingers stopped moving, wrapped around his throat, and squeezed. Fox's face met his. His eye sockets were empty, but if Erik looked closely, he saw a faint, reddish glow amidst the darkness. Fox's mouth turned up into a rotten smile.

I will kill you, just like your cousin killed me.

It's a dream, Erik thought. *I can't die here.*

Fox laughed, a deep, raspy croaking laugh, and the others joined in, even the little girl who still pointed her finger at him.

Fool, Fox said.

Suddenly, the air was filled with the musk of incense, the perfume of rose buds. Erik looked up, and Marcus stood over him, Nadya next to him. Erik tried to plead for help, to reach for his friend, but his voice was silent, and his arms too heavy. The gypsy couple just stared at him as Marcus' face went from a pale, moonlit color to red as blood poured from every pore in his body. The same happened to Nadya as more gypsies stood around the couple. Then, as one, they moved in until their feet touched his body and they stared—just stared.

More slavers appeared, crawling on the ground like human-sized insects, and they clawed at the gypsies' legs and pushed them aside. They howled and hissed and spat and cackled. They ripped Erik's clothes and tore his skin as Fox squeezed even harder. He felt pain, unbearable pain. He had never felt pain in a dream before and opened his mouth to try and scream but as his lips and teeth parted, cold fingers shoved into his mouth and down his throat.

Erik's vision began to blur as all of the dead around him opened their mouths too. But instead of crying out, blood poured out and washed over him, searing hot and stinking. More blood poured from holes like sword wounds that multiplied rapidly over their bodies until they became walking, groaning mounds of coagulated blood.

Now a chorus of agony, screams, and pleas surrounded him, and every note shook his body and rattled his brain around his head like a stone in a metal bucket. Icy fingers pierced his eyes; his vision went black, and his breathing stopped. There was nothing. Only death. Black, icy, cold death.

The moon blazed as Erik opened his eyes and his body jerked. Tears streamed down his cheeks as he gasped for breath and grabbed his throat. Nothing. No blood. No scratches; just sweat and tears. He gave a heavy sigh as he wiped the tears away from his eyes.

Staring up into the nighttime sky, he could still see remnants of smoke blown in front of the moon by errant winds. They had camped away from the ruins of Aga Kona, for fear that mountain trolls would still be about, watching them, attacking them by the cover of night. Erik was glad to camp away from the tomb. It was, however, a thing of contention. Drake wanted to stay. He wanted to bury the dead, even if it took days. Befel and Bryon couldn't understand why he was so upset.

"These were his people," Erik had said. Miners. Their families.

They would have known some of the dead, certainly. This was the destination of the miners from Marcus' gypsy caravan. The smell of burnt flesh... the sight of burnt flesh had made Erik vomit, but he did it privately. The last thing he needed was Bryon chiding him for being childish. He wondered if his cousin even cared about the dead.

He looked to his side and saw Turk, sitting back on his haunches. His axe was gripped in one hand and his other hand touched the ground as if it steadied him. Erik lifted his head and tried to prop himself up on his elbows, but a hand caught his shoulder and pushed him back down. Switch pressed his face close to Erik's and put an index finger to pursed lips.

"Roll onto your stomach," Switch whispered.

"What..." Erik began to say, but Switch covered his mouth with his free hand.

"Be quiet, you stupid bastard," Switch hissed. "Roll onto your stomach and crawl next to Turk. Or close your eyes and go back to sleep. But shut your mouth either way."

Erik nodded, and Switch removed his hand from his mouth. Erik rolled onto his stomach, and as he was crawling towards Turk, he noticed Switch taking the same stance as the dwarf, a long-bladed dagger held in his left hand.

As Erik pulled himself next to Turk, the dwarf looked down at him and smiled. His face was clear in the moonlight, although his beard looked almost white; there was no mirth in that smile. The dwarf pointed two fingers at his eyes and then pointed out into the darkness.

Erik squinted as he sought to focus on whatever was beyond their camp, but despite the bright moonlight of a clear night, he saw nothing. He shook his head, rubbed his eyes, and looked again. Nothing. But then, the slightest of movements. A shifting of a subtle shadow like black smoke floating through an unlit room. And he saw it.

Yellow eyes, like a wolf's. The moonlight caught them just right, and they glowed in the darkness. That's when he sensed the eerie silence. Erik hadn't noticed it until now, but the typical chirping of nighttime birds, crickets, and the distant yelping of wild dogs had fallen quiet. Then he heard it. A loud sucking sound of air being drawn into a narrow tunnel. Sniffing.

The yellow eyes closed and, as Erik squinted, he saw the shadow of a large, human-like head tilt skyward. He heard the sound again. It was smelling, searching.

Erik felt his heartbeat quicken. He ducked low, pressing his face to the ground as if that would help keep him hidden. His hand moved, causing the slightest of sounds as dirt shifted. The sniffing stopped, and the eyes shot open, looking in their direction. Erik heard the crunching of dry grass under a heavy foot as the eyes moved closer. One step. Two steps. Another step.

"You stupid son of a bitch," Switch hissed and then began searching on the ground.

The thief's fingertips brushed through small tufts of grass until he stopped and picked something up—a rock the size of an apple. He threw it over to their left, and Erik heard the slightest thud. The yellow eyes swiveled away in the direction of the sound, and the shadow jumped like a cat trying to pounce on a mouse. There was a quick snort and then Erik watched as the shadow slowly moved away until he couldn't see it anymore.

Erik heard Turk breathe a sigh of relief.

"It's gone," Turk whispered.

"Are you sure?" Switch asked, also in a whisper.

Turk shrugged and then shook his head. Switch nodded, lay on his belly, and started to crawl forward.

"What is he doing?" Erik asked.

Switch glared back at him, over his shoulder. Turk put a finger to his lips. The dwarf moved closer to Erik.

"He is going to go see if it is gone," Turk said.

"Was that…"

Turk nodded. He knew what Erik meant.

"Will Switch be alright?" Erik asked.

"I think so," Turk replied. "He's a sly one, craftier than a troll."

"I suppose so," Erik said.

"Go back to sleep," Turk said. "Morning will come soon enough."

Erik shuffled back to where he lay before but had no desire for more sleep and found himself still awake as the sun rose and Switch returned.

"It was one of them alright." Switch spat, kicking a rock.

"A troll?" Befel asked from behind Erik.

"Blood and guts and ashes," Switch said, turning on Erik's brother hard. "What else would it be?"

"I saw it," Erik said, standing up again.

"You saw…" Switch began to say but then stopped as his face grew red and he walked so close to Erik that their noses almost touched and Erik could smell the thief's foul breath. "You saw it? You stupid shite. You almost alerted it to our presence. You nearly brought that thing down on us in the middle of the night. It and probably several more. You cause more trouble than you're bloody worth; you know that?"

Switch turned on his heels and looked straight at Vander Bim, holding two fingers in the air.

"This is twice these young rat turds have almost gotten us killed," Switch said. "I don't care what you say. The moment we have a chance, we're getting rid of them."

"That's not your choice…" Vander Bim began to say.

"You best keep your eyes on them," Switch said, stepping a little closer to Vander Bim. Erik could see Turk and Nafer walking behind Switch. "Things happen out here in the wild. People go missing at night. And don't think I don't know you two furry tunnel rats are behind me."

Switch turned to face Turk and Nafer and, as he walked by them, made sure to bump Turk.

"Were there more than one?" Vander Bim asked.

"We only saw one," Turk replied. "If it was a scout, I doubt there were more. But still, one troll would have been more than a handful in the middle of the night, even for us. They need but a small sliver of light to see as if it was midday."

"What do we do?" Drake asked. His eyes were red, and his face looked tired.

"Do we have a chance?" Vander Bim asked. "Are we going to find ourselves attacked in the middle of the night tonight? Or tomorrow?"

Turk just shrugged and turned to the other dwarves, Demik and Nafer.

"Even in the employ of men," Demik said, "they won't want to be away from the mountains for long. Trolls working for men. Disgusting."

"That worries you?" Vander Bim asked.

"Trolls are primitive, tribal," Turk replied. "They attack out of necessity. They ambush in groups of two or three at the most. And they never leave the mountains. Five or six trolls, working together in a coordinated attack, under the guidance of men…well; we have seen the devastation that can cause."

"These men," Erik said, "they would have to be powerful."

"Indeed," Turk replied.

"The Lord of the East?" Erik asked.

"Why would the bloody Lord of the East hire trolls to destroy his own mining camp?" Switch yelled. "Why are you talking anyways? Shut your trap."

"Relax, Switch," Vander Bim said, although Erik could see the gathering annoyance in the sailor's face as well. "What do we do now?"

"I would say we travel a league north of the mountains for a while," said Turk who didn't look annoyed at all. "It'll be hotter, but I doubt the mountain trolls will venture this far from the slopes again. What do you think, Vander Bim?"

"I suppose," the sailor replied, "if that is our only option."

"I think so," Turk said.

They broke camp, and as they continued east, Erik watched the Southern Mountains pass by, seemingly doing so more quickly now that they weren't right next to them.

"It's funny," Erik said, "how they look so simple, so much less intimidating."

"What?" Befel asked.

"The mountains," Erik explained.

"They still look intimidating to me," Befel replied, making arm circles and trying to work out the soreness in his wounded shoulder.

"I don't think so," Erik said with a smile. He knew that the hurt in Befel's shoulder made him grumpy, and he did his best to ignore it. "You can't see the large peaks and shadows, the rocky crags."

"Are you scared of shadows?" Befel asked. He certainly sounded irritated, and Erik could sense the chiding in his brother's voice.

"Now?" Erik replied, stopping to think for a moment. "Yes. After seeing one last night with its yellow eyes, I think it's smart to be afraid of shadows."

Towards noon, both the temperature and humidity of the Plains of Güdal rose. Erik felt the stickiness of sweat on his back, under his arms, and in between his legs and the horse's saddle. A salty droplet here and there would even sneak from the tip of his nose to his mouth and, through tiredness, it annoyed him more than usual. He just wanted to sleep... but then again, no. He wondered if he would ever look forward to sleep again.

Erik looked over his shoulder to find billowing gray clouds and thunderheads forming behind them, a chorus of chirping and crackling and clicking rising with them, the insects of the plains reveling in the high temperatures. Buzzing gnats were annoying, but flying stingers and ants were even more so, and Erik felt the red bumps rise along his arms and on the back of his neck as they began to itch.

"When we stop," Turk said, "I have a salve that will calm the itching of those bites."

"Thanks," Erik replied. "I try not to scratch them, but it's almost impossible."

"Well, until we stop," Turk said, "try not to. Open them up and make them bleed out here, and you'll find yourself with an infection."

"Right," Erik said with a nod.

"And, I have another salve that will help keep the insects away," Turk added. "Lather yourself up with that, and you'll find a quick reprieve from pestering stings and bites."

Erik heard a rumble behind him. Looking over his shoulder again, he saw the clouds growing taller and fuller and darker.

"Blood and guts and thunderstorms," Switch cursed.

"Do you think we can outride the storm," Drake asked.

"Doubtful," Vander Bim replied. "You don't realize how fast that storm is traveling. It'll be on us in no time—probably before nightfall."

"That's all we need," Switch continued, "to get bloody soaked while we sleep and ride around with wet clothes."

"Never being able to dry off in such a hot and humid climate; I'd be more worried about fevers and illness," Demik replied.

"Who decided we should travel here," Switch asked, "a league away from the mountains and where we can get rained on every night?"

"It was me," Turk replied defiantly, "and what does it matter if we travel close to the mountain or a league away? The rain will still reach us."

"The mountains would offer a bit of shelter," Switch argued.

"Would you like to trade the rain for mountain trolls?" Turk asked. "For the wetness we might avoid, we would have to contend with what you know very well is lurking in the shadows of trees and boulders just above the mountain foothills."

"Damn tunnel diggers," Erik heard Switch mutter as the thief kicked his horse hard in the ribs, spurring the animal forward and away from the rest of the party.

"Maybe, if it rains I'll stay awake," Erik muttered to himself.

The heat of the day finally subsided, and Erik shivered as he felt smatterings of water on the back of his neck. He couldn't tell if was sweat from his hair or errant raindrops carried by the strong wind.

Sleep, please stay away.

Erik shook his head, knowing it was a false hope.

Chapter 2

PATÛK AL'BANAN LOOKED OVER HIS shoulder for one last glance at Warrior. He hated going into battle without the giant of a war horse; the beast had proved almost more of a reliable weapon than his sword. Those hooves could easily crush a man's skull. But, being in the hills of the Western Tor, Warrior would have been more of a hindrance than a help.

A short time later, from behind a rock, Patûk watched as Terradyn interrogated one of Patûk's men. Patûk had not seen the Messenger's henchman for a while, and he looked as if he hadn't aged a day in the last twenty years. Patûk watched the large servant to the Messenger of the East remove yet another finger from his scout's hand.

Patûk growled but did not wince. To most, the interrogation might have been hard to watch, the large man mercilessly beating the two captors and removing appendages at will, and often they would die, and they would be glad for it. If the Messenger's enforcer let them live, Patûk would serve much worse —punishment for being captured.

"We move," Patûk whispered, looking to his personal guard, Bao Zi.

They inched closer, silently and unseen. The General looked to his left. Lieutenant Sorben Phurnan looked nervous. He should have left him behind, in the camp. He was becoming a liability.

Sorben seemed surprised when Patûk said he would be leading

the attack himself. But who would he put in charge? Sorben Phurnan? Certainly not. That would prove catastrophic. Captain Kan was east, towards the center of the mountains, and Lieutenant Bu was busy tracking fools willing to serve the Lord of the East. Bu would have proven an excellent commander for this skirmish. All in due time. Besides, it had been a while since Patûk had been in a fight, and he needed his men to see him in action. They needed to know he was still willing to shed blood. He needed them to respect him…and to fear him.

A scream caught Patûk's attention. He had been watching the ground before him as he inched closer, crawling on his belly and taking cover under brush and behind rocks. Staring through the thin branches of a yellow-flowered shrub that grew waist high and clothed itself in thin gray leaves, he watched as Terradyn drove his two-handed sword into one of his men's bellies. The captured soldier spat blood across the henchman's face as the Messenger's man lifted his blade. Patûk heard cracking as the blade easily cut through bone and eventually sliced through the soldier's shoulder, splitting him like a fileted fish. The other captor began to cry and shriek as his companion's intestines spilled over the ground and blood soaked his pants at his knees where he knelt before the large interrogator.

"Damn the gods," Patûk muttered.

He had planned on inching closer before they attacked, but the remaining captured soldier would talk now and reveal the location of the camp from where he came. Patûk's men were loyal and well-trained—all thirteen thousand of them—and the vast majority of them would withstand any interrogation, keeping their mouths shut in reverence of their devotion to the General. But Patûk had interrogated enough men to know when they were about to crack. This man—already missing a hand, both ears, the tip of his nose, and now staring at the entrails of his companion—was at that point.

Patûk nodded to Bao Zia, and his trusted guardian lifted a hand. It was the only signal the archer needed. An arrow passed through the remaining prisoner's neck, and he fell forward, dead. A quick command from Terradyn brought twenty soldiers forward, their shields interlocked in practiced precision. The ensuing volley of arrows bounced harmlessly off the steel that glared at Patûk's force with the emblem of the Messenger of the East.

Patûk Al'Banan prided himself in strategy, but even so, he had made a fair number of logistical mistakes in battle. Every military leader had. Only a few had proven disastrous, and he always made up for them with great victories and total devastation. This was quickly proving to be one of those miscalculations.

A frontal assault on one hundred Soldiers of the Eye was folly, even if Patûk's numbers were four times that, his men would struggle against the elite personal guard of the Messenger. But, he had no choice. They had captured two of his men—those fools—and, in order to protect vital information, Patûk had given up their position. Today would be a defeat, but it was to protect the resistance, the locations of his camps, and to put the Lord of the East on his guard.

"I am done hiding in the shadows," Patûk Al'Banan grumbled.

He nodded his head, and Bao Zi whistled. The arrows stopped, and full attack commenced. There was no battle cry, the General thought that stupid. Why have a bunch of men waste their energy screaming and yelling? Go to battle. Do your job. Kill the enemy and be done with it.

Four hundred men, led by Patûk Al'Banan and Bao Zi, raced down a gently sloping hill and towards the waiting forces of the Messenger of the East.

"Black magic," Patûk groaned as the sky above them grew dark and a thick fog rose before them. He spat into the dusty earth. "Cowards."

The fog that clouded their path did not hinder the vision of the Soldiers of the Eye, and as the ground around the feet of Patûk's soldiers moved and swayed, turning to mud, he knew his enemies' feet stood firm on solid ground. Rain began to pour down on the General's men, but it was not cool like the recent rains of the monsoons but hot as if some god above them was pouring water on them from a cauldron taken from a fire. He felt a few drops hit his face, and his skin sizzled. He felt the blisters rise almost immediately but ignored them.

"You have no honor!" Patûk yelled to the sky. "You never did!"

A boom of thunder cracked overhead, but it wasn't thunder—it was laughter.

That's when the screaming started. Arrows loosed from within the ranks of the Soldiers of the Eye found their mark among Patûk's men, and he knew they wouldn't just be arrows. They would burn or freeze the blood of the man they hit or turn him to stone—some further enchantment from Andragos.

"Bao Zi," Patûk Al'Banan said. His guard turned to him. "When we retreat, which we will have to, whoever from our ranks is captured, make sure they do not live."

Bao Zi nodded.

Patûk tried to lead his men around the wall of soldiers, hoping that they might flank them, but the Soldiers of the Eye had formed a box around their carriages. In honor of his eastern heritage, the General decided to attack the eastern flank. Perhaps the gods of Golgolithul would look kindly on him for doing so and give him some little semblance of a victory.

Man after man fell under the spear or sword of the Soldiers of the Eye. Patûk's force crashed and fell against the wall of soldiers like waves against a rock cliff. They were able to pull one of Andragos' men away from the wall, cutting him down even as he took four more with him. Bao Zi killed at least one. And the General killed three. The enemy were well trained, by the gods they were the best trained in all Háthgolthane, but they were not as well trained as Patûk Al'Banan. For every parry, he struck twice as hard and fast. For every feigned attacked, he predicted where the real attack would come from. And as one of Andragos' soldiers would plan three moves ahead, Patûk would plan six.

"You are a gutless pig, Terradyn!" Patûk Al'Banan shouted, watching the giant of a man stand behind the wall of soldiers and direct the fight. "Where is your equally craven companion, Raktas? Or should I call him Rat's Ass!"

"Why don't you come and find him?" Terradyn called back.

Patûk watched as a smile spread across the man's face as the wall of soldiers parted, offering up an opening and a direct path to Terradyn. The General was no fool, but many of his men proved to be. As they rushed into the opening, they met a swift end at polished steel.

Patûk nodded, and Bao Zi whistled. Flaming arrows flew through the sky, daring the burning rain. Two boulders, covered in burning brush, rolled down the hill. The arrows thudded into the ground and the boulders crashed by a parting wall of soldiers to strike a carriage and burst its wood into flame. The confusion was intentional and organic, and this smoke was not magic.

Even as a sudden wind rose up, blowing the smoke away from the Messenger's caravan, it was all Patûk needed to escape unseen. As he did, he claimed one last victim, a soldier that had broken from the ranks of his comrades. The General drove his sword hilt deep into the man's belly, retrieved his blade, and then—as the soldier fell to his knees—removed his head from his neck.

When Patûk Al'Banan felt comfortable enough to stop his retreat, he looked down upon the battlefield from a tall hillock covered in large ash trees. Nearly all four hundred of his men lay dead down there, some by his own men's arrows. It seemed a waste, all those men. But it was a necessary sacrifice.

"They now know we are strong," Patûk muttered, "and that we are no longer afraid."

"Yes, my lord," Bao Zi replied with a quick bow.

To many, this might have seemed an overwhelming defeat, but to have killed a tenth of the Black Mage's soldiers—if one *truly* understood the prowess and the Soldiers of the Eye—could be measured as a victory.

Patûk watched as Andragos emerged from his wagon. The fires had died, and the dead were now piled in a large heap, the wreckage of the carriage with them. The Messenger walked about the battlefield and approached one of his soldiers. The man looked injured, clutching his stomach and crimson covering his legs and arms. The Black Mage touched the man's shoulder, and the soldier stood straight, uninjured and strong.

"Black magic," Patûk grumbled yet again.

Andragos looked in the General's direction. Patûk's keen eyes thought they saw a smile creep across the Messenger's face.

"You couldn't possibly see me," Patûk said. But then, he realized it was the Messenger of the East he was talking about. "Well, if you can see me, then you can hear me. Know this, we are strong, we have allies in the east, and we are no longer hiding in the shadows."

"Are you all right, my lord?" Terradyn asked.

Andragos sighed.

"Just tired," he replied as he rubbed his temples with his thumb and forefinger. "Magic seems to take more out of me than it used to."

Andragos could feel Terradyn staring at him. He looked up, straightening his back a little. He couldn't tell if the concerned look on Terradyn's face was one of fear or concern.

"I'll be fine," Andragos said with an insincere smile. "What are our casualties?"

"Ten, my lord," Terradyn replied. "It would have been eleven, but you... Why did you heal him? He could have been replaced."

"It seemed the right thing to do," Andragos replied with a shrug. "Do you think I am getting soft after all these years?"

"Hardly, my lord," Terradyn said. His voice sounded defensive.

"I'm assuming the interrogation yielded no results," Andragos said.

"No, my lord," Terradyn replied, shaking his head.

"I didn't think it would," Andragos said. "A waste of time. More eastern blood spilt."

"Traitors, my lord," Terradyn said. His voice was now hard, stoic, and proud. "Hardly easterners. They turned their back on Fen-Stévock. They turned their back on their lord. I gutted one while the other wept and pissed himself and then..."

"Then Patûk had him killed." Andragos finished Terradyn's sentence. Then his voice dropped to an inaudible whisper. "Is it so hard to imagine someone turning their back on Fen-Stévock?"

"What was that, my lord?" Terradyn asked.

"Nothing," Andragos replied. "We will have to replenish our ranks when we return home."

"There are plenty willing to serve," Terradyn replied.

"Aye," Andragos said, "but I think I might be more selective this time."

"My lord?" Terradyn said.

"You admonish these men for turning their backs on Fen-Stévock and their lord," Andragos said.

Terradyn bowed in response.

"But whom do you serve?" Andragos asked.

"You, my lord," Terradyn replied.

"And who do the Soldiers of the Eye serve?" Andragos asked.

"You, my lord," Terradyn replied again.

"You—and they—do not serve Fen-Stévock and the Lord of the East?" Andragos asked.

"Well, of course," Terradyn replied. "But, so do you, my lord."

"Aye, but who do you serve first?" Andragos asked.

"Well, I serve you first, my lord," Terradyn replied.

"And Raktas?"

"He serves you first as well, my lord," Terradyn replied. "My lord, forgive my brazenness, but what are you getting at?"

The look on Terradyn's face was one of true concern. Andragos let the man stare for a while and then finally shook his head with a smile.

"Do not trouble yourself with my inane questions," Andragos said. "Patûk Al'Banan has become bold."

"We will follow him," Terradyn replied. "We will track him and kill him."

"So easily?" Andragos asked.

"My lord?" Terradyn replied with a question of his own.

"He, alone, killed five of my men," Andragos explained, "and his servant, Bao Zi, killed another two. Two men killed twice as many soldiers as it took four hundred to kill. He is a cockroach. You can step on him, poison him, crush him, and he will live on. We are only ninety, plus you and Raktas. He is...How many men does he command?"

"Our last intelligence says ten thousand, my lord," Terradyn replied, "but that was several years ago. It could be more."

"We are outnumbered," Andragos admitted. "It would be too much, even for the Soldiers of the Eye."

"Even with you?" Terradyn asked. "With your power?"

Andragos laughed silently.

"It will take me a while to regain my full power, Terradyn," Andragos said. "I feel drained. It is odd, I suppose. I have never felt this way. But I might prove a hindrance, as my soldiers would sacrifice themselves to protect me. No, we will continue to Fen-Stévock, and we will report back what has happened here."

"And what exactly will we report, my lord?" Terradyn asked.

"We will report that Patûk Al'Banan is growing strong and bold," Andragos replied. "We will report that winds of change are on the horizon."

Chapter 3

"I COULD DO WITHOUT THESE damn bugs," Bryon muttered. He slapped his neck hard. He missed whatever six-legged creeper had been resting there and winced at the quick sting. He heard Erik chuckle. "What are you laughing at?"

"Nothing, cousin," Erik replied. "I just think it's funny, you constantly slapping yourself."

"I'm so glad my misery amuses you," Bryon said.

"Oh, please, cousin," Erik said. "Your misery is self-inflicted. Ever since I used Turk's salve, I've barely felt a bug. Befel too."

"Yeah, well, you both smell like shit," Bryon retorted. "Befel even more so because of that cream the dwarf has him put on his shoulder too."

"Maybe," Erik replied with a quick shrug of his shoulders. That look of indifference that Erik had been giving recently, especially to Bryon, infuriated his cousin. "But at least we don't look like idiots, slapping ourselves every few moments."

"At least I don't smell like pig shit," Bryon replied. He glared at Turk. "I'll not give in to their tricky ways."

Erik shook his head and rode away from Bryon.

"You're the reason I left the farm," Bryon muttered as something buzzed about his ear. "You and days after days of grueling work in the sun. I don't know if this is any better."

He tried to swat a bug and almost fell out of his saddle. He heard Switch laugh.

Bryon felt his face color with embarrassment. He hated that man. Was this any better indeed?

But it was an improvement because the end result would be better. Gold. Women. Fame. Days of hard work and abuse on the farm meant nothing, just more of the same on the morrow.

The clouds built early the next day, shading the men and dwarves just past noon and bringing errant sprinkles of water. A distant wall of rain covered everything under the clouds. There was no horizon, only grayish-blue that Bryon knew was a downpour that would be flooding the already soaked Plains of Güdal. The bottoms of those thunderheads looked black, casting a premature night just several leagues behind them. Then, the clouds that billowed skyward turned white like goose down or freshly cleaned cotton. At the very top of the ever-growing clouds, the sun's rays fought through, illuminating the edges of white with golds and reds.

As the day darkened, and the sun fell farther behind the clouds, the pretense of light and goodliness, given by the feigned aura the sun created behind the clouds, finally faded. More and more smatterings of quick rain wet them; clouds that traveled on an especially quick gust of wind reached them first.

"Is it time to make camp?" Bryon asked.

"No," Befel replied. "It's barely afternoon."

"It's so dark," Bryon said.

"The clouds are thick," Befel added.

"Clearly," Bryon said. He felt sour.

"No need to be short with me, cousin," Befel said, and before Bryon could retort, added, "just because Switch gave you a tongue lashing earlier."

"I'll beat you bloody," Bryon said.

"I don't think you will," Befel replied.

"You son of a..." Bryon tried to say, but Befel cut him off.

"Careful, Bryon," Befel said, "we come from the same family. Cursing me and my origins does the same to you."

The smile Befel held on his stupid face was all Bryon could take. He took in a deep breath, ready to yell, jump from his horse, and throw Befel from his, but a shout from Switch stopped him.

"Sard! Stint your damn claps!" Switch yelled. "I see something ahead. You see it too, tunnel digger?"

Turk nudged Nafer, and the two nodded to one another.

"What is it?" Erik asked.

"I said, shut your damn mouth," Switch hissed, never taking his eyes off the horizon ahead.

Bryon leaned forward in his saddle, happy that it was Erik who now took a tongue-lashing from Switch and not him; not that he was afraid of the Goldumarian. He didn't see anything until something in the distance flickered.

"Is that a torch," Bryon muttered.

"Blood and guts and village idiots," Switch cursed.

Then, Bryon saw it, as if a shadow from the ensuing clouds had somehow hidden it. But suddenly it was as clear as day. Evidence of a small village glared like a blinding beacon in the darkness of a stormy afternoon. The faintness of torch fire began to come into view, and there it was.

"Is that bad?" Bryon asked no one in particular.

"I guess it depends," Drake replied.

"On what?" Bryon asked.

"On whether or not they want to kill us," Drake replied.

Bryon saw a mill, a barn, some homes, a great hall with gray smoke spilling from the ceiling, and rows of crudely made, wood colored fences—perhaps a wall.

"I doubt this place even has a name," Bryon said.

"Maybe not to us," Drake replied, "but the inhabitants here most certainly have a name for their little hamlet."

"You sound worried," Bryon said.

"Aye," Drake replied. "You never know in these little villages. The small folk that live in these places are often a proud people, unawares of anything going on in the world around them. And they fear anything that challenges their own little domain. They can often be very untrusting and violent towards outsiders. They'd as soon kill you as feed you."

Unaware of anything going on in the world around them... Bryon decided that sounded like himself before he left the farm.

"The thought of a warm, cooked meal is a good one, though," Bryon said.

"Aye," Drake said, "but if they offer one, make sure you check for rat turds and rocks."

The thought made Bryon grimace, but then he smiled.

"The thought of a soft farm girl sounds nice as well," Bryon added with a boyish grin. "I know how pleasant that can be!"

Drake looked at Bryon, meeting his eyes with his own.

"You keep your cock in your pants and your mind on the mission, you little shite," Drake said. It was the first time the man had ever been short and direct with Bryon, and it took him by surprise.

"They find you sticking one of their daughters, or worse, you get one of them pregnant, and you'll find yourself in a place that is worse than the hellish halls of the Shadow. If you know these people so well, you know how serious they take that sort of thing. They'll beat you, rape you, and cut your balls off before they kill you, and that's if they're being nice."

Bryon swallowed hard. He tried being defiant at first. What could some village ass do to him, but Drake spoke the truth. He couldn't imagine what his father would have done to some traveler who he caught sticking one of his sisters. He couldn't imagine what he would have done to someone he caught. They were annoying little cumberwolds, but they were his sisters.

"Halt," Vander Bim said.

"Damn it," Switch hissed.

Bryon wondered who or what Switch was cursing at, but then he saw a dozen flickering lights moving towards them. Torches.

The men holding those torches soon came into view. Bryon recognized these men—scared farmers and small folk, carrying whatever weapons they could muster from pitchforks to wood axes. Men like his father, his uncle, and his grandfather. He used to be one of them too. He couldn't much see their faces in the failing light and in the distance, but they didn't look happy to see them.

"Peace!" Vander Bim yelled, cupping his hands around his mouth. "We come in peace! We mean you no harm!"

The small mob of villagers didn't stop. In fact, Vander Bim's calls seem to spur them on faster. Bryon saw Turk put his hand on his axe. He saw Drake ready his pickaxe and Switch retrieve two of his many daggers from their hiding places. He even saw his cousins rest their hands on the handles of their swords, as if they would make a difference.

"Oh, here we go, boyos," Switch said. There was a hint of glee, pleasure even, in his voice. "You boys ready for a fight. I am."

"A fight is the last thing we need right now," Turk said, and Drake gave him a grunt of agreement.

"Speak for yourself," Switch replied. "I need to let off some steam."

When the villagers came into full view, they slowed down until they all together stopped. Bryon could see them talking amongst themselves, heard their mutters and warbling, and couldn't help thinking that they looked apprehensive at best, maybe even scared.

A very tall and broad-shouldered man walked to the front of the group of villagers. He was truly a large man, and when he looked to Vander Bim, he lifted his chin.

"We mean you no harm," Vander Bim said. "We're just looking for shelter from the rain."

The rain had started to fall steadily, and Bryon felt rivulets of water run down his back. His hair matted around his face, and he constantly blew water from his moustache. The large villager didn't answer for a moment, and then he spoke in a language Bryon didn't understand. From Vander Bim's look, he didn't understand either. Bryon did notice, however, Turk looking up as the villager spoke. He whispered to his dwarvish companions.

As the dwarves spoke, Vander Bim continued to try and communicate with the villagers, but he only seemed to make things worse.

"I don't think they understand you, mate," Drake said.

When Vander Bim turned in his saddle and lifted a hand with his forefinger and middle finger extended—an impolite gesture meant for Drake—a shout came from the villagers, and they lowered their makeshift weapons.

"A little bold for lowly villagers," Switch sneered, looking at a lowered boar spear pointed at his face. "How many do you think I can kill before I get a scratch?"

"Stop it," Vander Bim replied in a whispering voice. "You're only agitating them more."

"Good," Switch said with a smile of finality. "Besides, if you haven't noticed, they can't understand us anyways."

The presumed leader of this band of villagers spoke in hurried tones to his companions. They all replied and then inched forward.

"Here we…" Switch began to say, but Turk's voice cut him off, an unusual gruff tone to it.

"Shut up," Turk snapped, leaning forward in his saddle. Then, he said something in Dwarvish.

"What are you get—" Switch began again, but this time, Demik drew his broadsword and pointed it at the man.

"Shut your damned mouth," Demik hissed, "before I run my steel through it and jam what little brains you have out the back of your skull."

Switch closed his mouth hard as his face turned red. He shrugged in his saddle and stayed relatively quiet, but Bryon could hear the man cursing under his breath.

"I'd like to see you try it, you little bearded maggot," Switch whispered through his teeth, so low that Bryon had to strain to understand him.

As Turk spoke again, the village leader appeared to listen as if they shared the same language.

"What, by all the gods, has this world come to?" Switch asked no one in particular, although Bryon overheard him. "Men speaking Dwarvish. Never thought I'd see the day."

"You're a fool," Drake replied. He must've heard Switch as well.

"Oh, look who decides to chime in," Switch said. "All bloody good, but can you even read?"

"What does that matter?" Drake asked.

"You're no better than these small folk," Switch replied. "Can't read. Don't know your asshole from a hole in the ground. Is your wife your sister?"

"Coming from a dirty street rat," Drake retorted, "that doesn't mean much."

"You don't have the balls to do what you know we should do," Switch said.

"And what's that?" Drake asked.

"Command them to feed us," Switch replied. "Lead us to some farm girls. Been awhile since I've shagged."

"You're foul," Drake said, his lip curling.

"Piss on your grave," Switch cursed. "You're lucky we're not by your little village. I'd be shagging everything in sight. How would that make you feel, watching me stick your sister…or your wife."

Before Drake could leap off his horse and wrap his strong hands around Switch's throat, the village leader nodded and motioned to Turk. The dwarf clearing his throat to get everyone's attention.

"Let me take the lead, Vander Bim," Turk said.

The sailor paused for a moment and then relented.

"That's all we need," Switch grumbled, "a bloody tunnel digger in charge."

The villagers surrounded the party, escorting them to their hamlet.

Bryon smelled a familiar smell, the thick scent of tallow. Looking down, he saw a man next to him holding a torch. He suddenly felt the heat from the torch, especially in the rain as it picked up and began to bear down on them harder with each passing moment. The flame sputtered in the wetness but burned strong, and that strong smell of cow fat hit Bryon's nose like a fist, bringing back memories of home, reminding him of the smells of his mother's kitchen, her mint garden, and his father's orange brandy. Bryon's stomach twisted and knotted.

The tall villager spoke again, his voice resonating from deep within his keg of a torso and bull's neck. His voice was curt. He didn't seem angry, but he spared little civility on Turk, even if the dwarf could understand the man's language, at least somewhat.

"What are they saying?" Vander Bim asked.

"It's hard to completely understand them," Turk said with a quick shake of his head. "Their language is similar to our southern dialect of Dwarvish, but not the same. I think they are harboring some of the survivors from Aga Kona."

"Survivors?" Drake asked, spinning around in his saddle.

"Aye," Turk replied. "A large group of them came upon this village—they call it Stone's Throw—just yesterday. These men thought we were the same soldiers who had attacked Aga Kona. They thought we were leading the trolls."

"So what do we do, tunnel digger?" Switch asked.

"They're concerned about giving us shelter," Turk replied, give Switch an irritated sidelong glance. "They don't know if they have the resources to feed us, and they don't know if they trust us."

"What's not to trust?" Switch asked.

"You," Demik replied.

"They are a simple people," Turk said, "who barely make a living here in the Plains of Güdal, carving out an existence against terrible odds. They are alive because they don't trust most people."

"They think they don't have enough food?" Vander Bim questioned. "Tell them we have our own rations."

"And what of their distrust of us?" Drake asked.

No one seemed to have an answer.

"Tell them we'll give up our weapons for the night," Bryon said. It seemed a good idea, and he didn't see a need for weapons around these people. He knew these people. They were traditional, lowly farmers simply trying to survive.

"I told you to shut your bloody mouth," Switch hissed.

"That's a good idea," Vander Bim said.

"Are you daft?" Switch asked.

"Will you stop your constant bitching!" Vander Bim shouted, turning halfway in his saddle. "I want to get out of the rain and away from the prying eyes of trolls. And if I have to give up my sword for a night while we sleep amongst innocent country bumpkins, then so be it."

The villagers seemed startled by Vander Bim's shouting, but Turk spoke with the leader nonetheless. The large man didn't say anything for a while and then nodded. The leader turned and walked closer to the village, between some sticks stuck into the ground and sharpened at the end sticking out.

"A meager barricade," Bryon said, "considering what the mountain trolls did to Aga Kona."

"It's all they could muster, I bet," Drake said. Bryon could hear sadness in his voice.

As they passed through what Bryon presumed to be the front gate, the villagers that had escorted them collected their weapons. Bryon saw Erik stuff his jeweled dagger into a saddlebag. He didn't blame his cousin. That was a prize even an honest farm boy might find hard to resist. Then he saw Switch, slowing his horse and dropping to the back of the company. No doubt he was stuffing any number of daggers and knives away to someplace no simple villager would think to look.

A pretty farm girl came to fetch their horses. The rain had plastered her dark hair against her face and soaked her dress so that it clung tightly to the curve of her breasts. Bryon couldn't help staring, but she caught his eyes, snapped her fingers, and pointed angrily. Bryon felt like a boy being scolded by an older schoolhouse teacher.

"Oh, son, you got caught," Switch said with a whistle, and as the girl passed by him, he winked and pinched her behind, also prominent under a wet dress.

When the girl turned hard and glared, Switch smiled and blew her a kiss. A younger village man walked up behind her and also glared at Switch. The Goldumarian could have cared less, pressing past both of them and making sure to nudge the man with his shoulder.

He means to get us killed, Bryon thought.

Chapter 4

THE MAIN HALL OF STONE'S Throw was nothing more than a large home that had been converted to a meeting place. A fire raged in the hearth, the only stone fixture in the whole structure. Even though only several dozen men and women crowded the hall, it might as well have been a hundred. At first, Erik found the warmth of the raging fire and bodies crammed together welcoming, a stark contrast to the cold of the raging storm outside. Now, it seemed unbearable.

"How much longer will this thatched roof hold up to the storm?" Erik wondered as another boom of thunder shook the walls of the hall and the glow of lightning flashed through the cracks of the room's doors.

"I think that roof has held up much longer than you would think, Erik," Demik replied.

A broad-shouldered man with a barrel chest and a large gut sat in a chair in front of the hearth. His bushy white beard spread over his chest haphazardly. This man clearly sat in a place of leadership amongst the people of Stone's Throw, but he looked sickly and immobile. His breathing was labored, and a gurgling grunt accompanied every breath.

"Is he their leader?" Erik asked Demik while Turk stood in front of the fat old man being interrogated. "Their chief?"

"Yes," Demik replied in a hushed whisper. Whenever one of the village men or women caught them speaking, they would glare at the two with disapproving eyes.

"Some leader," Erik muttered.

"Looks can be deceiving, Erik," Demik replied.

That was truly a lesson Erik had learned more than once since he had been away from home. Marcus' face popped into Erik's head, and he smiled. Then, he remembered a dream when Marcus' kind face had turned white and pale, his kind eyes blank and unknowing.

The fat chieftain leaned forward, trying to fight against his own girth, and spoke to Turk in a gruff, harsh tone. Spittle collected at the corners of the man's mouth and every half dozen words, he had to stop to take an extra-large breath. As his eyebrows frowned, the white tufts of hair shadowed his piercing, blue eyes, making them look even harder. They were judging eyes: Those were the eyes of Hámonians who watched his father ride into Bull's Run with his harvest in tow. Those were the eyes of nobles passing by in Venton, watching him throw slop to pigs. Those were the eyes of the people of Waterton, watching Marcus' gypsies with fearful glances.

"What is he saying?" Erik asked.

"The man who led us into Stone's Throw is named Arynin Flatenfer," Demik replied. "This man who is their chieftain is Arynin's father, also named Arynin."

"He sounds angry, this Arynin the Second," Erik whispered.

"He is," Demik replied. "And stubborn and unyielding. He thinks we are spies and collaborators of trolls."

Erik paused a moment as the elder Arynin stopped interrogating Turk and the younger one picked up.

"But, you're dwarves," Erik said.

"I hadn't noticed," Demik said with a smile. "They are accusing the Southern Dwarves of being distant, discourteous. They are accusing us of breaking an ages-old pact between Stone's Throw and Drüum Balmdüukr."

"A pact?" Erik asked.

"Who knows?" Demik replied. "Certainly, these men had, at one time, traded with dwarves. Their language tells us that much. But a pact…it is doubtful. And if there was one, it is long passed, before this fat one's great grandfather. They are angry and, even more importantly, scared."

"Of what?" Erik asked.

"Trolls. Men. Dwarves. Thunderstorms," Demik replied. "This is a small village, and these are small folk with big superstitions."

Stone Throw's chieftain cut off his son as Arynin the Second grew loud and animated. This time, as the chieftain spoke, his voice was softer and calmer.

"The chief doesn't believe we are spies. He even apologized for the accusation," Demik explained as Turk bowed several times.

"He says that, despite Stone's Throw being a small village, An has blessed them with many young ones, so they are hopeful for the future. But his people are scared," Demik added. "The survivors from Aga Kona have depleted their stores of food and fresh water, and they do not have the ability to care for all the injured and sick."

"Does the Chieftain want us to help with the injured and sick?" Erik asked.

"Aye," Demik replied. "And he wants to make sure that all of the village's virgins remain virgins while we are here."

"They'd never know." Switch's whispered response caught Erik by surprise. The ever-eavesdropping thief had sneaked up behind them.

Turk nodded several times and bowed low again to the Elder. Arynin scratched his bearded chin and stood, speaking.

"Formalities," Demik said with a shrug. "He is saying that we can only stay here tonight and that we must help the sick and injured. He is making sure that his people know this is his command."

Turk bowed low again, and Vander Bim followed suit. As the Elder and his son left the hall, an older, gray-haired woman began serving a meal to the mercenaries—hard bread and vegetables that were undercooked, but they were hungry and ate it despite Bryon's grumblings.

"Well, shall we go see these survivors and see what we might do for them?" Turk asked as they finished their hurried meal.

Arynin's son met them at the door of the mead hall, the rain coming down at a steady pace as the thunder and lightning passed them over and traveled north. He led them to a large longhouse outside which, two men, little more than villagers armed with boar spears, stood guard.

"By the Almighty, what is that?" Erik put his arm to his nose.

"Sickness. Death. Fear." Demik looked at the young man and gently grabbed his wrist, lowering his arm from his nose.

Erik didn't understand at first, but then he saw him—a little boy of no more than five. His face was covered in dirt and blood. The boy looked numb and ignored the dwarves and men as they walked into the room. He just stared into space. His clothes hung in tatters from his shoulders, and he looked skinny, sickly. His right hand clutched his left close to his body, only... there was no left hand. Just a stump wrapped in what once was white cloth, now brown with the color of dried blood.

The longhouse was relatively quiet, despite thirty or forty women and children crowding its floor, sleeping on tables covered in straw and in makeshift cots. Erik heard only the whimpers of children, a baby crying, and a mother quietly singing what was perhaps a lullaby.

Turk turned to Arynin and spoke to him in Dwarvish. Erik looked to Demik.

"He is asking for some supplies," Demik said. "Herbs, village medicines, and the like. Your cousin needs to go with Arynin to help gather what Turk needs. You and your brother will gather water and bread. You will feed and give water to these people. Only water and bread, nothing more."

Erik heard Bryon sigh and groan, but as Arynin left the longhouse, he followed. Erik found two water pails sitting in the corner of the building. He handed one to his brother.

"Sailor, you will help us with the bandages," Turk said. "Miner, help the sailor. Thief... where did the thief go?"

It didn't surprise Erik that Switch was nowhere to be found.

Erik gathered rainwater while Befel retrieved bread from the mead hall and then they went about the longhouse giving some to each person. One little boy who spoke Westernese asked for butter.

"I'm sorry my little fellow," Erik said, patting the little boy on the head.

"But bread always tastes better with butter." His whine was piteous.

"I know, but there isn't enough for everyone, and if you're to get any better, you can't have butter. Just plain bread and water. And Turk and Demik and Nafer over there will make you right as rain, and after that, you can have butter on your bread."

"Will they make Davey better too?"

When the boy said that, the woman on whose lap he sat—a spitting image of the boy—started to whimper, tears running down her cheeks.

"And where is Davey?" Erik smiled at the boy and gave him another piece of bread.

"He's back in the camp. He told us to run. He was well when we left, but I'm sure he's hurt. He's big and strong, he is. He's eight, you know. But even so, I'm sure he needs some tending."

Erik's stomach knotted. The dried bread and water he had eaten and drunk rose in his throat. The boy's mother clutched him tight to her, fully weeping now. He didn't know what to say. He just smiled at the boy and gave him another piece of bread.

It seemed that most of the women and children in the longhouse needed just simple attention—a healing salve on this cut, a cooling ointment on that bruise—and Turk advised Arynin and his father to move the less injured survivors to another place, other homes perhaps if the citizens of Stone's Throw were willing.

"You can go," Turk said, walking up to Erik. "Get some rest, young Erik."

Erik tried protesting, but Turk put up a hand.

The Elder had all the men housed in different huts. Erik figured that was for the safety of the village. They still didn't trust them. Erik walked into a hut with an older man and woman and, much to his surprise, the little boy crying for Davey and his mother. The man, gray-haired and wrinkled, watched Erik with weary eyes. The woman, presumably his wife, brought the boy and his mother soup. Erik smiled, bowed, and shook his head when she tried to offer him some.

"Do you speak their language?"

"No, sir." The boy's mother shook her head.

"Please, you don't have to call me sir."

"You're very kind." She wouldn't look at him, just slurped her soup and, when that was gone, patted the bowl with a piece of bread.

She was barely older than Erik. With an eight-year-old boy, she must've been married and pregnant by the age of twelve. Erik's mother would have killed his father if he had allowed his sisters to marry at twelve.

With dark, curly hair and a slight body, she reminded Erik of Marcus' daughter without some of the curves most gypsy women had. Her face was dirty and her hair a mess. Her clothes lay in almost tattered rags, but despite that, she looked pretty.

Erik cursed himself for thinking such a thing. Here, this woman sat, son dead, husband dead too, presumably, and he was thinking about how pretty she looked, how even prettier she could look.

"What's your name?"

"Mari, sir." She looked up from her bowl and bread, and when she met Erik's eyes, she looked down again. "Sorry. Mari."

"And your boy?"

"Willy." Her son chimed in before his mother could answer.

"Willy," Erik repeated. "That's a good name."

The boy smiled at that.

Erik looked at the old wife. "Do you have a place where I can bathe?"

She just looked at him blankly, gray eyes and a kind, weathered face.

He tried to motion himself washing, under his arms and on his chest. The woman understood then and with a smile, brought Erik to the kitchen where a black cauldron sat over the glowing embers of the day's fire. Water sat in the iron bowl, and she handed Erik a piece of cloth that might serve as a washing rag.

The water was hot, but it felt good. Erik only spent a few minutes wiping under his arms and on his neck and chest. As he walked from the kitchen, Mari and Willy walked in. She stared at him as he passed by her, his chest naked. His cheeks burned, and he hurried by.

From what he gathered, they were to sleep in the dining area. Beside a bedroom and a kitchen, it was the only other room in the small hut. As Erik sat down on a makeshift bed of straw, Willy ran into the room, face cleared of most the soot and grime and dirt that had collected there. Erik thought that maybe the young boy would keep him up all night with talking and questions, but as soon as the boy hit his bed, he started snoring gently.

Erik closed his eyes, but when he heard the gentle trickle of water, he opened them halfway. Mari, her naked back to him, was running a clean rag along her arms. Her skin looked soft. She wasn't curvy at all, but Erik had been in the company of men for so long…

She turned around. She didn't see him watching her. He saw her, her breasts. His eyes met hers.

He closed his eyes. When he opened them again, Mari stood over him. She watched him. She didn't look angry. She didn't look happy. She didn't look like she felt any emotion.

"I saw you," she said in almost a whisper.

Erik sat up. "I'm sorry."

She put a hand on his chest. She sat, slowly, in his lap. She ran a finger down the side of his face, across his forehead, along his lips. She kissed him.

He had kissed Simone, the woman from the farmstead next to his whom he knew he would marry—had thought he would marry—the woman who held his heart. She was the only woman, up until this point, that he had kissed. Mari's lips were thin. They weren't bad, just thin, and cold. She pressed them hard against his. She straddled him and rubbed hard against him. He groaned and felt his manhood stiffen. Her hands brushed his chest again, then down to his stomach, then…

Erik grabbed her shoulders and gently pulled her away. Simone's kisses were always gentle, warm, welcoming. Mari's were forced.

"You don't have to do this," Erik said.

"It's all right. I want to," she replied.

No, she didn't. Erik wasn't as good with women as Bryon was. He was never the smooth talker, the flirter, the flashing hero who would make their hearts flutter. But he could tell that Mari, given a different circumstance, wouldn't have paid Erik a moment's thought.

He closed his eyes for a moment, letting Mari kiss his neck. She started to play with the tie at his pants. His eyes shot open. He pulled her away again.

"No, you don't. You don't really want to do this," Erik said.

Maybe she thought Erik could protect them, her and little Willy. Perhaps she thought they could go with him. Maybe she was simply grieving so badly that she just needed to be with someone, feel something. He had heard of that before. A grieving mother or wife running to the arms of a man, a grieving husband or father running to the arms of a whore—all simply to feel something familiar, something natural, something normal.

"Be with your son, Mari. Be with Willy," Erik said softly.

Erik half expected her to slap him. The other half expected her to cry. She simply stood and smiled. Her smile seemed odd, a blank smile. Was it gratitude, thanks for not sticking her when she really didn't want to? Or was it just a look of numbness? Whatever it was, she went to lie next to her son. Erik lay back, closed his eyes, and, thank the Creator, dreamt of nothing.

Chapter 5

"WE SHOULD JUST WAIT HERE," Maktus said. "We should wait for him to return."

"No. We can't just wait for him to come to us," Del Alzon replied. "I'm not some sneaky slaver. We'll find him and his group of dogs, call them out, and fight him like men."

He had looked to Yager, the Nordethian huntsman.

"Do you think you can track them?"

"Fer sure," the simple hunter replied.

"Then where to, my friend?" Del Alzon asked.

Yager walked around the slaver camp, almost sniffing as he went. He would bend down here and there, touch the ground, taste the dirt. Finally, after a few moments, Yager stood and pointed his bow to the east. "This way."

Del Alzon looked to Danitus, looked back to the other dozen or so men who were still with him, shrugged, and jerked his head in the direction Yager pointed.

Even leading their horses most of the way, with such a small force of men, it had taken only a day to reach the eastern edges of the Blue Forest and the Southland Gap. After another day, Yager's tracking had led them to the outskirts of Finlo.

It had been years since Del Alzon had smelled that pungent smell of sea salt, heard the squawking of seagulls and the splashing of waves against a beach. Too long, perhaps since he felt the salt and sand in every gust of ocean wind beat against his face.

"Gypsies and Samanians?" one sailor replied as Del Alzon began his inquiries around the coastal city. "So many people come through here but sure, I've probably seen some gypsies and Samanians. Also seen dwarves and gnomes. Ogres too. By the Shadow, I've probably even seen an elf or two."

"If I was looking for a particular gypsy or Samanian, who would I ask?" Del Alzon queried.

"*The Drunken Fin*," the sailor replied. "One of the largest pubs in the city. Morgan is the main keep. If you are looking for anyone in particular, he might have heard."

Del Alzon couldn't help smiling when he walked into *The Drunken Fin*. It was like any other large inn, and he coveted the smells and sights and sounds, but he didn't have any time to revel in the familiarity. He made his way to the bar and a younger man standing behind it who he presumed to be Morgan. He pushed one Katokien out of the way—jumping and prancing around while playing his pipes—and raised a hand to a smaller than usual gnome before the little pipsqueak could even get a word out, sending the annoyance running in the other direction. When Del got to the bar, he found Morgan deep in conversation with one of the serving wenches.

"You Morgan?" Del said curtly.

The younger man behind the bar ignored him. Del Alzon cleared his voice.

"Eh, you Morgan?" he asked again, this time a little louder.

The man looked at Del lazily.

"Yeah," he replied and then turned back to speak with the woman.

"I've got a question for you," Del Alzon said.

Morgan gave an exasperated sigh, which made Del scowl, but when the barkeep looked at the merchant from Waterton, he seemed less annoyed. Perhaps it was Del Alzon's own look of annoyance, or the fact that Del had placed his dagger on the bar, pointed at the keep, that softened Morgan. It could have been those, or it could have been the sparkling Hamonian pound that Del placed on the bar, along with his dagger.

"Well," Morgan said, all but ignoring the serving wench, "maybe I have an answer."

"If you do," Del Alzon replied, "the pound is yours. If it's an answer I like, I have another one for you. I'm looking for gypsies and Samanians."

"Really?" Morgan said, although he seemed less surprised. "This is a large city. We get folk from all over."

Del Alzon grumbled.

"Not gypsies like these," Del said, "and not Samanians like these either."

"Do you see that man over there?" Morgan said, pointing to a table in the corner of the bar occupied by a single man.

Del nodded.

"He had a run in not too long ago with a Samanian," Morgan said. "He was a barber. Burned his shop down and cut off one of his fingers."

Del Alzon slapped another Hamonian pound on the bar and made his way to the man sitting in the corner. He was drunk, halfway asleep, and murmuring incoherencies when Del Alzon sat across from him.

"I hear you had a run in with Samanians," Del Alzon said.

"Samanians," the man mumbled, coming out of a stupor for a moment. Then he began talking to himself, drooling over a shirt that looked dirty and soiled.

"Yes," Del Alzon said. "Samanians. I am looking for Samanians. And Gypsies. And three boys, not that anyone would notice them here in Finlo."

"Gypsies," the man said as if the word suddenly sparked some recognition, and he seemed to sober just a little. "And boys."

He looked down at the table. One cup, toppled over and its contents spilled, lay in front of him, another one on the floor. A broken pair of spectacles lay next to the overturned cup. He then lifted both his hands up, inspecting them. One of his hands was wrapped in cloth, a patch where his pinky finger used to be stained brown with dried blood.

"Samanians burned down my shop, took my finger," the man said, "took my life."

"Where'd they go?" Del asked.

"Burn them," the man said, still clearly drunk.

"Tell me where they went," Del Alzon said low and clear and deliberately.

"To the Shadow with them," the man said, and he started to cry.

Del Alzon grabbed the man's hand, the one with the missing finger. He was about to scream when Del Alzon clamped a big, meaty hand over his mouth.

"Stuff your crying," Del Alzon said, "and your self-pity. Now, tell me where these Samanians went. I'll avenge your finger and your shop and your livelihood. By the gods, I'll even come back here with their heads and their coin so you can build another shop."

Del Alzon released the man's wrist. He rubbed it this time, sobered a fraction more and nodded.

"There is an inn," the man said, "on the outskirts of the eastern part of the city. I don't know the name. It's rundown and broken, and no one hardly goes there. You'll know it by its looks. The Samanian was looking for three boys, just like you. That is where they were staying. Don't know why. But that is what I told the Samanian—to go there."

"Thanks," Del Alzon said as he stood.

"Buy me a drink for my troubles," the man said, looking up at Del Alzon with pitiful eyes.

Del Alzon looked about the table and then at the man.

"It looks like you've had enough to drink," Del Alzon said. "Whatever extra coin you have, use it to clean yourself up. And I meant what I said. When I kill that Samanian, I will bring you his coin...unless you are still sitting here drunk."

After they passed some of the worst areas of the old, ocean-side city, staring at a windswept plain of beach sand and small tufts of grass, they came across a sad looking inn, surrounded by a broken, white fence, and a makeshift stable attached to its northern side.

Del Alzon passed through the opening in the fence and looked to his right. A pile of rags lay there that moaned and moved a little when touched by Del Alzon's boot. The smell of stale brandy and a malodorous body hit his nose.

"A pleasant place," Danitus offered, squeezing between the drunk and a fence post.

"My kind of place," Yager said with smile, waiting for Del Alzon before they entered the inn's yard.

The weathered steps of the inn creaked with strain under Del Alzon's weight, and he advanced with caution for fear of the wood actually breaking. Yager and Danitus followed, the rest of the men staying with their horses. Del Alzon stopped at the front door and sighed. He didn't quite know why.

"This place reminds me of something," he said, sorrowfully.

"What was that?" Danitus asked.

"I feel like I've seen this place before," Del Alzon clarified. "In some country. Maybe with a girl, or a friend. Maybe I had a fight there."

"The years have made you forgetful." Danitus laughed.

"And brandy and spiced wine," Yager added.

"And tomigus root."

Del Alzon huffed a quick, insincere laugh as he pushed the door open. Three tables stood in the middle of a modest room, each surrounded by four rickety chairs made of splintered wood and covered in a faded blue paint that had started to chip away long ago. They sat empty. The bar was a slab of wood with too many dings and bruises and cracks to count. A hallway stood to the left of the bar. On the wall behind the bar, a single shelf held just three bottles that all looked to be of the same gray glass, disguising the liquid inside.

A large man—not as large as Del Alzon—stood behind the bar, wiping the same spot repeatedly with a dirty, brown rag. He didn't bother to look up at the group of three men as they entered the inn. Del Alzon stepped forward, the floor—a mishmash of warped wooden planks that struggled to fit together—creaking with every step.

"What can I do ye for?" the man behind the bar said, never taking his eyes from his cleaning.

Del Alzon recognized his accent. He sounded like a seaman, but not any old sailor. That soft rolling sound suggested a sailor from the east, another Golgolithulian, perhaps.

Del Alzon stopped, put his left hand on the handle of his sword, and straightened his shoulders.

"We're looking for some young men." Del Alzon paused. "Them and one other man, really."

The bartender stopped cleaning but still didn't look up at the three men.

"Most people don't come around these parts. Chances are I haven't seen 'em."

"I think you have," Del Alzon replied.

The innkeeper's sausage-like fingers gripped his rag tightly, and he finally lifted his head, showing a row of yellowed teeth bordered by blackened gums. His bald head turned a deep red and glistened with sweat. The black beard that silhouetted his face, albeit speckled with gray, seemed to deepen the darkness in his thick, eyebrow-laden eyes.

"You're in the habit of telling people what they have and haven't seen?" the bartender asked quietly, but his voice was full of menace.

Del Alzon lifted his hand from the handle of his sword and showed the innkeeper his palm.

"I meant nothing by it. I apologize." Del Alzon took a step back. Yager gave him a crooked sidelong glance. It wasn't often he saw the big man back down from someone. "You might not think a young man would be noticed in such a big city, but his presence seems to have stood out among some more unsavory company."

The barkeep's face seemed to soften, only for a second, then his eyebrows coiled like a black dragon on his forehead and shadowed his hard eyes.

"Go on." The bartender reached under the bar—slowly, carefully.

"When I first got to town, I heard talk of a southerner, a Samanian, and a group of gypsies and some lads from the west, from Waterton who seemed to be hanging around here. It just so happens that this man I'm looking for is Samanian, following a group of gypsies that had a group of lads from Waterton traveling with them. And, from what I was told, they all passed by here."

"No idea," the bartender said with a shrug. "Haven't seen anything like that."

"I don't believe you," Del Alzon said.

"I don't care," the bartender replied. "You can piss off now."

"Sailor," Del Alzon said softly in Shengu, the language of Golgolithul. The innkeeper shot him a dirty look. "Could I have your name before we leave?" Del Alzon added.

A wry, crooked smile crept across the innkeeper's face.

"Shengu, eh?" the bartender said before switching over to the language of the east himself. "Spoken like a true Easterner."

Del Alzon returned the smile.

"No. I think I might be mistaken," the sailor added, still speaking in Shengu. "Spoken like an Eastern officer."

Del Alzon's smile widened.

It had been a long while since Del Alzon had tasted cheap, salty brandy, let alone three bottles of the stuff. The first few glasses churned his stomach, but he got into it again like it was only the day before. He rubbed his face hard with a callused hand.

"I can't feel my lips," Del Alzon said.

"I think maybe you've had a bit too much, mate," Rory the bartender replied.

"Is it hot in here?" Del Alzon asked.

"Aye, a bit warm," Rory replied. "But we've also drunk three bottles of my best brandy."

"Best?" Del Alzon questioned.

"Aye," Rory replied with a cocked eyebrow. "You have a problem with my brandy?"

"No," Del Alzon replied. Then, a smile cracked his lips. "Not if you're trying to pass hog's piss off as brandy."

Rory looked at Del Alzon with hard eyes for a moment, then broke into fits of laughter. He slapped the table hard and slapped Del Alzon's shoulder even harder.

"If fermented hog piss only tasted this good," Rory finally said, still chuckling.

"I'd be drunk all the time," Del Alzon added, lifted his cup, and toasted the old sailor.

They had traded stories about serving Golgolithul for hours, stories of fighting too many men to count and bedding too many women to count. Del Alzon found himself lost in the tales. It had been many years since he had sat and drank with another man who had served. It felt good.

He looked down to see a single strand of sunlight creeping under the crease of the front door and across his boot. It reminded him of blonde hair. It reminded him of Siri, a long lost, fond memory.

"With a smile like that," Rory said, "you must be thinking about a woman."

"I didn't realize I was smiling," Del Alzon replied.

"Women do that to a man," Rory said.

"Aye, that they do," Del Alzon said. "Is it really morning?"

"It looks that way, mate," Rory replied.

Del Alzon shook his head and rubbed his face again, this time with a heavy sigh. He now just wished he could get the information he came for and go and sleep with the stinking drunk outside. It seemed like Rory had read his thoughts, or perhaps he too had drunk enough.

"So," Rory said, "the lads you've been looking for."

"Aye," Del Alzon said, "the lads I've been looking for. They were here?"

Rory took another draught of his brandy and tore off a piece of the loaf of bread sitting in the middle of their table.

"Aye, they were here," Rory replied.

"Foolish lads," Del Alzon muttered.

"Foolish indeed," Rory agreed.

"What makes you say that?" Del Alzon asked.

"Those young fools," Rory said, "came to Finlo wanting to sail east—to join the armies of Golgolithul."

"Aye," Del Alzon said. "I encouraged them to do so. Said service does a man good."

He decided it would be prudent to leave out mention of his ulterior motives for encouraging the boys to join a gypsy caravan.

"I agree," Rory said, "the East isn't the same East we served, Del Alzon. It's changed, and not for the better in my opinion."

"Dangerous words," Del Alzon said, "even in the west."

"Bah," Rory snorted. "I'm too old and tired to worry about dangerous words. You and I both know it's true and burn me if I'm going to worry about speaking truth. Anyways, the stubborn one…"

"Bryon," Del Alzon said.

"Aye, Bryon. Well, he was dead set on sailing east," Rory explained. "It seemed that Befel had resigned himself to the same fate as well. Although he spent a good deal of time in town, getting his shoulder looked at."

"Getting his shoulder looked at?" Del Alzon asked.

"Aye," Rory replied. "Had a hurt shoulder. Took a knife in the joint. It seemed to get better over the week they were here. But that young one…"

"Erik," Del Alzon said with a smile.

"Aye, Erik," Rory replied with a smile of his own. "He's a thinker, a follower of his heart. He sat right where you sit, and we talked for a whole night. Brandy loosened my tongue, and I told them The Messenger of the East was due to visit my bar."

"The Black Mage?" Del Alzon asked in astonishment.

"The very same," Rory replied. "He was due to come, looking for mercenaries to perform some task in service to the Lord of the East."

"They're no mercenaries, Rory," Del Alzon said.

"That they're not," Rory agreed, "but they are now porters to a group of mercenaries."

"You might as well slit their throats." Del Alzon slammed a fist on the table. Yager stirred, but didn't wake, and some of Rory's brandy spilled.

"Hold your temper." Rory seemed unmoved by Del Alzon's apparent, sudden concern. That angered Del Alzon even more. "It was either that or sail east in a cramped ship with a bunch of fools, half of which might die of dysentery before they ever reached the western shores of the Giant's Vein. Do not think I didn't care for those lads, especially Erik. There's something about him; he's a good man, will one day be a great man. It was the best choice for them: Either that or go home, and that didn't seem to be an option at all."

Del Alzon sat back. He closed his eyes and breathed slowly. It was a technique he had learned during battle when the blood lust rises and all a man wants to do is remove heads from shoulders, bowels from stomachs, and limbs from joints. It calmed him, allowed him to lead, allowed him to fight with composure.

"Where did they go?" Del Alzon finally asked.

"North," Rory replied. "I am pretty sure they would've stopped in Dûrn Tor. And then, from what I gathered from the Messenger's meeting, they would go east, and then into the Southern Mountains."

"Must've been serious for the Messenger to find himself away from the walls of Fen-Stévock," Del Alzon said.

"Aye," Rory replied. "Something about lost treasure, an heirloom dear to the Stévockians, and a lost dwarvish city."

"Dwarves," Del Alzon grumbled.

"There were four here," Rory said. "Three of them actually agreed to try and find this treasure. They seemed like right fellows. Never had much experience with dwarves, save for the smiths who worked on the ships on which I sailed."

"I had plenty of experience with them east of the Giant's Vein," Del Alzon said. "Dwarves from the Black Hills. They'd sooner crack your skull with a hammer than ask you your name or give a dying man a handful of water."

"Well, anyway, north they went," Rory said, "then east."

"Dûrn Tor?" Del Alzon asked.

"Aye. Dûrn Tor," Rory repeated.

Rory nodded with finality, and Del Alzon slid back his chair and nudged Yager with the toe of his boot. As Del Alzon stood and threw Rory several silver nickels, the old sailor chuckled. "Here. No need. I had as much fun as you did. If you find those lads, give 'em to them. A present from ole Rory."

Del Alzon nodded.

"If you go north, watch out for those Samanians," Rory added, and Del Alzon sat down again. In the brandy haze, he'd forgotten about them.

"You know where they went?" Del Alzon asked.

"Aye. They went north as well," Rory replied. "They seemed right intent on finding Erik and his cousin and brother, just like you."

"Slavers," Del Alzon muttered.

"Come again?" Rory asked.

"They are slavers," Del Alzon replied, "the Samanian and his crew."

Rory spat on the floor. He looked completely disgusted.

"Figures," he said. "Killed a whore that used to hang around here, just for the fun of it. Had a few dealings with Samanians. I suppose, like anyone, there are a few good ones, but didn't meet many."

"I hope I meet them," Del Alzon said.

"I hope you meet 'em, too," Rory added. "That one is crueler than most."

Del Alzon nodded and nudged Yager, waking him and then Danitus.

"Time to go," Del Alzon said and then turned to Rory. "My thanks, sailor, for the brandy, the hospitality, and the information about Erik."

Del Alzon turned and started for the door to *The Lady's Inn.*

"I have to ask, though," Rory said, just as Del Alzon turned the handle of the door, "why are you so intent on finding those boys? They don't seem to want to be found. I wish you luck, and I wish 'em good health and safety. Just wondering."

"Penance," Del Alzon replied and gathered up the others.

"Where to?" Maktus asked when they were outside.

"Dûrn Tor," Del Alzon replied.

"Are you still hoping to find those boys?" Yager asked.

Del Alzon shook his head.

"I think we could search all over Háthgolthane and not find them now."

"Then why not just go home, back to Waterton?" Maktus asked.

"I suppose for one last hope," Del Alzon replied, "for one last piece of information that will tell me I'm not an unsalvageable bastard and that those boys are still alive."

"And what of Kehl?" Yager asked.

"What of him?" Del Alzon said.

"What if we should meet him on the way?" Yager asked.

"We kill him," Del Alzon replied matter-of-factly.

"And what if we miss him?" Yager asked. "What if he goes home to find his brothers dead?"

"I am sure he'll want revenge," Del Alzon replied. He knew he would.

"Will he come looking fer you? Fer us?" Yager asked.

"Probably," Del Alzon said.

"And when he finds us?" Yager queried.

"We kill him."

Chapter 6

THE HUT WAS STILL DARK when Erik awoke to the smell of cooked oats and bacon. Despite the scratchiness of the straw, he had slept soundly, better than he had in a long while, thank the Creator. He sat up and found a clean shirt neatly folded next to him. It looked new, but it was his.

Someone, probably the old wife, had sewn up the holes and tatters and removed the worst of the stains. It smelled of mint and lavender, but there was still the distant stink of sweat and blood.

After eating, Erik walked into the sunlight, bright and hot with the constricting muskiness of a day after a heavy rain. Citizens of Stone's Throw, along with survivors of Aga Kona, bustled about, taking little notice of the young man. He walked to the longhouse where the village housed the wounded and found Vander Bim just outside the door, arm lying across a wooden chair, head resting on his arm. He was asleep. The door opened, and Turk walked out. His shirt lay against his body, soaked in sweat, and he wiped his hands clean with a dirty rag.

When Turk saw Erik, he smiled. "We lost three. Two more are questionable. Another night and An's will, and we will see."

"I'm sorry," Erik said.

"For what?" Turk asked.

"For the three you lost," Erik replied.

Turk shook his head. "Four dozen women and children, beaten

and bruised and burned, and we only lost three, maybe five. I count that as a blessing. I thank An for guiding my hand, and the hands of Demik and Nafer and the sailor here."

"I'm sorry for not being here to help, then." Erik had slept soundly, comfortably, and here, all night long, Turk and the sailor and the other dwarves labored over the sickly and the dying.

"I told you to go. No apology is needed. I trust you slept soundly," Turk replied.

Erik smiled wide. "The best I've slept in many months."

"That is good. I think it is my turn," Turk said.

"Do you need me to do anything while you rest?" Erik asked.

Turk shook his head.

"Rest. Arynin has agreed to let us stay another night. For that, I am glad." Turk nudged Vander Bim. "Come, friend, let us find a place to rest."

With a short cough, Vander Bim woke, blinked hurriedly, smiled at Erik as he stood over him, and fell back asleep.

"Have you seen Switch?" Erik asked.

"No, and I am also glad for that," Turk replied.

Erik didn't see Turk or the other dwarves for the rest of the day. As he walked around the village, he saw Drake trying to help, seeking to tend to the wounded however he could—fetching water and food, changing bandages, just talking to people. Erik could understand why Drake wanted to help. These people, in a way, were his people. Certainly, miners were not some different race of people, some different ethnicity like dwarves or Samanians—at least Erik didn't think so. But it was apparent to Erik that Drake felt a kinship with these survivors. He felt bad for the miner. The man just wanted to help, and all he seemed to do was annoy these people, who just wanted to sit in peace and rest and be left alone.

Unseen in the night, Erik discovered the village's farmlands and orchards, sprawling lands of fruit trees, wheat, and cotton. Erik suspected his father would be planting wheat right now, and the thought made him want to help.

Erik picked up a hoe and tilled in front of a man spreading seed. The villager—an older man—looked at Erik just once, but when he did, he smiled and nodded. Hours must've passed as Erik helped, and the sun hung at its zenith in the sky as he wiped the sweat from his forehead with the back of his arm. A young girl came around with a bucket of water, and Erik cupped his hands, sipped some, and splashed the rest on his face.

It felt good to work. Erik knelt down and touched the earth which was moist and rich. He scooped a healthy amount into his hand and smelled it before he let it fall through his fingers. The old man he worked with saw him and smiled.

"It's good soil," Erik said and then remembered the man couldn't understand him.

"Yes, good soil," the man replied to Erik's surprise.

"You understand me?"

"A little," the villager said. "I am old. Have met many people. I learn language of west."

"I envy your soil," Erik said, smelling it again.

"An has blessed us for many seasons now."

Erik nodded.

"Indeed."

They went back to work. Erik looked to a nearby orchard and saw Mari. She worked diligently with the other women, picking nuts from the trees. Erik recognized them as pistazi trees, little nuts with hard, poisonous shells, but the greenish fruit inside was sweet. Even though they grew plentiful around Rikard Eleodum's farmstead, Erik learned that the people of Hámon were willing to pay quite a price for just a handful.

Mari didn't see him, and he watched her for a while. Something inside of him longed for her. He now suspected she had kissed him, had offered herself to him, because she wanted to feel normal, wanted to do something that felt normal. Maybe that's what he wanted? Simone's face flashed through his memory, the feeling of her soft lips and the warmth of her body against his.

When Erik went back to the hut in which he had slept the night before, the old wife was there. He knew she couldn't understand him, but he remembered the word of thanks Turk had taught him.

"Yethan."

She seemed surprised by that. She hadn't really paid him much attention, but to the word of gratitude, she smiled and poured the young man a glass of goat's milk. He drank it graciously, although he would have preferred another piece of that bacon.

Erik woke before sunrise and, with the help of his brother and cousin, readied the horses. Arynin and his son met them with supplies, gifts of bread, goat's cheese, dried fruit and goat meat, and extra food for their horses, rewards for their honesty and help.

"Yethan," Erik said.

Arynin laughed, slapped his belly hard, and started speaking to Erik as if the young man understood.

Erik shook his head. Arynin understood and replied with a simple bow and said, "Yethan."

Switch finally returned. Erik didn't bother to ask the thief where he had been. He didn't really care.

"Are we off yet? This place bloody stinks."

"It smells like home," Erik said quietly to himself.

Just as the cock began to crow, the company mounted up, and Erik watched as Vander Bim looked over the party, counting heads. He watched Drake look to the mass of sleeping huts, hurt and sadness in his eyes. He watched Befel and Bryon stare at the farm fields. While they would never admit it, they missed home also, the smell, the feeling of soil between their fingers. Erik could see the longing in their eyes.

Turk bowed his head before they left, his lips moving silently. Erik bowed his head and said silent prayers as well.

"Are we ready?" the sailor asked.

"By the bloody gods, I've been ready for an age," Switch muttered and spat in the earth.

The sun began to peak over the eastern horizon just as they passed the last tree in Stone's Throw's orchards.

"An olive tree," Erik said. He had seen them in Hamon.

He looked over his shoulder, and she was nowhere in sight, but the image of Mari stuck in his head. It was not of her body or her naked breasts, but her face, those thin lips and gray, numb eyes.

Chapter 7

LIEUTENANT BU EYED THE THREE men. Mercenaries. The word left a bitter taste in Bu's mouth. These three had left Finlo with the Messenger's task in hand, along with all the other fools who had met the Black Mage in that dung-heap of an inn. Patûk's orders were simple. Find out why the Lord of the East had them hired and then kill them all. This group of three were some of the only ones left.

Bu hid behind a large white-barked pine tree. The three riders had been traveling swiftly but had recently slowed. They looked different than the other mercenaries—more formidable and dangerous.

"Are these the ones that speak Shengu?" Bu asked.

"Yes sir," Corporal Ban Chu replied, standing behind Bu.

"They are soldiers," Lieutenant Bu said. "At least, they used to be."

"Eastern soldiers?" Ban Chu asked.

Bu nodded.

Most mercenaries looked little better than dogs, finding the rigidity and discipline of a real army too much. They fought little better than dogs, too.

"How do you know, sir?" Ban Chu asked.

"Watch them," Bu replied, "the way they carry themselves and move. They are disciplined, well-kept, well-fed. There is order to them. This will not be easy."

"But, sir," Ban Chu said. Bu could see the Corporal giving a quick bow from the corner of his eye. "We outnumber them. And we have the…"

"I know our forces," Bu replied, cutting his corporal off. "Never underestimate an opponent, Chu."

"Yes, sir," Ban Chu said.

"It can be a fatal mistake," Bu added, a small smile touching the corner of his mouth.

It was a lesson General Patûk Al'Banan taught all of his officers—a truly important lesson. But it was a lesson Bu had learned even before being graced with the title of officer in the service to Patûk Al'Banan. Bu remembered too many times, as a young boy growing up on the streets of Fen-Stévock, being small. He remembered older, bigger boys thinking he would be an easy target. He remembered smiling over those bigger boys as they cradled broken arms and held broken noses and cried over lost coin. That coin would buy Bu and his mother supper.

When his mother sent him off to fight for Patûk Al'Banan, many men underestimated him. Many men found themselves with knives in their backs, throats slit, and necks stretched—crimes committed that would have normally gone unnoticed but somehow reached the ears and attention of commanding officers.

"Sorben Phurnan," Bu muttered, the name tasting sour in his mouth. His lip curled. "That entitled, self-righteous prig. He underestimates me. It will be to his demise."

"Lieutenant Phurnan, sir?" Ban Chu asked.

Bu's head snapped to the side. He glared at the Corporal.

"What did you hear?" Bu asked.

"Just the Lieutenant's name, sir," Ban Chu replied, backing up a few steps and bowing low.

Bu smiled, but then caught himself. That was what Phurnan did—frighten his men, make them feel worthless, degrade them and berate them. He was not Sorben Phurnan.

"Just thinking aloud, Corporal," Bu said, trying to soften his face as much as possible. "Nothing with which to concern yourself."

Ban Chu simply bowed.

"Let's move," Bu said. He jerked his head to the side and, silently, eleven men followed him down the mountain slope.

"Should I signal the…" Ban Chu began to ask, but Bu put up a hand.

"No," he whispered. "Not yet."

They tracked the horsemen for a while, slowly descending the slope until they were within striking distance. Bu crept closer, hiding underneath a bushy shrub. He slowed his breath, closed his eyes, and began counting. When he reached twenty, he would signal an attack. It was his way of calming himself before a fight. He reached eighteen when he heard the snapping of a twig.

Bu looked back and saw one of his soldiers standing still, face pale with fright. The Lieutenant didn't have time to say anything. A heavy snort said the mercenaries heard them. Already, the mercenary leading the group of three had turned his horse to face the mountains.

"There's something there," the mercenary said.

Bu could hear the mercenaries speak, as they turned their attention to the mountains, to him and his men. They were speaking Shengu, the language of the east.

"What do we do?" Ban Chu whispered.

The hand signal Bu responded with said "bowman."

"What do you see, Tedish?" Bu heard one of the other mercenaries ask.

"Nothing yet," Bu heard the man he named Tedish reply. "But there's something there."

"Be ready," the third mercenary said.

Bu clicked his tongue. He didn't think it would work, but perhaps a volley of arrows would at least make up for the lost element of surprise.

Two arrows flew from the trees of the mountain slope. One bounced off the breastplate of the man in front and the other thudded into a shield quickly raised.

"Run or fight, Wrothgard?" the third mercenary asked.

"I don't much like running," the man named Wrothgard replied.

"That's what I like to hear," called Tedish.

That's what Bu wanted to hear as well. He and his men burst from the cover of the shrubbery, six to the front and Bu and five to the back.

These men were soldiers, their movements precise and calculated. Rather than race out to meet Bu and his men, they backed their horses up so that they were flank to flank, then backing their horses away from the slope.

"Attack the horses!" Bu cried.

"Shengu. An Easterner," the one named Wrothgard said. "Let me guess, Patûk Al'Banan's lackeys."

Bu didn't reply, but the accusation made his blood boil. One of his men lashed out at the legs of that mercenary's horse, but the animal was as much of a weapon as the man's two swords. The horse kicked out, catching the soldier in the face, and leaving a bloody mess where his left cheek and eye used to be. Both swords then came down, crossed towards their tips, easily slicing into the soldier's neck and removing his head. A high-pitched scream came from another one of Bu's men as he turned, a gash exposing ribs and lungs slashed into his torso from his chest to his navel.

Bu realized these men were fools and ill-trained. Most of them—all except for Ban Chu and Da—were Sorben Phurnan's. Bu whistled quickly, catching the attention of his two men, and they knew what he wanted. They pressed their attack on the lead mercenary, seemingly acting recklessly, jumping in and out, stabbing and dodging. The other soldiers followed suit, another two meeting their end at the tip of a sword. Bu didn't care.

Bu crept behind the horse of the mercenary named Wrothgard. He was so consumed with the pressing attack, Bu thought for sure he could take him by surprise. The Lieutenant flicked his wrist twice, but Wrothgard saw him, leaning backwards as Bu's two thin-bladed daggers flew past his face. One flew some ways away, hitting nothing, but the other, as it missed this mercenary, found a mark in the armpit of the mercenary in the middle.

The man screamed as Bu's poison, although not fatal, worked quickly. A burning sensation would be coursing through the man's veins. He would feel feverish; his skin would crawl, and he would sweat profusely.

"Samus!" the man named Wrothgard yelled as the other mercenary fell from his horse. He hit the ground with a thud, and the two remaining horsemen closed in around him, guarding him.

These truly weren't mercenaries. Mercenaries cared little for anything, especially other mercenaries. These men—Tedish, their leader, Samus, the one poisoned, and Wrothgard—had been soldiers…once.

Another one of Bu's soldiers fell, his jaw hanging slack from the rest of his face.

"We are going to lose this fight," Bu spat.

"Sir," Ban Chu said, "should I call them?"

Bu scowled. They disgusted him. The very fact that they used them made his stomach turn. But without them, they would lose this little skirmish. He nodded.

Ban Chu turned and whistled loud. A growl and a thud came from the dense brush and trees of the mountain slope, and with a great howl, a mountain troll burst from the foliage. It raced towards the horsed men on all fours, knuckles slamming into the ground as its massive legs pumped and propelled the beast four times farther in one leap than any man.

The troll took Wrothgard by surprise. The beast slammed its shoulder into the mercenary's horse. The mount crumpled to the ground, taking Wrothgard with it. Falling from his horse, he landed atop Samus, who in turn screamed. The poison must have been in full effect now.

Samus' horse reared up, but the troll grabbed it by its neck and, with both hands, wrestled the animal to the ground before he twisted hard and broke the animal's neck.

Another troll burst from the mountain forest, this one carrying a large club—a thick branch the size of a man's thigh with the smaller branches trimmed and fashioned into spikes. It lumbered towards Tedish, the leader of the three mercenaries and still on his horse. Bu hated these creatures, but their size and muscularity amazed him. They looked like giant men, but then they didn't.

The mercenary looked to his companions on the ground and spurred his horse forward, barreling towards the club-wielding troll. As the troll swung its club at the horse's head, striking the animal dead, the mercenary leapt from his saddle. Tedish brought his sword down on the troll's shoulder. The blade might as well have been a small thorn from a thistle bush.

As Tedish hit the troll, the beast swatted the man away as if he were a fly. The mercenary, hitting the ground hard, gasped as the troll's club struck him in the chest. Bu watched as the mercenary struggled a bit more, but another strike from the club, and he went limp.

Bu saw two men running—Samus and Wrothgard—out of the corner of his eye. This other man, Tedish, had given his life so that they might escape. How noble. His death would be in vain.

"Go after them," Bu said.

"Yes, sir," Ban Chu replied.

"And take *our* men," Bu commanded.

"As you wish, sir," Ban Chu replied with a bow.

"This is why I hate these creatures," Bu muttered.

"Sir?" Ban Chu asked.

"The mountain trolls," Bu added. "Look at the devastation. We could have used the horses. They were clearly well-trained. And that mercenary, now destined to become troll shit, might have made a good prisoner."

"I thought General Al'Banan didn't take prisoners, sir," Ban Chu said.

"He would have taken one like that," Bu said, watching the troll peel away the man's dented breastplate. "Take them with you."

"Yes, sir," Ban Chu said with a bow.

Bu looked at the other troll, chewing on horse flesh, over his shoulder. He turned hard, grunted, and kicked the beast. A collective gasp consumed Bu's soldiers. That was a death sentence.

The troll growled and stood to its full height, a whole half a man taller than Bu. Blood smeared its face, and entrails matted its black, stringy hair. It glared at the Lieutenant with its yellow, black-pupiled eyes. Any other man would have shitted his pants.

"They are weak," Patûk had said. "They fear strength, they revere it, and will follow it. Show no fear, and they will obey you."

"You let them get away!" Bu yelled. He drew his sword and jerked his head sideways. "Go. Get those two. Feast on them."

The two trolls rushed away, Ban Chu and Da after them. The other soldiers followed and in just a hundred paces, Bu's other men would join up with them as well. His own men would take care of those mercenaries—his men and the trolls.

He saw the soldier who had stepped on the twig, alerting the mercenaries to their presence, lagging in the back. Bu flicked his wrist, and another thin blade flew from underneath his sleeve, striking the man in the back of the neck. The soldier collapsed to the ground.

Bu slowly walked to the man. His foolishness had caused six deaths. He groaned and grunted as he squirmed on the ground, trying to reach back and retrieve the knife.

"You are a fool," Bu hissed, turning the man onto his back with his boot. "Your foolishness killed six soldiers and made me use those wretched beasts."

"I'm sorry," the soldier struggled to say as the knife's poison coursed through his body and as he still tried to pull it from the back of his neck.

"I don't want your apologies," Bu replied. He placed the tip of his sword at the base of the man's throat. The soldier's eyes went wide, and Bu slowly pushed.

At first, the tip barely broke the skin, but as Bu pushed harder, the soldier's eyes grew wider. He tried to mouth something, but only gurgled. The Lieutenant made sure to press slowly, very slowly.

"No more mistakes from you," Bu finally said when the soldier lay dead.

Bu walked into a small clearing bordered by tall, white-barked pines and ironwoods. Only a short distance up the mountainside and the air had a biting chill to it. The Lieutenant pulled his cloak tight around his arms. The remnants of thunderclouds hung overhead, wisps of gray mist twisting through the upper extremities of trees, blocking the sun, and casting eerie, ghostly, hand-shaped shadows in front of Bu. He closed his eyes and sucked in the sweet smell of rain mixed with pine. The sting of sweat and dirt then invaded that sweetness, his eyes opened, and a growl rolled from his throat.

A retinue of men dropped to one knee in front of him, dipping their chins to their chests and covering their hearts with a closed fist. He glanced at each man, and they waited as he counted. Eight.

"Where are the rest?"

When no one spoke, he looked to Ban Chu, his trousers soiled and caked with wet dirt, blood staining his leather breastplate. Two deep grooves traveled from the left shoulder to right hip. Those were new. Bu needed no answer to his question. He asked again.

"Corporal, where are my other two men?"

"Dead, sir." Corporal Ban Chu never lifted his head or moved his position but spoke quickly and concisely.

"Even with trolls at your side?" Bu asked.

"Yes, sir."

The Lieutenant heard a deep grunt and a snort—like a sneezing dog—from behind the small troop. The two trolls sauntered into the grove, slowly moving around the men. One stopped to sniff the hair of a young soldier. Bu didn't know his name. He was new, young, but he was one of his. The snort blew the hair aside. The soldier never flinched.

The trolls came to stand, rather, lean forward on their hands like gorillas in front of Lieutenant Bu, looking around, picking their noses, pulling their stringy, black hair, paying little attention to the officer.

"Weak." Bu's whisper was inaudible. "For all your strength, you are weak."

They both looked about, side to side, snorting and sniffing, even snarling at the eight kneeling men. But neither one of them would look Bu in the eyes. Weak.

Leaning on their fists, directly in front of Bu, he realized how much they reeked. Bu couldn't place the smell, worse than cow shit. Something between chicken shit and the eviscerated intestines of a deer brought down by a lion and then left to rot. He saw the young soldier gag.

The largest of the two, the one that carried a club with it, sneezed. He was a brute with faded, whitish scars riddled over his body and a fresher, jagged, red one running from the middle of his forehead, through his bushy, disheveled, black eyebrows, along the corner of one beady, yellow-black eye, and down his cheek. Black and gray phlegm spewed from its nose and collected at Bu's feet. A stench even worse than its body odor poured from its open mouth. The young soldier vomited.

He noticed the other troll lingered back, favoring its left arm as it leaned upon its fists. Bu pushed past the first one, moving it with his elbow and stood before the other one. It looked away, like a beaten dog, while Bu inspected it. A deep gash seeped puss and blood from its shoulder, just where the muscles of its neck met the joint. The wound flowed slowly, but the soldier could see that a copious amount of its old blood had already dried and dyed its gray skin a deep crimson, flaking off with its small movements.

"What happened here?" Bu asked.

"They were stronger than we anticipated, sir," Ban Chu replied. "They were certainly trained soldiers at one point, as you had surmised, sir."

"Clearly." Disappointment and sarcasm riddled Bu's voice. "So strong they killed two of my own men and severely wounded a mountain troll."

The Lieutenant prodded the wound with the index finger of his right hand. He could see Ban Chu staring at him from the corner of his eye. Fear contorted the Corporal's face, but Bu paid that emotion no mind. The wound on the troll's shoulder wasn't its only hurt. As Bu walked behind it, two stab wounds on its back were dried and cracked, along with a shallow slash across its broad chest.

"This is more than displeasing." Bu felt a bit of his hair falling loose of the leather thong that held it back. He brushed it off his face with the back of his bloodied hand.

"And the bodies? Did the trolls feed?" Bu asked.

"They live, sir," Ban Chu replied.

"What?" Bu hissed.

"They severely wounded one of our trolls," Ban Chu replied, "and killed two of our men. I thought it prudent to retreat."

"My men," Bu corrected as he felt rage rise up in his chest.

"Two men severely wounded a troll and killed two of my men," Bu said, "men I personally trained and you…you ran away."

"They knew how to fight, sir," Ban Chu replied. His voice sounded pleading almost.

Bu again inspected the troll's wound while his Corporal spoke. He knew what the soldier was about to admit. He was ready for it, as much as it pained him to hear, as much as it disappointed him. Who was he fooling? It enraged him, made him want to take the Corporal's head with a single swing of his long sword. Perhaps that was why he jabbed his finger deep into the cut on the troll's shoulder. His finger went knuckle deep and still had farther to go. The creature screamed and snarled and snapped at Bu's arm. The Lieutenant pulled his hand back quick enough to avoid the attack and in the same instant unsheathed his steel and slammed it into the same laceration, clear to its cross guard.

Through it all, Bu's expression never changed. No emotion.

He stared at the gray lump of stinking flesh huddled before him, its foul blood dripping slowly from the blade of his sword. He wiped the filth off on the skin of the dead troll, cleaned what little stubborn bit clung to the steel with a rag he always kept in his belt pouch, and sheathed the long sword. That would have to appease his want for Ban Chu's head. Ban Chu was a good soldier. It would take much more than this to make Bu actually kill him.

Bu looked at the other troll. He could feel it staring. It caught his gaze and looked away.

"The General will not be pleased by this. Go back to camp," Bu commanded. "Take the men and troll with you."

Corporal Ban Chu stood and bowed quickly. "Yes, sir. And that troll?"

Bu looked at him with a raised eyebrow.

"The dead one, sir?" Ban Chu clarified.

"What of it?" Bu asked.

"What shall we do with it?" Ban Chu asked.

"What would you have me do with it?" Bu's voice was hard and impatient, and he was immediately angry with himself. Emotion equaled weakness. The General's voice would be more even, it would have remained steady and calm. Stern, but calm.

"Leave it," he concluded. "Leave it to the wolves and squirrels and beetles and worms."

"As you wish, sir," Ban Chu replied.

The Corporal commanded the other seven men to stand, and he marched them back into the dense woods towards their camp, only two miles away. The troll followed at a distance, never looking at Bu, and sniffing at its dead companion as it passed it. The clouds and tall trees shadowed the soldiers and the surviving beast, despite the day being just past noon, and Bu lost sight of them within a few moments.

The soldier looked down at the dead troll.

"Despite all that muscle and your stench and your great girth and height, you were still weak."

Chapter 8

KEHL WALKED TWENTY PACES AHEAD of his men, ignoring the low hanging branches that slapped him in the face as he went. A thick, white line of sweat stiffened the edge of his cloak's hood, and new sweat darkened the black wool around his shoulders and neck. He scratched his nails along his cheeks and through his beard, now curling into tight kinks. He hadn't cared to shave daily or straighten the hair with oil as he normally did.

Kehl held his curved sword tightly in his left hand, not caring to use it—there was nothing to kill, and he cared not for the foliage in his way. He just held it, his knuckles growing white and bloodless, hurting he held it so tight. He ignored the pain, refused to feel it. He felt numb, his own breathing sounding shallow and distant, his vision narrowed and tunneled. Everything happened at a distance. He heard things as if they were aloof shouts down some unending channel. Smells were bland, washed out. Tastes were plain, weak, mildly putrid, and touches merely a breath of soft wind, nothing.

He stopped when someone grabbed his arm. In one movement, he plunged his sword hilt-deep into the man's belly, and when he looked up, he stared into Kaysin's dying eyes. The man had come to Háthgolthane with him, they had grown up together and shared beds as young boys, japes and jokes as youths, and women as men.

Kaysin's eyes asked the same question Kehl asked.

"Why did you think you could touch me?" Kehl asked. "I am Im'Ka'Da."

Stupid fool thought Kehl as he spat. He looked into those eyes again and saw hurt, disappointment, and sadness. There was no fear, no anger…only death. He slid from Kehl's sword to the ground, and the slaver said a quick prayer for the man.

"I commit you to Sha'Sûn," Kehl said. "I give you to his Sun Army where you may bask in the desert oasis, away from this cursed land of sickly whores and blue-eyed cunts. There, you will live eternity in honor as you fight for Sha'Sûn."

Whatever remorse or guilt Kehl felt for killing the man went away after he had finished praying. It was more than the man deserved, even if he was one of Kehl's companions and friends. Kehl looked up, through the branches of elm and oak. Noon? No, past noon. Wisps of cloud intermittently darkened the already gloomy forest.

"Kellen better have supper ready," Kehl muttered. He looked down at Kaysin, curled around his feet in death like a beaten dog. "When we get back to camp, I will kill a younger slave, one of the children. It will make me feel better, and perhaps it will appease Ner'Galgal."

He looked to the sky again, then back to the body. He could already see flies buzzing around a pool of blood, beetles crawling on the man, ready to burrow into his flesh.

"Sha'Sûn works quickly. It has been a long time since I have sacrificed anything to you, my Lord of the Sun," Kehl said. "Is that why you allowed my brother to die? Is that my punishment for my lack of piety?"

As the murmuring behind him grew, Kehl kept walking.

"I will rectify my wrong. Even if it takes the sacrifices of all the prisoners," Kehl said.

His men would be unhappy. His prisoners—their prisoners—would fetch a high price in Saman.

"But Sha'Sûn and Ner'Galgal care not for money," Kehl said to himself. "They care only for blood. The bodies of warriors are the currency of Sha'Sûn and blood is the currency of Ner'Galgal."

Kehl thought he saw his camp through the low-hanging branches of several old and gnarled elm trees, one tilting so badly, he suspected it might uproot with a strong gust of wind. The thought of a hot supper and spiced wine, a woman—the young gypsy woman he captured, perhaps only a year past her flowering—and a blood sacrifice moved his feet faster and his men fell farther and farther behind him. He pushed past bushes and branches, again ignoring the scratches they brought to his face.

That little gypsy bitch might struggle at first—they always did, especially that young—but that was half the fun, the excitement, the arousal. Then she would relent, and that proved sweeter than any struggle. The look in her eyes as she understood her fate and accepted it, the same look a wild horse gave a man the moment he broke it. Her brown eyes, her olive skin, the tight, black ringlets of her hair, they reminded him of the women back home. His blood boiled, his face blushed, his palms sweated, his heart quickened. He wiped a bit of spittle from his smiling lips with the back of his left hand.

Kehl saw a fire, its faint glow poking through the darkness of the forest. He almost ran. He was close. It was there. He could taste roast meat, the wine, the gypsy's skin. Just there. A few more steps. The fire was just there. The sound of men talking, joking, and laughing. The flute and harp. He was almost there. A few more steps. Past that tree and the next. Through this bush. He could hear his brother's voice throwing japes at their prisoners. Kehl laughed. A few more steps. The warmth of the fire hit his face. His mouth watered. His muscles tensed. His eyes widened. He pushed aside a branch and…

An old fire glowed somberly, tiny flames holding on to their last bit of life. A broken spit and overturned kettle lay next to it. A dead man, face down, next to them. What? Flies buzzed over his head. Next to a log once used as a seat, he found a head. Jossem, the Fin.

Foxes and squirrels and maggots had already been at him; one of his eyeballs was gone, the fleshy parts of his cheeks gnawed to the bone, his ears torn off, his skin blackening and oozing with puss. He slowly looked around through 360 degrees, and truth dawned. Only the dead remained, and there was not a single slave in sight.

"Ner'Galgal, Lord of Death, Slayer, Condemner," Kehl prayed, "you have abandoned me, forsaken me for my insolence, my sin against you, my irreverence."

Then Kehl found his brother—Kellen—his body and head separated. He shook as a shiver trembled through his body. He knelt beside the head and picked it up. Despite the maggots and rot, he kissed its face and held it to his chest as a mother might hold her newborn babe. He looked to the sky and wanted to cry out, ask why. But he knew why.

"I will burn your body, brother," Kehl said. "You, I will give to Sha'Sûn as well. You were always good and loyal, and the god of the sun will welcome you into his shining halls."

He looked about the rest of the camp, all who had once followed him were dead.

"The rest of you I will bury face down," Kehl continued. "I will give you to The Slayer so that he might feast on your bodies every night. That will be your punishment for failing me and my brothers."

He spat. But then he remembered it was his failure, his lack of piety. He would still bury his fallen men face down and give them to Ner'Galgal, but he would have to atone for his sins as well. Kehl knew his surviving men stood at the edge of the encampment, watching as he built a pyre out of the broken pieces of cages and wagons.

"What do we do, Kehl?" one of his men finally asked.

Kehl didn't answer for a long time, not until he finished Kellen's burial fire.

"Count the number of dead, excluding my brother," Kehl commanded. "Once you have done that, dig that many graves, but do not put bodies in them. Then, I want you to dig five more graves."

His men obeyed. He could taste their apprehension, but they did as he asked without a word. When they finished the graves, Kehl carried his brother's body to the pyre and placed his head where it should have lain had it not been excised from his body.

"Sha'Sûn," Kehl quietly prayed, "I pray you welcome my brother to your holy place. Nan'Sin, goddess of the night and the stars and the moon, I pray you show my brother the way to the sun god's shining halls. And Ner'Galgal, I pray that you stay your hand from my brother's body as he makes his journey."

He put a torch to the pyre and it blazed, the wood crackling and the hair and skin smoking with putrid incense. For the other dead men, he commanded his slavers to drag their bodies to the edges of their graves. Before they threw their bodies in, he pissed in each grave, spat, and said a silent curse.

"May The Slayer and his minions feast on your body for all eternity," Kehl cursed, "and may you know endless sorrow, pain, and suffering."

"Wha' 'bout these other graves, Kehl?" one man, Gilga, asked.

Kehl didn't answer his question, but instead barked orders.

"Gilga, Zima, Hiskos, Pierce, and Mika, you stay with me."

He looked to his men. He only had ten left. It would be a costly sacrifice, but that's what The Slayer wanted, needed, required. His sacrifice would appease Ner'Galgal, and he would then bless him.

"The rest of you, spread out, through the forest. If the men who did this are still near, I want them," Kehl commanded, "alive."

"With only five men?" a man named Len asked, but before any more questions could come, Kehl backhanded the man.

"Just do it," he hissed.

As the men he had sent away dispersed into the forest, he gathered his remaining five to him. Kehl retrieved a wineskin from his belt and passed it to the others.

"Take and drink," Kehl said. "You are thirsty, and you have served me well."

Each man took a hearty draught and passed the skin to the next.

"I pray to you, Slayer, that my sacrifice will be pleasing and wash away my transgressions," Kehl prayed in his native language.

His five men lay dead at his feet within only a matter of moments. The poison, venom from the black adder, worked quickly. It was painless, silent. Kehl moved quickly, disemboweling the men, setting their entrails to flame, and then burying the bodies in the five, empty graves. The others would be back soon, and empty-handed.

"Where are the others?" Len asked. Kehl knew Pierce was his friend. He had seen them conversing and sleeping next to one another just the night before.

A'Uthma, another Samanian, but not one who had originally traveled to Háthgolthane with Kehl as Kaysin had, looked at the pyre and smelled the burning bile. The Samanian looked at the five graves, empty when they had left, now filled.

"Ner'Galgal will be pleased," he said. The others didn't understand.

"Let us hope so," Kehl replied. "That is my prayer."

"They are facing skyward?" A'Uthma asked.

Kehl nodded.

"And you said the blessing?" A'Uthma added.

"Of course." Kehl hoped his smile didn't look childish. He cared little to learn about this man, A'Uthma, but it pleased him he worshipped the same god.

"They will serve The Slayer's army well," A'Uthma said. Then he spat in the direction of the other dead, the ones they buried facedown. "And they will suffer the cannibalism of The Slayer's army every night. Ner'Galgal will bless us with treasure worth three times the worth of these men."

Kehl nodded. "And men fivefold and slaves tenfold."

"What the bloody four furnaces are you bloody talking about?" Len said, raising his voice. "Where, by all the gods, are Pierce and the others?"

Before Kehl could say anything, before his curse left his mouth, A'Uthma opened his.

"You will cease to speak to your master in that tone, you fatherless dog," the Samanian cursed, "or you will find out what happened to your *friend*."

Kehl smiled. The Slayer worked quickly. He had already blessed him with a new lieutenant.

He would shed more blood and burn more entrails and rape more women in the name of the Slayer than he had ever before, and Ner'Galgal would continue to shower him with blessings.

"Where to, Im'Ka'Da?" A'Uthma asked.

The last person to call Kehl master in their own tongue was his brother, Kelben. The thought of both his dead brothers finally brought a tear to his eye. Who could have done this to his camp, his men, his brother? He looked about the camp. He saw a body he didn't recognize, one that had been buried but then dug up by wolves and foxes. The dead man had the look of a westerner, one of those transient sons of whores from Waterton. With that, just one thought came to mind.

"Del Alzon," Kehl said quietly.

"Im'Ka'Da'?" A'Uthma asked.

"The men of Waterton are treacherous," Kehl said. "They have betrayed us, sold us slaves, and then stabbed our backs. I want to see that town burn."

Chapter 9

THE CLOUDS ROLLED OFF THE Southern Mountains as if eager to maximize their effect, but the rain came on more slowly for a while, nothing more than misty wisps of water floating through the air. The noonday breeze blowing through the precipitation brought on a much-appreciated coolness at first, but as was so common with monsoons, the rains quickly built to a near deluge, and any praise for the cool rain dissipated as quickly as clothes were soaked.

Erik pondered on the early arrival of the showers this year as he looked back over his shoulder. He didn't really know what he was hoping to see. Stone's Throw, maybe, and a warm straw bed, albeit itchy, a small roasted chicken and a cup of honey-sweetened goat's milk. Mari, her naked body. Her kiss, as cold and numb as it was. The touch of another person—a woman. Perhaps he was looking towards home, thinking he might see his father and mother and two little sisters, hoping his dreams were mere terrible fantasies. Simone and her warm body, the sweet smell of roses that always trailed after her, her soft kisses. He knew he wouldn't see comfort like that for a long while. He looked to the ground.

"There's another pile of horse apple," Erik said.

"Is it fresh?" Drake asked.

Erik squinted. That might be hard to tell in the rain. The other droppings he had seen were at least a few days old. A disheartening-ing thought, especially if these travelers were mercenaries from *The Lady's Inn.*

"I don't know," Erik replied.

"Get off your bloody horse and check," Switch commanded.

Erik looked over to see the mercenary riding next to him, glaring angrily.

"I said…"

"I heard you," Erik retorted, cutting off Switch. Erik knew the thief would kill them if he could. In Switch's eyes, they were proving more trouble than they were worth as porters.

They had found the remnants of a camp just the day before, and now the rain picked up as Erik inspected the droppings with a stick. He shivered when a cold wind rolled off the Southern Mountains and he heard Befel groan. The change in weather wreaked havoc on his brother's shoulder.

"What is he doing?" Turk asked.

"Checking to see if the horseshit is fresh," Switch replied. "Come on, boy. Use your hands."

Erik stood. He suddenly felt ridiculous.

"Get back on your horse, Erik," Turk commanded. Erik could tell the dwarf was irritated. "This is a waste of time."

"Who are you to say what is and isn't a waste of time?" Switch asked.

He squinted hard at Erik.

"Is it fresh?" Switch asked.

"Don't know," Erik said with a shrug. "Go check yourself."

Erik had half expected a slew of curses, but, instead, Switch just smiled and started laughing. Sometimes he was as unpredictable as he was predictable.

They rode on for a while and then something else caught Erik's eye.

"More horseshit?" Bryon asked when he saw Erik slow his horse. "You have such an eye for dung."

"Something shiny, glimmering on the ground," Erik replied.

"It's nothing," Befel said. "Just moisture in the air and the heat playing with your eyes."

"No, it's not nothing," Erik said as he looked for this mysterious shimmering object.

"Oi! There it is," Switch exclaimed as he jumped from his horse.

The thief stooped low to the ground and unsheathed one of his knives. He dug it into the ground and flipped something up, catching it and closing his fingers around the thing. When he opened his hand, he revealed a piece of metal, polished and glimmering and as long as the width of his hand, broken at one end and tapered to a point at the other.

"What is it?" Drake asked.

"Iron." Vander Bim's response was almost a question as much as it was an answer.

"Looks too shiny to be iron," Erik said. "Silver?"

Switch turned his head and looked at Erik. Erik expected a glaring look, a condescending look, but the thief shook his head with a small smile and a quick wink.

"No," Switch said. "Not bloody iron, and not bloody silver. It's steel—good steel."

"A sword?" Erik questioned as he stepped down from his horse.

"Aye," the thief replied, "at least, the tip of one."

The thief threw Erik the piece of sword. He caught it, scratching the index and middle fingers of his left hand as he did. It was sharp. Erik sucked the little bit of blood on his two fingers and watched the thief intently. Switch had uncovered several other shards of sword, small enough for dirt to hide.

"A fight," the thief muttered softly. "Recently too."

A bundle of bushes with tiny purple flowers and white leaves grew close to the area where Switch found the shards, and the thief walked to them; in a matter of seconds, he found a small leather pouch stuck in the branches of one of the bushes. He tossed it to Erik. Empty. The thief knelt and gave a snicker. Standing, he showed

Erik his palm. Three Finnish nickels and a gold, Hámonian pound. He quickly closed his hand and stuffed the coins into a pouch on his belt.

"Finders keepers," he said with a laugh.

Turk and Demik dismounted, as well as Vander Bim.

"Look here," Switch said, pointing to the bush.

"Blood," Erik said as he leaned in to look. "Dried blood."

"Aye," Switch agreed.

"What are those?" Erik said, pointing to what looked like bent pieces of iron.

"Links." Switch picked a few up and held them in his hand, inspecting, before dropping them back to the ground. "Links from a mail shirt. Good iron. Hard to break."

"And yet, broken," Turk added.

Erik didn't like the sound of that. Turk's voice sounded somber, dulled, scared almost.

"What could break a mail shirt?" Erik asked.

"A sturdy axe. A mace." Switch seemed to shrug as he spoke.

"Men from *The Lady's Inn?*" Erik intoned.

"Probably," Switch replied. "You saw the normal people that live around here. They don't carry swords or wear mail armor."

"So, you think they got into a fight with other men from *The Lady's Inn*?" Erik asked.

"If I could bloody see into the past, I would tell you," Switch replied and was then more tolerant. "But I don't know. It is possible, however."

"Dwarves maybe?" Vander Bim's question earned him a disapproving grunt from Demik.

Switch laughed. He so loved chiding the dwarves.

"Also a possibility," Switch replied.

"Probably not," Turk said, looking about for a moment—the blood, the iron links, the shards of sword. "Where are the bodies?"

"Buried," Bryon said.

"Why would one group of mercenaries worry about burying

another group of mercenaries?" Turk asked. "Why would wayward villagers care? Why would dwarves care for that matter?" Then, his voice turned to a growl.

"A cougar then," Erik said.

Turk shrugged.

"I would hope a cougar. By the Creator, I would hope for a herd of cougars over what I am thinking," the dwarf said.

"And what is that?" Switch asked.

"Mountain trolls," Turk replied with a growl.

"Blood and guts!" Switch exclaimed standing and putting his fists on his hips.

"We need to keep our eyes on the mountains, keep our eyes keen, and our ears open," Turk said. "If this is the work of mountain trolls, An help us."

No one ate that night, and certainly, no one drank. They just all watched the mountains. Despite the buzzing of insects brought on by the rains, or the cries of the plain's dogs, or the crackling of a blazing campfire, all seemed so still and quiet in the tension of the night and the knowledge that a mysterious and violent death might be waiting and lurking in the shadows of the Southern Mountains.

Erik leaned back against his saddle, trying to block out the silence. How silly that sounded. He slid his hand into his saddlebag, felt the smooth woodworking, and laid it in his lap. Marcus' flute lay there, waiting and wanting, untouched for weeks now. Erik smiled, imagined something that might scare away the looming thought of death, and smiled. He put the flute to his lips.

"What are you…" Switch began to say, but Turk put up a hand and stopped the thief, only slightly shaking his head. Then he looked to Erik.

"Play, Erik."

Erik stood on a battlefield, soldiers all around him, wearing a multitude of colorful tabards and surcoats, the coats of arms of a thousand families, ten thousand households, stitched and etched and emblazoned and enameled over dazzling, brilliant suits of gleaming, iron mail and steel plate, polished to a brilliant reflection. Spears and axes, war hammers, swords and halberds all lifted in the air with a mighty cheer as the sound of a hundred thousand booted feet started to march. The war horns blew, and the war drums pounded. The ground shook. He saw dwarves and men, flags and standards flying high in the air, flapping ardently in the wind, snapping to attention with every gust, the banners of their houses and castles and countries showing clearly. The march halted, and shields went up as their enemy approached. An army of mountain trolls stood across the field. Erik didn't know what they looked like. He had only seen their shadows. So, his ethereal trolls stood there, hunched, shadowy figures with piercing yellow eyes. They had no true form, and as they marched, their skin moved about like wisps of smoke.

The men and dwarves charged. They crashed into the trolls with the deafening sound of a hammer hitting an anvil. Soon, men and dwarves began slaying trolls, every single one of them. All the while, the horns blew and the drums beat, and Erik played a tune on his flute that made the men dance as they fought—a warrior's dance, moving to and fro to dodge swiping hands, lunging here and there to strike a death blow. A step to the right to block a shadowy fist, a twist to flank the enemy, a blow to bring a sword across the enemy's back.

Erik played, and the shadows stayed away... at least for a night.

Chapter 10

In Mardirru's gypsy caravan, Bo sat on an overturned barrel, opting for a stiff back and uncomfortable seat over the soggy wet ground. He took a deep breath. The air seemed tight, heavy, burdensome. A constricting warmth hung just above the ground, a snake slithering about. With it, however, came the sweet musty smell that rain so often brought in the western regions of Háthgolthane.

The gypsy watched the glow of the city, dull and yellow, and yet too bright in the middle of a moonless night. What hour was it? Men in the east divided their days by numbers. Men past the Giant's Vein simply divided their day by what meal they might be eating at that time. Gypsies told time by what animal would be active, out and hunting. The hour of the bat at dusk, the hour of the morning dove at first light, the hour of the owl at first moon break, and the hour of the eagle when the sun sat at its peak. This was the hour of the wolf, the dead of night when the prowling thief and his companions found leisure to hunt whatever they might find resting unawares or going about under the supposed cover of darkness.

The radiance from Bull's Run was only a dim glimmer, perhaps several taverns and two brothels to serve the few weary travelers passing through, or one of the many stockyard workers who needed such distractions to forget their otherwise hard and dismal lives. Many things might drive a man to Bull's Run, but riches and ease of life were not two of them. Underneath the shadow that hung on this night, however, those lanterns and candles coming from humble inns and the whorehouses glared like beacons.

"Have you been?" Bo asked.

Mardirru turned to Bo, his father's falchion on his lap and a hollowed gourd of sweet water in his hand. The curved eyebrows were all the answer Bo needed.

"Of course not. You're too young," Bo said. "I will say this—it's an interesting city. Big enough for a man to get lost in a crowd but not big enough for a gypsy to get lost in a crowd, if you know what I mean."

Mardirru nodded his head. Big cities didn't necessarily welcome gypsies, but their sheer size meant they cared little for who entered their streets. Small villages and towns were not as complacent. Superstitions, gossip, and rumor hung heavy in a small village or town and, typically, they were no place for Bo and Mardirru's kind.

"This type of night makes me feel uneasy," Bo said.

"How?" Mardirru asked.

"I don't know," Bo replied. "The air is thick. It is as if a shadow, an extra blanket of darkness, has been laid over the night sky. No moon, no stars. I don't like it."

"It's just the clouds," Mardirru said.

"Is it? You cannot say you don't feel it," Bo said. "A movement in the air. A foul stink despite the rain."

Mardirru looked to the sky, then to the faint glow of Bull's Run, then to the ground. He took a sip of his sweet water and then leaned over and picked a blade of grass, crushed it between his thumb and forefinger, and then smelled it. Bo smiled. He was so much like his father—a thinker, a contemplator.

"I feel it," Mardirru finally replied. "But what do we have to worry about? We have our family. We have the Creator watching us."

"It is not us I am worried about."

Bo looked to the sky again as if he would see anything other than the blackness that had been there all night. He scratched his chin underneath the thick, dark bramble of his beard, and then wiped a bit of sleep from his eye. Was that a tear?

"You think they are all right?" Bo asked, breaking several long moments of silence.

Mardirru took twice as long to answer. "No. They are in grave danger. Their wills, strength, and faith are being tested. But they are alive, and I have a feeling—perhaps a hope—that they will survive their ordeal."

Bo wished he could be so confident. He wished he could have the same faith Mardirru had.

"Are you sure?" Bo asked.

"My friend," Mardirru said, "that might be the only thing I am sure about at this moment."

Bo smiled. "So now may not be a good time to ask you where we are going?"

Mardirru gave a short laugh and shook his head with a wide smile.

"I think we will go north and then east. I hear there are villages north and east of here that are not so fearful of gypsies. And, of course, in the north we will be able to trade with both the dwarves of the Gray Mountains and the ogres."

North and east, Bo thought with a smile. It had been a while since he had been north. It would be a good change. Anywhere would be a good change as long as this shadow stopped following them.

Chapter 11

BEFEL WENT TO WIPE AWAY the sweat forming on his brow in the hot, humid, pre-noon day, but stopped, remembering it would only serve to spread it over his face and into his eyes, which already stung. He felt something soft hit his shoulder and drop into his lap. He looked down to see a dry rag sitting there, bouncing atop the horn of his saddle. He picked it up and looked to his left. Vander Bim rode next to him, smiling.

"That should serve," he said, "at least for the next few moments."

Befel laughed. Next few moments indeed. That's all it would take for this dry piece of cloth to become drenched and as useless as the back of his forearm.

"Thanks," Befel replied, holding the rag up and then wiping his face.

"Don't worry, lad." Vander Bim looked to the sky. "The clouds will roll back, and the rains will come, and they will wash away the heat; at least for the afternoon."

"Until tomorrow," Befel replied.

The smile on Vander Bim's face disappeared a little. "Aye, until tomorrow, but that is the way of things. Ebb and flow, come and go. You must take the good with the bad, the joyful things with the sorrowful things. It all balances out in the end."

"Hog piss," Switch said. "We all wind up dead. We all wind up worm shit."

"Maybe my body," Turk said, "but my spirit will live on, forever in…"

"Oh, here we go again," Switch said, rolling his eyes, "with the Creator and heaven."

"You would do well to listen," Turk said, "or both your body and your spirit will wind up worm shit."

"Oh ho." Switch laughed, "The upright dwarf curses."

"It seems you men have been a bad influence on me," Turk grumbled.

Befel laughed at the banter, but as he stared forward, he saw shadows in the distance, wavering wisps of heat rising from the ground. But they began to take on shape, like far away ghosts. And as he leaned forward in his saddle, he squinted and saw them—the silhouettes of men.

"Men," Befel muttered.

"Yes," Turk said. "You men…"

"Men!" Befel yelled.

"That is what I said…"

"No, you fools!" Befel yelled. "Men, on the horizon!"

"Oh, blood and guts and fool's ghosts, it's just the bloody heat and moisture in the air." Switch spat on the ground and glared at the farmer. "Can we get on now, or are we going to stop and chase phantoms? Let me know because I have to piss."

"It's not the heat," Befel said. "Two men. There."

"I see them," said Turk. "Yes, good eyes, Befel. Two men, just on the horizon."

They continued, slowly.

"I think they see us," Befel said. "It looks like they are waving their arms."

"Do you hear that?" Vander Bim asked.

"Aye," Turk replied.

"What is it?" Befel asked.

"Voices," Turk said.

"They're calling to us," Befel said. "Perhaps they need our help."

"Or they're bloody goading us into a trap," the thief added, his words almost a hiss.

Befel looked back at Switch and saw the expression he gave Turk. A quick nod and a wink. He gave the same to the sailor and Drake. Turk said a quick word in his own language to his dwarvish companions. Demik slid his broadsword from its scabbard, and Nafer laid his mace across his lap. Vander Bim and Drake readied their weapons as well, and Befel's brother and cousin caught on, unsheathing their swords too. Befel simply shook his head.

They mean to kill these men. We don't even know who they are, and they mean to kill them.

The men became more visible, waving their arms and calling out, but Befel still couldn't hear what they were saying. A slight breeze had picked up, blowing against their backs, and for that, Befel was grateful. Even though the air felt warm, it cooled the sweat that had collected on his face and brow. But with every breeze, the thief grew more fidgety. His hand gripped tightly around one of his daggers. The dwarves too looked nervous, and Nafer, Demik, and Turk rode close together, almost flank to flank.

He looked to Vander Bim. The sailor never took his eyes off the two men, never hinted to knowing what they said.

"So what? Do we just kill them and hope they meant us ill will?" Befel asked,

"Hush, Befel," Vander Bim whispered.

"Doesn't that seem rather rash?" Befel pressed.

"I said be quiet." Vander Bim paused a moment, and then added, "This is the way of things in our profession. They are competition."

"Shut your flaming mouths," Switch said in a hissing whisper.

They finally got close enough to clearly see and hear the two men. They called out "Ho" and "Help" and "Friend." Of course, none of Befel's companions believed them, evident by the tightened grips on their weapons and the clenching of their jaws, ready for a fight. The farmer could see one man leaning against another. They had weapons—swords—sheathed as far as he could tell. The men wore armor, it seemed, for they glimmered slightly in the sun.

"What competition are these men?" Befel asked. "There are two of them, and one looks to be hurt."

Vander Bim glared at Befel, pursed lips and curved brows, but the farmer thought he saw a hint of understanding, agreement, in the sailor's blue eyes.

"They might have others waiting to ambush us," the sailor conceded. "They seem innocent enough, but as soon as we let our guard down, play into their game, out come their comrades to slit our throats and take what treasures we have."

"That's bloody right." Switch leaned forward in his saddle and glared at the two men. "Now don't make me bloody say it again. Shut your flaming, sheepherding mouths. And if I have to tell you again, you tick-filled, cow-loving farmer, I'll cut you open from balls to throat."

The men were a hundred paces away, maybe less.

"Be ready," Switch whispered.

"This doesn't feel right," Befel said to Vander Bim.

"No, it doesn't," Vander Bim replied, seemingly pondering Befel's statement. "You're right. Come, Befel, ride to them with me. Let us greet them before we get into a fight that need not happen."

Befel nodded with a grin, and while Switch, Turk, and Drake spoke quietly of their plan, both the farmer and sailor spurred their horses and galloped towards the two men.

"Eh!" Switch yelled, trying to stop the two men. "Vander Bim! You old fool of a sailor!"

"Ho," Vander Bim cried out as they neared the two waving men.

"Ho," cried back one of the men.

They stopped a dozen paces from the two men. The one who had called back—a man of middle years with a face showing signs of at least two weeks without a razor—held up one hand, the other wrapped tightly around his companion's waist, propping him up against his hip, the other man's arm draped around the first's shoulders.

"These men don't look like a threat," Befel said.

"No, they don't," Vander Bim replied, "but nonetheless, be careful and ready."

"They both look beaten," Befel added.

The first lowered his hand for a second to brush a bit of his wavy brown hair from his face, revealing a forehead full of tiny cuts and caked with dried blood. Despite the brown stubble on his face, Befel could see spots of yellow where the skin rose in soft puffiness.

"Bruises," Befel muttered.

"Aye," Vander Bim agreed.

"Ho there," the man said again, and Vander Bim replied in kind.

The men looked like they could fight, once, both with polished breastplates and greaves and vambraces of high-quality steel. Shirts of mail poked through the armor's joints and below their cuirasses. At the first man's waist hung two long swords, one on either side, matching scabbards of well-worked leather and wood embroidered with silver scrollwork and a dagger with a similar sheathe hung next to one of the scabbards. The other fellow—the injured one—also had a single sword hanging from his left hip, its handle a thick piece of spiraling wood bound in leather and tipped with a golden orb etched to appear like the sun.

"They truly look like they mean us no harm," Befel whispered as the injured man started slipping off the first's hip.

He was barely conscious, blood caking his blond hair and beard. His battered face was evident by puffy cheeks and a left eye that was black and swollen shut.

"I agree," Vander Bim replied, also with a whisper, "but we still need to be careful."

"Thank you," the first man finally said, a wide smile splitting his face and showing two rows of whitish teeth, cleaner than Befel might have expected from a traveling warrior. "We wouldn't have lasted another day, and most men in these areas probably would've ridden us down rather than stopped."

Befel gave the sailor a concerned look and tried to glance over his shoulders at the rest of the party.

"Throw down your weapons," Vander Bim commanded, his voice hard and direct. "Slowly."

The first man opened his arms, palms facing outward. He looked beyond Befel, who turned in his saddle to see the rest of their party joining them, weapons at the ready.

"You'll excuse us," Vander Bim said, his voice softening. "You are obviously well-trained warriors and, as you said, out here, most men might have ridden you down just as most men might feign injury to lure several trusting travelers into a trap."

The man straightened his shoulders a bit, pulling them back and pushing out his chest, revealing a body of lean muscle. Despite the possible attack on his pride, the man never lost his smile and gave a dismissive shake of his head.

"Please, no apology needed." The soldier said something to his companion that Befel didn't recognize.

"Is that Shengu?" Switch asked as he arrived alongside them.

Befel looked at Vander Bim.

"The language of Golgolithul," Vander Bim replied.

"Aye," the man said, his smile fading a bit, but still present, however fake it might be.

"You're an easterner, then?" Switch's words were more an accusation than a question, but he still put it to the soldier to answer.

"Aye, both of us. Does that concern you, my good man?" the Easterner asked.

"Just lay your weapons on the ground," Vander Bim said before adding, "please."

As the one who spoke helped his injured companion, they did as Vander Bim bid, slowly drawing their swords and laying them before their feet. Their swords were beautiful, wonderfully worked pieces of steel and polished and sharpened to a gleam. One of the two swords of the first man was broken just a couple of hands-span from its cross guard.

Befel saw Erik riding up next to him.

"I know these men," Erik whispered. Befel waved him off as if he were an annoying gnat.

"That's all of them?" Switch asked when the first man threw his dagger to the ground.

"An honorable soldier does not hide weapons," the man replied.

"Well, you'll bloody excuse me, but we don't find too many honorable soldiers out here," Switch replied.

"They were at *The Lady's Inn,*" Erik whispered. "The one with the broken sword even spoke to me."

"Erik, please," Befel replied as he saw Vander Bim shoot him a hard look.

"But there were three of them," Erik added.

"Are you sure?" Vander Bim asked.

"Yes," Erik replied. "Without a doubt."

"You were at *The Lady's Inn*," Vander Bim asked. "You heard the Black Mage's message?"

"Aye, we were, and we did," the healthier of the two men said. "I remember seeing you there."

He pointed at Erik.

"What happened to you?" Vander Bim asked. "Was there not a third?"

"There was," the Easterner replied, his voice laden with sadness.

"And where is he?" Switch asked, cynicism ripe in his voice.

"Soldiers attacked us," the Easterner replied, "three days ago—a day as the crow flies. They killed our friend."

"What kind of soldiers?" Vander Bim asked.

"Eastern soldiers."

"And why would men from the same country you are currently serving attack you?" Switch asked.

"Men loyal to Patûk Al'Banan," the Easterner replied.

"Were mountain trolls with them?" Turk asked.

"Aye, master dwarf," the Easterner replied. "In fact, that is the only reason they were able to take down our friend, Tedish. When they killed Tedish, Samus and I ran. I am ashamed to say it, but we had no choice. They followed us—the trolls and soldiers. We killed at least two of the soldiers, and my sword is broken because of the deep wound I gave one of those trolls."

"Blood and guts and queen's ashes," Switch said.

"Poor Tedish," the man muttered. "He was a good soldier and an even better man. He didn't deserve to die that way. Curse the gods for their follies. I have been soldiering for a long time all around this world, and yet never had seen such a sight as mountain trolls working with, or for, men."

"What is your name?" Vander Bim asked.

"Wrothgard, Wrothgard Bel'Therum," the healthier man replied, "and my friend's name is Samus Sunrider. We are, as you can tell, soldiers by trade."

"Soldiers turned sell-swords, aye?" Switch's tone always had an edgy hardness to it.

"Aye, 'tis true, whether I like to admit it or not," Wrothgard replied, "the life of a simple soldier can be a short one, and if a man happens to outlive his usefulness, well, there is little else for which he is qualified. I would like to think that, despite carrying the title of mercenary, we still practice the honor we did as soldiers."

"Soldiers for the Eastern Kingdom," Turk said. His voice sounded hard, irritated, and disapproving.

Wrothgard Bel'Therum nodded.

"There is little honor in that." Switch laughed, showing his yellowed teeth. "And even less as a sell-sword. Don't try to fool yourself, or us."

"A point well taken," Wrothgard replied. "Certainly, many military actions taken by the Lord of the East have stained his country's reputation, and those who serve him. And, no, I suppose there is little honor in being a mercenary. However, we are both strong men…when healthy."

"And what do we care, however strong you are?" Switch hissed.

"We have much experience in the way of soldiering, sword and shield, the spear, the bow. I feel that, perhaps fate has brought us together."

"You wish to travel with us, join our company?" The answer seemed obvious, but Vander Bim had to ask anyway.

"Aye," Wrothgard replied.

Vander Bim looked to Switch and Drake and the dwarves. Befel could see the slight shake in the thief's head. The miner shrugged. Demik grumbled, and Nafer said something to Turk in Dwarvish.

"We will have to confer as a group," Vander Bim told Wrothgard. "Give us a moment."

The soldier bowed, and the party followed Vander Bim as he rode a dozen paces away. Everyone circled up, even Befel, Erik, and Bryon.

"Cut their throats and leave them here for those damn trolls," Switch said.

"I think we should let them into our company," Vander Bim voted. "We watch them for a day or two, help the injured one heal up, and make our final judgement that their word is true. If it is, and they actually are the soldiers they say they are, then we offer them a partnership. Equal shares. If that fellow served for Golgolithul, he certainly has more fighting experience than me."

"Aye, and me," Drake added.

"They seem trustworthy," Befel said.

"Eh, you, my son, just shut your mouth," said Switch, true to form as usual. "You have no say in this, and you and your kin have bloody well said enough already."

"Will they slow us down, though?" Drake said. "They're both injured, one badly. Dwarf, can your medicine heal him?"

"If he is willing," Turk said, shrugging. "I would have to look him over. Maybe. Their eastern roots are what concerns me."

"Aye," Demik said.

"And not just easterners," Turk added, "but eastern soldiers. Too many dwarves have lost their lives to the treacheries of the Eastern Kingdom for me to so easily trust these men simply because they say they are honorable."

"Saying honorable man is like saying clean mud," Demik added, to which Switch whistled. Turk said something to his dwarvish friend in their native tongue.

"It should be unanimous," Vander Bim proposed. "You know my vote, and you know what must be done if we vote not to allow them into our company."

"I don't really care either way," Turk said. "You know my concern. I will keep a watchful eye on them. However, if the vote is to leave them, that is fine with me as well. If we leave them, I am not, however, comfortable with killing them."

"We are already behind," Drake said, "but if they can keep up, then so be it. The first sign of falter, though—I am not a greedy man, but this is about money and about seeing my children again."

"I say they will slow us down," Switch added. "They're injured. I say kill them or leave them. Let the trolls occupy themselves with these fools while we make a clean break."

"You are truly heartless," Befel said.

Switch just shrugged his shoulders.

"I can live with that," Switch replied. "Listen, I'm not going to bloody argue about it. If you fellows want them, fine. Nevertheless, their seeming so honest makes me think they aren't. But then again, who am I to judge? Like the miner said, though, they slow us down and I'll just cut their throats in the middle of the night, along with these three idiot porters."

Chapter 12

VANDER BIM RODE OVER TO the man who called himself Wrothgard.

"We'll let you into our company, if you wish," Vander Bim said.

"We do," Wrothgard replied with a quick bow.

"We have porters with us that will serve you as well," Vander Bim said, "and two packhorses you and your friend can use."

"May we have our weapons back?" Wrothgard asked Vander Bim.

"Why don't you let Turk take a look at your wounds first?" Vander Bim replied.

"The dwarf?" Wrothgard questioned.

Demik grunted at the inquisition.

"Aye," Vander Bim replied, "he is an exceptional healer."

"Very well then," Wrothgard said. "Have him look at Samus first. I have been in battle many times and have many times seen wounds such as his. They look grave to me."

Turk nodded, tending to the blond-haired man who seemed to have trouble simply keeping his eyes open. Erik remembered the man being an imposing figure with well-kept hair and a trimmed beard, broad shoulders, and a barrel chest. A muscular man then that had the prowess of what the young farmer expected to be a seasoned soldier, but now? Presently, he looked little more than a cripple, or some old, weathered beggar that might inhabit the streets of Eastern Finlo.

Erik looked to the sky. Not a cloud in sight. Just crystal blue staring back at him, so crisp and bright that he had to blink after only a short while.

"If the sun stays out," Erik murmured, "perhaps it will burn away all the moisture. That would be nice."

"I wouldn't get your hopes up," Drake said as he walked past Erik, eyeing the two new members of their party suspiciously.

"Not good." Turk's words caught Erik's attention.

"What is that, master dwarf?" Wrothgard asked.

Turk probed Samus' ribs. The mercenary would fall asleep, only for a moment, and then snap awake with a shrill cry or a low grunt as the dwarf pressed down.

"Erik," Turk said.

"Yes," Erik replied.

"Get the blue jar out of my bag, along with several strips of cloth and the round, clear bottle," Turk commanded.

Erik complied, bringing the dwarf what he asked for.

"Master dwarf," Wrothgard said, "what is wrong with Samus?"

"His ribs are certainly broken," Turk replied, opening the mouth of an unconscious Samus and pouring in the clear liquid.

"Not to second guess your medical expertise," Wrothgard said, "but I already knew that. We have all probably had broken ribs."

"Aye," Turk acknowledged, "but the real problem is that I think his broken ribs have punctured a lung."

Erik heard a low groan come from Wrothgard.

"That is a death sentence," Wrothgard muttered. "Should I give him a quick death to subside his pain?"

"You mean to kill your own friend?" Erik asked, exasperated.

"It is because he is my friend," Wrothgard replied. Erik noticed the glimmer of tears in the man's eyes. "My best of friends, that I would do this for him. A punctured lung is incurable—certain death—and I could not stand to have my brother in arms linger for a few more days in agony. I will give him a quick and honorable death."

Erik saw Wrothgard's hand go to the handle of his dagger.

"Not necessarily," Turk said, putting up a hand to stay Wrothgard. "A punctured lung is no small thing, but not certain death. If we were in Thorakest, our surgeons could heal him. I can too, but out here? We must seek to immobilize his broken ribs. Ideally, he should stay still and rest, but that cannot happen if you wish to join us."

"So, he may yet live?" Wrothgard asked.

"Aye, despite his lung. And his cuts are infected," Turk added. He poured the blue liquid over the lacerations on Samus' ribs. The wounds hissed and bubbled as the liquid spilled over his skin. "Surely, this humid weather is partially to blame. Erik, get me the yellow salve in the short, fat jar."

Erik did as he was asked. Turk scooped a healthy portion of the salve onto two fingers and spread it over Samus' many wounds, taking the strips of cloth and bandaging them as best he could.

"He has a fever," Turk said.

"Will he last the night?" Wrothgard asked.

"Tonight will be the test, I think," Turk replied. "I will tend to his wounds once more before we stop for the evening, and I will give him a tincture that should quell his fever and relieve some of his pain."

"Please, master dwarf," Wrothgard said, "if his fate looks certain, you must tell me. I must end his suffering if there is no hope."

Erik couldn't help thinking the look on Turk's face was one of disapproval, but nonetheless, he nodded.

"I will tell you if I believe there is no hope," Turk said. "Now, let's have a look at you."

Turk tended to Wrothgard's cuts, Erik helping him by fetching this vial of liquid and that cream, along with bandages. The soldier's wounds seemed simple in comparison to those of Samus.

"I'm sorry about your friend," Erik said.

"Thank you," Wrothgard replied with a smile. "He is a good man. Tedish was a good man too."

"I will pray for him," Erik said. "Him and Samus."

"To which god will you pray?" Wrothgard asked. "I have prayed to Ga'an Yû, the god of war, Ner'Wu Ta'Shin, the goddess of healing. I even prayed to Chago and Tugo, our brother gods of wealth and prosperity. None seem to answer."

"I will pray to An," Erik replied.

"I don't know that god," Wrothgard replied with a smile, "but I do appreciate the prayers."

"He is the one dwarves believe in," Erik said. "We Westerners too, although we simply call him the Creator."

"I see," Wrothgard said, that smile still on his face, although, Erik wondered if it was authentic. "Well, I will cherish those prayers."

"What route have you chosen?" Wrothgard said after a few moments of silence. He drank some water Turk had given him after the dwarf had finished bandaging a wound along his chest.

"Which route had you chosen?" Turk asked in return.

"Ecfast," Wrothgard replied.

"Ecfast?" Turk said with surprise.

"What is Ecfast?" Erik asked.

"An outpost," Turk replied, "that sits along the feet of the Southern Mountains and towards the easternmost reaches of Drüum Balmdüukr."

"Aye," Wrothgard agreed.

"And how would you pass through a dwarvish outpost?" Turk asked.

"Tedish, our fallen brother, knew a southern dwarf working as a silver and goldsmith in Goldum," Wrothgard explained. "He had given Tedish a token—a gift for his friendship in an otherwise unfriendly land—saying that if he ever needed passage into dwarvish lands, he was to present that token, and he would travel unharmed."

"Do you have the token?" Turk asked. "They usually bear the family name of the dwarf. Do you know the dwarf's name?"

"I do not remember the dwarf's name," Wrothgard replied, "and, unfortunately, the token was lost with Tedish."

"That is too bad," Turk said.

"Can we not still take that course?" Wrothgard asked. "After all, you are dwarves."

"Simply being a dwarf does not allow you into all dwarf lands," Demik answered, sitting only a few paces away and obviously overhearing their conversation. "Does simply being a man allow you into Fen-Stévock?"

"An outpost will not allow anyone, even a dwarf, through its doors without a writ of passage or token," Turk explained. "I was hoping you still had that token. It would have made our journey a bit easier. We will stop in Aga Min and enter the mountain from there."

"I would be careful in Aga Min," Wrothgard said.

"Why's that?" Vander Bim came to join them as well, sipping on rum and biting into half a loaf of stale bread that looked to have spots of mold.

"Master Cho, the Chief Miner of Aga Min, is not known for his hospitality, that is all," Wrothgard explained. "He is far less hospitable than Arnif."

"Arnif?" Erik asked.

"Aye. Master Arnif, the Chief Miner of Aga Kona. Did you not meet him when you passed through?" Wrothgard asked. "I am assuming you passed through Aga Kona."

"It was…is gone," Vander Bim replied softly.

Wrothgard looked to Turk, and the dwarf nodded, as did Erik.

"Gone?" The bewildered look on Wrothgard's face was one of both misunderstanding and mirth as if he believed Vander Bim was playing some cruel jest.

"Aye. Gone," Demik added.

"I don't understand," Wrothgard said.

"The camp was gone when we got there. Destroyed," Vander Bim explained. "It looked like…"

Vander Bim paused as if the word was too much. It stuck in his throat, refusing to leave his lips.

"Mountain trolls," Turk finished.

"That saddens my heart," Wrothgard said softly. "And the people who lived there?"

"Many of them dead," Vander Bim replied. "Some had escaped—to a small village a day's ride east of Aga Kona."

"That is terrible," Wrothgard said. "The things that one man can do to another."

"But it wasn't men," Erik said. "It was mountain trolls."

"Led by men," Wrothgard replied.

"Do you think these were the same trolls that attacked you?" Vander Bim asked.

"Undoubtedly," Wrothgard replied without hesitation. "We meant to stay a night, Samus, Tedish, and I. I waited outside Arnif's tent, as he engaged another man in conversation. He had, as usual, guards posted outside his tent, but one of those men did not belong. He bore the look of a true soldier—a clean face, well-groomed hair, the lean body of disciplined training. He wore a heavy, cowled cloak to cover his armor, but when he moved, I saw, only for a glimmer of a moment, something I had not seen in years emblazoned on his steel breastplate."

He paused a moment, took a bite of jerky and a drink of water.

"What was it?" Erik asked.

Wrothgard smiled. "The conversation inside Arnif's tent became heated. Anyone within twenty paces could've heard that. A tall man with gray hair exited, visibly frustrated. He had the same look as the soldier guarding the entrance. And then I recognized him. Like the emblem on the soldier's breastplate, I had not seen this man in many years and thought I would never see him again. Those cold, gray eyes. They were unmistakable."

"Who was it?" Vander Bim asked. Erik, the sailor, and both dwarves had now stopped to listen to Wrothgard's story.

"I had the honor of receiving a commission in the Eastern Guard—an elite company of soldiers only bettered by the Soldiers of the Eye and the personal guard of the Lord of the East—at a young age," Wrothgard explained. "In fact, I was one of the youngest lieutenants ever in the Guard's ranks. My commander, perhaps one of the greatest generals in all of Háthgolthane in a century, was Patûk Al'Banan. General Patûk Al'Banan exited that tent in Aga Kona."

"The bloody Shadow take us all," Switch cursed. He had walked by just as Wrothgard had said the General's name.

"Who?" Vander Bim asked.

"Who?" Switch said with exasperation. "Patûk bloody Al'Banan, that's who. Only one of the greatest generals to ever serve Golgolithul."

"I thought you might recognize the name," Wrothgard said with a mirthless smile.

"You bet your bollocks I recognize the name," Switch replied. "The champion of the Aztûkians, going around and earning titles like *Scourge of the East* and *Champion of Death* and *He Who Makes the Skies Rain Blood.* Even a bloody gutter shite knows who he is."

"I know of him as well," Turk said.

"Aye," Demik added. "He orchestrated the death of many of our kin."

"The emblem I saw on the General's guard's armor was that of a cobra, coiled and ready to strike, hood flared, and fangs bared," Wrothgard said. "If it were on a standard, the cobra would have been black, save for red eyes and white fangs, and it would have been centered on a purple field."

"The Aztûkians," Switch muttered.

"Aye," Wrothgard agreed, "the Aztûkians."

"Who are they?" Erik asked.

"The family that held the seat of High Lord Chancellor for three hundred years before the Stévockians regained control," Wrothgard replied.

"It was Rimrûk Aztûk who signed the peace treaty with King Agempi I at the Battle of Bethuliam," Turk added, "ending the Great War."

"Aye," Wrothgard said.

"Families?" Erik questioned.

"Feudal politics many of the free folk of the west never have to worry about," Vander Bim explained. "A wicked and treacherous game of power and family ties."

"That it is," Wrothgard replied, "but much is the way of the developed nations of the world."

"Even the dwarves face these political issues," Turk added.

"Well, if tunnel diggers experience it," Switch chided, "then it must be real."

Turk ignored Switch, just shaking his head as Demik grumbled.

"The Lord of the East is a Stévockian," Wrothgard explained. "They are enemies of the Aztûkians and ruled Golgolithul before the end of the Great War. The Stévockians regained power—the Lord of the East's father—through treachery and deceit, murder and corruption. It is, unfortunately, the way these political games work.

"To avoid civil war, he allowed many Aztûkians to remain in his High Council and allowed the Eastern Guard to keep the Aztûkians' standard as their own—the cobra ready to strike on a purple field. General Patûk Al'Banan was a loyal servant to the Aztûkians, as were most of the high-ranking officers and knights in Golgolithul's armies and guards. I remember some of them, for they were still allowed to bear their standard when I received my commission.

"Five years later, the High Lord Chancellor was dead, and his son, the Lord of the East, assumed the title of High Lord Chancellor. Five years after that, he dissolved the title of High Lord Chancellor, crowned himself emperor, and disbanded the High Council. His first order of business as Golgolithul's despot was to change all military standards, save for the Soldiers of the Eye, to that of his family—a clenched fist, black as pitch, holding an arrow, black fletching and blood red tipped on an ash gray field. He made it illegal to fly any other standard as high as his own, and any noble marching to battle must fly the Stévockian crest above his own or face death as punishment. Needless to say, many dissented, including Patûk Al'Banan, and those who were not executed in the streets for their opposition, fled."

"I remember that day," Turk said with a solemn voice.

"Aye," Demik replied, a hint of disgust in his words. "Many dwarves died as well, any who would not fly the Stévockian standard above their shops and homes. They were labeled spies for enemies of the East."

Demik spat as Wrothgard nodded.

"That was twenty years ago," Wrothgard continued, "and many have suspected that those who did flee have been plotting to overthrow the Lord of the East ever since, fighting some hidden, shadowy civil war, using whatever means necessary, including enlisting trolls into their ranks. Easterners killing innocent easterners. It makes my stomach churn."

"So why would they bother with you?" Switch asked.

"Disrupt the business of Lord of the East? Find the ancient city for themselves and use its wealth to fund their army? Exert their control in Háthgolthane and present themselves as a legitimate force?" Wrothgard said with a shrug. "All of these, probably. Maybe even more. General Al'Banan is smart, cunning, ruthless, and powerful."

"And what of Aga Kona?" Vander Bim asked. "Why would they bother with Aga Kona?"

"It is supposedly the richest mine owned by Golgolithul," Wrothgard replied. "Copper, iron, and gold like we haven't seen in years. That's what people said, at least. I think Patûk wished to buy it, or at least buy the miners and then have them abandon the mine."

"Those people were not soldiers, though," Erik said. "They were women and children?"

"General Patûk Al'Banan is known for many things, my friend," Wrothgard said. "Compassion is not one of them."

Chapter 13

"When will we be at Aga Min?" Befel asked.

"Three days," Vander Bim said.

"Not soon enough," Erik said. Befel couldn't agree more, but, of course, their cousin took the opportunity to scold his brother for complaining and whining like a little boy.

The look Erik returned Bryon said that he was more than willing to have it out. The last time they fought, Bryon could have killed Erik if he had wanted to. He certainly beat him silly. Befel didn't think that would happen again. He wasn't even sure Bryon would best his brother. Muscles had started to show clearly in his brother's arms and legs and shoulders and back. He suspected Erik was now taller than him by a good hand's width, and their time away from home had hardened him. It saddened Befel, just a little. Erik had always been gentle and kind, and now there were moments when Befel only saw a toughened traveler, a mercenary in the making.

As they settled down for the night, Befel could see shadows in the mountains; large shadows, troll-shaped shadows.

"Are they really there?" Befel whispered. "Does anyone else see them?"

They must. Befel looked to the faces of Drake and Demik, Turk and Switch as they too stared into the mountains. It now seemed that this was all everyone did at night as if sleep were a thing of the past.

"You see what you want to see," his father once told him, "especially when you are acting out of fear rather than faith."

"I don't even know what a troll looks like," Befel muttered.

"What's wrong with you?" Erik asked.

Befel knew he had been tossing and turning, despite the quietness of the night. His shoulder, the suffocating humidity, his homesickness the hot, wet ground—they were all contributors along with the nagging sense that some monster stared at him—just him—from behind a rock.

"My shoulder," Befel replied. "My skin. Under my arms and in between my legs are raw and red from the rain. I'm just uncomfortable."

Befel pulled a blanket given to him by the gypsies up to his waist as he spread a cooling cream Turk had given him on the skin of his inner thighs. He looked to his right and saw no one. Then to his left, just at the edge of the firelight and mostly hidden by the shadows of the night, stood a man. Drake. He held something in his hand—a jar. Rum. He swayed back and forth. Drunk. The miner looked up to the mountains. Befel followed the man's gaze but saw nothing in the darkness.

"I'll follow you up there. I'll bloody kill you all." Sobs interrupted his slurred words. "Bloody bastards. I'll kill you. I'll kill you all."

"Who are you talking to?" Befel asked softly.

"Trolls," Drake muttered. He looked at Befel then looked away, swaying so far to one side, Befel thought he might fall. "Trolls. I'm talking to trolls. Don't you see them? Don't you? Up there. Watching. Waiting."

Drake looked back to the mountains and pointed. Shadows flickered across Drake's face. He ran the back of his right hand across his nose and then across his cheek. He snuffled.

"We must kill them," Drake said. Befel thought Drake looked at him now, but the miner's gaze looked unsteady. "Those people. Poor people. They deserve it. They deserve more. They deserve vengeance."

"I don't think—"

"No one cares what you think!" Drake's voice was a slurred hiss, but Befel noticed that it caused the rest of the mercenaries to look their way.

"Oi!" Switch shouted. "Shut your bloody mouth."

"Come over here, Drake," Vander Bim said. "Come near the fire and away from the lad. Let him rest."

Drake seemed reluctant, still looking at Befel, but he eventually took another draught of his rum and huffed.

"No one cares what you think," he muttered as he passed the young man. "No one cares. They have to die. All of them ..."

His voice trailed off, and Befel sighed, glad for the sailor's intervention.

Befel's stomach twisted as he watched Drake stumble to the fire, crying. The sailor put a hand on the miner's shoulder, helping him sit. He heard the miner say something about haunted dreams and dark memories. Befel had suffered his own dark dreams of late, visions of his grandfather, dead in a box made of oak and pine. His face was pale, and he looked like he had lost weight, his normal, stout face drawn and gaunt. Befel had seen plenty of animals, dead and rotting, maggot-infested with ribs and cheekbones exposed, but nothing could compare with what he had seen in the last two months. Burned bodies, eviscerated corpses, women and children slaughtered, chewed upon. It was no wonder they haunted his dreams.

He lay down, head on a rolled-up blanket, shirt sticking to his chest. He would have taken it off, but weariness weighed him down, and to take off his shirt without hurting his shoulder too much proved a laborious process, delaying further the onset of sleep. He would be lucky if restful sleep ever came back to him. It never did now. He would dream a dark dream, and then he would wake to an aching shoulder. It would take him at least a half hour to get back to sleep, and then the cycle would repeat itself.

He looked to Erik, sleeping next to him. His tiny shivers and sweat-soaked shirt told of a similar experience. He knew his brother had dark dreams, too. Befel laid his head back and stared at the stars overhead, most of which hid behind gray wisps of cloud. The snapping and cracking of wood in the fire served as a lullaby while sleep pulled at his eyelids. Amidst the chorus of popping, and the faint chirping of crickets, he tried to hear his mother's voice telling him a bedtime story. But then he closed his eyes, and darkness came, and the dead were there to greet him.

Chapter 14

ERIK WAS LISTENING TO ANOTHER story about Drake's wife when the scratchy, almost hissing voice of Switch chimed in.

"By all the bones beneath the ground," the thief said. His voice sounded like that of a scolding father, loud enough to gather someone's attention, but not a shout. "Could we please listen to another bloody story rather than one about your bloody wife?"

His sarcasm was not lost on Drake, and he stopped for a few moments. Vander Bim had slowed them to a crawl and was already turning his horse to face his companions. Erik heard the dwarves behind him speaking in their native tongue and then heard the familiar thump of boots hitting the ground. He saw Nafer tying his horse's reins to a knee-high shrub growing lonely amongst hard ground. Befel sighed, and Switch grumbled, spitting and cursing about the slow goings and injured men and dead weight.

"If it was his decision, he'd slit Samus' throat in the middle of the night and be done with him," Erik said.

"That he would," Befel said.

"Probably ours too," Erik added.

"Most certainly ours," Befel replied. "I'm sure he would slit mine first."

Befel looked at his shoulder and made arm circles.

"I don't think so," Erik said, shaking his head. "He would probably slit Bryon's first."

"You're probably right," Befel said with a short laugh. "Then mine. Then yours. Then Wrothgard's. And then…maybe even the dwarves."

"Not the dwarves. They are too smart," Erik said. "And so is Wrothgard."

"You don't even know the guy," Befel said. Erik could see that exasperated look forming on Befel's face, the one he wore when he thought Erik was being childish.

"No, I don't," Erik said with a shrug, "but I think I like him. He seems like a good fellow. I remember him from *The Lady's Inn.* He was kind, helpful. Not like the other mercenaries."

"Erik, please," Befel said.

"Stop talking to me like I'm a child," Erik spat. "You think I'm still some young, ignorant fool on the farm. Two years and some has done a lot, Befel. I can read people. I could have told you from the beginning that Switch is a rat turd. And I could have told you that Vander Bim, as kind as he tries to be, is a lost, hopeful leader who will never amount to that which he wants. And I can tell you that Wrothgard is a good and kind man."

Befel walked away, shaking his head and muttering to himself while Erik stood by his horse, drinking warm water and watching Turk tend to Samus. He noticed his cousin brushing his horse's hair, whispering to it like a lover, and Switch, off in the distance spitting and kicking rocks like some little disgruntled kid. The other two dwarves—Nafer and Demik—conversed in their own language, while Wrothgard listened intently to a jovial conversation between Drake and Vander Bim. Erik couldn't hear much of their conversation, but he did hear the miner say something about his mother-in-law and to that, both the sailor and the soldier threw their heads back and laughed loudly.

Amidst the laughter and Switch's cursing, Erik heard another sound, something like an odd laugh, loud and piercing. He looked about to see where the sound came from, but it turned to a screech, and then a whimper, and then a gurgling, grotesque sound like bubbling water passing through a narrow spout. Then, at the edge of their makeshift camp, Drake's horse was flailing about on the ground, its hooves slamming hard against the dirt, kicking up a choking cloud of dust. When it stopped, Erik saw its head, a bloody mess of black mane, a broken jaw lolling to one side, and broken teeth and bits of the rock that had felled it scattered about.

Demik shouted something spoken in a harsh, cursing tone in his own language and, in response, a bestial growl echoed from the mountains. Demik pointed, and Erik followed the dwarf's finger to a spot in the slopes of the Southern Mountains—and there he saw it. It caught his breath for a moment—something he expected to see and then something he thought he would never see at all. It looked like he thought it might, but then again, much worse.

"Trolls!" Wrothgard yelled.

Two stood there, among a small copse of ironwoods and boulders. One was half-hidden behind a tree while the other stood in the open, clearly defiant as it looked down on the group of men. It's back hunched over, slouched at the shoulders, and almost leaning on its knuckles. Its arms were as long as its legs and both rippled with muscle that cast shadows along its gray skin every time it moved. Even from a hundred paces away, it looked monstrously large, perhaps six heads taller than Bryon if it stood straight up. Its head of stringy, black hair that spilled over its shoulders like thick, sticky mud, sat atop its shoulders seemingly without a neck. Below its sloping brow of disheveled, bushy, black eyebrows sat two beady eyes, too small for its massive head and set too close. They stared at Erik and, with a malicious grunt, the beast showed a row of sharp, yellowed teeth set in a jaw with a severe under bite.

The troll in plain view gripped a rock in its one hand that would've taken Erik all his own strength to lift just a hand's-width off the ground. With a wolf-like howl, it lifted the rock over its head, snorted from its snot-filled, flat nose, and heaved the missile well past where anyone in the party stood. It shattered in a spray of rubble. Everyone just stared.

The monster snorted in disgust—it had missed its mark. Its comrade grunted and spoke in an ugly language. The first moved down the mountain's slope, and its saunter was one of indifference as if it really didn't care that the mercenaries stood there, watching. However, every step it took caused Erik's heart to beat faster, harder. He could see the thing's leg muscles flex and move under the torn and stained wool pants it wore, cut at the knees. Still eighty paces away, Erik could smell its putrid stench, that of shit and offal and unwashed flesh.

"What are you fools doing?" Wrothgard cried, retrieving his long sword from its sheath. "Arm yourselves. Get ready. Fight for your lives."

His voice stung like a switch across the back of Erik's legs, and his mesmerized trance broke. He looked back to his brother and drew his own sword at the same time. He saw his cousin doing the same, Switch racing after his frightened horse and pulling his bow from behind the saddle when he finally caught it, and the dwarves readying their weapons. He saw Drake, flat on his backside, scooting away from the dead horse he had been grooming and then pushing himself into a crouched position. The troll was only sixty paces away now, with another rock in its hands, this one smaller than the last one. Drake realized he was weaponless and made for his pickaxe, but as he lunged forward, the monster threw its own weapon and the rock crashed against Drake's right knee with a deafening crunch. The miner's face hit the ground hard as the rock took his legs out from under him. As soon as he pushed himself up, his face covered in blood and dirt, a scream erupted from his mouth. He tried to stand but collapsed immediately, his leg a twisted, mangled thing underneath his body.

"Help me!" cried Drake. Erik thought he heard the troll laugh. "My leg! It's broken!"

"No bloody kidding," Erik heard Switch say and turned to see the thief taking careful aim with his short bow.

While Vander Bim made his way, sword in hand, towards his

friend, Switch loosed two arrows towards the first troll, both missiles striking its meaty chest and doing little more than causing a low growl. It slammed its fists into the ground hard and, using all four of its limbs, raced towards Vander Bim, who now had Drake's collar in his hand and was dragging the screaming miner away from the fight.

The other troll now started down the mountain slope, and Erik noticed this one carried a spear, the shaft a long, thick pole of crooked ash tipped with a bent bronze dagger. It barked at its comrade, and the first troll replied with crude grunts and howls.

Erik heard the sound of hooves behind him.

"Move aside!" yelled Wrothgard. He galloped hard towards the trolls, digging his heels into the horse's flanks. As he passed Erik, the young man heard him yell, "For Tedish!"

"Get to your horse," Befel said, pulling himself into the saddle of his own mount.

Then he heard Vander Bim plead to him, "Help me. Help us."

He looked to the sailor. He cried as his friend flailed about like his dead horse did only moments before. Erik could see bloody bone sticking from the miner's pants. His foot twisted behind him. Vander Bim stopped pulling him and cradled his head, trying to hush him as if Drake was a child just awoken by a nightmare.

"I'm no good to them," Erik muttered.

"Here," Befel cried. Erik turned to see his brother holding the reins of his horse. "Mount up. Hurry."

"I can't fight from horseback." Erik took the reins. He looked into the eyes of his horse. Fear. It stamped its hoof hard and neighed, jerking its head so hard, it almost pulled the bridle from Erik's hands.

"You had better try," Befel replied.

Erik looked to the troll. Even on all fours, it stood several heads taller than he did. Erik mounted, and as he turned his horse to face the monster, he saw Wrothgard race past the beast. His sword sliced across its shoulder. Thick, darkened blood erupted like a fountain and poured over the troll's gray-skinned arm, but it didn't seem to notice, even as two more arrows thudded into the opposite shoulder.

Then, as Wrothgard raced towards the second troll, a throwing axe bit deep into the creature's thigh.

"Turk," Erik muttered. The dwarf ran to the troll, shield at the ready, another throwing axe in his hands.

"Let's go," Befel said, and spurred his horse towards the oncoming troll.

Erik saw Vander Bim dragging Drake again, pulling him as quickly as he could away from the monster and making almost no ground. Turk rushed to their aid, battle-axe now in hand. Erik saw Bryon ride up next to Befel. He saw a beast with an open mouth of blackened teeth, sharp as daggers, salivating as it closed in on the sailor. Two more arrows thudded into its ribs, but the troll ignored them as one might ignore a gnat. Instead, it lifted its arm, a massive hand curled into a fist which it shook as it roared.

Bryon passed Befel, passed Turk, rode hard to the troll, and raked his sword across its underarm. It stopped and swatted at Bryon, missing. When it turned back around, Vander Bim had made his way to the beast. He plunged his sword into its side, a finger's-length deep. The troll brought the thick back of its hand across the sailor's face with a deafening thud. The sailor flew backwards, heels over his head, his sword still stuck in the troll's flesh. The troll pulled the blade from its side and threw it away like an annoying splinter. Erik could see its gaze turn to Drake.

"No!" he yelled.

As Bryon turned his horse around to attack again and Turk raced towards the troll, the beast continued to make its way to Drake, who pushed himself backwards as fast as he could, screaming in agony with each jerk of his body, but spurred on by the adrenaline. As the monster hovered over him and reached for his neck, the miner pulled a dagger from his belt and plunged it into the troll's hand. The iron blade ripped through the beast's hand, poking through the back. The troll howled like a demon wolf. It brought its face close to Drake's and yelled, covering the man's face with sticky saliva. The miner still gripped his dagger, so the troll grabbed his wrist, and with a simple shake, Erik heard the snapping of bone. The miner cried, but the beast slammed its sloping forehead into the miner's face and an explosion of blood silenced Drake's shrieks. The troll gripped the man's throat and lifted him off the ground. It shook him like a straw-stuffed doll and then threw the miner to the ground, his body limp.

The troll stood over the miner's body, lifting its hands in the air, ready to slam its fists into Drake's chest. The beast merely flinched when Bryon's sword sliced a red line across its back but roared when Turk's half-moon axe blade thumped deep into its flesh. For the first time, Erik saw the troll falter as it bent to one knee, but it popped up again, swinging at the dwarf twice, Turk easily ducking out of the way. Both Bryon's and Turk's blades cut the troll again, another arrow thunking into its chest.

"Erik, don't just sit there," he heard Befel yell. He turned to see his brother riding after Wrothgard toward the booted troll.

He had been sitting and watching, doing nothing.

"Do something, you fool," Erik hissed, cursing himself. "You coward."

As he rode to the aid of his cousin and Turk, he could hear Bryon's curses as he dodged attacks from the troll and tried to jab and cut with his own weapon. He saw the other two dwarves from the corner of his eye, rushing over to help, Samus close behind them, hobbling with his sword and shield in tow. Blood seeped from dozens of the troll's wounds, but it still fought, and hard. A kick to the chest sent Turk rolling backwards. Another backhand to the face knocked Vander Bim, who had gathered himself and taken position over the body of Drake, off his feet. Bryon's horse reared, and the troll rushed in and punched the steed in the chest. It looked as if the creature would roll backwards, over Bryon, but it came down resiliently on its hooves, Bryon barely hanging in his saddle.

Erik rushed in, swinging three times. He felt the tip of his sword bite the troll once. His heart raced, and goose pimples rose along his arms. He raised his sword above his head, ready to bring it down hard on the troll's shoulder, but an errant arm from the troll caught the young man across the face and chest. He flew from his saddle, over the flank of his horse. The ground came up fast and hit Erik. He couldn't breathe. His face felt hot. He looked up to the sky overhead, clouded by dust. The clouds seemed to run away, growing smaller and smaller. Erik's vision narrowed, black crowding in on all sides until the blue sky became a tiny pinpoint that finally disappeared into nothing.

Chapter 15

WROTHGARD COULDN'T HEAR ANYTHING. HE knew a hard fight raged behind him. He didn't care. He couldn't care. There was only *it*. The second troll. The murderer. White scars mottled its chest. Its spear, bronze tip bent, stained with old blood.

"Tedish!" Wrothgard screamed, releasing the tension in his body. A wild, madman's scream. His air ran out, he coughed, breathed, and screamed again. And his foe simply stood its ground, a hideous grimace its version of a smile.

"I will kill you!" yelled Wrothgard as he dug his heels into his horse's ribs.

The troll understood his promise, and it shook its head ever so slightly as it gripped its spear with both hands.

Forty paces, thirty paces, twenty paces, ten, lift the sword and…

Wrothgard leaned away from the bronze tip of the troll's spear and brought his sword down, hard. Not a solid strike. Not as solid as he would have liked. It cut deep into the creature's shoulder, however. His steel pulled away a chunk of flesh. He could hear his enemy scream behind him, and he turned to attack again.

"What man is a match for a mountain troll?" Wrothgard asked himself. "I am."

The shaft of the troll's spear met him when he turned, the thick wood smacking him across the face and sending him backwards over the flank of his horse. He fell to his stomach, his face buried in the dirt. His vision blurred for a moment.

He could feel the troll's hot breath pour over him and knew he only had a few seconds. He pushed himself up and rolled to his right. The bronze blade of the spear drove deep into the ground where Wrothgard had been lying. He looked up to see the troll staring at him. It screamed, retrieved its spear, and thrust it into the shoulder of Wrothgard's horse. The creature cried and shrieked as it bucked. The troll then grabbed the horse by the head and twisted, straining the animal's thick, muscled neck, its eyes wild and scared. Wrothgard finally heard the loud snapping—like a thunderclap—of a horse's neck breaking, and the beast fell limp to the ground. Fifty men wouldn't have been able to do such a thing.

Wrothgard picked up his sword and drew his other one, the broken one. His head pounded, throbbing from the base of his neck to the back of his eyeballs. The mountain troll standing in front of him blurred, turning into two monsters for a moment. Wrothgard tasted blood in his mouth but refused to spit it out, refused to show signs of hurt or weakness. Wrothgard thought the troll would charge; it would have been the easiest thing for it to do, after all. But it didn't. It seemed to study him, perhaps even overestimate him. It jabbed its bronze-tipped spear at the man a few times, Wrothgard easily dodging. These weren't meant to kill, wound even. It was playing with him.

Wrothgard could hear the sounds of battle behind him—the cries of men, the screaming of horses, the howl of the other troll. He ignored them. Another spear jab, this one more serious. Wrothgard stepped to the side. The soldier spit at the beast and lunged forward, the tip of his good sword barely scratching the troll's skin.

A snort, a growl, and another jab. He leaned to one side, then to the other, stepped forward, crouched, put his broken sword up over his head as if it were a shield, and then jabbed. This one bit deeper into the troll's leg, just above the knee. The beast howled and stood to its full height as it flexed its massive chest, bared its blackened teeth, and slammed the butt of its spear hard into the ground. Wrothgard braced himself for the onslaught about to come, caring little for the outcome, only caring that his steel would bite the whole time.

Then he heard four boots slapping the earth, driven by stout, well-muscled legs, and the slapping of iron-shod hooves on hard-packed earth. He saw them from the corner of his eye—Demik and Nafer and Befel, broadsword and mace and rusted sword ready. The troll turned and saw them too. At that instant, Wrothgard attacked, driving his sword deep into the beast's thick side. It twisted hard, ripping the blade from its flesh, and swung the back of its hand. The soldier ducked. At the same time, the troll swung its spear at Demik. The dwarf rolled forward, bringing his sword up into the underbelly of the troll's arm as he found his feet again.

Wrothgard saw the exposed chest and raked his sword across it, cutting from shoulder to hip. Nafer's mace crashed into the troll's knee, and the soldier heard the crunching of meat and bone. Any other creature would have collapsed, but the troll still stood. Despite another blow from Demik's broadsword, it brought the spear shaft down hard, cracking the dwarf on the side of the head and sending him rolling sideways. It then kicked out at Nafer and the dwarf, though nimble, caught a boot to the chest and landed on his back.

Wrothgard brought his good blade down on the extended leg and scratched the broken blade along the monster's ribs. A bronze blade sailed just above his head as he ducked another attack, and then he jumped as the troll brought its weapon low. Demik was up again, blood reddening his hair and beard from a lesion just above his ear. Demik's blade bit again. He deflected a spear attack with his shield and struck once more. The soldier brought his sword up along the monster's hamstring and then down along the back of its ribs. Nafer, woozy but on his feet, jabbed with his mace, the spike at the top of the steel ball digging into the troll's thigh.

The beast stepped back, and for a moment, Wrothgard thought

it didn't know what to do. It seemed confused. Maybe even... scared. No. It was evil. It had killed his friend and then eaten him. It killed innocent men and women and children. It deserved to die.

He saw Befel leaning forward, hard, in his saddle. He raced at the troll, sword high above his head.

"No!" Wrothgard shouted. "You fool! No!"

The injured beast swung up with its weapon, taking Befel from his saddle. He fell hard to the ground. The young man jumped to his feet quickly, ducking one attack as Nafer and Demik and Wrothgard moved around the troll, but then another hard swing caught Befel's shoulder. Wrothgard saw the shoulder drop from its socket. The next attack was a grazing blow along the top of his shoulder, skin and flesh erupting in blood from the brute force of the strike. Befel went down, unconscious. He would have been dead but for the two dwarves stepping over him, jabbing and prodding the troll backwards a few steps.

Wrothgard looked to the troll. Blood covered its skin, wounds exposing muscle and tissue. He looked into its eyes, those black, beady pupils. Was it fear, determination, sorrow he saw there? No. Rage. Pure, malicious, wicked rage.

It charged. Wrothgard ducked out of the way. He saw two arrows sail into its chest. It barreled past Demik, knocking him to the side and ignored Nafer as he swung at the beast with his mace again. The soldier chased after the troll. It howled when two more arrows thumped into its chest. Wrothgard wondered how the beast still stood.

Wrothgard leapt onto the troll's back. He gagged at its stench. Holding his breath, he plunged his broken sword into the troll's flesh just at the base of its neck. The creature howled and screamed as the broken blade dug in cross-guard deep. It dropped its spear and reached back, digging its nails into its own flesh as it grabbed for Wrothgard. Its exposed chest lay bare for several more volleys of arrows as well as a half-moon bladed battle-axe, sailing shaft-over-head through the air until its steel sunk to the troll's sternum.

The troll finally fell to one knee, and Demik's broadsword crashed into its shoulder twice. It shuddered, still trying to grab at Wrothgard, the soldier twisting his broken blade back and forth. He heard his teeth grinding, echoing through his pounding head. His face felt so hot that perhaps the tears streaming from his eyes might have evaporated as they touched his cheeks. He felt wetness on his lips—spit and blood.

"Die, you son of a bitch." His curses hissed through his teeth. "Die. Die. Die!"

It began to oblige. The troll fell to the other knee, its hands now falling to its side. It lurched sideways when Nafer's mace smacked its ribs, bone crushing under the force. Wrothgard jumped from the troll's back, leaving his broken sword in its place. He gripped his other sword in both hands, lifted it high over his head, and swung, repeatedly, creating a red mess of the troll's back. The creature barely flinched.

"Oh, no. You are not going to lose your senses before this ends." Wrothgard spat as he walked to the troll's front.

He bent down to look the creature in the face. The troll didn't look up. It simply stared at the ground, shoulders lifting slowly as it took long, labored breaths.

"Hey!" Wrothgard yelled in the troll's face. It didn't move. He spat at it. It still did not move. He punched it in its head. Still nothing. He stood up, sheathed his sword, and removed the glove on his right hand. He eyed a deep wound on the beast's shoulder and jabbed his index finger in, knuckle deep. He heard it, then—a growl. It lifted its head, eyed the soldier, and snapped at him. He leaned back, out of the way, and smiled.

"Do not torture it." Wrothgard caught a glimpse of Turk walking up behind him.

"Did he give my man, Tedish, the same courtesy?" Wrothgard asked.

"Probably not," Turk replied. "But it is a wicked thing. A creature of the Shadow. Lawless. Foul. It is evil. We are soldiers. We fight by a code."

"An easterner's code is as good as no code at all," Demik muttered, and Wrothgard heard him.

Turk said something to his companion in Dwarvish, but Wrothgard could tell it was an admonishment.

"He is right, my dwarvish friend. What weight does an easterner's code carry?" Wrothgard asked.

Wrothgard drew his sword again and held it loosely, so that its tip touched the ground. The troll slouched in front of him, slow, short breaths. It was near death. Something was wet on his cheek. He wiped away the tear with his left hand.

"I am sorry, my friend, my poor Tedish. I have let my anger defame you. I am sorry," Wrothgard said. "You would have done better."

The troll moved, putting both its fists on the ground, its breaths even slower.

Wrothgard gripped his sword in both hands again and moved to the troll's side, the blade hovering just above the beast's neck.

"Wait," Turk said. He walked in front of the soldier, reached under the troll, and, with one hand, retrieved his battle-axe from the monster's chest. He stood and looked to the easterner, handing him the weapon.

"It will be cleaner, quicker," Turk said.

Wrothgard paused for what seemed to him a long while. He nodded, sheathed his sword, and took the half-moon bladed battle-axe. Gripping it in two hands, he eyed his mark, lifted the weapon over his head, and brought it down. He repeated that same motion four times before the head rolled from the troll's shoulders.

Wrothgard smirked, looking at the pool of blood collecting under the still unconscious Befel.

"At what cost?" Wrothgard asked.

"What was that?" Turk asked.

"Our victory. At what cost did it come?" Wrothgard repeated.

He looked to Befel again. Then he saw the young man named Erik also lying unconscious and the tall one—Bryon—kneeling next to him. He saw Vander Bim holding Drake, cradling the man's head in his lap. Wrothgard knew how that felt all too well. He knew what it was like to watch a friend die, to hold him in your arms as he breathed his last, to hear the pain in his voice as he cried out to his mother or his wife or his children or whatever god he thought might forgive his last sin. That was a feeling like no other, a helpless feeling that twists the heart and stomach. Suddenly, that feeling struck him once more. He looked about. He saw the dwarves, the young men. He saw Switch and Vander Bim and the dying Drake.

"Where is Samus?"

Chapter 16

Erik pressed the palms of his hands against his temples. The harder he pressed, the more it hurt, but at least it seemed to help his headache go away. The ground was hard and hot, but every time he stood, his vision blurred, and he felt like throwing up. Even sitting down, he was woozy.

Turk walked by him. He seemed busy, but Erik spoke anyways.

"I thought I wouldn't wake up," Erik said. "As I passed out, I thought that was it."

Turk stopped and turned. Erik looked up and met eyes with the dwarf. Turk smiled.

"Do not worry, my young friend," he said. "You would have woken up. It may have not been here. It may have been that, praise An, you would have woken up in the halls of the Almighty, but you would have awoken nonetheless."

Erik held back the tears as best he could, but something inside him wouldn't let him stop. He felt foolish, childish, and tried to cover his face but then felt the strong hands of Turk rest on his shoulders.

"It is all right to cry, Erik," Turk said. "It is all right to show emotion. We had a hard fight. Men died. Men we know are dying."

Erik followed Turk's eyes as the dwarf stared at Vander Bim, sitting on the ground and cradling Drake's head, face broken and bloody, in his lap.

Erik looked over at Drake and then up at Turk. The dwarf looked down at him and shook his head.

"You will rest here while Turk comes with his healing salve," Vander Bim said. "Then we will forget this treasure map nonsense. We will pack your horse and send you to your wife and children."

"My boys," Drake whispered. "Where are my boys? Where are they?"

"They are here. Close by. On their way to see…"

Vander Bim's voice cracked, and he began to sob.

Drake coughed, and when he did, his whole body cramped as he let out a silent scream.

"My wife." Drake turned, resting his face against Vander Bim's thigh and hugging the sailor's knee. I want my wife."

Vander Bim leaned down, putting his forehead to Drake's temple. He kissed his friend's blood-wet hair.

The miner reached out as if his wife was there, reaching back. Then, he shuddered once more. His body went slack in the sailor's arms, and he slid from Vander Bim's lap to the ground in a bloody heap, lifeless.

"Should we do something for Vander Bim?" Erik asked.

Turk shook his head. "Let him grieve. He needs time to grieve, time to mourn and remember the life of his friend. Are you all right?"

"My head hurts," Erik replied. "But I'm sure there are worse than me."

"I would imagine so. Here." Turk pulled a small vial from a pouch on his belt and handed it to Erik. "Drink this and find a quiet spot. Your head will feel better soon."

"Thank you," Erik said.

"I have to help our friends now," Turk said. "If your head doesn't clear, let me know."

Erik had found a spot away from the rest of his companions where he could drink the contents of Turk's vial. It tasted like nothing, like water, and shortly after he drank it, he felt tired, and he was soon in a deep, dreamless sleep.

His headache gone, his body feeling refreshed, his mind clear, and his spirits much higher than before, the first person Erik saw when he walked back into the midst of his companions was Wrothgard. He stood quietly over the body of his friend, Samus. He then crouched, sitting back on his heels. Erik put his hand on the soldier's shoulder. It's what Turk had done for him.

"Are you well?" Wrothgard asked.

"Yes," Erik said. "Turk gave me something that cleared my head and took away my pain."

"He was like my brother, you know." Wrothgard stroked the blood-soaked hair and beard of Samus. "We served in the Eastern Guard together, with Tedish. We traveled into the wilds of the east and battled the men of Mek-Ba'Dune, side by side. And for what? To die by the hands of simple mountain trolls commanded by the very men to whom we paid allegiance. Samus and Tedish were as strong and skilled warriors as I have ever seen. Their skills were far beyond mine. It should be me lying here, dead. It should be me."

"I am truly sorry," Erik comforted. "Perhaps the Almighty has something else in store for you."

Wrothgard waved him off with a little, mirthless chuckle, one filled with derision.

"I didn't mean any harm," Erik said, removing his hand from the soldier's shoulder.

Wrothgard shook his head. "No, I am sorry. Continue to believe in your god if that is what brings you comfort. I have lost all faith in any gods, or religion. To me, it is naught but misplaced hope. I have lost two brothers in a matter of days, and countless more in all my years. What god would allow this? What god would allow such death?"

Erik didn't know what to say. The soldier stood and bowed his head. Wrothgard said something in his eastern tongue and put his right fist to his left breast.

"Do not mourn them," Wrothgard said, turning to face Erik. "Applaud them as warriors. Let their memory live on in our lives as we fight, eventually, to glorious deaths. Tonight, I will drink to their lives, and tomorrow, we will continue on."

They buried the two men, and Erik was glad for it. They deserved at least that.

"Is that for the pain?" Erik asked Turk as he gave Befel, who leaned against his saddle, some liquid from a hollowed gourd.

Turk gave Erik a quick nod.

"I don't think it's working," Erik added as Befel groaned loudly and visibly shook.

"He is in a lot of pain," Turk replied. "I don't know if I have enough to dull all of it. And then if I did, he would be in a stupor greater than any rum could cause."

"What about what you gave me?" Erik asked.

Turk shook his head.

"That is a very different medicine and not suited for your brother," Turk explained.

Befel dug his heels into the dirt and gritted his teeth as the dwarf prodded and probed about his wound.

"You must relax, Befel," the dwarf said. Befel replied with a yelp.

"Brother," Erik said, "you must listen."

A groan and then a long moan of pain escaped Befel's mouth as a reply.

His left arm lay limp, his shoulder drooping low, farther than what was natural.

"It is out of socket," Turk explained. Erik didn't know if the dwarf spoke to him or his brother, or to himself. "And before I can continue to work, I must set it. This will hurt."

He tried feeding Befel more of his numbing liquid, but the young man spit it out with another groan. Turk placed both hands on Befel's shoulder, one in front and one behind. Then he waited, head stooped, chin to chest.

"What are you doing?" Erik asked. "Why are you waiting?"

Turk didn't reply. Then, without a word, he lifted his head, gripped Befel's arm firmly with both hands, pulled, pushed, pulled, and then pushed again. Erik heard a clicking sound, followed by a subtle pop, and Befel screamed while his face went paler than before. He clutched at his pant leg and jerked sideways.

"Hold him, Erik," Turk commanded.

Erik complied while Turk hushed Befel like a mother trying to sooth a crying baby.

"You will be all right, brother," Erik said, holding him tightly and pressing his head into his chest. Befel began to cry.

The dwarf cleaned the wound. He smeared his cooling salve on the wound and then stitched it as best he could; Erik held his brother the whole time, preventing him from jerking and writhing about.

"Will he be okay?" Erik asked when Turk finished and Befel had fallen asleep.

"We will see," Turk replied. "It was bad before. Now it is even worse. Now, he may definitely not use his arm again."

"But there must be something you can do?" Erik said.

"I am sorry, my young friend," Turk said. "I hate to say such a thing. And I certainly would not say that to Befel, at least for now. I will do everything I can, use all the gifts and skills of healing with which An has favored me with—that I can promise you—but the best surgeons live in Thorakest. When we reach my city, An willing, they may be able to look at his shoulder and save his arm. Meanwhile, when we reach Aga Min, I will redress the wound with clean cloth. That is most important right now. The quicker we can do that, the surer I am that we will stem any infection."

Erik gave him a blank look.

"If it gets infected, he may not only lose the use of his arm, but he may lose his life."

As they finally mounted and readied themselves for the road again, Vander Bim moved over to where Erik was settling Befel on his horse, as Bryon looked on.

"I haven't discussed this with any of the others," Vander Bim said, loudly enough so that everyone could hear him, "and they may not like what I am going to say, but if they don't, then they can just piss off. I don't give a troll shit if they don't like it. You three proved yourselves today, to be more than just servants. I believe you saved my life, at least, and that's good enough for me. I am making you full partners. Whatever riches we find, whatever commission the Lord of the East pays us, we will split with you. Evenly. And you too, Wrothgard."

Erik looked at the dwarves. They were nodding, and he saw Wrothgard nod as well. And then he saw Switch. He gave a slight shrug of his shoulders, a wry smile barely breaking the corners of his mouth. When he saw Erik staring at him, the thief gave him a single wink, and for once, Bryon seemed speechless.

Chapter 17

ERIK LOOKED BACK AND SAW the purplish shades of dusk dwindling away, giving space to the darkness of night and the twinkling of stars overhead. The clouds of early monsoons had all but disappeared for now. Erik could occasionally see them in the distant west, lit up by the quick flash of some faraway lightning.

"Is that the camp?" Bryon asked.

"I hope so," Befel replied. The last two days had been hard on Erik's brother.

"Do you?" Vander Bim hissed, glaring at Befel under shadowed eyes as he spoke. "Will it be so welcoming when we find that glow is the fire of men and women and children burning?"

"Must you be so dark?" Switch said, and Erik thought that somewhat contradictory.

"Death is typically dark," Vander Bim added as he spurred his horse forward. It was clear that the loss of his friend was still very much in his mind.

Rather than destruction, they found a camp of semi-permanent buildings and dirt roads full of people despite the night. Even though there was no wall or fence, two men stood at what looked to be the main road, dented and rusted half-helms resting on their heads and tall halberds in their hands. When they noticed the party, they went from leaning on their pole arms to standing at attention.

"Stop there!" yelled one of the guards.

The party rode a few paces further before complying.

"Ho," Wrothgard replied.

"Ho yerself," said one of the men. In the light, Erik could see he had graying hair and a stubbly face. He extended his halberd so that the curving blade stopped just short of Wrothgard's horse's snout, his thin jaw tightening.

"He's nervous," Erik whispered.

"Aye," Befel said with a nod.

"We mean no harm," Wrothgard said. "We're simple travelers from the west—"

"Yer no simple trav'lers," said the gray-haired miner's comrade. He had thinning red hair and a belly that hung sloppily over his belt. "We may be ign'ant miners, but we ain't that ign'ant, thank ye very much. Ye've got three tunnel diggers, yer no simple trav'ler."

"What business have ye got in Cho's camp?" the gray-haired man asked.

"Our business is ours to know," Wrothgard replied. Erik could hear a flatness in Wrothgard's tone.

"No. Sorry. That won't do." The gray-haired man nodded to the other. Erik saw the redhead moving towards a large bell that hung from an iron hook on a chest high wooden pole along the dirt road that acted as an entrance to the camp.

"It's a signal," Erik whispered. He knew Wrothgard had heard him by the sidelong glance the soldier gave him. "A signal to warn a militia maybe?"

He then heard the subtle, soft sound of iron sliding against leather and knew that Switch rode just behind him. Erik twisted, just ever so slightly in his saddle, to see Switch, hand firmly gripping the handle of one of his daggers.

"That's not necessary," Wrothgard said before the redhead could ring the bell. Erik knew the soldier spoke to both the guards and to Switch.

He stopped, and both guards looked to the soldier. Wrothgard waited a while.

"Well," the gray-haired guard finally said, "what's yer answer? What be yer business?"

"We are accompanying our dwarvish companions as they journey to visit their families in Thorakest," Wrothgard offered.

"What is men doin' trav'lin' with dwarves?" the redhead asked.

"They are our friends," Wrothgard offered. "Can dwarves and men not be friends?"

Erik saw the two miners confer with one another. They were trying to be quiet but doing a poor job at it. He heard one whisper, "I don't think dwarves live in these parts of the mountain."

"Aye, they could be lyin'," the other one said.

Wrothgard cleared his throat, "Excuse me, but don't you think dwarves would know whether or not dwarves live in this part of the mountain?"

The graying guard looked to his redheaded companion, who still stood within arm's reach of the bell.

"That may be, but to go into the mountain, ye must first talk to Cho. This be his mine."

"Very well. We will speak with him in the morning. Where's the nearest—" Wrothgard started to say, but the gray-haired guard cut him off.

"No. Tonight." The gray-haired guard finally lowered his weapon. "Ye can stable yer horses at *The Golden Miner*. Not all of ye need to be visitin' Master Cho, so the rest of ye can bed down there, or visit Madame Ary's. Really, just ye need to go."

"Very well. May we pass?" Wrothgard asked.

"Aye, ye may pass," the guard replied.

Erik let out a silent sigh and heard, again, the sound of iron sliding against leather. As he passed the two miners, they looked nervous. He heard the clink of a fingernail on metal and looked back to see the thief flipping a coin to the miners. Perhaps they thought him generous, giving them a copper coin, but Erik knew he meant it as a slight.

Despite the busyness of the street, most of the commotion came from the east of the camp.

"That must be the tavern?" Erik said.

"What gave it away?" Bryon snorted. "Was it the shouting and laughing, or the shouting and laughing?"

"Say whatever you need to say, cousin," Erik said, but he knew Bryon couldn't hear him, having moved towards the front of the group, "to make yourself feel clever."

Aga Min proved more a village than a simple mining camp. It had all the requirements one might think of, save for tents in place of thatch-roofed houses. They saw a smithy and a small mill, and along the main road on which they rode was a small marketplace. Carts of fruits and vegetables and meats were shuttered for the night and several tents that looked like makeshift temples for different religions.

"There are more people here than Stone's Throw," Erik said. "That must be *The Golden Miner* and Madame Ary's."

Erik pointed to two permanent buildings resting at the eastern edge of the camp.

"I would guess so," Wrothgard replied.

"Madame Ary's is an odd name for a store," Erik added.

"I don't think it is a general store, Erik," Turk said with a chuckle as a half-naked woman doing her worst to cover her breasts emerged from a three-storied building chased by a shirtless fellow with a huge smile on his face. The shirtless man finally caught her and dragged her back through the front door. In the darkness, Erik blushed at his naivety.

The Golden Miner was another permanent building sitting to the left of Madame Ary's, five stories of golden stained wood with a covered porch of polished rock. As the double doors of the entrance opened, the loud din of laughter and drinking exploded from the building. A few men emerged, and they mostly staggered into Madame Ary's.

"You all get several rooms," Wrothgard said. He threw Switch a small purse that clinked of coin when it hit the thief's hand. "I will pay for tonight's stay."

Wrothgard looked to Vander Bim and slightly jerked his head. The sailor nodded and pressed his heels to the side of his horse.

Before they left, the soldier looked at each one of his companions. He locked his eyes on Turk.

"I am sorry, master dwarf," Wrothgard said. "I would normally have you come with us to meet this Master Cho, but I do not know what his feelings are towards you and your ilk. I hope you understand."

"Aye," Turk said coldly, but his anger was not aimed at Wrothgard.

Wrothgard then locked his gaze on Erik.

"You," he said curtly. "Come with us."

Cho's villa—another permanent building, a single-story home of brick and wood and polished stone—sat away at the farthest, north-eastern corner of the camp. A reddish-stained, wooden fence with a post every several paces and a single rail surrounded the home. A torch stood at every other post along the fence in the front of the house, the light revealing a lawn of well-tended grass, rosemary bushes, and several orange trees. The torches stopped along the front, however, and nothing illuminated the rear of the house. The only reason Erik knew a stable sat towards the back of the home was the faint whisper of a horse's whinny.

Two guards—true guards, in leather brigandines and carrying long swords—stood at the front of the path. Erik met one guard's eyes, and the tip of the man's spear dipped, pointing at Erik's chest. He said something quickly, in a language Erik didn't understand. Wrothgard replied. A back and forth conversation ensued then Wrothgard nodded to Vander Bim and Erik. They dismounted and handed over the reins to their horses to one of the guards.

Erik smelled the rosemary as they walked along the brick path. Mixed with the smell of orange blossoms, it created a rich, sweet aroma that reminded him of his uncle's orange orchards and his mother's rosemary bread.

The front door—a thick piece of dark oak with carvings of bears and lions and giant eagles etched into it—didn't seem to fit with the rest of the house, with its brick and golden pine. The guard knocked on the door. Within moments, a large man opened the door. His head was shaved, and his oiled beard was trimmed close to his face. His colorful robes shimmered in the light.

The man paid no attention to the three men. Rather, he spoke in a hushed whisper to the guard. Regardless of the volume of his speech, Erik thought his words sounded scornful, chastising almost. Eventually, the guard bowed and returned to his post, leaving the mercenaries with the large man at the front door.

"You wish to meet with Master Cho," he said in a nasally voice. "You wish to ask his permission to stay within his camp, yes?"

"We do," Wrothgard replied.

"Who is calling at such a late hour?" His voice was void of any emotion, and his stare was a listless, half-lidded look of indifference.

"My name is Wrothgard Bel'Therum, of Kamdum, and this is Vander Bim from Finlo and Erik, from . . ." Wrothgard paused, not knowing from where Erik hailed.

"Waterton," Erik interjected, "Erik Eleodum from Waterton."

"And you wish to enter the mountain?" the robed man asked.

"Several of our companions are dwarves. They are traveling to Thorakest to visit kin," Wrothgard replied.

"I don't care why you wish to enter the mountain. Although, it is a curious thing that men would be traveling with dwarves."

"We are their friends," Wrothgard replied. "That is all."

The doorman looked at them for a long moment, again through those half-closed, condescending eyes.

"One moment please," he said before he shut the door. Erik could hear the man walking through the house. He heard voices. Then, the door opened again.

"Please follow me." The attendant opened the door fully and nodded for the three men to enter the house.

From what he saw of the dwelling, Erik could tell this Master Cho had expensive tastes. They walked down a long hall, stepping on thick, soft rugs. Every few paces, an oil painting hung from the wall, depicting any number of scenes from nude women to war and battle. Tables of ebony and of golden oak stood against the walls as well, each holding a ceramic vase scrawled with blue or red inking, or a golden bowl, or a statue made of silver or brass. It all looked so elegant, so expensive, and yet, it seemed out of place to Erik. Each piece of art, each table, each vase, by itself, was something to hold any rich man's attention. But combined they created a smattering of trinkets and treasures that spoke of a man trying to buy acceptance, trying to portray a sense of nobility he could never truly earn. It looked more like a store than a home.

The hall opened into a large room that, much like the hallway, offered a mishmash of paintings and tapestries and vases and other treasures collected, perhaps, throughout a lifetime of travels. Centered in the room, at the end of a long, brown and blue rug, sat a large seat, ebony carved with a deft hand. The scroll work on the armrests and at the head clearly depicted the heads of lions, their eyes set with blue emeralds and their teeth made of small, yellow topaz.

A broad-shouldered man sat upon a large cushion on the chair. A bit of loose skin on his neck shook as he turned to see the three men. He leaned forward and gripped the lion's heads of the armrests hard until his knuckles turned white. Those hands could have crushed a man's skull. He snorted, the air from his nose causing his bushy, peppered mustache to flutter. His jaw, hard and well-defined despite his apparent age, flexed and his eyes narrowed into small dark pools shaded under thick, black eyebrows. They seemed to stop on Erik, and the weight of his stare caused Erik to take a step back, and he bent his back a little in deference.

"I am Cho." His voice was a deep war drum. "And this is my camp, mined in service of the Lord of the East."

Wrothgard bowed, and Vander Bim followed suit. Erik stayed standing for a moment, but when he caught that stare again, he quickly complied, staring at the ground, and breathing quickly. A drop of sweat trickled along the back of his neck.

"You may stand." Cho remained at the edge of his seat. "You hail from the west, and yet, you," he pointed a thick index finger at Wrothgard, "have the look of an easterner."

"Aye, my lord," Wrothgard replied. "I am originally from Kamdum."

"And your reason for leaving the east?" Cho asked. "Your reason for leaving your home?"

Wrothgard paused. Erik thought he looked worried. Cho gave the soldier that same stare, although he didn't seem to bend as much under its weight.

"Those reasons are . . . well, they are of a personal nature," Wrothgard finally replied.

"Perhaps you are a murderer who has fled his homeland for fear of the noose. Or, maybe you are a traitor, a spy for Gol-Durathna. How do I know?" His massive shoulders shrugged. "Maybe you are a gypsy or some damned sell-sword."

"Do I have the look of a gypsy or sell-sword, my lord?" Wrothgard asked.

The thin lips under that bristling mustache turned into a frown, and Master Cho stared at them for a long while. Then, he sat back in his seat, running his hand over the top of his balding head, straightening the patch of black and gray hair that still sat just above his ears and at the back of his head. He chuckled.

"How do I know what a gypsy or mercenary looks like? By the gods, how do I know what a murderer looks like?" Cho asked. "I probably have several in my employ right now. And what do I care?"

He leaned forward again.

"I don't. But you see, I must ask, for this truly isn't my camp. It is that of the Lord of Fen-Stévock, and if he were to ask, I must at least be able to say I asked. As if he would ever really check. I make him money, and he cares little for what we do beyond his borders."

Wrothgard bowed with an insincere smile on his face.

"So," Cho sat back again, draping one leg over an arm of the chair. He wore a sarong of reds and gold and purple, and when he put his leg up, some of the cloth revealed a thick leg covered in dark hair. He lazily reached over to a table standing next to his chair and picked up a golden, jeweled cup between his index and middle finger. "You have dwarves in your company."

"Aye, my lord," Wrothgard replied.

"I am not overly fond of dwarves. They are greedy. They think these mountains belong to them, as well as the riches that lie within. But," Cho said with a shrug and a quick drink from his cup, "I suppose we are just as greedy. How long do you wish to stay?"

"One, maybe two nights," Wrothgard said.

"And you assure me that you are going into the mountain to visit these tunnel diggers' kin?" Cho asked.

"Aye," Wrothgard simply replied.

"If I find out otherwise, I will kill you." Cho dropped his leg and leaned forward again, the wry smile and nonchalant look on his face disappearing, replaced by narrowed eyes and pursed lips. "You have the look of a soldier, but do not think your skill with a sword will do you any good against a hundred pickaxes."

Wrothgard nodded.

"Keep your dwarves at *The Golden Miner*. They are to stay there for as long as you stay here. They are not allowed at Madame Ary's. Only *The Golden Miner*. Do you understand?"

He spoke as if the dwarves were their pets and could be leashed and muzzled.

Wrothgard nodded again.

"If I find them walking about, I will kill them myself," Cho threatened. "It has been a long while since I've blessed any blade with dwarvish blood."

Erik stared at the large man, his muscled arms despite the skin loosening with age, the stern jaw, the hard eyes. He couldn't imagine most men being able to kill a dwarf, especially after watching them in battle. But this man…if there was a man who could do so, Erik thought it would be Cho. He wasn't lying about having killed a dwarf before. It was his eyes. Those eyes didn't lie. Those were the eyes of a man who told the truth no matter what. If he bedded a nobleman's wife, and it meant his death, he would tell the truth. Erik's father had those same eyes.

"You are most kind," Wrothgard said with a bow. Cho flicked his wrist and the three turned to follow the master's seneschal out when the master of the camp cleared his throat.

"Waterton, eh?" Cho said.

Erik looked over his shoulder. His heart quickened, beat against his chest with a deafening sound that everyone must've heard. The vein in his neck thumped against his collar.

"It hasn't been too many years since I have passed through Waterton. I don't remember any Eleodums. It's a small town. You would think I would have heard of the name. Although…" Cho paused for a moment. "Yes, I vaguely remember the name."

Erik let out a relieved breath.

"But not from Waterton. No, it was in Venton I heard the name. Yes, Venton. What did you say you did in Waterton?"

Erik turned and met those hard, truthful eyes. "I…I didn't, my lord. I-I was…I was a barkeep."

Cho may have never traveled west. Why would he? He may be testing them. But, then again, he may not. The mining boss nodded, one side of his mouth turning in a slight smirk. He didn't believe Erik. The young man could tell that much in that smirk and those eyes.

"You weren't a farmer?" Cho asked.

"No, my lord. A barkeep, at *The Wicked Beard.* It was my father's before he died," Erik lied, "killed trying to break up a fight. His family hailed from the north. I don't know if it was Venton or where. He didn't speak of them much. But, no, until now I've lived my whole life in Waterton, working in our family's tavern."

"*The Wicked Beard.* That name rings a bell. I don't think I ever had a drink there," Cho said. "There was this place—*The Green Dancer*—I settled there a few times, with its owner, Flemming. He had the most beautiful girls, and considerably skilled."

Erik remembered that place. Did he? Yes, but it wasn't *The Green Dancer.* No, it was *The Blue Dancer.*

"You must be referring to *The Blue Dancer,* my lord," Erik said. "But you could not have been there."

"Oh," Cho said, sitting back in his chair with one raised eyebrow and the fingers of both hands pressed together just under his chin, "and why is that?"

"Because Flemming detested whores," Erik replied. "And to say a woman in Waterton is beautiful, well, you must not have seen many women in your lifetime to say that."

Cho let out a thunderous laugh and slapped his knee so hard, Erik flinched.

"Truly. Truly. You have yourself a restful night, Erik Eleodum of Waterton," Cho offered.

The master of the camp took another drink from his jeweled cup and continued to laugh as the three men left the house. Erik sighed, his head in a daze. He hadn't grown up in Waterton, but he had certainly lived there long enough to know most of its citizens. It was, as Cho said, a small town.

Chapter 18

WROTHGARD SAT SLOUCHED IN HIS chair, elbow propped against the arm, chin resting on his fist. His other hand lay loosely on the table, index finger picking at a splintered hole. His cup of beer had lost its frothiness, and the suds that had spilled over the rim and down to the wood were now just a small puddle collecting around the mug's base.

He sat and listened. He listened to Switch and Bryon argue about anything they could. He listened to the dwarves speak in their native language and couldn't help thinking they were always arguing too, with the way their language sounded, and yet the smiles on their faces said they were not. He listened to some of the other customers and their talk of this woman, that backstabbing bastard, why the hell there would be dwarves in their bar.

Another sip, and a drink, and then another sip, and his beer was gone. He signaled for the waitress, a pudgy, yet pretty, woman shorter than Wrothgard normally found desirable but not so short that he wouldn't bed her down for a night of company. She came over, somewhat slowly as if she didn't much care for him or the rest of his party. She had a little button nose and rosy cheeks with dimples, but she didn't smile.

She barely paid him a glance as she filled his mug from a large jug, carelessly spilling some beer on the table. At first, that irritated him, angered him even. But that secondary, sidelong glance she gave him with her piercing blue eyes made him smile, and he grabbed her wrist as she turned away. She let out a grunt as she spilled some of her pitcher on the floor and turned to face him full on, cheeks now red, eyes squinted, and a strand of sandy hair escaping the bun that held the rest of her hair so tightly. The strand whisked across her face.

"You know, if you smiled, I might give you an extra coin for your service," Wrothgard said.

She pulled her arm away. She was strong.

"My *service* demands more than an extra coin," she replied.

Her voice was hard and sharp.

"You are a bold one, with so many hardened men drinking your beer," Wrothgard said. "You think you'd be a little nicer."

"I don't do nice. And believe me," she said, "I've been around men harder than you. And bigger."

She cracked him a tiny smile, one no one else could've seen. There she was, opening up to him, if only a little.

"Really," Wrothgard said. "We'll see."

"Oh, will we?" she replied, turning and walking away.

Wrothgard took a drink. This mug tasted a little better.

Sitting back and savoring his drink, Wrothgard saw Vander Bim walk over to his table. He took a seat across from the soldier, his own mug of beer in his hand, and leaned forward.

This looks like it's going to turn into a conversation I don't want to have right now, Wrothgard thought.

"What's going on here, soldier?" Vander Bim said, his voice as cold as his stare.

Wrothgard cocked an eyebrow.

"I have been a sell-sword," Vander Bim lowered on the word, "for long enough to know that this is turning out to be something far more complicated than just finding a simple treasure for some lord."

"To truly understand this," Wrothgard set his mug down and opened his hands as if offering up something, "one must understand the history of Golgolithul."

Wrothgard had hoped his answer was complicated enough that

Vander Bim would stop asking, but the continually questioning look on the man's face said otherwise. The eastern soldier sighed and took another drink of his beer. Somehow, it didn't taste as good anymore.

"The Lord of the East's father—Mörken—was the first Stévockian to rule Golgolithul in almost three hundred years, since the peace treaty at the Battle of Bethuliam. Like any other kingdom or country, Golgolithul has several ruling families that are very powerful, always vying for power and position. And as one takes more power, the others plot against them. It's all very complicated to me. I am a simple soldier after all."

Vander Bim continued to stare at Wrothgard, and he knew the sailor would not let that answer suffice.

"The Aztûkians and the Stévockians are the two most powerful families in Golgolithul, each controlling their own cities—Fen-Stévock and Fen-Aztûk. All the other citizens align themselves to these two families," Wrothgard said. "Like any change in power, when Mörken Stévock became High Lord Chancellor, the opposition claimed treachery and deceit. And truth be told, there always is. However, this last change in power—especially after three hundred years of the same family ruling—was messier and bloodier than usual. Many in the east know our history, when the Stévockians last ruled, and know the tales of black magic and constant war. But, then again, others consider the Aztûkians weak and blame them for Golgolithul's dwindling power."

"What does this have to do with us?" Vander Bim asked.

"Like I said," Wrothgard replied, "I am only a simple soldier. Political espionage and secret civil wars are beyond me. I would prefer a head on fight to any of that. But ever since the Lord of the East's father took power, the Aztûkians have secretly worked to overthrow him and his family. It seems our simple mission is wrapped up in this feud, much more than I would like it to be."

"So, do you support the Lord of the East?" Vander Bim asked.

"He fills my purse with coin," Wrothgard said with a smile. "That is what concerns me most these days. Truth be told, I supported his father. High Lord Chancellor Mörken started raising Golgolithul to its former glory. Háthgolthane began to remember the strength that lives in the east. We had become weak under Aztûkian rule. But what is the price of such power? The Aztûkians could be brutal, but the cruelty of the Stévockians is legendary. Mörken all but crushed any family that openly opposed him. And the Lord of the East—whose name only his inner circle knows—is becoming the most ruthless Stévockian in all the ages."

Wrothgard shuddered as he thought of some of the Lord of the East's brutal tactics, memories he didn't dare share with his companions.

"I don't know," Wrothgard said, lifting his cup and hoping that young beer maiden would hurry over so he might flirt with her some more. "Perhaps, it was when the Lord of the East did away with the Senate Council and the title of High Lord Chancellor that I began to question my loyalties. Like I said, this is greater than me. I serve gold now and try to care little for which fool rules over other fools. Patûk Al'Banan and the Lord of the East and anyone else will wage their wars, and we are just unfortunate enough to have been caught in the middle of some of it."

The serving girl came by again and filled Wrothgard's cup. He slid a hand around the back of her thigh and winked. She gave him a hard look at first, but then, she smiled.

"Enough about the history of our homeland, eh Vander Bim," Wrothgard said, lifting his cup of beer towards the sailor, Switch, and the others, "Gentlemen, to more gold than we can imagine and pretty beer maidens."

Chapter 19

BRYON HAD NEVER SEEN A tavern with so much light coming in, and the bright noon sun that spilled through the many windows of *The Golden Miner* revealed the golden hue in the wood that gave the inn its name. The innkeeper knew his establishment's worth, that was certain, for he watched everyone with an eagle's eye and was quick to scold anyone banging on his tables or scratching their chairs across the floor.

Bryon sat with his sell-sword companions, eating a midday meal when a boy—maybe two seasons from having his first hair on his chin—walked into the bar and directly to Wrothgard at the other end of the table. Bryon didn't recognize the lad, but the soldier seemed to as the boy leaned towards him intently. The boy whispered something into the easterner's ear, and when he had finished, Wrothgard placed a coin in his hand. The boy bowed and ran out of the inn, and Switch came over next and the two men talked. Bryon squinted and leaned forward as if that would help him hear what they had to say. It didn't.

Finally, once Switch and Wrothgard finished talking, the soldier motioned for everyone to come closer to him.

"That boy is a servant in Cho's house," Wrothgard explained. "Late last night, many hours after we entered Aga Min, another party of three men came requesting a night's stay in the camp. Apparently, the hour was so late that the camp's guard would not take them to Cho, so they camped just outside Aga Min's perimeter and went to see the camp's master this morning."

"What does this have to do with us?" Bryon asked.

"They are sell-swords. They were at the Messenger's meeting," Wrothgard explained.

Demik groaned, Switch ground his teeth, and Vander Bim cursed under his breath.

"They told Cho why they were here. They told him they were mercenaries and for whom they worked," Wrothgard said. "Now, it is in Cho's best interest to let them stay for a day, since Golgolithul owns this camp, but the boy said Cho despises sell-swords and cares little for the Lord of the East."

"And we should be concerned by this?" Befel asked.

"Yes," Wrothgard replied. "First, we are too close to our competition. In this game, when the competition is too close, there is only one solution."

"I think I can guess what that solution is," Bryon said, to which Switch smiled.

"Secondly," Wrothgard continued, "it is rather suspicious that two groups of men enter a camp within hours of one another, both seeking entrance to the mountain. Cho already does not like mercenaries. Now, he knows he has one party of sell-swords dwelling within his camp and is probably, at this moment, suspecting that we have lied to him about the nature of our journey. He may be no warrior, and he may not have what one might call a garrison or a guard, but nonetheless, he is a powerful man with enough men willing to fight for him. Our skill in battle would matter little to the numbers that would come to kill us."

"So, what do we do now?" Bryon asked.

"Leave before dawn tomorrow morning. Avoid Cho. Take care of our competition," Wrothgard replied.

"Dawn," Bryon muttered. He had slept well, his bed comfortable, the whore from Madame Ary's rather pretty. A few more nights would have been welcomed. He looked at Wrothgard. "Why did that boy come and tell you all this?"

"I gave him a gold coin and told him if he hears anything that I might find interesting, to come tell me," Wrothgard replied.

"Always have your eyes to the horizon and ears to the ground," Switch added.

Bryon felt sweat trickle down his cheek. As the sun dipped west into the afternoon—the hour of the snake, Bryon guessed—it grew hot and uncomfortable. The dwarves sat behind him, whispering in their native language. Vander Bim and Wrothgard also spoke quietly to one another. And Befel and Erik sat beside Bryon, talking here and there. But Switch just sat and stared, his eyes unblinking and body unmoving save for the shallow rise and fall of his chest as he breathed. Bryon's collar was already damp, and by the end of the day, it would be soaked. Even the innkeeper and serving girl stood, just behind the bar, still and quiet, staring. Watching. Waiting.

The three other men sat, just as still, although they rarely looked to Bryon's companions, especially Switch, and when they did, they turned away quickly. Whenever that happened, Bryon thought he saw Switch smile just a bit.

"They have been sipping on their ale for over an hour now," Bryon whispered to the thief. "They wish to stay sober."

One man with a bushy, black beard mouthed something to another, this one with long, spiked hair running down the middle of his head. The third nodded before turning to face Switch. His face looked crooked, and by the curvature in his nose and scarring on his jaw, Bryon suspected he had broken both at some point.

"What the bloody 'ell do you keep looking at?" Crooked Nose said.

His voice reminded Bryon of an old farmer named Benji, several leagues from his father's farm. It was low and gruff and almost unintelligible.

Switch said nothing. Wrothgard, who sat just to the side of the thief, put his hand on the thief's shoulder and whispered. He could just hear what he said.

"Remember, we don't want a fight here."

"Didn't you 'ear me, you shit," Crooked Nose added, his voice growing louder. Switch still said nothing.

Finally, the man stood, knocking his chair to the ground. He was a giant of a man, larger than anyone in the company with which Bryon traveled. He towered over Switch and must have been three times as heavy.

The man's mail shirt clinked as he stood. He rested one hand on the long handle of his hand-and-a-half sword while the other he lifted in front of him, fist clenched, leather gloves creaking.

"He's speechless," said Bushy Beard as he leaned back in his chair, one elbow on the table and his other hand resting in his lap.

"Maybe he thinks you're cute," Mohawk added. He sat as well, leaning on his elbows. His voice sounded muffled and nasally as if he had bread stuffed in both cheeks. "He's got the look of a woman, all small and skinny."

Switch's face grew red, but he didn't say anything, didn't even move.

"Although, that one looks softer," Mohawk said. "I bet he would be fun. He would fight a little, but then I bet he would give in. He might like it."

Bryon didn't realize at first that the mohawked mercenary was talking about him, not until the man blew him a kiss.

Bryon clenched his fists and stood. Mohawk and his two companions only laughed.

"Sit down you bloody fool." Switch's whisper sounded a venomous hiss.

"Does your boy need a spanking, worm?" Crooked Nose stood tall and cocked his head to one side, a smirk now on his face. His clenched fist had dropped, and he stuck a thumb in his belt, letting it rest there. He joined Mohawk in blowing kisses at Bryon. "I'd be happy to spank your little friend."

"Sit down, Bryon. This is what they want," Wrothgard whispered. "Calm down before you find yourself dead."

Bryon looked over at Crooked Nose. His blade was out, held easily in one hand. The other two men were on their feet as well, swords drawn.

"If this is what they want, why not give it to them?" Bryon asked quietly.

They outnumbered these three men. They had the dwarves, the soldier, the experienced mercenary sailor; but then he looked at Befel, his left arm in a sling, tied tightly to his body. He looked to Vander Bim, dark circles around his eyes, weariness strewn across his face as plainly as the blond stubble on his chin. He looked to Erik, eyes hard, and yet worry hidden in there as well. He felt his own ribs, still sore, still not wholly healed.

"What's the matter, maggot?" Crooked Nose said, looking straight at Switch. "You lose your balls to that young one?"

Switch spun on his heels and faced the three mercenaries.

"When I slide my steel across your neck," Switch hissed, "before you die, I'm going to stick a knife up your ass."

"Why not now?" Mohawk incited. He pointed his broadsword at the thief.

"Enough!" The yell rang through *The Golden Miner*. The barkeep stood, now in front of his bar, rigid, pale-faced and stern. He gripped a large cudgel in his right hand, its end, an unfinished piece of wood with the stubs of branches still present. There were other men, miners hardened by work, that stood as the barkeep yelled, moving to back the man up.

"I've stood 'ere long enough listening to yer pissin' contest. I'll no' have no fighting in me bar," yelled the bald man. "Soldiers or no soldiers, I'll beat your brains out of your skull if ya disrupt me bar anymore. Eat till yer fat. Drink till yer drunk. Go next door to Madame Ary's and fuck 'til yer cock's sore. Or get out."

Mohawk glared at the bartender with squinted eyes. His face and head turned a pale red, all but the white scars that dotted his face, which stood out like white roses among a blackthorn bush. He let the tip of his blade drop to the floor as he drummed his steel breastplate with the fingers of his left hand. He gave the bartender an exaggerated half bow, glaring at Switch the whole time.

Bushy Beard jerked his head to the side, and as he left *The Golden Miner,* his two comrades followed. He stopped at the door and looked to Wrothgard.

"You best keep your dog on a leash." He gave Switch a quick smile. "Else he might try to bite a bigger dog."

The other two men laughed loudly, and as Mohawk followed the other two mercenaries out the door, he blew Bryon a kiss.

Bryon walked along a darkened edge of Aga Min. No torches. No miners. Just stars and solitude and the sound of the distant howls of wild dogs. His green bottle of wine hung loosely in his hand, and as he looked around, he had forgotten how he got to where he was. He held up the bottle. It reminded him of home, of his father.

"Damn you," he cursed.

Why had he started walking? His cousins were boring. The dwarves only spoke to each other, and in their own language. Wrothgard was too busy flirting with some bar wench. And Vander Bim and Switch seemed to want to have nothing to do with him. He had gone to Madame Ary's, but the whore he had bedded the night before was taken and the others weren't to his liking. So, that left only one good alternative... drinking. Only, now, he had lost his way. How hard could it be to find an inn and brothel in a small mining camp? Bryon shrugged. He supposed it mattered how drunk he was.

His thoughts trailed off to Switch, that little weasel of a man who thought himself so smart and cunning and worldly. Bryon would show him... one day. He was certainly angry with Bryon, for standing up to those men in *The Golden Miner.* But he wouldn't do it. Neither would Wrothgard or Vander Bim. Or the dwarves for that matter.

"Yellow-bellied cowards," Bryon said as he took another draught from his bottle.

What had Switch said as Bryon left the inn?

"I'll stick my knife up his ass. Teach him a thing or two."

As if to add lemon juice to the sting of Switch's words, Wrothgard had added, "Leave him be. He's only a boy."

Bryon felt his face grow hot. He shook his head and drank yet again.

As Bryon tilted the bottle up, it shattered. The green shards sparkled in the bright moonlight, some of them scratching his face. But that wasn't what sent him tumbling backwards. Something hard hit his cheek. His head hit the ground, and when he stared up at the stars, they danced and bobbled back and forth. Something shadowed them, blocked them out. When his vision normalized, he saw a face in the pale glow of the moon. Mohawk.

"Trying to act all tough earlier," Mohawk said. There was something about his smile in the faint light, something almost fake, like his skin was made of porcelain. Bryon thought the man might go for his sword, but instead he saw Mohawk tugging his belt, loosening it. "We'll see how much of a man you are, boy."

"What by the Shadow are you doing..." and then Bryon realized.

Bryon pushed up to his elbows and dug his heels in the ground, sliding backwards a few paces. Then he went for his sword. He had been foolish enough to go for a walk by himself and to drink himself into a mild drunkenness, but he hadn't been foolish enough to go without his sword.

Before he could reach his weapon, someone caught his arms and pinned them to the ground. He looked up. Crooked Nose put the full weight of his frame—a whole two heads taller than Bryon—against Bryon's shoulders, and he found himself motionless.

"You should've stayed with your friends, boy," Crooked Nose hissed, "or better yet, stayed home. Too bad you won't live to learn your lesson."

Mohawk dropped his belt to the ground and walked to Bryon, still struggling, even though it proved futile.

"This isn't happening," Bryon cried. "Son of a whore, this isn't happening."

"Did you know my mother?" one of the men replied with a laugh.

"Oh, it is happening," another one said.

He kicked out at Mohawk as the mercenary loosened the tie on his own pants.

"Oh, boy, keep fighting. It just makes the meat all the sweeter."

The mercenary dropped his pants, grabbed one of Bryon's ankles as he kicked out, and jerked his leg up. The man licked his lips, a bit of drool rolling from the corner of his mouth and collecting on his chin.

"Please, no. Gods, please, no. The sailor's gods, the soldier's gods, Erik's God, please, any of you, help me." Bryon's cries only made the three men laugh more.

Just then, a quick glimmer, almost like a shooting star, flashed in front of Mohawk. The mercenary, still smiling, dropped to one knee. He even chortled, and leaning forward onto one hand, his dull eyes met Bryon's. Then, he dropped Bryon's leg. He felt Crooked Nose's hold on his shoulders loosen.

"What's wrong with you, Poc?" Crooked Nose asked.

Mohawk—Poc—looked to his comrade. The smile on his face faded, although he still drooled incessantly. But, no, it wasn't drool. In the pale light, Bryon could see. It was blood. A stain along the collar of his shirt grew as a thin line appeared across his neck. In a moment, blood poured from his wound, and the mercenary, eyes wide and pants around his ankles, dropped face down to the ground, breathless.

Bryon scooted away from Crooked Nose and rose to one knee. He saw Bushy Beard standing off to the side, sword drawn. He heard steel on leather and saw Crooked Nose draw his sword as well. He growled at Bryon and gripped his sword with both hands. It gleamed, almost purplish, in the night, and Bryon knew that blade could take his head off with half an effort. He saw a shadow move, and as Bushy Beard ran to him, Switch jumped from seemingly nowhere onto the mercenary's back, covered his mouth with one hand and plunged a dagger, blade almost as thin as a needle, into the man's neck.

"Who is the dog now?" Blood sprayed across Switch's rictus snarl as he pulled out the knife and plunged it into the man's flesh again, and then again, and then twice more.

Crooked Nose stood, only for a moment, stunned, sword down. Bryon knew this was the moment and, with sword drawn, lunged at Crooked Nose. The mercenary saw Bryon's attack, if only a little late, and brought his sword up to block the farmer's. It prevented Bryon's iron from striking deep into his gut, but he still managed to drive the weapon into his enemy's shoulder. Before Crooked Nose could cry out, a knife thudded into his neck.

Crooked Nose coughed, spewing blood all over Bryon's face. He pulled the knife from his neck with a grunt and grabbed Bryon's blade with his gloved hand, preventing him from retrieving his weapon. With his long arms, the mercenary reached out and grabbed Bryon by the shirt, pulling him close. He dropped his sword and both his hands worked their way to the young man's throat.

Bryon felt the squeeze, felt air leaving his lungs. He swung up, catching Crooked Nose in the chin. It did nothing. He stepped down hard, his boot heel catching the man's instep. Nothing. Then, suddenly, Bryon heard, of all things, his father's voice. It was a time when Bryon had had enough of his father, enough of his drunken rants and his put-downs. He decided he would show his father he was a man. He had stripped off his shirt and put up both fists.

"Come on, old man," Bryon had said.

"Are you sure you want to do this?" his father had asked. Bryon had replied with a simple nod.

Before Bryon knew what had happened, his father was in on his legs, lifting him off the ground and driving him back to the ground hard. Bryon had gotten a hold of his father's head, squeezing it between both arms, but a quick pinch to the inside of one arm made him let go. A knee drove up into his groin, and then he felt another knee press on his neck, hard enough so that he could not move but not so hard as to stop him from breathing.

"Are you done?" his father had asked.

"You didn't fight fair," Bryon had replied.

And then the words Bryon heard in the back of his head.

"There is no such thing as a fair fight. Fight to win, at all cost. One day, it may mean your life."

Bryon drove his knee up hard. He could feel the soft flesh of Crooked Nose's groin give way, feel the man's balls crushed under his kneecap. The mercenary let go. Bryon saw Switch creep up behind the man, a dagger in his hand. He slid the dagger across the man's hamstring, and Crooked Nose promptly fell to his knees.

"Remember what I said," Switch hissed into Crooked Nose's ear, wrapping one arm around the man's giant head and pulling it back, exposing naked neck.

Bryon saw fear on Crooked Nose's face.

Switch's blade slid across the soft flesh of the man's neck and as a thin, red line trailed the steel, Bryon saw the thief keep his promise. Crooked Nose reeled forward, wanting to scream, but Switch clapped a hand over the man's mouth and kept it there until he stopped breathing.

Switch walked to a large tent, the flap of which was held open by a heavy cord.

"We'll stuff these bastards in here," Switch said.

"How did you... where did you..."

Bryon's arms felt like lead. He couldn't move. Numbness overcame his body. Blood covered the ground, in great pools of inky black under the bright moon. He looked around the unlit portion of the camp, visible under the bright moon. Tents lined the walkway along with lean-tos resting against the trees that grew here and there, tall and bushy. This was certainly a part of Aga Min that people didn't spend much time in.

"When you left the inn, I followed you," Switch explained. "I suspected these prigs were up to no good, wanting to send a message and show force. After that drunken sod leaning against his meat cart gave you his wine bottle, I saw them."

"Why didn't I realize they were following me?" Bryon asked, as much to himself as to Switch.

"They are cunning warriors and you're not," Switch said with a shrug. "Pretty simple if you ask me. Anyways, when I realized what was going to happen, I snuck ahead of you and hid in one of these tents. It was easy. They're equipment tents, and no one comes around here much. When they jumped you, I used that as my opportunity."

Bryon shook his head. He felt his hands shake. He looked at Mohawk's dead body. He was going to... Bryon shivered.

"Bloody Shadow," Switch exclaimed as loud as he dared. "You are undefiled and alive. Praise the gods and the saints and the seasons and whatever else you bloody want to thank. We need to cover up the blood and hide these bodies and make sure they stay hidden until we leave."

"Drag them into the Plains?" Bryon asked.

"Nah," Switch said. "That'll take too long. No one checks these tents. This one here is full of bags of sand and barrels of coal. We'll stuff them under those bags. It'll be weeks before anyone finds them."

After they laid the dead men towards the back of the tent and piled as many bags on top of them—stacking barrels, then, in front of the bags—Switch threw three swords down at Bryon's feet. Bryon eyed the swords.

"Take them," Switch said. He jerked his head towards the resting place of Bryon's attackers. "They don't need them anymore. Spoils of war, if you will. They're too big for me."

Bryon eyed Crooked Nose's hand-and-a-half sword. It was a thing of beauty with an odd, eerie tint to it, almost as if it reflected black, purplish light rather than the normal, dull gray of steel. He took it, sheathed it in its scabbard, and stuffed the scabbard into his own belt.

"Leave your old one. You don't need it with your new one, and it's a rusted piece of cow shit anyways."

Bryon threw down his old sword.

"Don't know if you care or not, but you might want to grab the other two swords for your cousins," Switch suggested. "They're a far sight better than what they're carrying now. And, the gods know, we'll need decent weapons where we're going."

Bryon nodded and grabbed Mohawk's and Bushy Beard's swords.

Switch gathered the men's purses, pouring their contents into his hand and stuffing it all into his own purse. He grabbed the knives on the dead men's belts and put them on his own. He searched through their pockets, their boots, inside their shirts, under their armor. He shook his head.

"What are you doing?" Bryon asked.

"Men hide their valuables in the queerest of places, but these bastards have almost nothing. They're even scarce on their coin." Switch kicked Mohawk and spat on his dead body. "I figured they'd have a good deal of coin, perhaps even something magic."

"Magic." Bryon took a step back.

"Aye, not that I'll use it, but anything magic, especially a blade, can fetch a handsome amount of gold in the right market," Switch explained.

"You can tell if something is magic?" Bryon asked.

"Aye, a little. I am no expert, but a thief has to know what to keep and what to throw away," Switch replied. "Otherwise, he wouldn't be a very good thief. Now, before we go, we must cover up the blood with dirt."

Switch and Bryon, getting sober by the minute, slowly walked back to *The Golden Miner.* Wrothgard was the only one in the bar, a barmaid Bryon noticed him talking to the night before sitting on his lap, giggling as the soldier whispered something into her ear. The easterner saw the two walk into the inn and met the thief's eyes. The thief nodded, and Wrothgard returned the nod.

"Was this all planned?" Bryon asked softly, not to Switch but to himself. "Was I used as bait?"

"Aye," Switch replied in a whisper. "Don't feel bad. Our plan worked well."

Bryon felt his face go hot. A flash of anger coursed through his body. But then, it went away. What difference did it make? It was over and done with, and he was alive. As he walked up the stairs to his room, Switch leaned against the bar, a pitcher of ale in front of him, as if nothing had just happened.

"Bryon," Switch said.

The farmer, halfway up the first-floor stairs, stopped and turned. It was Switch, pitcher in hand. The thief drank from it like it was a mug.

"Come here," the thief commanded.

Bryon hesitated. Was he going to stick a knife in his belly? Bryon wouldn't put it past the man. He descended the stairs to face the thief.

"Hold out your hand," Switch said.

Bryon complied. The thief pressed something into his hand and then walked away. The young man looked down and saw three gold pieces sitting there. Bryon cocked an eyebrow. He didn't understand this game.

Bryon walked up the stairs and to his room. He opened the door. Erik lifted his head from his pillow, eyes still half-closed from sleep, saw it was Bryon, and dropped his head back to his pillow. Befel sat on the edge of his bed, exercising his shoulder as best he could. His face contorted and grimaced as he made circles with his arm and stretched it across his chest.

Bryon could see Befel eyeing the two swords he held in his hand, watched them questioningly as he leaned them against the wall next to the door.

"They're for you," Bryon said.

Erik sat back up. "Which one is mine?"

"Don't you even care where he got them? Where did you get them?" Befel asked.

"I don't want to argue. They're good swords," Bryon said. "Don't worry about where they came from. Just take them."

Erik shrugged and nodded his head, but Befel gave Bryon a disparaging look. "No. I want to know from where they came."

"Damn it," Bryon hissed. "Why do you always make things so difficult? The three mercenaries from this afternoon attacked me. They're dead. These were theirs. Now they're ours. I took one too."

He unsheathed the sword he took for himself and held it out for Befel and Erik to see. The steel caught the light from the room and, again, sparkled with a purplish glimmer. He looked closer in the room's light and saw pictures, letters, some sort of carvings along the blade.

"Interesting," Bryon said and smiled to himself.

"I don't think I want it," Befel said. "I appreciate it but, well, I just don't think I want it."

"Don't be a fool." Bryon sheathed his own blade and glared at Befel. He left Befel and Erik's swords leaning against the wall and walked to his bed, crashing against the mattress without even taking off his boots.

Chapter 20

"ARE YOU COMING?"

Serving the General Lord Marshall of Gol-Durathna, and following mercenaries heeding a call from the Lord of the East, had led Ranus and Cliens deeper into the Southern Mountains, and Cliens wondered if, despite his desire to serve his country and Creator, the mission was worth the trouble.

"You grew up in a swamp," Cliens replied. "You're used to this."

Ranus had a very real ability to annoy Cliens, despite their friendship. The rain had been coming down for days now, and their trek up into the Southern Mountains had slowed to a crawl. Some of the steeper slopes proved almost treacherous, and even the flat surfaces had turned to such a muddy mess that Cliens thought he might sink knee deep with a wrong step. Ranus didn't have the same problem.

"I could help," Ranus said.

Cliens found it hard to understand his friend, his language made up of clicks and clacks, chirps and hisses, through the monsoon deluge, so for a moment he just stared and tried to decipher what he had said. Finally, he figured it out and shook his head.

"I don't want your help."

Cliens watched Ranus, a good dozen paces ahead of him. The rain seemed to part above him, split just as it was about to hit his friend's head and flow to each side, not a single drop touching him. Truly, he stood as dry as a sun-bleached bone even though everything else around him stood soaked beyond comprehension. Even the ground under his feet sat dry as if the rain had never been there.

"It's just a little charm," Ranus said with a smile, "a prayer I give to the Creator."

Cliens shook his head. "Whatever you call it, its magic, and I don't like it. Nothing good can come from magic."

"It's a gift from the Creator, which is only good," Ranus replied, laughing. "I pray, and he gives."

"And if he doesn't give you this . . . this little charm?"

"I walk in the rain," Ranus replied.

"Has he ever not given it to you?" Cliens asked.

"No."

"And how do you know it's the Creator giving this…charm to you and not something else?" Cliens asked.

Ranus shrugged. "I just know."

"Right," Cliens replied.

They hiked long through the night, the rain never leaving. There were moments when the rain seemed to lighten, only to regain its strength and dump more water than before on Cliens and Ranus…well, at least Cliens. The Durathnan watched as the water simply spilled around his companion. He shook his head.

Damned magic, Cliens thought.

"What are we looking for, anyway?" Cliens asked.

"A level path," Ranus replied. "Something that will allow us to make it to the great ravine that splits the north and south ranges."

"And if we don't," Cliens called to Ranus. Amidst the heavy rain, he found himself yelling half the time. "If we don't find a level path?"

"Then we keep climbing," Ranus replied.

My legs are going to be twice as thick as they are now if we keep this up, Cliens thought.

"Are you sure climbing into the Southern Mountains was a good idea?" Cliens yelled over a thunder strike. "Those other fools went all the way to Aga Min."

"That's why they are fools," Ranus replied.

Right now, we look the fools, Cliens thought.

"This is best," Ranus explained, "if we wish to remain hidden."

Just then, a loud crack of thunder caused Cliens to jump, and even the stalwart Ranus ducked his head a little. The lightning that accompanied the boom bathed the whole mountain in white, electric light. Cliens hadn't realized how far up into the mountain they were, as he looked down over the edge of the slope on which they traversed and saw boulders and trees and, far below, the feet of the Southern Mountains and the Plains of Güdal.

More thunder reverberated through the peaks of the Southern Mountains and more lightning flashed and lit up the whole mountainous landscape. They were on top of one another—the thunder and lightning.

"It's close," Cliens yelled. Ranus hadn't heard him. Cliens walked faster, even ran, up to this friend. He crossed into Ranus' magic—or charm—and the rain stopped beating against his shoulders and face. "That's pleasant."

"What was that?" Ranus asked, turning to see Cliens.

"Not having a river of rain beating against me," Cliens said, "is nice."

"Do you see?" Ranus asked. "Now, would you like me to pray for a charm for you as well?"

Cliens thought for a moment, almost forgetting why he had run to Ranus.

"We need to find shelter," Cliens said finally. "The lightning is close, right on top of the thunder."

Ranus nodded. A bolt of lightning struck a tall pine tree nearby. The sound was deafening. Cliens clasped his hands over his ears. It almost created a vacuum, and he couldn't even hear himself scream. The tree exploded in flame, and the fire dared the torrential downpour to extinguish it.

Ranus grabbed a handful of Cliens' sodden shirt and half-lead, half-pulled the man as they searched for shelter. Cliens never could figure out how long, thin fingers could be so strong. Finally, they found a pile of rocks and boulders leaning together and squeezed in between a tight copse of trees that created a small cave. Just as Cliens stepped inside, he heard the low growl of a dog. He looked up to see the yellow eyes of a wolf.

The wolf bared its teeth, the gray-black fur on its back bristling. Three other wolves stepped up to its side, all growling and snarling.

"Wolf den," Cliens said, his hand going to the handle of his sword.

Ranus stopped Cliens from drawing his blade.

"Look," Ranus said. He pointed to the back of the cave where, huddled together and under some pine needles, half a dozen wolf pups lay, eyes barely open, all whimpering.

Ranus crouched low, both hands held out, and began to speak calmly to the wolves in his language of clicks and chirps and whistles. It was a slow process, but the wolves began to calm. First, they stopped growling. Then, their ears stood up and their fur smoothed a bit. Finally, they simply paced back and forth, whining and whimpering. Eventually, one of them stepped forward and licked Ranus' hand.

"Do the same," he commanded Cliens.

"So they can bite me?" Cliens asked exasperatedly. "So they can taste my blood and find they have a liking to it?"

"Do it, or they won't trust you," Ranus said softly, still crouched and staring intently at the wolves.

"Fine," Cliens said, stepping next to Ranus and squatting.

At first, none of the wolves would come forward to Cliens. They all stayed back, near the pups. But, eventually, they did the same with Cliens that they did with Ranus.

"We can sleep here tonight," Ranus said as a crack of lightning sent the pups into frantic whining and caused more anxious pacing by the adults. "But, we must move on by first light."

"Did the wolves tell you that?" Cliens asked.

"In a way, yes," Ranus replied.

"More of your magic?" Cliens accused. "Or, I'm sorry, charms?"

"No." Ranus shook his head. "Just knowing how to understand a frightened animal."

"So, am I going to wake up with a wolf's fangs at my throat because you think you know how to speak with frightened animals?"

"We will see," Ranus replied. "Are you brave enough to stay? Or should we take our chances in the rain and thunder and lightning?"

Cliens scoffed. He hated it when Ranus did that—gave him a choice when Cliens knew there was none.

"No, of course we'll stay in here," Cliens replied.

When the morning came, Cliens did not find wolf fangs wrapped around his neck. Rather, he found the small den of wolves fast asleep, the young pups nestling and rummaging at their mother's teats. He looked up at Ranus, who was already ready to go. It took Cliens only a moment before he was ready as well.

"How did you sleep?" Ranus asked.

"Surprisingly well," Cliens replied, "although, I am a little hungry."

"Here," Ranus said, handing Cliens what looked to be a handful of crackers.

Cliens' lip curled at the sight.

"Then go hungry," Ranus replied, moving to put his crackers back in the pouch that hung from his belt.

"No, no," Cliens replied. "Give them here. Stop looking so hurt. It's not my fault that I have no taste for your dried bread."

"What makes you think I have a taste for them?" Ranus asked with that crooked, almost sarcastic smile of his.

"You don't?" Cliens asked.

"Of course I do," Ranus said, smile still on his face.

"You can be a piss ant, you know that?" Cliens replied.

Ranus laughed. Cliens popped one of the crackers in his mouth and chewed slowly. The cracker became soggy instantly and seemed to slide down his throat. Cliens almost gagged.

"They're so dry," Cliens said, "and they taste like moldy, bland dirt clods."

"And you know what bland, moldy dirt clods taste like?" Ranus asked.

"Well, no," Cliens replied. There it was again, that condescending questioning Ranus did when he knew he was right.

"Only a couple of crackers will keep you sated for a day," Ranus said.

Cliens threw a couple more in his mouth, chewed, and smiled sarcastically at Ranus.

"And," Ranus said, putting up a long, slender finger, "they are nutritious. It is like eating a day's worth of fruits, vegetables, meats, and milk all in one bite."

"Well, lucky me," Cliens said, his voice somewhat muffled by a full mouth.

Cliens looked over his shoulder at the wolves. They looked peaceful. Funny, how something so deadly could look peaceful.

"Do you think they'll make it?" Cliens asked.

"Who?" Ranus asked with a quick click of his tongue.

"Those fools marching into Aga Min," Cliens replied.

"I saw two companies headed to Aga Min," Ranus said. "The one with the dwarves…I think they have a chance, especially if they make it to Thorakest."

"You think they're heading to Thorakest?" Cliens asked.

"That is my best guess," Ranus replied, "and with the help of the dwarves, they have an advantage."

"The dwarves of Thorakest would help them?" Cliens asked with a tone of disbelief. "Being in the employ of the Lord of the East?"

Ranus shrugged.

"Only the Creator knows," Ranus replied. "These are desperate times for many people, though, including the dwarves. Dangerous times call for drastic measures."

"We had better get going then," Cliens said.

Chapter 21

ERIK SAT ON HIS BED, new sword resting in his lap. It was longer than his old one, straight with few chips and dings to speak of, and the edge looked sharp. He was almost asleep before Bryon had opened the door, exclaiming he had killed three mercenaries and confiscated their weapons. Now Erik couldn't sleep. All he could do was think about what a mountain tunnel might look like. Would it be hot? Cold? Wet? What monsters lay in wait for them?

He sheathed the sword, leaning it against the table next to his bed. Erik produced two large, smooth rubies, bobbling them in his hand. He put them up to the light. They seemed to drink it in, consume it all, and reflect nothing. They were dull and brilliant at the same time. Their worth must have been great, and every time he looked at them, he wondered why Mardirru gave them to him.

He held them up to the light again. They were something special. He reached under his pillow and pulled out his flute, the thing that puzzled him more than the rubies or the reason why Mardirru gave the stones to him. The magic of the flute scared him. Was it magic? If it was, wouldn't Mardirru have been able to play the thing? He slid the instrument back underneath his pillow and pulled his hand back quickly.

"Damn it," Erik hissed.

He sucked a little bit of blood from his index finger, coming from a small puncture wound at the finger's tip. He was sure he had left his dagger sheathed.

A tingle crawled up his spine. Erik jumped from the bed, stripping his shirt off, and flinging it around his head.

"What are you doing?" Befel mumbled, his voice muffled with his face buried in his pillow.

Erik couldn't find a spider, but the tingle came again. Then it moved to the back of his head as if someone was running their hands through his hair. He looked at his brother.

"Just a spider crawling up my arm," Erik explained. "I guess I overreacted."

Befel's snoring told Erik his brother wasn't listening anymore. His cheeks began to tingle.

His flute and dagger lay on the bed, exposed, the pillow that once covered them now on the floor. He eyed the dagger. Its golden-gilded scabbard lay next to it, and he sheathed the blade. Erik turned and bent down to pick up his pillow, and when he turned back, his dagger lay again, blade exposed. Erik raised an eyebrow. Was he going crazy? He shook his head. Then he felt another tingle . . . and a voice in his head. His thoughts, but, not. His voice . . . but not.

His head buzzed as if he were drunk. That tingling sensation spread over his whole body, almost hurting. Goose pimples rose along his arms. The hair on the back of his neck stood on end. He heard the voice again. Erik looked to the golden-handled knife . . . no, it was a dagger. He shook his head again. How did he know that? Because the dagger had told him . . . in his head . . . through his thoughts. And the gold wasn't really gold, but an Elvish metal that looked like gold.

Forcing himself to accept he wasn't going crazy, that this was really happening, he decided he needed to pay more attention to his dagger. It wasn't just some toy, or simple weapon. Erik pressed the heels of his palms against his eyes. All these thoughts rushing through his head, and they weren't even his own thoughts. The dagger would make a deal with him, protect him, guide him, even teach him…as long as he paid it more attention.

Erik's hands dropped to his sides. The vision of a mighty warrior stood in his mind, plain as if he were looking at his own reflection. It was a man—broad shoulders, thick chest, strong legs. He was stunning, with shining armor and a great sword at his hip, the wind whisking through his hair. It was him, standing atop a hill, overlooking all he had conquered. And there, on his hip, sheathed next to the magnificent sword that had helped this warrior conquer all he saw, was a golden-handled dagger.

"All right," he said quietly and tingling left as quickly as it came. As he dropped the pillow back on the bed, the dagger was sheathed once more.

Chapter 22

BRYON LET BUCK EAT THE apple from his hand. He scratched him behind the ear as the horse pressed its nose into the man's hand and then into his chest.

"You'll be all right. They'll probably end up selling you to some rich bastard that uses you as a stud for the rest of your life. No matter what, if I survive this, I'll find you, I promise."

He traced his finger down the white stripe that traveled down the horse's head from between his eyes to the nose. How would he find him? How would he tell it was him? Bryon shrugged.

"I'll be able to tell if it's you," Bryon said.

"Bryon, we're leaving," Erik said.

Bryon looked at Erik and nodded.

Walking to the rest of the party, he heard Switch talking to Wrothgard, Vander Bim, and Turk.

"We should just leave him," Vander Bim said. "He'll only slow us down."

"I hate to say it, but he won't be useful in a fight right now," Wrothgard replied.

"Everyone goes," Bryon said, passing by the group and walking with Erik to the mine's entrance. He knew they were talking about Befel. He looked over his shoulder. "He's a member of the company, right, Vander Bim?"

Vander Bim nodded, somewhat reluctantly.

Bryon walked next to Erik, looking over his shoulder to the sailor, and then looking to his cousin.

"We will need to watch them, especially the thief," Bryon whispered. Erik nodded. Bryon added, "That sword looks good on you."

Erik smiled, tapping the pommel of his new blade before he stepped into the darkness of the tunnel and the smile quickly faded.

Thick oak beams shored the opening, but, that didn't make him feel any better. He felt for his brother, brushing his arm in the darkness, and Befel flinched before he pushed the hand away; Erik resigned to keeping his hand on the smooth wall of the mineshaft. The shaft took a sudden left, and there was welcomed light, with Demik holding two torches. Wrothgard and Vander Bim stood at the front of the party, each holding a torch as well.

"Take the rear with me," Demik said. He handed Erik a torch.

The tunnels of the underground were wide and even at first, the sides of the walls and ceilings supported by wooden columns and rafters. Picks, shovels, and buckets littered the mineshaft and at regular intervals lanterns—some lit and some extinguished—hung from an iron hook hammered into a wall or wooden post. The tunnel declined gently at first, but then became steeper. Erik could feel the pounding in his chest and the clamminess of his palms as he heard his breath quicken. The light from the torch in his hand danced as his hand shook, and the only consolation to Erik's apprehension was that a dwarf was leading them through the mountain.

As a child he'd hated small, dark spaces, and sweat poured from Erik's forehead, stinging his eyes, and dripping into his open, panting mouth, leaving an acrid, salty taste that only made him thirstier.

"This heat is worse than the heat of the Plains," Erik said, seeking to focus on something tangible.

Erik heard Demik grumble at his complaint, but then felt a rough hand on his elbow. He looked over his shoulder and saw the dwarf handing him a water skin.

"Drink water," Demik said.

"I'm all right," Erik replied. "Thank you, though."

"You think you're all right. But this heat is dry," Demik explained. "You'll sweat out all your water before you know it, and then you won't sweat anymore. When that happens, it's too late."

Erik nodded, took the water skin, and took a hearty draught even though he didn't feel he needed any.

"Thanks," Erik said.

"Don't worry," Demik added. "It will grow cooler, once we get deeper. It will almost feel like a cool spring day."

"That's nice—and welcomed," Erik replied, but he wasn't sure he meant it.

"Aye."

Erik heard something in the pressing darkness, a distant echo, and his chest tightened and pulse quickened. He felt dizzy, and the next step, lost his balance and leaned against the tunnel wall for a moment.

"Don't worry," Demik said. "It's nothing. Probably a rock falling from the wall. A miner perhaps."

"A miner?" Erik questioned.

"Aye. I wouldn't worry much," Demik said. "Just keep an eye out."

Demik patted Erik on the shoulder, which took him aback a bit. The dwarf wasn't necessarily known for being overly friendly to any of the men in the company.

"You're in dwarves' hands now," Demik said with a certain amount of mirth.

Erik tried to smile.

Chapter 23

"Are those fools still in my camp?" Cho lifted a silver chalice up to his lips, holding it between his index and middle finger. He slung one leg over the arm of his chair and loudly sipped.

"Which fools?" Cho's seneschal replied.

"Any of them," Cho replied with a hint of irritation.

"No," the seneschal replied.

Another man, Cho's personal manservant walked up the few steps to the dais where his throne-like chair sat, a silver pitcher gingerly held in both hands. He lifted the pitcher, and Cho responded with a quick shake of his head. The thin manservant hugged the pitcher to his chest and bowed, his wispy, gray hair floating in front of his face.

"Good. I hate mercenaries," Cho said.

"So you said, my lord," his seneschal said. "Do you believe the group with the dwarves is truly a group of mercenaries as well?"

"If those three barbarians are to be believed," Cho replied.

He sat up in his chair and leaned forward, elbows propped up on armrests carved into lions' heads and cup held tightly between both hands.

"Can one truly trust a sell-sword?" Cho asked before he took a sip of his wine.

"If the group with the dwarves is a group of mercenaries, does that not mean they lied to you?" the seneschal asked.

Cho knew where this was going. He narrowed his eyes and straightened his back.

"I cannot very well kill those who are in the employ of my employer."

"As you say, my lord," his seneschal said with a quick bow.

Cho threw his cup to the ground. The silver chalice clinked along the floor, and a healthy amount of wine splashed along a gold and red rug he had bought from Wüsten Sahil some years ago. The stain made him growl. How much had that rug cost?

The thrown cup caused two guards to flinch and sent Cho's manservant rushing in with a cloth. He fell to his knees and aggressively dabbed at the stain. The seneschal didn't move a muscle. Those half-closed eyelids infuriated the master of Aga Min. They made him want to punch the man in the face, or perhaps take a pick to the back of his head. However, there was not another man he could trust more, trust to be truthful, trust to help make his mine profitable, trust to keep the Lord of the East at bay and out of his business.

"Did they enter the mountain?" Cho composed himself. He looked at his manservant, still desperately trying to remove an unmovable stain from the rug. "Stop that, Anton. Leave it be. Fetch me more wine."

"Which party, my lord?" the seneschal asked.

Cho folded his hands under his chin, "Either one."

The seneschal sighed. "We have reason to believe the first, those with the dwarves, did enter the mountain, either early this morning or late last night. The second has not been seen since early evening yesterday."

"Where would they be going?" Cho asked. "The first lot."

"There are parts of the mine that have not been explored for some time," his seneschal replied. "It has been here for many years, before you arrived, my lord."

Cho squinted hard at the seneschal, to which the bald man replied, "Of course, its true success arrived with you."

It was true. Aga Min had sat relatively unproductive until Cho had arrived a decade ago. It was also true that many parts of the old mine had lain unexplored and unmined for some years now. It was plausible, however unlikely, that some hidden passageway existed there in the darkness, unused or undiscovered.

"I don't like agents of the East coming through my camp," Cho said. "Do you think he's spying on us, Li?"

The seneschal shrugged his shoulders. "I would not put it past him, my lord."

"What do you think, Anton?" Cho asked his manservant.

The seneschal lazily looked over to the manservant with contempt, still on his knees dabbing at the rug despite the command of his master. The servant quickly looked up at Cho, something akin to fear in his eyes.

"I…I don't know, m'lord. I think…I think he might."

Cho loved Anton, but he was a fool. Li was a better choice as his seneschal, for sure, despite his pompous airs. He was smarter, bolder, unafraid of upsetting Cho. He rubbed his knuckles hard against his chin. He stood.

"My lord?" Li questioned.

"Get my armor, Li," Cho commanded. "Anton, ready my horse. Those mercenaries have given me an uncanny feeling. I will ride to Aga Kona and meet with Arnif. It has been a while since we have talked."

"Is that wise, my lord?" Li asked.

"I don't care if it is wise," Cho said. "It is my wish. Make it so."

Both Li and Anton bowed.

Cho walked along the golden-bricked walkway of his villa, his cuirass reflecting less of the noonday sun than it did a dozen years ago. It fit tighter around Cho's waist and not as tight around his chest as it once had. It felt heavier than he remembered.

Li handed him his mace, a long piece of *hotong*—a tree many in the west called hickory—capped by a large, steel ball. Cho knew hotong for two things: smoking meat and making weapons. It gave off a smoky flavor when burned and was the toughest wood he had ever seen. He lifted the weapon up and inspected it.

"How many years has it been, my friend?" Cho asked his weapon.

Anton brought Cho his horse, a gray Durathnan with a black nose and white fetlocks. With the help of two other servants, Cho climbed into his high saddle. Three men joined him in front of the fence that surrounded his villa, all armored in mail shirts and carrying long spears. Anton brought them horses as well.

"We are to travel to Aga Kona," Cho explained.

His three men nodded.

"Anton, Li will be in charge in my absence."

The manservant bowed low again, and if he held any contempt for the master's decision—he had been with Cho for two decades after all, and Li had only been in his employ for three years now—he never showed it.

They hadn't ridden but a few paces when he heard a "Ho!" and the jingle of belled reins. He sighed when he saw six men, all clad in polished armor, riding down the camp's main road towards him. Their light, gilded quarter horses bounced nimbly, even under the weight of iron breastplates, round shields, and long swords. These six men represented a constant thorn in Cho's side—half the guard donated by the Lord of the East himself, given to the master of Aga Min to protect his investment. Cho wouldn't mind the men if they didn't want to know his every move. He had, after all, successfully run mines for most of his life without the constant intervention of some other man's soldiers.

"Trying to leave without us?" one of the guards asked.

Cho growled to himself. The guard must've been twenty-four years old at the most, and as pompous an ass as he had ever met. The sergeant's close-cropped, black hair, fair features, and noble lisp pegged him as a member of Golgolithul's elite. His father had probably bought his rank for him, and this dull post was a temporary one meant to hold his family over until a better position opened up, one with more prestige—at which time the sergeant would leave, and

The Lord of the East would *grace* Cho with yet another pompous shit born into more money than he would see in his lifetime.

"Of course not. I was just coming to get you," Cho replied.

"I am sure," the sergeant replied with narrowed eyes. He walked from behind the six horsed guards and looked up at Cho. "Where are you going?"

"I am going to meet with Master Arnif, in Aga Kona," Cho replied.

"Why?" the Sergeant asked.

"Because it has been a while, and that is what we masters of mines do," Cho replied. "We meet every once in a while. Li will be in charge in my absence."

"I wish you wouldn't call yourselves masters," the sergeant said with a short snort. "You are anything but."

"My apologies, Sergeant Andu. It is a small compensation for the meager lives we live." Cho bowed from the back of his horse, a sly smirk on his face.

"I will stay behind," Andu proclaimed, "and help Li."

"A wise decision," Cho replied.

Andu bowed and turned to the guards. "You will follow Cho's lead. Travel well."

"As if they had a choice," Cho muttered.

Cho led his men through his camp. Yes, his camp. He saw a squat, Goldumarian man leading a group of miners towards the mine's main tunnel, barking orders and cursing every other word. Apart from his short stature and limp, he looked like a bull.

"Shall we dig deeper today, Osl?" Cho called.

"Aye, my lord." Osl squinted through one eye involuntarily and spat the stinky, black residue of Night Leaf. "Gonna find Dwarf's Iron today. Make you a rich man."

Cho laughed. It would indeed make him a rich man. It would also be impossible. Only dwarves had an eye for Dwarf's Iron.

"Step to, you lazy pigs," Osl called back to the miners following him, "and bow to master Cho as you pass him."

Cho smiled as each man passed him and either bowed or tipped their hat. How sweet it would be if Osl ran into those fool mercenaries in his tunnels? He would show them a thing or two.

"It will be good to travel again," Cho said to himself. "It has been too long since I've taken a little journey like this."

Cho halted to take a final, easy breath before his ride to Aga Kona. A light breeze blew off the neighboring mountains and touched his face. The smell of the mountains was the smell of his youth. He smiled. Harder times. Better times. Something hit his nose, and his smile disappeared, his lip curling into a slight snarl. It was a foul smell, something from a distant memory. It started slow, faint, but then hit him in the face like a gauntleted fist.

"No!"

A distant cry, and the sound of timber and earth crashing and crumbling met his word. He turned to see the limp body of Osl, lying just feet from where the mouth of the camp's main tunnel had stood a mere moment before, now blocked by rock and wood. He looked up, to the slopes of the Southern Mountains, and saw what he had hoped he would not see.

"Mountain trolls!" Cho cried. He looked to his three, armed servants. "Gather what women and children you can. Ride with them to the north."

"How far?" one asked.

"As far as you can go. To arms!" As he yelled, a large rock caught one of the eastern guardsmen in the chest and knocked him from his horse. "Arm yourselves with whatever you have."

Cho saw Andu, the other six guardsmen with him, running about, yelling at frantic miners, and cursing them when they ran away, weaponless.

"Andu, don't worry about them," Cho said. "Those who will fight will fight. Rally your men to you. There are two trolls in the cliffs. I expect there will be more attacking the camp from ground level."

The cries behind him said the trolls were attacking the camp from all sides. In front of him, he saw four more of the evil-smelling giants crashing through the camp, Four men—one horsed—were behind them, all clad in purple cloaks and barking orders in some archaic language. Horses, goats, women, children, the trolls cared little for whom or what they bludgeoned with their crude clubs, which were barely more than broken tree branches. Cho saw another guardsman go down under the weight of a troll fist and yet another break and ride hard north, only to be caught by another large rock hurled from the arm of one of the trolls hiding up in the cliffs.

"Fight if you will!" Cho cried. "Flee if you will not fight!"

Within what seemed like moments, the volleys of boulders and swinging clubs reduced his camp to rubble. The dead numbered more than the master miner could count as he urged on his horse to go here and there, seeking to rally support or save the unarmed and defenseless. He ducked as another rock came his way and then saw *The Golden Miner* and Madame Ary's go up in flames.

Other purple-cloaked men ran both the surly barkeep and the mistress through with swords before tossing torches through broken windows. He saw his villa in flames as well. Poor Anton. A woman clutching three children close to her body ran in front of his horse.

"Woman, flee north," Cho commanded. "Take your children and flee into the Plains."

Who knew what would happen to her out there, but at least there, she had a chance. Here, she and her children would only feed these beasts.

"We must flee as well," Andu cried.

"Flee and then what?" Cho replied climbing down from his horse and helping the woman up into the saddle, handing her each one of her children in turn.

Andu simply stared at him.

"Do you think the Lord of the East will welcome us with open arms after losing him the wealthiest of mines in the Southern Mountains?" Cho slapped the flank of the horse and, with a loud whinny, it raced north. "Do you think your father will welcome you with open arms? You will be a disgrace, and the Master of Golgolithul will do far worse to us than these monsters ever could. Gather your remaining men and prepare to fight and die as a noble soldier of the east."

Andu looked back at him, chin quivering, hands shaking, eyes watering with tears.

"Fear will do you no good here, boy," Cho said. "Meet your last moments with courage, not fear. Fate has dealt the cards this way and, even though we wish they were different, we can't do anything about it."

Cho walked towards the attack, Andu and his men—eight still stood—following. What few miners remained and had the courage to follow their master joined their brigade, taking up positions behind the guards. The trolls saw the makeshift army and howled in delight. Their growls seemed like chuckles.

The volleys of boulders stopped upon the order of the horsed attacker. With the flick of his finger, the two trolls in the cliffs climbed down, one joining their comrades and the other sneaking around to the rear of the defenders. It growled, and those miners in the rear turned to face the beast just as it pummeled through most of them with its vicious fists. A dark-haired guard gripped his sword, ready to meet the creature head on. Even though he drove his sword deep into the troll's chest, it struck him so hard in the face that the blow snapped his head back so hard his neck broke. The troll had no time to celebrate, though.

Cho and the guardsmen attacked the beast. The troll caught one of the servants by the neck and squeezed until its fingers ripped into the soft flesh, but as it turned its back to Cho, he took a mighty swing, bringing his mace against the back of its head. The beast stumbled forward, falling to a knee. Two more quick blows crushed its skull, killing it.

A club crushed the skull of one guard while another troll threw its stone-tipped spear at another guardsman. The spear struck him in the middle of the chest and hit him so hard it sent him off his feet and back several paces. The three miners who remained, along with a guardsman, panicked and ran. They got to the northern boundaries of the camp before purple-cloaked men cut them down.

"Stand down, Cho, master of miners." The horsed attacker spoke perfect Shengu. He removed his helm and rode to the front of his attacking beasts. His shaven face showed a man with a Golgolithulian look, and his pointed nose seemed to hook. The bit of gray just brushing the edges of his hair spoke of a man in his early middle years.

"You know my name," Cho replied.

The man squinted his small, brown eyes. "One would be a fool to not know Cho, Master of Aga Min."

"Noble pleasantries will do you no good with me. Try them on this sergeant here." Cho nodded to Andu. "But do me the courtesy of saving your breath."

The man seemed to inspect Andu. "His family holds allegiances with the traitor."

Cho looked at Andu's breastplate, seeing three moons rising over a clenched fist emblazoned on his armor. Andu looked at the horseman with a questioning curve of his brow, but Cho laughed.

"Aztûkians," Cho said. "You are Aztûkians. Haven't you figured out that you have lost?"

The horseman growled.

"I have been commanded to accept your surrender. I will let you live," the horsed soldier said. "My lord, the merciful and just Patûk Al'Banan, has commanded it. Give up your treasures, and I will stay my beasts from eating you alive. You cannot win. With the snap of my fingers, all of you will be dead before the first drop of blood hits the ground."

"You know that I will not live long," Cho replied. "The Lord of the East will do far worse to me."

"He is not the Lord of the East!" the man cried, indignation rich in the tone of his voice. "He and his family are usurpers, thieves, nothing more."

"Nevertheless," Cho replied, "you know what he will do to me."

"Lord Patûk will take you into his employ," the man said.

"I know your Lord Patûk," Cho replied. "Trade one slaver for another? I think not."

As Cho shrugged off the man's offer, a young blond guard looked around at his comrades. He shook uncontrollably in his armor, and his bladder loosened. He caught the blue eyes of another young guard. His chin bore the signs of an attempt to grow a beard, several weeks in the trying. Simultaneously, they threw down their shields and swords and walked towards the horsed man. The corners of the horsed man's sharp mouth curled into a smile. The trolls they passed growled at them but left them alone, and they walked behind the horse of the obvious leader of this attack.

"At least there are some in your group who know what is best," the horsed man cried out. "What about you, Master Cho? Will you not throw down your weapons and choose reason over madness?"

"I am no fool," Cho yelled.

"You are," the attacker replied. "Oh yes, you are. You had men come through your camp that work for that imposter who pretends to rule our land. They work for your lord as mercenaries, and you are too stupid to know they were here. Did he not tell you they would be coming? Doesn't it infuriate you that he so readily employs vermin? Doesn't it sicken you?"

Cho knew they were there, but it wasn't worth the argument. These fool Aztûkians. Idealists. A real man knows when he has lost. Cho knew he had lost.

"I am no fool, traitor," Cho hissed.

"Better a traitor than someone's lapdog," the soldier said. "And that's all you are. Now, you are a fool if you choose to fight. So, I will give you one more chance to surrender."

Cho shook his head, but as he did, Andu threw down his sword.

"I wish to surrender," Andu shouted.

"Even a nobleman loyal to the Stévockians knows when he has been beaten," the horsed soldier said.

Cho shook his head. Disgusting. Andu wouldn't look at him. Of course not, he was a coward. Never worked a day in his life.

"Oh, I know I've been beaten," Cho muttered to himself. "I just have some pride left in me.

Cho stood there with one other man, an older guard who had the look of a man perhaps only ten years Cho's junior. This was a man worth dying next to. This was a man who worked and bled.

Cho would've guessed the guard had no chance against the charging troll, but he held his footing for a good while. Eventually, the beast ripped the shield from his arm and tossed the man's sword aside. He met his death with a cry of "Your mother's a pig whore!" and then leapt into the troll's waiting arms where the thing crushed him until he stopped breathing. Cho smiled. Good man.

Cho batted away a spear with his large shield and swatted away another one with his mace. He caught a hard jab in the head, and his scalp split in a rush of blood. Bite marks and dents began to mark his armor. Eventually, one troll ripped his shield off his arm, and he had nothing left but his weapon and a suit of armor that was now falling apart. He remembered his cuirass holding up better in his younger years. Back then, it was fresh off the forge; the steel was strong and the leather strapping that held it together new. No matter.

Cho looked to the dead guard, the last to stand with him, and smiled. "I'm going to shove this mace up your asses!" he screamed.

He charged into the waiting arms of three large mountain trolls. He managed to draw blood, but the trolls beat him to the ground in only a matter of minutes. He stared at the clear sky above.

"At least I died in the open air," he said through labored breaths. "So many of my brothers have died under the earth. This is a better way to go."

Chapter 24

SORBEN PHURNAN WALKED TO THE entrance of the mine.

"Damn," he yelled. "Stupid animals. Now we cannot enter the mine."

He slapped one of his trolls with the broad side of his sword, and it recoiled back in fear. He pulled his purple cloak closer around him as he walked through the camp. Blood soiled the ground, and he stepped around the bigger puddles, trying not to dirty his sandals.

"Stupid animals or incompetent leader?" a voice behind him said.

Sorben spun, sword ready to strike down whoever spoke those words, but saw Bu standing there.

"Several weeks ago, I would've had your head for saying such things," Sorben said.

"And several weeks ago," Bu replied with a smile, "I would not have said it."

"What are you doing here?" Sorben Phurnan asked.

"Checking up on you," Lieutenant Bu replied.

"On whose orders?" Lieutenant Phurnan asked.

"The General's, of course." Bu smiled again. "I am also to bring any prisoners to him."

"We have these three. That is all," Sorben Phurnan said. "One of them is a nobleman. House of Gházjûka."

"This is a good prisoner to have," Bu said.

"It is a lesser house," Lieutenant Sorben Phurnan said. "I was going to feed him to the trolls."

"But you said…" the nobleman said. That was all the prisoner was able to say before Bu's gauntleted fist struck him across the face and sent him reeling to the ground.

"You will speak when asked to speak," Bu commanded. "He will not be food for the trolls. Nor will these other two. Give them horses. They will come with me."

Sorben Phurnan clenched his fists and ground his teeth.

"My lord, we have two more," a purple-cloaked soldier said, pushing a richly-robed bald man with lazy eyes and pulling an elderly man with gray, wispy hair and a slender, if not almost emaciated, frame.

"Who are you?" Bu asked before Sorben could do the same.

Who does he think he is? Sorben Phurnan thought. He wanted to punch Bu or command his trolls to eat him.

"Li. Master Cho's seneschal," the lazy-eyed man replied.

"He is no master," Sorben cursed, but Bu put his hand up to silence him.

"Do you wish to live?" Bu asked.

"Oh, very much so," the seneschal Li responded.

"And what of you?" Bu asked the thin, gray-haired man.

Sorben thought he was going to answer the Lieutenant, but as soon as he saw the dead body of Cho, he began to weep uncontrollably. Sorben Phurnan saw Bu shake his head, and the guard dragging the man brought his blade down hard along the back of the man's neck.

"I will take this seneschal with me as well." Bu turned around and looked at Sorben with hard eyes. His eyes trailed down to the Lieutenant's hand, the one grasping the handle of his sword. Bu smiled.

Bu did as General Patûk Al'Banan commanded and he left, prisoners in tow. As the small party moved away, Sorben Phurnan walked to Cho's body, spat on it, and kicked it as hard as he could.

"That will be your body one day, Bu."

Chapter 25

When Erik first entered the mountain, the air was thick, warm, and constricting, but now it had cooled and become a more constant temperature, reminding him of a cool summer night back home. He asked Turk about it.

"Natural vents," Turk said. "As the air outside heats and cools, the air in these tunnels moves as well, replacing old air with new air."

Running off the main tunnel were dark and seemingly unused side tunnels, all sheared with the same oak beams. Even though they looked safe, the dwarves encouraged a speedy trek down the main shaft of the mine until the tunnel eventually forked. Two lanterns hung from iron hooks screwed into one of the wooden shore beams running along the ceiling, illuminating the tunnel to the left, a wide tunnel with a heavy cart sitting at its entrance. As they looked down the tunnel, which took a slightly steeper grade than the one they were on, they saw at every twenty paces another two lanterns hanging from iron hooks on either side of the wall. Erik wondered who had lit them but didn't voice the question.

Almost perfectly in between each set of lanterns were more vertical shoring beams holding the tunnel to form, and at least as far as they could see, horizontal wooden shoring beams supported the ceiling by running with the tunnel in the ceiling's corner, with cross beams every two or three feet. A thick rope lay coiled next to the cart and another rope pulled taut at chest level ran from a wheel pulley, firmly attached to the mountain wall by an iron plate and four iron screws, down into the steep tunnel. A simple hook anchored its end to the floor.

"Must be attached to another cart down there somewhere," Turk said.

The right side also boasted heavy timber braces and two lanterns illuminating and supporting the entrance, but that was it. The walls were narrow, and it looked sparsely used.

"Which one do we go down?" Vander Bim asked in a whisper.

Everyone looked to the dwarves.

As Turk started to answer, Demik hushed him and held up his hand, signaling the others to be quiet as well.

Erik leaned forward and closed his eyes as if that would help. He heard the ring of iron picks against stone. Then, he heard voices carry from somewhere beyond, somewhere deep in the lit tunnel, echoing off the walls. That was who lit the lanterns.

"Damn it," one said, voice amplified by the hollow tunnel, "that damned Cho said he would have us relieved by now."

"They're always late," said another voice amidst the clanging and chittering of pickaxes and shovels and hammer, "Osl's crew is."

"Aye, and yet, Cho's favorite," said the first voice.

"Piss on him I say," said yet a third voice. "He can stuff his damned cursing and damned barked orders and his damned grunts of disapproval, and his damned ugly face for that matter."

"Ole Osl," continued the third voice, "is supposed to break through that other tunnel. Ten weeks crews have been trying to break through that damned rock, and he thinks he's going to do it in one shot. Piss on that I say. He says there's Dwarf's Iron in that tunnel, that's why the wall's so hard. Piss on that, too."

"What are they talking about?" Erik asked in as hushed a whisper as possible.

Turk put his finger to his lips. The littlest sound in these tunnels could sound like war drums reverberating against the walls.

"What was that?" the first voice said. Their picking stopped.

Switch turned on Erik, fist clenched, jaws tight and flexed.

"It's nothing," said the second. The sound of iron against stone said they had gone back to working.

"Well," the third man's voice elevated as he spoke, "if someone is here and it's Osl, he'd better hurry up."

"I heard Osl say once," echoed the first voice, "that dwarves used to use these tunnels all the time. He said old Cho just stumbled across them, unrefined cave tunnels full of iron ore and copper, and turned it into a mining camp. Old Osl said dwarves used to spy on us from here. Supposedly, Cho even ran into a couple of tunnel rats once—lopped their heads right off according to his manservant, Anton. Kept their beards as trophies."

"Hush you fool," the third voice reprimanded. "You don't talk about dwarves in these mines. It's bad luck."

Erik saw Demik's hand tighten around the handle of his broadsword and Turk catch his wrist. Turk nodded down the right passage, the dark one that was narrower. They had barely walked a few moments past the edge of the torches' light when the tunnel dead ended.

"Oh great, tunnel digger," Switch said. "Fine job you did of leading us."

Turk ignored the thief and ran his hands all around the walls and the rock face that ended the tunnel. It looked uneven and rough, not refined and smoothed like the walls and ceiling. Dust and pieces of stone and rock lay at its feet. The holes from miners' attempts to chip away the rock dotted its surface. Turk continued to search the crude wall, getting down on his hands and knees. After a moment, he grunted and chuckled.

"When I heard them say," Turk said, still on his knees, "Cho found these tunnels and that they used to belong to dwarves, I knew we had found the entrance."

"The entrance to what?" Erik asked.

"I probably shouldn't say *the* entrance, but an entrance—to our lands in Drüum Balmdüukr. Dwarf tunnels normally have openings not so evident to the naked eye, especially gates into our lands."

He stopped talking as he reached about the bottom of the wall now, feeling about, grunting as he did so.

"One of the things we pride ourselves on," he said with a last grunt, "is secret doors made of what those men called Dwarf's Iron and made to look like cavern walls."

A quick click sprung up from the floor, and a hissing sound like steam escaping a geyser, echoed through the tunnel. The door creaked and scraped, stone against stone, and Turk turned around to his companions and gave a broad smile, making sure Switch was the first to see.

"So," Switch said.

Turk turned back around and pushed on the wall. It slid backwards a pace or so, producing a small opening, and as it did, a sudden gust of wind howled through the tunnels, almost extinguishing the party's torches.

"That ought to frighten those fools plenty well," Vander Bim said.

Turk slid through the opening, the rest following suit. Erik and Demik were the last to go through. The young man looked back at his dwarf companion, eyes wide, sweat building along his brow.

"Go," Demik insisted.

Erik didn't move.

"It will be all right." Demik's tone was a little softer. "Go."

The other side of the secret door was much different from the areas the miners had touched. The walls looked rough and ancient, curving with the natural motion of the mountain. They became narrow then wide and then narrow again. The ceiling was rounded instead of squared, allowing the formation of small stalactites. The ground, as well, remained uneven, dotted by clusters of stalagmites here and there.

"This is so different," Erik said. "It looks as if no one has been here for a while."

"Oh," Turk explained, "dwarves have probably been here more recently than you think."

"We pick naturally formed tunnels," Demik said. "We allow the earth and mountain to tell us where to go. We do little to our tunnels, as little as possible. You can see we rounded the ceiling, that's about it."

Nafer rubbed his hand along the wall, and his fingertips brushed the edge of the ceiling, just low enough for him to reach. Erik could see a smile creep across his face in the dim light. The dwarf grabbed the young man's wrist of his torch hand and pulled it close to the wall. There, Erik could see etchings, runic carvings. Nafer said something to Turk in his native language.

"They are simple directions," Turk said, a smile also on his face. "This one tells traveling dwarves to keep this door closed."

Turk and Demik pushed the door closed, as the directions said. It made a loud yet dull banging sound like that of a bass drum. They continued, their pace quickening with the excitement of the dwarves.

"Ah," Turk sighed, "we will be at the entrance to my people's kingdom soon."

"How long?" Wrothgard asked.

"One week," he replied. "I know it seems like a while, but our pace will be less than half that of surface travel. We'll be lucky to walk three leagues a day, and most of that will be up and down as the tunnel shifts."

"Will we have enough food? Water?" Erik asked.

"Oh, yes," Turk replied. "We will have to be careful, but after our resupply in Aga Min, we should have enough."

"Your cities really are not that far from the lands of men," Befel said.

The dwarf chuckled a bit. "No, we keep well hidden from men and other things. You just need to know which turns to make, which rocks are not so real. As you can see, my people have watched these miners for some time now, hiding by cover of secrets and shadows."

"Kind of like a thief. Eh, tunnel digger," Switch said.

Turk grunted, "No, I think not so much like a thief."

Switch giggled at his pestering.

"They will eventually get too close, though," Demik said, "mining farther into the mountain. It will be war."

"War?" Erik's voice cracked at the word.

"Demik," said Turk, his tone disapproving, "that's enough. Men and dwarves have not been friendly with one another for many years—and many inequities have been done on both sides—but there have been serious hostilities."

The dwarves seemed to argue for several minutes when Erik heard a throat-clearing cough from Wrothgard. Turk and Demik stopped and looked to the soldier.

"Perhaps we should be moving," Wrothgard suggested.

Turk nodded and led the party deeper into the mountain.

"What was that?" the young miner asked.

A howl echoed through the tunnels and a gust of wind, as if a storm brewed within the confines of the mountain, hit his face.

"Hush," Saba, the senior miner for this group, commanded. His eyesight was almost gone, but his other senses took its place. He listened intently, rough hands cupping around his ears, and the gray hair that surrounded them stood on end. He took one hand away and wiped sweat from the tip of his nose. Another roar rattled through the tunnel.

"Piss on this," Saba said, "we're getting out of here, Osl or no Osl."

He and two other men, the young miner and an older easterner ran to the entrance of the tunnel they mined, gripping their picks just in case they had to use them as weapons. They stopped at the tunnel's fork, and Saba stared down the right passageway, hearing something that sounded like the sliding of stone. He continued towards the surface, heart pounding and feet faster than before. Each causeway they passed, some with lit entrances, and some shrouded in the blackness of the mountain, Saba would stop and call down to the men who worked that part of the mine. Only moments after the call at each tunnel, three or four men came rushing up to Saba and his two companions, lanterns in hands, and picks, hammers, or shovels gripped tightly.

As they neared the entrance, fifteen men in all, they didn't see the normal brightness they yearned for after a week underground. In fact, the tunnel grew darker—and then they saw it, the fear of every miner. A mess of boulder, rock, and wood blocked the entrance. Two dead men, miners from Osl's crew, lay in front of the rubble, and an arm, cut and bloodied, protruded from the wreckage, the rest of another body imprisoned.

"Come on!" cried Saba, his voice commanding. "We need to clear this out."

"Ryce, Ven," he called to the two men who worked with him. "Go back and get some wood braces so the ceiling doesn't cave in again as we clear the entrance.

They ran back, and as they did, the rest of them put their shoulders and backs to clearing away the entrance of the mine.

Chapter 26

A DAY'S HIKE, A NIGHT, and then half a day brought them to a change in the cave. The channel they walked through slowly opened into a large cavern, with ceilings so high the torchlight didn't reach it. A small fissure appeared on the floor, which eventually widened into a larger crack and split the cavern in half. Turk instructed them to walk on the right side, and it was a good thing. That crack became a chasm wide enough that the other side grew invisible, as did the chasm's bottom. The floor turned into a ledge wide enough for single file marching, almost a catwalk along the dark gorge. Erik wanted to look over the edge, curiosity eating at him, but he remembered what Rory had said, "Curiosity skinned the gnome," and elected to stay where he was, his shoulder almost brushing against the cavern wall.

Erik looked up every once in a while, even though he could see nothing. He wondered how the ceiling kept from falling on them, and how this great chasm in the center of the mountain came to be. It was so wide and open, and yet he felt as if he sat in a jail. He could only move but a few feet to his left before he would be tumbling to his death in the blackness.

"I am surprised at how comfortable the air is in here," Erik said. He wiped the sweat from his forehead. The air in the cavern was certainly damper.

"Aye," Wrothgard agreed, "although the moisture in the air is going to make my breastplate rust if I don't get some oil on it soon."

"A good set of dwarf armor could last months in this climate without rusting," Demik said with a disapproving grunt.

"And what climate makes you shut up about good ole dwarvish this and good ole dwarvish that?" asked Switch. "What it would be like to be a tunnel digger? Life would be just bloody grand."

Demik groaned loudly, and Erik chuckled silently, although he refused to show the dwarf he thought Switch's comments funny.

Turk bent over the edge of the walkway, steadying himself with his left hand and pointing at a dull, wide, silvery line that contrasted against the black slab that made up the mountain cavern. He rubbed his rough, dwarf hands over the cool, smooth rock.

"Ah, look at this," he said. "Bring the light closer."

Erik obliged by carefully tiptoeing up to the edge and putting his torch's flame next to Turk's face.

"Closer," Turk said, and Erik slowly got down on his knees and put his light next to the rock to which Turk pointed. The lighter rock reflected the torch light and a bright radiance, almost like a small star in this black place, sparkled through the darkness. In an instant, it reflected against another strand of the rock, curving like a thin silver hair through the cavern wall across from the company. That light then caught another band, which caught another and then another. Within moments, the mountain lit up like a wave of sunlight, released from dark clouds to crash against a black sanded shore. Now the company no longer needed their torches to see.

"The gods must've hidden some of heaven's stars right here," Wrothgard said, "for I have never seen something so magnificent."

"A dawning sun on a cool spring morn coming over the calm horizon of the sea cannot match this," Vander Bim gasped.

Turk simply smiled. He could see for hundreds of yards in every direction and still could not see the ceiling or the floor of the cavern. The intricacies of the walls, the crags and rocks, the lone ledges and small caves lay bare in the silver light.

"This is Dwarf's Iron," Turk said. "It is most sought after by miners and smiths alike."

Turk continued to inspect the strand of metal, smiling as he did so.

"Years ago," he explained, "when men first started delving into the mountains, started realizing the treasures the earth had to offer, well, it wasn't too long until they found us dwarves—or we found them, whichever way you look at it. I think most people think us a suspicious lot, but we had watched men in secret for many years, and when they stumbled into our mountains, we just figured it was the Creator telling us to help the men. We helped them understand the treasures the earth could offer, how to work with earth and stone, how to mine, how to extract ore from rock. We showed where to find kûhther and siber—copper and silver."

He saw Erik mouth the words as he spoke them.

"We showed you where gold was and how to extract iron. We even showed you how to forge iron into stahl, which you would eventually call steel. But the mountains hold one secret we would not show you. We would not show you how to find Rhimstan, also called Hildenstahl in our northern dialect. Of course, your ancestors eventually found it, but still we dwarves would not give up its secrets, and even then, we did not reveal how to smelt it and forge it."

"I have heard of this stone, or metal," Wrothgard stated. "What makes it so special?"

"It is so strong, stronger than any other iron or steel men can forge. Even stronger than legendary elf steel," Demik replied. "A blade made from Hildenstahl can bend farther than any other blade and not break, and yet, it will come back true. To have a dwarf forge you anything from this metal is a treasure you would never receive in ten lifetimes."

"No wonder the secret door guards this tunnel," Turk said, "and no wonder dwarves have been here recently. This is a find that is uncommon, especially in Drüum Balmdüukr. Rhimstan is common in the north, but not here. If those men could get to this, within days, a thousand miners would be here taking it back to Fen-Stévock. It seems Osl was correct."

Turk looked at Erik, still kneeling in awe, his torch next to the original strand of Dwarf's Iron Turk found.

"Take your torch away now, young Erik," Turk said. "The dwarves patrol this area often, I am sure, but there are always things in the deeps of mountains to both be respected and feared."

Erik took his torch away and stood. The light slowly dimmed as a wave of darkness took control of the cavern again.

"How many thousands of years has this cavern sat here, dark and black?" Erik asked.

Turk smiled. "Many, my young friend. Many. It is good to be home."

As they continued, Turk wondered if it really was good to be home. Were there still people in Thorakest who thought him an upright dwarf? They would've thought more of him than he thought of himself, even if Nafer constantly admonished him for thinking such things. But he still could not set aside his guilt—guilt for leaving his father to die alone, guilt for leaving his homeland, guilt for selling his skills as a warrior to the highest bidder. His shame seemed unbearable, and he knew there would be those from his city that would not so readily welcome him with open arms.

Saba saw a single ray of dimming sun poke through a thin hole in the rubble.

"Put your backs into it, boys," he cried. "We're almost there."

The ringing of hammers and picks hitting rock quickened as men close to exhaustion pushed themselves past fatigue, sensing open air, sensing freedom.

Then Saba knew something was wrong. He did not hear the sounds of men working on the other side. No one called to them to see if they could get an answer.

Rock and rubble began to fall away, and Ryce threw down his pick, digging at a larger pinhole of light with his hands. He pulled off stone, pushed away splinters of wooden beams, anything he could do to get out. Other men followed, ripping away debris now that it seemed loosened.

"Watch it men!" Saba yelled. "We don't know how stable the mountain is. Watch it. We might just bring on another cave-in."

His miners ignored him, anxious to be free.

"I said watch it, you fools," he yelled again. "You might get us killed in here and ..."

A sharp yell from Ryce cut him off as the wreckage below Ryce gave way, and he tumbled over rock and stone to the outside. The remains of the entrance followed him and covered him with dust and small rocks.

"Ryce," Saba called. No answer. He called him again, still with no answer. "Damn it. I told you idiots what might happen if we didn't do this slow and right."

They all worked to remove the rest of the debris, more carefully this time, and within moments, a narrow path was made so the miners could climb through. They all shouted with joy as the waning sun hit their faces and they caught a breath of fresh air, but then their cheers died. They saw Ryce, kneeling and staring, tears streaming down his face.

Horror. Saba looked to Ryce, then to the camp. So many dead, eaten, torn, ripped apart. They lay in the dying sun, rotting, food for ravens and buzzards. Saba heard the distant calls of wild dogs. The smell of death and rot and blood carried far.

"What by the bloody Shadow," Ven muttered, his voice trembling so badly with terror his words barely escaped his lips.

Saba looked down amidst the entrance rubble and saw Osl's dead body. He saw Cho's body, in the distance, lying alone. The miner did not have the heart to walk over to his master and see what happened.

"We have to leave."

"But some of these men had, have families here," Ryce pleaded.

"Then if they want to stay, they can," Saba said loudly so all could hear. "If they are still alive, they have surely escaped north and east, back to Golgolithul, or Nordeth, or Gol-Durathna. If not, then I am sorry, but I am not waiting here."

Saba spotted a good-sized brown gelding—white stripes running between its eyes to the end of its nose—still tied in the camp's stables. The animal seemed skittish as the man neared it, but seeing that he was not a troll, neighed and pushed its nose into Saba's outstretched hand.

"Will you flee with me, my friend?"

The neigh and bobbing head were enough affirmation for the miner. He mounted the horse. Behind him, he heard other horses. He looked over his shoulder. Van and Ryce had also found horses. They followed, along with several others. Some men searched the rubble, searched the dead. One cried. Saba looked to his left. One of his men threw himself onto a broken spear, jutting upwards from the ground. His family must've been dead. He must've had nothing left to live for. Saba felt sadness, pity, but he wasn't waiting around to mourn. He fled north, some of his miners following, away from Aga Min, away from death.

They had walked perhaps half a day's travel, it was so hard to tell in the mountain, when Turk stopped the party and knelt, feeling the tiled ground. Bryon sighed with relief, rubbing his legs.

"This road has seen little use recently," Turk said.

"Does that worry you, dwarf?" Wrothgard asked.

"I don't know," Turk replied, "yet."

A dwarf worried in a dwarvish tunnel. Bryon didn't like the sound of that. The whole point of joining up with the dwarves was the very fact that they could navigate these tunnels and get them to the lost dwarvish city without incident. Just then, Bryon heard a sound. It might have been dripping water in the distance—simple wetness collecting on the ceiling before plummeting to the ground—or a loose rock tumbling from the wall. Whatever it was, Bryon's hand went to his sword, drawing it from its scabbard.

Bryon would've run away from himself if he could. Certainly, everyone else in his party stepped several paces back from the young man. A purple glow, bright and brilliant, reflected along the farmer's face, shining on his wide eyes. Scared eyes.

"Blood and guts and magic wands," Switch said. "I can't believe I missed that."

"What is it?" Befel asked.

Bryon just shook his head.

"Magic." Turk moved closer to Bryon. "What kind, I do not know, but definitely magic."

"Did you know about this?" Befel looked at his own sword, the one Bryon had confiscated for him. He pulled it halfway from its leather scabbard, and it clearly didn't glow with any magical brilliance, but, he looked nervous.

Bryon shook his head again.

"A magic dagger and now a magic sword...I don't like it," Vander Bim said, glancing furtively at Erik.

"There are worse things to worry about," Wrothgard said. He didn't seem remotely concerned.

"Let us move," Turk commanded. Bryon, looking almost ashamed, began to sheath his sword. "Bryon, keep your sword unsheathed. I am sure the extra light will be welcome."

They did indeed come across intersections and other passageways, but they did as the Dwarvish directions said and continued straight. It seemed that they had walked for days in this road hewn from the mountain rock when Turk finally stopped the party at an area of the road that widened and created an intersection of five other roads.

"We will camp here."

Chapter 27

A FIRM SHAKE WOKE BRYON, and he found himself looking up at Demik's face.

Bryon sat up to see Turk standing in the middle of the companion's small encampment.

"I will be continuing from here with just Nafer," he said. "Demik will stay with you until we return."

"I don't know," Vander Bim said. "I don't like the thought of splitting up."

"Dwarves are not above setting traps," Turk explained. "It will be easier to spot them with just two dwarves."

"One of us should go with you," Vander Bim said.

"One of you men, you mean," Demik said.

"It's not that I don't trust you, Turk," Vander Bim said, "but I think it only appropriate."

"I don't trust you," Switch muttered. It sounded as if he meant for everyone to hear him, even though he kept his voice low. "Why should I?"

"I do trust you, master dwarf," Wrothgard said, "but I agree with Vander Bim. One of us should go with you. I will go."

"No," Turk replied. "You need to stay. You are the most seasoned warrior besides Demik."

Turk looked around to his companions. His eyes stopped on Bryon.

"I will take Bryon with us," he said.

Bryon's heart stopped. It hadn't been uncomfortable in the tunnel, but suddenly sweat pooled around his neck, his face grew hot.

"Good choice," Wrothgard said. Vander Bim nodded his head in agreement.

"Don't I have a say in this?" Bryon asked.

"You don't want to go with us?" Turk asked.

"I don't know," Bryon said with a shrug. "I don't know what good I will be. Why not take Vander Bim?"

"We have a limited number of torches," Turk said. "We can take Nafer's torch and then use your sword for light."

Bryon nodded reluctantly, stepping forward and unsheathing his sword. The purplish hew seemed stronger than before.

They walked briskly for more than an hour when Turk abruptly stopped, Bryon almost tripping into him. Turk looked at the mountain wall to his right, almost sticking his nose against it. Bryon brought his sword close, illuminating a myriad of markings that looked oddly different from the directions etched into the tunnel walls up to this point.

"They look...different." Bryon poked his face closer, almost next to Turk's face. "What are they?"

"Runes." Turk brushed his hand along the writing. "These are commands, written in our old tongue, a runic tongue. It's a language most southern dwarves do not know. I only know it because of my pilgrimage north. I am almost certain I have walked this road before, and I have never seen these here."

"Maybe you just missed them," Bryon said.

"No, I would not have missed these," Turk said. "Nafer, have you seen these before?"

The other dwarf just shook his head.

"Is that bad?" Bryon asked.

Turk shrugged. "It's a warning. It could be bad for those who don't heed the warning."

"Warning for whom?" Bryon asked.

"For anyone who is not a dwarf," Turk replied.

"Do men read Dwarvish runes?" Bryon asked.

"This is not here for men, my friend," Turk replied, shaking his head. "This is here for…"

He stopped again, falling silent. A moment later, he said something to Nafer in Dwarvish, and Nafer's reply sounded anxious and angry.

"It is a trap." Turk took a quick step back, holding one hand out to Nafer and placing the other one in the center of Bryon's chest. "A magical trap."

"I thought dwarves didn't like magic," Bryon said.

"Just because we don't like something doesn't mean we don't recognize its benefits," Turk replied.

Turk motioned for his two companions to follow him. They walked slowly, inspecting every stone in the mountainside. They could not have walked more than a hundred paces when Turk stopped again. He, again, inspected the mountainside and found more runes—the same, more warnings, more signs of a trap. Then, they started walking again, slower than before.

"This is ridiculous," Bryon whispered. He felt constricted, like the darkness—despite the light from the torch and the purplish glow of his sword—was weighing in on him.

After a long while, the tunnel became a wide hall with carved stones visibly marking two sides of a street. Statues adorned both walls, crafted and placed into small alcoves. All of them were of stout dwarf warriors armed with battle armor and holding a mighty axe or sword or hammer.

"The artistry here is…" Bryon said, voice trailing as he gazed at the expertly carved statues.

Turk suddenly stopped Bryon and Nafer, shoving his rugged hand into Bryon's chest. The torch Nafer held and Bryon's sword glimmered off something lying on the floor. Turk inched towards whatever it was and eventually knelt down. Bryon heard him give a loud chuckle and then say something again to Nafer. Nafer replied with quiet laughter of his own. Turk motioned for Bryon, and he slowly walked to the dwarf and found him kneeling next to a large lizard. Its skin was dark-gray, like mountain rock, and its body the size of a large dog. Its head was gone.

"What, by the Shadow, would hunt this?" he muttered.

Nafer snapped at Bryon in his native language, and Bryon stepped back.

"Do not invoke the Shadow down here," Turk said. "Things that live for and serve the Shadow live down here. Now, about this thing. Lizards are common in these areas of the mountain, although they seldom come close to dwarf settlements."

"I thought you said we were safe camping in the dark," Bryon said.

"Oh, these creatures will not come near any man or dwarf," Turk reassured. "Though, they could hurt, if not kill, a single dwarf. Look at it claws."

Bryon stared at the lizard's feet, bearing five toes ending in curved, long, black, claws.

"Some dwarves domesticate these creatures," Turk explained. "They aren't as easy to train as bears, dogs, or wolves—but when they are set to something, like protecting what they see as their family, they can be vicious foes."

"Was this a domestic lizard?" Bryon asked.

"No," Turk replied. "It would have a collar bearing its clan's name if it was."

Bryon saw the severed head, and it was fresh, its spilt blood still wet. Bryon saw the nearest stone statue—a dwarf with a long beard, an impressive breastplate, and a long-handled battle-axe clutched between both hands. The stone blade of the axe looked...wet.

"It is fortunate that you have dwarves with you, no?" Turk asked with a smile.

"And why is that?" Bryon asked.

"This poor creature seemed to walk into a trap meant for something...or someone else," Turk replied.

Bryon gave him an odd look. Turk stood up and walked over to the nearest statue. He placed his hands together as if he were going to pray and closed his eyes. He then opened up his eyes. He took a silver coin from his belt purse and placed the coin at the foot of the statue. Then he grabbed his knife from its sheath and sliced a small cut in his left palm. He squeezed his hand over the silver coin, causing a few drops to drip onto the money. Nafer followed Turk, repeating the same steps.

Both dwarves, together, recited something in their own language. The wall that held the statue shook, and gray smoke, a barely visible mist, surrounded the stone carving. A blue light filled the stone dwarf's eyes, and its head began to move so it could look at Turk. It slowly turned its head to Nafer, then to Bryon, and then back to Turk.

Bryon took a step back, lowering his sword so that it pointed to the stone statue. The stone dwarf's voice boomed in Dwarvish, shaking the hall's walls. As it spoke, little bits of rock chipped and fell from the corners of its mouth.

"Turk Skäd Crûsher," Bryon heard Turk reply, "der clan Eorthfolk."

"Nafer Rûndshild, der Helvegar," Nafer said.

The statue then looked at Bryon, still speaking.

"Stone Axe, or rather the statue of Stone Axe, asks if you are a slave," Turk explained with a chuckle. "I told him you are a friend, and he seemed somewhat perplexed by that, as you are a man."

The statue continued to stare at Bryon.

"Am I supposed to say something?" Bryon whispered.

"In a moment. He says we may pass," Turk explained to Bryon. "You must offer treasure and blood first, though. Do as I did."

Bryon hesitantly walked towards the statue. He sheathed his sword and accepted Turk's knife. Bryon grabbed his small leather purse, took out a coin, and placed it gently at the foot.

"Do I really need to cut my palm?" Bryon asked.

"Aye," Turk said with a smile, "unless you want to end up like that lizard."

He cut the palm of his left hand, flinching as he did so, and squeezed a few drops of blood at the foot of the statue.

"Now say these words as I say them," said Turk. "Maġenacen Magorin."

"Do I really have to?" Bryon asked, cutting Turk off and looking pessimistically at the dwarf.

The blue eyes of the stone statue brightened. Bryon needed no more encouragement. He repeated the first two words.

"Offrion min feoh und blôd beorga weġ," Turk continued. Bryon repeated the words. When he finished, the statue nodded its head, dust and flakes of stone crumbling to the ground.

The stone dwarf warrior became inanimate once again, and the blue faded from its eyes. As smoke covered and then faded from the statue, Bryon saw that the chips that fell from its mouth, leaving small cracks and holes, were no longer there, replaced with fresh stone, as if it never spoke.

"What, by the..." Bryon paused. "What by the Heavens was that?"

"The trap. Those who did not offer up blood and gold, as these instructions here say," Turk said, pointing to some runes next to the statue, "the two things dwarves value the most, would die by Stone Axe's blade."

"Who is Stone Axe?" Bryon asked.

"The statue. Of course, it is not really him. He died many years ago," Turk replied.

The dwarves and Bryon hurried back to get their companions. They were sleeping again, and it took a while to wake them. They followed Turk to the statue of Stone Axe, and both the dwarf and Bryon explained what they had to do.

"I'm not bloody giving money to a flaming statue," Switch hissed.

When Stone Axe came to life, however, Switch seemed all too willing to give the statue his money, and Erik seemed more than ready to cut his left hand.

"We will camp here for a little while," Turk explained. "We do not need to hurry right now. We are safe here."

Turk inspected the statue of Stone Axe when he could hear Demik snoring and Bryon groaning as he dreamt. He didn't really feel ashamed for marveling over the effigy, just a little silly, childish maybe. He preferred no one see him do it.

"Is this what you really looked like? You remind me of my grandfather." He smiled and ran his fingers along the stone beard that hung in a braid to just above the knee. He traced the intricacies of the hair that flowed from underneath the skullcap helm worn on the statue's head.

"You reunited the North and the South, and here you stand, a statue to watch over us. What was it like when you lived? How do we reunite our people once again? Is that why you are here? We are so despondent. Could it ever happen?"

He watched the statue, motionless, for a while longer.

"Or are you here for another reason? In our disparity, have *they* returned? Have they?" Turk looked to the darkness above him. "An, I pray to you that they have not returned."

Chapter 28

ERIK AWOKE TO FIND TURK dressed for battle. Demik and Nafer had followed suit. As concerning as the sight might have been, Erik was glad for it, having dreamt of dead men again, crawling at him through the darkness of the mountain tunnel. No matter how fast he ran, they were right at his heels, and dead arms poked through the mountain walls, grasping at him and tearing at his clothes.

"Ready yourselves," Turk said. "Things don't seem right."

"Even with the dwarvish traps to protect us?" Bryon asked.

"There are things that can slip past dwarvish traps," Turk replied.

The crude mountain tunnel turned into a well-worked hall, wide and with pillars carved straight from the rock walls.

"Stay here, and stay close to one another," Turk commanded.

"What the bloody flaming sheep's guts is happening now?" Switch asked.

"Bryon and Nafer," Turk said, "come with me again. Wrothgard, stay here and be ready."

"Ready for what?" Wrothgard asked.

"Just be ready," Turk replied.

The three, led by Turk, disappeared into the darkness, the light from Nafer's torch and Bryon's sword fading away.

"Are you all right?" Befel asked.

"I don't know," Erik replied.

"You don't look all right," Befel said.

"I don't feel all right," Erik replied.

"What's wrong?" Befel asked.

"Is that a serious question?" Erik asked. "We are stuck underneath a mountain, only the Creator knows how deep. We thought that having dwarves with us would be the answer to safe passage through these mountains, and yet, here we are, preparing for a battle with who knows what. On top of that. I can't sleep without dreaming of dead men attacking me and dragging me to the Shadow. Almost everything that could be wrong, is wrong."

Erik looked to his brother. Befel looked disturbed, almost upset, but didn't say anything.

Turk finally reappeared in the torchlight, alone. He breathed hard and sweated profusely. Wrothgard snapped to, ready for battle. He ran to Turk.

"Where is Bryon?" Erik said softly, and then he raised his voice. "Where is Bryon? And Nafer?"

Switch shot him a glaring look.

"Hush," hissed Vander Bim.

"Where are they?" Wrothgard repeated.

"We are here," Turk replied.

"What are you bloody talking about?" Switch asked, moving up next to Wrothgard.

"Thorakest," Turk said. "The guards allowed me to come back for you only if I left Bryon and Nafer as collateral. They are safe. Bryon is a little worried, perhaps, but safe. Follow me."

They did as directed and Erik saw his cousin, standing in an illuminated area surrounded by oil lamps on tall, iron poles. Two tall, heavy, wooden doors loomed behind Bryon. Burning sconces rose along the wall on either side of the doors, showing a shadowed ceiling void of any natural cave formations.

Five dwarves, armored in plate mail, waited behind Bryon. Erik had never seen anything like these dwarves, their armor glistening in the light. He had seen a full suit of armor once, in a storybook his mother would read him when he was younger, but the splendor in that book did not do these warriors justice. Steel—or perhaps Dwarf's Iron—covered the dwarves from foot to head, layered in overlapping plates of metal. Four of them wore heavy helmets, their eyes barely visible through crossbars running horizontally in front of their faces, and held long spears, as tall as Bryon, with broadswords at their sides.

One dwarf wore no helmet but covered his head with a piece of cloth, like a handkerchief, which held his hair off his face. He held a war hammer in his right hand, its wide head not flat but rather fashioned to a dull point. He held a thick leash in his left hand, and at the end of that leash, a thick, leather collar studded with iron spikes held a mountain lizard. It calmly watched Bryon, flicking its forked tongue in and out.

As Erik and the others reached the lights of the entrance, the four helmeted dwarves grabbed their spears with both hands, extended the sharp, iron tips that gleamed in the lamplight. As they tightened their grips, their leather gloves squeaked against the polished wood. The lizard handler flicked its leash and said a single word in Dwarvish, to which the reptile immediately straightened its tail and opened its wide mouth, giving an eerie hiss. It then snapped its mouth shut. Its closing jaws sounded like a blacksmith's hammer and anvil.

"Sheath your weapons," Turk said.

Erik looked to Wrothgard. The soldier shook his head and tightened his grip on his sword. Erik saw Vander Bim lower his sword, but he didn't put it away. Switch smirked.

"They do not trust men," Demik said, "and fighting would only be to your folly. Sheathe your weapons as you were instructed. Surely, by now, you believe you can trust us."

Wrothgard waited for a moment and then slowly nodded. Everyone put away his weapon. Turk bowed to the guards and let the lizard sniff his hand like a dog. He even petted its head as he and the guards conversed. Most of the conversation sounded like an argument, and both Nafer and Demik came up to be alongside Turk and joined in the discussion. Finally, what looked to be a serious conversation turned into merriment.

"What's happening?" Erik asked.

"I don't know." Wrothgard put his hand back on the handle of his sword and left it there.

"Tunnel diggers. I don't bloody like this. Some flaming dwarvish trickery." Switch fingered the hilt of one of his daggers.

"Onbreg!" one of the guards shouted and then knocked on the door three times.

"Come on," Turk said with a jerk of his head.

Bright light peered between the two opening doors and drowned out the dim torchlight that illuminated the guards' post. Erik put his hands up, shielding his eyes.

As the blaze of light flooded out from behind the doors, two armored dwarves walked past the party and took up position in front of the doors, replacing two of the original guards. Those two then escorted Erik and companions through the doorway, and as soon as they had all passed the front gate, the doors started closing.

They stood in a hall nearly one hundred paces wide and three or four times that in length. The light in the hallway originated from large, oil cauldrons and fire pits along with hundreds of torches and lanterns.

Erik looked to Demik, who wore a wide grin as he tilted his head back, sniffing the air. He sighed.

"I don't know if I've ever seen you smile," Erik said.

"It has been many years since I've been home, lad," Demik replied.

"It's amazing," Erik said.

"Aye, quite amazing," Wrothgard agreed.

"This is only the entrance." Demik laughed.

"Welcome to Gröde Handenhall," Turk said. "The Great Trading Hall in Westernese."

All around them, visiting shops built right into the wall, Erik was fascinated as he watched a ceaseless stream of busy dwarves walking in and out of the shops, carrying food, clothing, tools, and other supplies one might buy from a city's market.

Also, around the walls stood the carts of vendors and artisans, selling anything from mining supplies to food, from clever artwork to weapons. Dwarves pushing wheelbarrows full of rock, dirt, and metal mined from the mountain rushed by the company, paying no attention to them, and into stores or into other, smaller hallways adjoining this one.

"Have all these shops been here a long while?" asked Erik.

"Aye," Demik said. "They've been here for ages, owned and run by the same families for just as long."

"On my mother, are those..." Erik's eyes widened. He couldn't even finish what he was saying as a dwarf carting a sturdy wheelbarrow full of large, uncut, unrefined gems passed by him hurriedly, almost running over his toes. Rubies the size of his fist and sapphires a deep, translucent blue. Erik looked at Demik who smiled back at him.

"Not in all my years of thieving have I seen such a beautiful sight," muttered Switch, almost drooling. "One of those buggers could make me a king."

"Where do those lead to?" Erik asked, pointing to a number of hallways adjoining the one into which they walked.

"To other cities eventually," Demik replied. "The hallways can take a dwarf all over Drüum Balmdüukr, they are much like the ones we passed coming to Thorakest."

"I would much rather travel through these ones," Erik replied, noting that most had armed guards standing in front of them as well as plenty of light.

Demik laughed and said something to Nafer in his own language. The other dwarf laughed as well.

"You men," Demik said. "You are so afraid of the dark and of things you cannot see. You have no faith, no trust."

Several groups of dwarves appeared beside them, leading oxcarts packed with tools, food, clothing.

"Oxen?" Erik questioned.

"What else would they use?" Demik asked in return.

Erik just shrugged.

Four dwarves, armored in mail, followed one of the ox carts, but it wasn't them that caught Erik's eye, it was the great, brown bear trailing behind. Rarely had Erik seen such animals around the farm, but when they did show, someone was sure to let loose a large bull, or several, to chase it away.

Several heads taller than Bryon if it stood on its hind legs, leather barding, as might be used on a large warhorse, protected its neck, shoulders, and hindquarters. It stopped when it saw the men, grunted, and roared. One of the dwarves scolded the beast, and it turned and trotted to catch up to its masters. The dwarf made eye contact with Erik, and as the young man smiled, the dwarf frowned.

"I would have thought the dwarves here would have been a little more... well, I don't know. How long has it been since they've seen a man?" Erik asked.

"Why? Are you so interesting that we dwarves should just stop what we are doing because you are here?" Demik asked.

"Demik," Turk called back to the dwarf. Skull Crusher gave his dwarvish companion a scolding look. Erik saw Demik roll his eyes.

"It is unusual to see men in the trading hall, but not too rare," Demik explained. "We dwarves often trade with the men who live in villages on the surface of these mountains or along their foothills, like Stone's Throw, and at times will entertain men from the north, Durathnans, and even Hargolethians. That trade usually takes place on the surface, or at one of our outposts. But from time to time, if the man is important enough, or what they want to trade is grand enough, dwarves will escort them to this place."

Eventually, they walked the length of Gröde Handenhall, coming to giant double doors again, these ones made of iron and preceded by an open portcullis.

More guards stood in front of them and, after a few moments of speaking with both Turk and the two dwarves who had escorted them through Gröde Handenhall, one of them knocked on the doors three times and shouted, "Onbreg!"

The doors opened, and the mercenaries stepped into a giant cavern, and as soon as they did, Erik heard Turk sigh and say, "Home."

"It looks like any other city," Erik said, staring at the groves of apple and orange trees and farmlands that lay before him as they walked along what he assumed to be the main road of Thorakest.

"What did you expect?" Demik asked.

"I don't know," Erik replied, wincing when he heard the oinking and squealing of pigs and smiling fondly when he heard the deep moo of a cow. "When someone tells you that you are going to visit a city built within a mountain, you don't think of farms and cattle and orchards. And irrigation."

"And this bright," Wrothgard added. "It's as if you've smuggled the sun in here."

"I suppose, in a way," Demik replied, "we have."

The dwarf pointed to the top most reaches of the giant cavern. Erik followed the dwarf's finger and was promptly blinded, temporarily.

"Ages ago, all we could grow down here in the darkness were different types of fungi, carrots, and potatoes, and the only livestock we could raise were reptiles and large rodents. Any crops like corn or wheat we grew on the surface or near our surface entrances were susceptible to raiding and plundering."

"A thousand years ago, our forefathers installed giant mirrors in this cavern," Demik continued. As Erik tried looking up again, squinting, he could see several of the mirrors, but beyond them he saw only darkness. "It is perhaps our greatest invention, and something we created before our northern cousins. These mirrors riddle the mountain, all the way to the surface, built into the mountain by our ancestors."

"I cannot imagine the engineering feat that would have been," Wrothgard said.

"Truly," Demik replied. "To this day, it is a masterpiece marveled by peoples all over the world. They catch the sun's rays and reflect them into our great cities. This allows us to farm and raise cattle like you do on the surface world."

Erik and his companions walked along the main road of Thorakest, passing through farmlands and then a large urban area just outside the city walls.

"Why does a city that was built within a mountain need walls?" Vander Bim asked. "The tunnels are not large enough for siege equipment, or a large army for that matter."

"There are things in these mountains," Turk replied, "that are far more dangerous and disastrous than siege weapons and armies."

Passing through the urban area of Thorakest, coming to the city's walls, dwarf soldiers eyed them from its top. A gatehouse and barbican preceded the wall.

"Look to the bartizans," Wrothgard said. Erik had no idea of what a bartizan was, but he followed the soldier's eyes to what looked like short towers with sloping, tiled roofs on each of the outer corners of the gatehouse. Dwarves peered out through the crenels, thick spears in hand, watching Erik.

The iron portcullis of the gate sat open, and the two dwarvish guards that had been with them this far now led them through the entrance into the neck of the barbican. As they walked through, a horn blew from the top of one of the gatehouse's towers, getting a response from another at the top of one of the city's towers. Within moments, ten dwarvish soldiers blocked both the front and the back of the company. They stopped, and the party's two escorts began speaking with a tall dwarf wearing a red tabard, Turk joining them after a few moments. After what sounded like a heated conversation, the tall dwarf signaled to his soldiers. The dwarves immediately stepped aside.

The dwarvish escorts and Turk bowed to the tall dwarf, and he returned the gesture with a quick dip of his chin. After a wave of his hand, another horn blew, and a second portcullis, at the other end of the neck, began to open. A dozen more armored guards marched through the new opening as the tall dwarf spoke to Turk again. The look on Turk's face showed irritation mixed with compliance, and he bowed, again. Turk turned to face his companions.

"You must give up your weapons here. They will keep them until we leave."

"I think not," Switch muttered. "Do dwarves have to give up their weapons to enter the city?"

"No, but you are not a dwarf," Demik replied. "However, Turk, Nafer, and I must give up ours as well."

Erik's companions loosened their belts, and they walked forward, presenting their weapons. Erik saw Switch had shuffled to the back of the line and pushed a short-bladed knife into his boot and then another down the front of his pants. He then saw the thief removing all his other knives and daggers and piling them into the dwarf's outstretched hands before he slipped his bow off his back and gave that up.

Erik felt a tingle at his hip and slid his dagger to the small of his back and pushed it low so that only half the handle would be visible if his rucksack wasn't covering it. He handed the dwarvish guard his sword, and as gray eyes glared at him from under the dwarf's helm, Erik could feel sweat along his brow, down his cheek, and around the neck of his shirt. The dwarf looked him up and down for what seemed like an eternity until Demik curtly said something to the guard in Dwarvish and, with one last passing look, the dwarf jerked his head to the side, signaling the young man to pass through the gate.

Erik released a sigh of relief as he passed into the walled city of Thorakest. As he looked up at the open portcullis, he felt a tingle at his lower back, and a sudden sense of approval overcame him.

Chapter 29

"WILL WE GO TO THE mayor's hall first?" Turk asked.

"Aye," replied the guard who was leading them through the city.

"I have missed this place," said Turk, more to himself.

As they passed among them, almost as if he was seeing them for the first time, Turk took in the stone and wood shops, the artisan and fruit carts, the small homes with little, short-fenced gardens on either side of cobbled walkways. He saw a large fountain centered by a statue of some stately dwarf holding a bucket pouring water into the well around the fount. It sat in the middle of a large courtyard. Several dwarves—reading, courting, relaxing—sat around the well. They eyed the party and ceased their conversation as they passed but didn't scowl or offer jests.

"Why did you leave?" the guard asked.

"It's a long story," Turk replied. "I forgot how large Thorakest is."

They came upon a large market center with fountains at every corner and carts and half-permanent structures everywhere. A tall, square keep of dark-gray stone stood at the center of the market square.

"Here it is," the guard said. "The keep of Fréden Fréwin."

Turk turned to his companions and spoke to them in Westernese.

"We will ask the mayor for passage to the castle and freedom within the city."

"Is not the king's steward the person who would give us that leave?" Wrothgard asked.

"It's a matter of respect," Turk explained. "Just because you can eat whatever you wish in a host's house, as an honored guest, doesn't mean you do so without asking for permission."

"Ah, I see," Wrothgard replied.

The doors to the keep stood open, a steady flow of dwarvish peoples walking in and out. Turk walked through the doors and into a large foyer, a rectangular room with a number of vendors and carts lined along its walls, selling many of the same goods that a market-place vendor might sell. Along with colorful banners, which hung from the ceiling, suits of armor lined the wall. They were clearly meant for decoration since most of the suits, with their elaborate fins and horns and spikes, would be worthless in battle.

Across from the entrance, Turk followed the guard through a set of huge doors and into the main hall of the keep. It was long and wide, and a carpet of red and gold led visitors to a raised dais, upon which lounged an older dwarf, many years past his middle years, with long, gray hair and beard. Dwarves that looked like dignitaries and business owners, aristocrats and minor nobles surrounded the older dwarf and his high backed, cushioned chair. He stroked the beard that reached to his chest as he listened intently to his guests, the large, open sleeves of his gold and silver embroidered, red robe flopping back and forth, making it look as if he only pretended to listen. He had emeralds sewn into his sleeves and sapphires sewn into the front of his robe, which he used as buttons.

"Fréden," Turk muttered.

The guard looked over his shoulder and nodded.

"Who?" Bryon asked.

"The mayor of the city, the steward of the civilian world of Thorakest," Turk replied.

They walked towards the chair of Fréden Fréwin, and he pre-tended to ignore them, but Turk could see his sideways glances. He gave the party several fleeting looks before putting up his hand to some richly robed dwarvish man with gold rings and diamond necklaces to silence him. The old mayor straightened in his chair, gripped the armrests with his hands, and then leaned forward. Turk saw the dwarf nod to two of his own guards, dwarves clad in mail shirts and carrying large, round shields and tall spears. They moved to the front of the dais as if to protect the mayor.

"Who are these…visitors?" Fréden Fréwin called to the guard who led the party through the keep. He hung on the word *visitors,* almost spitting it out.

"Surely, you know who they are?" the guard replied.

"Do I not deserve a city guard's respect?"

Turk could hear the guard sigh and groan.

"No, my lord. Apologies. I present you Turk Skull Crusher."

"Just Turk Skull Crusher?" the mayor asked.

"Turk Skull Crusher and his companions, my lord." The guard bowed, but Turk felt that it took much effort to do so.

"And his companions consist of men?" Fréden Fréwin asked.

The guard paused and quickly looked back at Turk.

"Yes, my lord."

"Turk Skull Crusher." Fréden Fréwin stood. "This is a name that I know, at least the surname. Although, the patron of this family, to the best of my knowledge, died several years ago. You must be his son, long lost to the lands of men. Do you speak for this group of…" The mayor's lip curled. "Do you speak for this group?"

Turk stepped forward and bowed.

"I do. Shall we speak in Westernese, for the sake of my companions your Excellency, the most respectable Fréden Fréwin? Out of respect?"

"And would they speak in our tongue if we were in their lands?" Fréden Fréwin asked.

"No," Turk said to Fréden's curt question, "but we have always taken pride in being more hospitable than men, have we not?"

Fréden Fréwin scoffed. He looked at the party of men.

"Aye. Who are these other dwarves you have with you, Skull Crusher?"

His broad, pale finger might as well have been a knife as he pointed to Demik and Nafer.

"Demik Iron Thorn." The dwarf walked forward and stood next to Turk, offering the mayor a short bow.

"Nafer Round Shield, Fréwin," Nafer said.

"Your names I do not recognize," Fréden Fréwin said, "have you been living in the lands of men as well?"

Neither dwarf took care to nod.

"And these men are—" began Turk, finally switching to Westernese.

"I care not who these men are!" Fréden Fréwin shouted in Dwarvish. "I should ask what your business is here, after living with the likes of these surface dwellers for so long."

"My business is personal," Turk replied, using Dwarvish again himself.

"Not only do you show up with these dogs, but then you choose to disrespect me in my own hall. Especially you, a member of such an esteemed family. Am I to be such a fool to believe that you are simply here on personal business?"

The mayor stood and took a step down from his dais. "The Duke of Strongbur executed a young warrior such as you—family highly respected—not two months ago. And for what, you might ask? Spying."

"For whom was he spying, my lord?" Turk asked with eyes squinted and a cocked eyebrow.

"Who else could it be other than men?" Fréden Fréwin shouted. "Who else could want the secrets of the dwarves, the secrets of our mines and treasures, the secrets of Dwarf's Iron?"

Turk could think of another people for whom a young, disenchanted dwarf might spy as disheartening as that might be, but he dared not say a thing in this place.

"My family has been honored by King Skella and the kings before him. This you know to be true," Turk said. "Do not call into question my integrity. It is simply out of respect that we ask you leave of the city."

"You would speak to me this way in my own hall!" Fréden yelled.

"Has the mayor taken up the crown since I have left my homeland," Turk asked, "and been given leave to pass judgment on the honor and honesty of a warrior?"

Fréden Fréwin's face turned red. Below his bearded cheeks his jaws clamped. His fists clenched, and if he stood close enough to Turk, he might have hit the dwarf. Fréden's guards slowly began to close in on the party, but the mayor gestured them away. Anger and disrespect did not give enough reason to order an attack on a dwarf warrior, whose family had close ties to that of the king's. Fréden Fréwin sat back down.

"You know the way to the castle," the mayor said to the party's two escorts.

Turk bowed to him, but the mayor did not acknowledge his courtesy. They walked through the rearward door in the keep, behind the mayor's seat, and entered the remainder of the town. Only a few blocks of homes past the keep, sat another courtyard similar to the first, its only difference being two fountains on either side of the road on which they walked and rose gardens beyond each fountain. Their escort turned and held up a hand, turned back around, and walked towards the keep of the castle.

"Where is he going?" Wrothgard asked.

"He is going to tell King Skella we are here," Turk replied and stopped to wait. His companions followed suit.

"I apologize," Turk said to them all, "Nothing was said that should concern you, and I'm sure that you can tell that dwarves are no different than any other peoples of Háthgolthane. Some feel they are superior to others. They feel we should exert our superiority. Clearly, Fréden Fréwin is one of those dwarves."

"From his demeanor, the mayor seems like a bitter fellow," Erik suggested.

"He comes from a long line of stewards here in Thorakest," Turk replied. "He has never trained as a warrior like many of us. He chose a life of diplomacy and politics, and many of those fools are nothing but pompous, elitist idiots."

"And many think like him?" Erik asked.

"Some do, yes," Turk replied. "But most do not. Mind you, many dwarves do have a general dislike for men, even those that are born and raised in a dwarvish city like Thorakest. But his views of dwarvish purity and dwarvish dominance are more than foolish—they are contrary to our traditions, contrary to the teachings of An, the Almighty and the scriptures he has left us."

"But there are others that feel the same way?" Erik insisted.

"Yes, but they are fools," Turk replied with a nod. "The whole lot of them. Fréden Fréwin is the biggest fool of them all."

Switch grumbled and spat and kicked dirt, while Vander Bim walked from one statue to the next, inspecting them, touching them, and marveling at them. Befel and Bryon seemed to bicker about something, which they often did—when they spoke. Wrothgard stared at the castle while Erik stared to the darkness beyond the mirrors of Thorakest. All the while, Turk just expectantly waited, reveling nervously at being home.

The dwarvish escort returned.

"King Skella knows you are here," the escort said. "He has many appointments, however. He has commanded that you be housed in one of the barracks until he is ready to see you."

Turk bowed, turned to his companions, and relayed the information, and they began to follow the guard again.

"Are we not important enough for him?" Switch asked.

"He is a king," Demik replied. "We are lucky he is seeing us at all."

"Being men doesn't put us at the forefront of his appointments?" Wrothgard asked.

"He is involved with men quite often," Turk replied, "certainly more than Fréden Fréwin and some of his citizens. You being here is nothing too alarming. What we have in our possession is probably more alarming than anything."

"And what is that?" Wrothgard asked.

"The map to Orvencrest," Turk replied.

"What do you mean?" Wrothgard asked.

"I will show King Skella the map," Turk replied.

"Truly," Wrothgard said and stopped walking.

"Of course," Turk replied. Everyone stopped, even the escort, as Turk confronted the soldier. "What did you think I would do?"

"I thought we were helping you traverse the lands of men," Vander Bim said, "and you would help us traverse the lands of dwarves."

"And that has happened," Turk replied.

"You lied," Switch said.

"I do not lie," Turk snapped. "I did... we did as we said we would. Showing King Skella the map is of no consequence to you. We will still find the lost city, and you will still fill your haversacks with more jewels and coins than you could imagine. But not showing him the map could be of grave consequence to my people."

"That's all well and good," Switch said, "when you will be here, in the protective confines of your mountain. What happens to us when the Lord of the East finds out we've given a map to the king of the southern dwarves?"

"I don't think he will find out," Turk replied, "and if he does, you are truly foolish to think that I would be any safer than you, even in the confines of a dwarvish city."

Chapter 30

Lieutenant Bu watched both the small group of men camping in the forest clearing and the half-dozen dwarvish soldiers who thought they were hidden by the cover of the adjacent trees. General Patûk had tasked him with searching out men who had accepted the Lord of the East's mission of finding some lost dwarf city. Most would have balked at such a task. Sorben surely would have and would say it was beneath him. However, Bu was different. He relished the opportunity to find favor in the General's eyes and show strength to anyone who might think of challenging his position.

The dwarvish soldiers were expertly hidden. Any untrained eye would have never seen them until it was too late. They were from these mountains—the Southern Mountains—after all. But Bu saw them. It would be a bonus, dispatching a dwarvish patrol along with agents of the usurper. Hairy rats that smelled like bear fat. He scowled as he watched the men's fire blazing high into the sky, crackling and spitting. No doubt, it was an attempt to deter wolves and cougars and bears, but all it did was attract a dwarvish patrol—most likely from Strongbur—and him.

"I am impressed," Bu whispered.

"By what, sir?" Ban Chu asked.

"That they made it this far," Lieutenant Bu replied. "Most of them died as they ventured into the mountains through the Western

Tor. The rest, save for one group, died along the Southern Mountains."

"The men traveling with dwarves?" Ban Chu asked. "They are the ones that survived?"

"Aye." Bu nodded. He ground his teeth and groaned silently. They were the ones that had gotten away. They were the ones that pompous prick Lieutenant Sorben Phurnan let slip through his hands.

"Did they really kill two trolls?" Ban Chu asked.

Bu simply nodded.

Bu watched this dwarvish patrol. They looked like scouts, from what he could see. They were soldiers, certainly, but probably tasked with following and that was it. He doubted they would attack unprovoked. That complicated things. Dwarves were sturdy warriors, adept in the art of war. Even the basic dwarvish foot soldier would be better trained than most Golgolithulian soldiers. And Bu could not very well attack these men—these mercenaries in service to the Lord of the East—without then inciting a response from the dwarvish scouts. Even though his men were well trained, he doubted they would get out of a direct fight with half a dozen dwarves without any casualties. They would have to sneak up on the dwarves, take them by surprise, kill them without exposing their position, and then kill the mercenaries. But it would not be easy.

"So, we attack the mercenaries?" Ban Chu asked.

"And expose our position?" Bu snapped. He didn't mean to sound harsh. Ban Chu was a good soldier, but the answer seemed obvious and the question foolish. "No. We attack the dwarves."

"Attack the dwarves?" Ban Chu questioned.

"Yes, but quietly," Bu said with a nod of finality. "We will assassinate them by cover of darkness. Hopefully, we can kill them without alerting our location to those fools in service to the usurper. We will wait until they fall asleep and slit their throats."

"Are you worried about more dwarves hidden somewhere?" Ban Chu asked.

"No," Bu lied.

Truly, he didn't think there was another dwarvish patrol nearby, especially if they didn't know Patûk Al'Banan's forces were close. Certainly, the dwarves were aware of the General's presence by now, but the majority of his soldiers were confined far east of where Bu and Ban Chu scouted. But he didn't know for sure. He had scouted the area thoroughly, but dwarves were crafty bastards, and they knew these mountain forests better than anything else.

Bu nodded to Ban Chu. The two moved silently, followed by ten other men. It would take them over an hour to reach the dwarves, but stealth required precision and patience.

Bu took a breath, held it, and slid forward a hair's length, body pressed into the ground. The close proximity of the dwarves was given away by their repugnant smell, one of bear fat and muskiness. He wanted to gag, and if he hadn't been a man of strong constitution—Sorben Phurnan—he would have, giving their position away. One of the dwarves shifted and whispered something to another one, speaking in their harsh, backwards language. Bu had never bothered to learn it but cursed himself for not doing so at that moment.

He waited, breathing quietly, holding his breath for many moments before slowly exhaling. Then, in the flutter of a fly's wings, he reached up, grabbed one of the dwarves' long braids, pulled his head back, and jammed a dagger into the side of the dwarf's neck. At the same time, Ban Chu jerked another dwarf's chin up and slid his own dagger across his neck. Another one of Bu's men thrust his short sword down into the back of yet another dwarf's neck.

They were fortuitous kills. Bu had told his men they would kill four dwarves before they knew what happened, but he didn't believe it. He thought they would be lucky to sneak up on one. Any other scout would have surely given up their position, or at least would have alerted the dwarves to some movement. But he was Bu, the best of all Patûk's scouts.

Three dwarves fell before the other three knew what had happened. As one of the living bearded midgets turned, Bu slammed his dagger into his neck. The dwarf's eyes went wide and blood burst from his mouth, splattering Bu across the face.

Bu felt that all too familiar excitement, staring at a victim's face while he breathed his last moments, feeling his blood on his own face, even tasting his blood, although dwarf blood always tasted foul. His heart raced, his breath quickened. It was a feeling he coveted even more than being with a woman.

The last two dwarves finally knew what was happening. One raised a broadsword, ready to swing at Bu, but Ban Chu jammed his thin, long sword into the dwarf's armpit. Bu would have easily dodged the dwarf's attack, but Ban Chu was loyal to him. It was a curse as the one living dwarf tackled Ban Chu, both of them bursting from the cover of the forest trees and rolling into the clearing where the mercenaries camped.

"Damn it," Bu hissed as the mercenaries, who looked to be falling asleep, immediately snapped to attention. "Attack."

A throwing knife thudded into the dwarf's chest, but that was clearly not enough to stop him. He came at Ban Chu hard, his broadsword dragging across the man's chest. One of Bu's other men charged the dwarf, tearing his attention away from the Lieutenant's corporal. The dwarf ran his blade through the soldier's belly but didn't see one of the mercenaries charging him with a spear. The spearhead sunk deep into the dwarf's side.

Ban Chu made quick work of the mercenary. It seemed like, as the mercenary stared at Ban Chu in disbelief, he thought they were allies.

"They think we are here to help them," Bu said with a growing smile on his face.

Bu drew his sword, drawing it across the dwarf's throat and removing his head from his neck.

The three remaining mercenaries backed up, almost into their campfire.

"Mercy," one of them yelled.

Bu growled as the man spoke the language of the far west, Gongoreth or beyond.

"What did he say?" Ban Chu asked.

"He wants mercy," Bu replied.

"Mercy," the man said again, this time in Westernese. "Please. We are outnumbered, and over our heads. We mean you no harm."

Bu laughed.

"Did he make a joke?" Ban Chu asked.

Bu shook his head.

"They are just fools," Bu replied. "They are right. They are in something that is far over their heads. It will cost them their lives."

Bu lowered his sword and stepped forward, raising a hand.

"As soon as I drop my hand," Bu said to Ban Chu, "kill them."

A quick pretense would help avoid any more casualties on Bu's side. He extended a hand and, in Westernese, said, "Peace."

The man who had been speaking nodded and smiled.

"Peace."

Bu returned the gesture with a nod. A small smile creased the corner of his mouth, and the other two men seemed to relax as well.

"Thank you," the mercenary said, lowering his own sword.

Bu winked and dropped his hand.

Chapter 31

ERIK LOOKED UP, AND THE night sky was black. No moon, no clouds, and no sounds. He reached his hands out to either side. Nothing. The floor felt cold, hard, and rocky. Barefoot, he walked to the side and finally felt a wall. Rock. It was wet and cold. A cave. He stepped forward and then turned, and as he did so, felt the skin of his hip brush the damp wall. He was naked.

As Erik walked, all he heard were the echoes of the slap of his footsteps. He walked far, loosing track of time. Sweat trickled down his cheeks, his chest, his back, down his arms and legs. His heart pounded in his chest, the arteries in his neck thumped against his skin. His breath quickened.

Finally, he saw a pinhole, a single dot of light. He ran, his feet plodding against the uneven stone, and the light grew wider and wider as it got closer. He reached a small opening partially blocked by piled rocks. He reached out, and they were cold and wet, covered in moss. Branches and leaves and roots grew in front of the small opening that was perhaps no bigger than his head.

Erik pushed the branches and roots out of the way and stuck his hand through the hole. He gasped at the feel of the night's breeze. He tore away at the rocks, and as they tumbled to the ground, he expected them to bounce against his legs and fall upon his feet, but as they fell away from the opening, they seemed to disappear. The hole grew bigger, and now he saw moonlight. As he ripped rock away faster, a cool breeze blew against his face. Faster. He heard crickets. Faster. The hooting of an owl. Faster. He pushed through the opening, tumbled down a mound of rock, and found himself sitting on wet grass.

When Erik looked up now, a large, pale moon stared back amidst high tree branches. He felt his hands, his knees, his elbows where they had scratched against the rock. Nothing. No scratches. No blood. He stood and looked back. Dark forest. No tunnel. No rocks. Just forest. The cave was gone.

The forest was thick. He looked up as he walked and, most of the time, tall trees blocked the moon. Pine needles and twigs crunched under his bare feet. He felt nothing. They should have poked and cut and scratched, but he felt nothing. The wind whistled through tree branches as dead leaves and fallen needles rustled about his ankles. Erik wrapped his arms around his naked body. He should have felt cold, but…he felt nothing. And heard nothing.

The sounds he heard before were gone. Everything that should have been there was gone except the darkness. No noises, no chill in the air, no pain from his scratched skin…No breathing. He touched a finger to his wrist, but his pulse was gone. He tried to speak, but his voice was gone. He started to panic.

He saw movement, a flicker of red and gold. Fire. He walked to it, pushed through trees, and the darkness. He stepped into a clearing, a ring of trees encircling a flat space centered by a large fire. He looked up again. No stars. No moon. No clouds. Just a solid wall of black. A single log, perfectly round with no knotholes, no bumps, no imperfections, sat next to the fire, and on it, sat a hooded man, all cloaked in black.

He called to the man. No voice. No sound. He tried again. Nothing.

Where am I? Help me, please.

The hooded head turned to face Erik, reading his thoughts. Now Erik heard the wind whistling again and felt the blast of a cold, nighttime forest breeze. Goosepimples raced up his arms, his legs, his spine. The sounds of the forest exploded through the trees in an eruption of howling and hooting and scurrying and singing. His hands, his knees, his elbows, his chest, they all stung. He looked down. Scratches covered his body. Blood smeared his chest.

"What is this place? Who are you?" he said out loud as he felt his heartbeat hammer in his chest.

A gloved hand, with black leather that creaked as it moved, put a finger up to the cowled head where a mouth might be.

"This is a place of silence." The voice was soft, and Erik strained to listen. He stepped forward, and his foot crushed leaves and needles.

"Silence!" The voice was thunder. Erik closed his eyes, covered his ears, turned away.

"You do not belong here," the cloaked man said, standing.

Erik started to say something, but then stopped. He shrugged his shoulders.

"Why?" Erik whispered.

"You should not be here," the cloaked voice whispered.

"Why?" Erik whispered back.

"This is a place for those who are lost."

"I don't understand," he muttered, looking at the ground.

When he raised his eyes again, the man was gone. He looked to his left, and there he stood.

"This is the way." The voice was almost inaudible. "The path."

"I still don't understand," Erik replied.

"I burn my fire so the lost can see," the figure said as if Erik hadn't asked a single question.

"Who? Who are the lost?" Erik asked, moving closer.

"The wanderers. Those who wander the dark. Those who are lost to the dark. Those who have been stolen by the night."

Erik shivered as the cloaked man prodded the fire with a long stick.

"Night has stolen them, and they wander the dark," the cloaked figure said. "They search for the light and the way home."

The fire flared and blazed high into the darkness overhead, and

Erik began to feel warmth in his body as his eyes followed the flames up into the darkness. The sky was no longer black but blazed with thousands of twinkling stars, and a moon, both pale and brilliant, seemed to dance through the wispy clouds passing silently overhead. The stars looked so close, and he poked at them with his index finger as if they were tiny bubbles and he could pop them. Then his stomach knotted and cramped.

"They come for the caravan," the cloaked man said, "the way home."

"What?" Erik asked.

"Don't you understand? They are lost in the darkness of night. They have wandered, their souls have been weighed, and now they seek the sun."

"Who?" Erik asked.

"Them." The cloaked man pointed to the encircling forest, to a section of heavy trees where the woods stood especially dark.

A man stepped into the clearing. He stood naked, his skin pale, his lips blue, his hair white, his fingernails and toenails purple. He walked towards Erik who felt his heart quicken again. The man walked right past Erik, and when he was close enough, Erik could see he had no pupils, just the whites of eyes sitting on an expressionless face. Erik could feel a chill from the man as if he brought winter with him wherever he went. Just as he had emerged from the forest, he disappeared back into the trees.

"Where is he going?" Erik asked.

"To the caravan," the cloaked man answered. "To the carriage that awaits him."

More men emerged from the woods, passing Erik and the man clad in black, and then disappeared back into the forest.

"Where is the caravan?" Erik asked.

"There." The mysterious man pointed.

It was as if the trees, the forest where he pointed, had never been there, and instead, stood a clearing. Another fire centered the clearing. Next to the fire stood a caravan of simple carriages. There must have been twenty or more, but as far as Erik could see, there were no horses.

"What kind of magic is this?" Erik whispered.

"No magic," the cloaked man said. "Or maybe the greatest magic there is."

A breeze blew through the dark forest, and the trees fluttered and bent and waved to and fro. Men, and now women and children, continued to flood from the woods. He saw a face he thought he recognized. Whose face? Yes, William, from the lumber mill just south of Waterton. What was he doing here? He saw another face. One of the young men that traveled in the Ion Gypsies' caravan.

"I thought they were all killed or captured," Erik muttered.

And then he saw him. That man was unmistakable. In his nakedness, he looked smooth, no hair on his body, no definition in his muscles. He still looked huge compared to anyone else, but in a way, he had been diminished, softened. His shoulders seemed less broad, his chest narrower, his arms smaller. He lumbered through the first clearing, his long hair—now white—bouncing on his broad shoulders.

"But, no," Erik said, his voice wavering, cracking, "you're dead."

Marcus walked past Erik without saying a word, without looking at him, without even hinting to the fact that the young man was there. His wife, Nadya, followed. Then he looked to the cloaked man.

"What is this?" he hissed. "They are dead."

"Are they?"

Erik thought he heard a chuckle escape from underneath the black cowl. He clenched his fists and ground his teeth. He squared up to the cloaked man.

"What evil is this?" Erik spat.

Erik felt the air around him whirl and then vanish. It became stale, and he choked as he tried to breathe. In a moment's breath, a gloved hand had wrapped around his throat, squeezing so hard, his neck surely should have broken, but it didn't. The hand just kept squeezing, gripping harder and harder. He looked up to see the cloaked man, the space underneath his cowl black. He pulled Erik's face close, so that it also was hidden under the cowl.

Erik saw no face. He only saw two flames where eyes should have been, and they blazed with a heat like he had never felt, a heat that surely should have melted his skin off his bones, but it didn't. The flames grew brighter and brighter, so bright that surely, he should have gone blind, but he didn't.

The hand gripped his neck, the flames burned his face and pierced his eyes. Then something—a hand—reached into his chest and grabbed his heart. Erik cried out, his screams so loud he should have gone deaf, but he didn't.

Then, the hands released, the flames dissipated, the screaming stopped. He was sitting, leaning back on his elbows, breathless, and looking up at the cloaked man.

"That is evil," the cloaked figure said. "That and much more."

"But they are dead," Erik said.

"Are they dead?" the cloaked man asked.

Then he turned and walked to the caravan. Erik followed him. The people—so many Erik couldn't count them all—were loading into carts.

"Marcus," Erik said as the large man stepped onto one of the carts.

"He does not remember you," the cloaked man finally said.

"Will he never remember me, then?" Erik asked.

In that moment, Erik did not see a cloaked man all in black standing before him, but he saw another, this one clad in a robe of brilliant silver and gold. He saw his face, but he could not describe it, for it was all the faces that Erik had ever seen—his mother and father, his sisters, every man that had ever walked past the sties of Venton, even his own—all at once.

"He will remember you, young Erik Eleodum, and you must remember him and the lessons he taught you." The man's voice was as gentle as a cooing dove.

Marcus stepped into a carriage with Nadya. Erik saw them sit there, motionless and emotionless. And then, the paleness of the gypsy's skin washed away, the white hair turned black, and he turned his head and saw Erik. Marcus smiled and winked at the young man.

Erik heard more men approaching the caravan. He stood and turned and saw a man that at one time may have been Fox. The cloaked man was clad in black once more as a score or more men walked to the carriages. A gloved hand stiffly pushed Fox in the chest and drove him backwards. Inside the hood, Erik sensed a shake of his head.

"You are heavy with sin, and it will consume you in darkness for all eternity," he said. "You are not welcome here."

The cloaked man then turned, walked past Erik, and stepped into the last carriage of the caravan.

"We will meet again, Erik Eleodum," he said.

With that, the caravan rolled towards the forest, and one by one, each carriage disappeared. As they did, Erik could see the pale purples and pinks of a dawning sun to the east. He saw that Fox still stood there, and what he now recognized as other dead slavers among the two score of men, pale and white-headed, looking dumb. As the last carriage entered the darkness of the forest, Fox fell to his knees, looking to the sky and screaming. His scream keened like the high screech of a hawk, and it pierced Erik's ears worse than nails on slate.

Fox's face went from pale to blue to a putrid color of yellow. His hair turned a dull red and clumps began to fall out. His blank eyes disappeared into their sockets. His teeth cracked and broke. His nose ripped away, leaving an open nasal cavity. His skin dried and peeled away from muscle, which peeled away from bone. Decay overcame his body as if he had been dead and in the ground for a week.

The same thing happened to the others. Some had necks that wrenched to the side. Others had limbs that disappeared or twisted in unnatural ways. Gaping wounds appeared in sunken stomachs—slit throats, cracked skulls, stabs, cuts, and slashes.

Then, Fox turned his decaying, eyeless face to Erik.

"You," he hissed.

Erik could smell his breath, the stench, the warmth.

"You," he hissed again. He pointed a bony finger at the young man.

Erik backed away until his heels hit the trunk of a tree.

Another one looked to Erik.

"Yes, you," he hissed as well.

They all lumbered towards him, jerky and clumsy. And then, as fast as a striking viper, Fox was in front of Erik, his face as close to the young man's as possible.

"You are to blame."

The others echoed, "Yes, yes, yes, yes."

"No," Erik said. He couldn't help the shakiness of fear in his voice.

Fox looked down at his body. He was no longer naked, but tattered clothes hung loosely from his ever-withering body.

"Yes, you are why we must wander the darkness."

Erik closed his eyes and shook his head, pressing his back hard against the tree behind him as Fox's breath was ever closer to his face. "No."

"You are why we couldn't take the caravan."

Erik heard the echo again, "Yes, yes, yes, yes."

He felt cold hands around his neck, pressing him against the tree, pushing him upwards.

"No," Erik said as he struggled to free himself from Fox's grip.

"Yes."

"Yes, yes, yes, yes," came the echo.

Erik's feet were off the ground. He struggled with Fox's arm, but the putrid hand, flesh rotting off in front of Erik's face, proved too strong. He clawed at the arm, ripping skin and flesh away. Fox paid no heed, and he felt no pain.

"You will die," hissed Fox.

"Yes, yes, yes, yes."

"And you will wander the darkness."

"Yes, yes, yes, yes."

"Your skin will rot, and I will feast on it."

"Yes, yes, yes, yes."

Erik closed his eyes as he found it impossible to breathe in any more air. He gurgled, struggled, cried.

"You will know true pain," Fox hissed.

Erik remembered the gloved hand around his neck, squeezing so hard it should've broken his neck, and the blazing flames, so hot they could have melted iron. He remembered the thundering, deafening sound of his voice and the hand around his heart. It should have crushed it, splattered it like a tomato. His eyes shot open.

"No!" he shouted. He found the strength to suck in a breath of air.

He wrenched the hand away from his neck, twisting the arm until he heard bones breaking and tendons snapping. He kicked out and caught Fox in the chest. As the dead man fell backwards, his forearm broke away from the elbow, and Erik held it up for all the dead to see. He then threw it to the ground. Then Erik reached down and grabbed Fox by the throat.

Fox screamed in pain as if Erik's touch burned his rotting skin. The young man pushed the dead slaver against the same tree. One dead man grabbed Erik's shoulder, but he swung backwards, and the man hit the ground, writhing in pain. The others stayed back.

"You are evil, and you will feel pain that is unimaginable, and it will be unceasing. You are here on your own accord."

Fox squirmed and screamed, grabbing at Erik's arm. As he touched Erik's skin, however, his already decaying flesh burned away, revealing the bone underneath.

"This is your punishment."

Erik released Fox, and he crawled away like a snake at Erik's feet, head cowering and eyes turned away. He disappeared into the dark forest, the other dead ones at his heels, and as the last of them disappeared, Erik could see the sunlight just over the tops of several trees now, and he smiled. Then, in the brightening sky, the warmth of a late spring morning touched his face, and he closed his eyes and awoke.

The final scene from the dream was still clear in his mind, and he knew he would see Fox's face in his dreams for the rest of his days, but he could haunt him all he wanted to. Erik now knew that, one day, he would walk past Fox in the forest and step up onto a carriage and it would carry him away to the sun, away home. Fox would watch in his never-ending darkness and experience never-ending pain, knowing that it was no one else's fault but his.

Erik had once felt pity for him, but that pity was gone. He would no longer fear Fox, would no longer run from him, it would be the other way around.

Fox, you will run from me. You will no longer haunt my conscience. You will run from me or I will crush you, and you will live out your eternity as dust blown on a cold wind.

Chapter 32

ERIK HAD NEVER SEEN ANYTHING like the throne of King Skella, a chair made of solid gold, set with sapphires and rubies and diamonds, covered in cushions that just looked soft and comfortable. A man could buy all the free lands of Western Háthgolthane with just a piece of that throne. Even more amazing than the throne was the dwarf who sat upon it. He had never seen a king, had only heard stories of what a king looked like. He imagined a gigantic man with a massive crown and glimmering armor. Or an evil looking man with menacing eyes and an oily beard wearing long black robes. And then he imagined everything in between. But none of those looked like King Skella.

An older dwarf, with a long, white beard that pooled in his lap, sat upon the throne. He had the look of a dwarf that was once strong and muscular, with a firm jaw and broad shoulders despite the white hair and wrinkles, but also a look that reminded Erik of his grandfather. The King smiled as he looked at the mercenaries, his hands folded underneath his chin. His eyes were trusting eyes. Erik didn't necessarily know what that meant, or what trusting eyes looked like, but those blue, piercing orbs stared at everyone in the audience, and Erik couldn't help thinking those eyes saw things, and that a man with integrity could believe those eyes.

"It was many years ago that I saw you, Skull Crusher," King Skella finally said, speaking in perfect, unaccented Westernese, "but these eyes never forget a face, no matter how young or old. You were probably too young, though, to remember your father bringing you here."

"I could never forget such a thing, Your Majesty," Turk replied with a bow. "Such an honor to stand before the King of Drüum Balmdüukr—both then and now."

The King put up a hand.

"I appreciate your politeness, Skull Crusher," King Skella said with a bold voice, although Erik sensed weariness there as well, "but it is unnecessary. When you were a child, you knew none the better. You sat there, where you stand now, playing with wooden toys while I spoke with your father, caring not for whom you entertained. I think that is the beauty of children."

"Your Majesty," Turk said with a bow. Erik heard sadness in the dwarf's voice.

"Tomek Skull Crusher was a good dwarf and a humble servant," King Skella said. "His death was a great loss for us all. Although, certainly, none of us feel that loss more than you."

"Thank you, Your Majesty," Turk replied. "My greatest shame is that my father had no family to sit by his bedside as he passed. I abandoned my family."

"It is unfortunate that you were not here for his passing," King Skella said, "but such is life. It is not for us to know when those we love will pass from this life to the next. Many things would be different in this world if we could know such a thing. He was strong of faith, and he was not alone when he passed. I made sure to that."

"I can never repay your kindness, Your Majesty," Turk said.

Skella raised his hand.

"Your family has served my family for generations," King Skella explained. "Service must be repaid with service. Kindness with kindness. Friendship and faith with friendship and faithfulness. It was the least I could do to sit next to your father in his last moments."

Turk bowed.

"So," King Skella said with a heavy sigh, "what is it that you have that is so important to our people?"

Turk straightened himself.

"We carry with us a map that leads to the lost city of Orvencrest," Turk said.

Murmurs erupted throughout the throne room, and they continued until King Skella held up his hand.

"And how have you come by this map, Turk Skull Crusher," King Skella asked, "when our own historians haven't been able to find the lost city for a thousand years?"

"The Messenger of the East gave it to us," Turk replied. "Our renown as mercenaries earned us an invitation to a meeting he held, some mission for the Lord of the East."

"Andragos," King Skella said, leaning forward. "That is his real name. A snake, a scorpion, and a practitioner of the dark arts. And certainly not to be trusted, especially by dwarves. Why would Andragos, the Black Mage, so willingly give you this treasure? Perhaps a better question would be how it is that men have found the location to a dwarvish city, lost by time and hidden away within dwarvish lands?"

"It wasn't just us, Your Majesty," Turk replied.

"I don't like him talking about our business so bloody freely," Switch whispered, and Wrothgard, standing next to Erik, nodded in agreement.

"Most of those petitioned for this mission were men, Your Majesty," Turk explained. "Supposedly, there is some treasure, some family heirloom of the Lord of the East's hidden away in the treasure room of Orvencrest."

"I highly doubt some family treasure of the Ruler of Golgolithul lies hidden away in Orvencrest," King Skella said, sitting back. "Andragos is a lap dog to the Stévockians. And the Stévockians are cunning and cruel and wicked."

"That I do not know, Your Majesty," Turk said.

"Well, I do, and very well," King Skella said, raising his voice a bit and leaning forward once more. "The dark magic of the Stévockians is the only answer to the question of how men found our—I repeat, our—lost city. And there is certainly some other reason than a lost heirloom that Fen-Stévock would send mercenaries to find Orven-crest."

"This does not sound like it is going well," Erik heard Switch whisper again.

"Be ready," Wrothgard whispered back.

"Without our weapons?" Switch asked. "Be ready for what?"

"To run," Wrothgard replied in a hushed voice.

Erik raised an eyebrow as he listened to the two men mutter to one another.

"I suppose another question I might ask is whether or not this map can be trusted," the King said. "I do not harbor the same distrust of men that some of my kin have," the king added, seemingly more for the men than anyone else, "however, Golgolithul I do not trust."

The King looked to several of the politicians and nobles that had accompanied them in the throne room. They murmured and muttered among themselves. The King turned up a lip, and an audible growl came from underneath his sweeping, white mustache.

"So, you have brought me this map," King Skella said. "Did your companions know that was your intention?"

Turk looked back at Erik and the rest of the mercenaries. Erik could here Switch grumble.

"No," Turk said with a quick shake of his head.

"I see," King Skella said.

"How does that make you feel?" King Skella asked and it took only a moment for Erik to realize that he was speaking to the rest of them... the men.

"Pretty damn pissed off," Switch said.

"As I imagine you would be," King Skella said. "I know I would be. But we will have to deal with that at another time. You have come to me with this map, Skull Crusher. What is it you want? I would say to hopefully help your own people, but I think it is more than that."

"Help us, Your Majesty," Turk said.

"In what way?" the King asked.

"Let us rest here for a time," Turk said. "Maybe a fortnight. Give us room and board and give my companions leave to walk about Thorakest as if they were welcomed guests."

The King leaned back again, steepling his fingers in front of his face. Louder murmuring rose up from the politicians and nobles in the room. King Skella glared at them.

"I will let you rest here, in my palace, as guests," the King said. "Although, it pains me to aid the endeavors of Fen-Stévock, I trust you, Turk Skull Crusher. I trust your family and your loyalty, despite some of the choices you have made. And I will give your friends leave to move about the city unhindered. However, they must understand that this is a large city like any other and, with that, brings its own dangers."

"Of course, Your Majesty," Turk said with a bow. "And then send us on our way so that we might find the lost city of Orvencrest and return a millennia worth of riches home to its people. Give my friends leave to take their fill of the treasure and, if that remains their desire, to return this heirloom to the Lord of the East, and Drüum Balmdüukr can have the rest."

"It is a novel idea," the King said with a smile, and then the smile disappeared, "but I fear your enthusiasm is misplaced. You are not as smart as I thought you were if you believe Golgolithulian troops wouldn't be swarming these mountains the minute they returned with whatever it is the Lord of the East wants, trying to lay claim to the rest of the treasure. We are already dealing with Patûk Al'Banan and his forces infesting our mountains."

Erik heard Wrothgard grumble.

"Why shouldn't I just take the map you have?" the King asked. "Why not send my own warriors to find our lost city and forget about the Lord of the East?"

Switch hissed. Erik could feel the tension surrounding his companions.

"Should I be so willing to part with treasure that belongs to the dwarves?" King Skella asked. "Have you become so bold in your absence, Skull Crusher, to ask so much of your King?"

"I am sorry, Your Majesty," Turk said with a quick bow. "I meant no disrespect."

"Who knows what still lies in the treasure rooms of Orvencrest," the King continued. "They may be barren for all we know. Although, if not, a single, small chest of gold from that treasure would last any of these men's families for generations. It is, perhaps, not an overly absurd request to allow these men to keep a small portion of treasure for themselves. However, my concern lies not with these men, but with Golgolithul. You have come to me in trying times, Turk Skull Crusher."

The King sat silent again for a while. Finally, he stared up at the nobles and politicians and aristocrats in the throne room.

"Leave us," King Skella said with a dismissive wave of his hand. "Varlass Usse!"

They all hurried out of the room.

"Vermin," King Skella said, not holding back the volume of his voice even as some of the politicians still lingered. "At least, most of them. I am sure within a matter of moments, gossip will have spread to the streets of Thorakest that I am allying with men of Golgolithul, and those who think like Fréden Frewin will be calling for a coup of my rule. You have given me much to think on."

"I am sorry, Your Majesty," Turk said.

"No, you're not," the King said with a smile. "And if you return without this heirloom?"

"Death," Wrothgard said, speaking over Turk. "Torture first, then death, Your Majesty."

"And if the Lord of the East knows you are colluding with dwarves?" the King asked.

"Probably the same, Your Majesty," Wrothgard replied.

"He probably already knows you are here," King Skella said.

"It is a chance I am willing to take," Turk replied.

"I am sure," the King said and then pointed to Erik and the other men, "but are they."

"What choice do we bloody have now?" Switch hissed but less quietly.

"True," the king said with a shrug. The look on Switch's face said he didn't mean for the king to hear. "I am not sure if I will let you go, yet. It is a grave risk on the part of my people."

"You condemn us to death if you do not," Wrothgard said.

"I am a king, no different than the Lord of the East," King Skella shouted, suddenly standing. "I can condemn you to death if I so choose. It is my right, is it not?"

The dwarvish guards in the room moved in, spears lowered at the mercenaries. Wrothgard stepped back and bowed.

"Yes, Your Majesty," the soldier said, "it is your right."

"However, I am different than the Lord of the East, and I would not so willingly take a life," King Skella said. "I do recognize that if I do not allow you to continue your journey, the Lord of the East will sign a death warrant for each one of you. With that in mind, if you so wish, you could stay here, in Thorakest, as citizens of my city."

"As prisoners," Vander Bim said.

"Perhaps, some might look at it that way," King Skella replied. It was again, an utterance not intended for royal ears, but they worked as well as a child's. "Fen-Stévock's claws can still draw blood even within the protection of my city, so there is no easy answer. I promise to have an answer for you soon."

"Can we get our weapons back, Your Majesty?" Wrothgard asked.

"No," King Skella said with a slow shake of his head. "I do apologize, but that is a privilege extended only to citizens of Thorakest. Rest assured, they will be kept safely within my own personal armory."

"I am so relieved," Switch mumbled, and Erik couldn't help agreeing with the thief's sarcasm. "Now I'll just go walking around a large city full of people who hate me with nothing but my balls and my fists to protect myself."

"Introduce me to your compatriots, Turk," the King said, sitting back down and leaning back, seemingly relaxing a bit.

Turk introduced them all, making sure to announce Switch as a former merchant from Goldum, rather than a thief.

"Eleodum?" King Skella questioned when Turk introduced Erik and Befel and Bryon.

"Yes, Your Majesty," Erik replied before Befel or Bryon could say anything.

"That is an old name," King Skella said. "One I recognize. A good name. Be proud of that name—and where it comes from."

"Yes, Your Majesty," Erik replied with raised eyebrows.

"The lands south of the Gray Mountains carry the blood of heroes, Erik Eleodum," King Skella explained. "Perhaps I can give you a history lesson sometime."

"Heroes…" Erik whispered to himself as he felt goose pimples rise along his arms.

Chapter 33

ERIK AWOKE TO A LOUD knock at his door. Turk didn't wait for anyone to get up, and before Erik could prop himself up on one elbow, Turk was entering the room, holding two swords.

"King Skella agreed to give me your swords for a time," the dwarf explained, leaning them against the wall, "yours and Bryon's. I thought I might take you to my friend and have him inspect the weapons. Something interesting happened when I retrieved them from the King's armory."

"Oh," Erik replied, looking over his shoulder to see both his brother and cousin still asleep, "and what was that?"

"I thought we should take that peculiar dagger of yours, as well, but when I asked the armorer about a golden-hilted dagger, one studded with jewels," Turk explained, "he hadn't the faintest clue what I was talking about."

Erik smiled, reaching under his pillow to retrieve his dagger.

"Careful, Erik," Turk said.

"Of course," Erik replied.

"The King finds out you've hidden that from him . . ." Turk began to say, but a sudden thought passing through Erik's mind assured him the dagger would stay hidden.

"Are you ready?" Turk asked.

"Let me wake Bryon," Erik replied with a nod. He walked to his cousin's bed and shook his shoulder.

Bryon simply snorted loudly and swatted Erik's hand away without ever opening his eyes.

"We're going to take your sword to Turk's friend," Erik said, "find out what exactly it is."

Bryon didn't move.

"If you aren't going to wake," Erik said, "I'm just going to take it for you then."

Bryon groaned and rolled over.

"I'll take that as permission given," Erik said. He nodded to Turk. "Let's go."

"Obviously, we want to keep your cousin's sword sheathed," Turk said while they walked through the castle grounds. "A glowing sword will cause unwanted commotion."

Erik laughed at that.

"But I will also carry your sword," Turk added.

"Why?" Erik asked, looking almost longingly down at the empty frog at his belt.

"It's just safer this way," Turk replied. "Guards and constables know men aren't supposed to be carrying weapons and would not know of the King's agreement. This will help us avoid unwanted attention."

Erik argued no further. However unwelcomed he had felt in the cities of Waterton, Venton, and Finlo, the feeling he got walking through Thorakest made those places seem like family reunions. He knew some of it was the simple fact that Thorakest was a large city by any measure, with thousands upon thousands of inhabitants, but Erik also knew much of that feeling came from the fact that he was a man, and thus, very much in a minority. If rumors spread here like they did in any other city, some inhabitants who had heard of their arrival might not be too happy about it given their 'mercenaries' label.

"Why did you ask the King to return my sword as well as Bryon's?" Erik asked. "It's nothing special."

"Before you start thinking that sword is nothing but rubbish,"

Turk replied, "do remember it may very well save your life. I simply want Ilken to see you with it and test whether or not it truly fits you. My guess is that it does not."

As more of its inhabitants shot him dirty looks, Erik did see other men in Thorakest. Even in a dwarvish city, he supposed it wasn't so odd to see a diversity of people. They were working with carts or standing in front of their storefronts. Most of them had families with them. He saw gnomes too. He even saw what he expected to be a pair of ogres—remembering Befel's descriptions of the giant humanoids from Finlo. Regardless, Erik was a stranger who stood out as he followed Turk through the busy streets.

They eventually stopped at a house with a clay-tiled roof and walls of yellow-painted wood. Smoke rose from the back of the house. Turk knocked on the bright blue door and stood back with a smile, thumbs tucked into his belt. The door opened, and a gruff dwarvish woman stood in the doorway.

Aside from the lack of a beard, she looked almost like the dwarvish men. She wore a yellow dress that covered her feet and a white cap that covered most of her hair—dark brown speckled with gray. She looked hard at Turk, and then Erik, and then Turk again. Turk removed his pointed, feathered cap, and bowed. She cracked a slight smile and grunted a few words in Dwarvish. Turk replied, Erik understanding nothing but the name "Ilken." The woman nodded and went back into the house.

Another dwarf returned with her, a graying fellow slightly shorter than Turk and wearing a pair of spectacles that hung at the end of a bulbous nose. He wore what little gray hair he had left in tufts just above his ears and along the back of his head. He kept it fairly short, unlike most other dwarves. As soon as he saw Turk, he gave a big grin and hugged him. When Turk pulled away, dark soot stained the front of his shirt.

"Oh my," Ilken, speaking in Westernese in deference to the visiting man, said, "you are not the little apprentice I remember, my young Skull Crusher."

"Aye, it has been far too long Ilken Copper Head," Turk agreed.

"I am sorry about your father," Ilken said, a smile still on his face, "but I am sure he is with the Almighty now. He was a faithful warrior, always saying his prayers and sitting in the same seat at chapel. It seems An has been good to you."

Turk just smiled.

"And you have brought a man with you," Ilken said. "Don't see many of them around here."

The woman who had opened the door said something in Dwarvish to Ilken in a somewhat scolding tone.

"Come now, woman, it is not a dog. *He* is a man. My wife, Lita," Ilken explained when he saw the crooked expression on Erik's face, "was asking if you have fleas or worms."

"Not the last time I checked," Erik joked.

"I have brought Erik to meet you," Turk explained, "he has several items—weapons—in which you might be interested."

"Good to meet you," Erik said, extending his hand. Ilken wiped his hands on the heavy, cowhide apron he wore and then returned the favor, practically crushing the young man's hand.

"I am always interested in looking at fine—perhaps even *unusual*—weapons," Ilken said, giving Erik a look that was almost one of mischief.

Ilken motioned for them to enter, and Erik and Turk followed Ilken and Lita through a simple house with a large living area filled with two benches and a tall shelf with little trinkets and glass figurines. A wall separated the living area from the kitchen, an equally large room with two large basins for dishes, a wood stove, and a simple box of iron covered in furs.

"It's a place to keep things cool," Ilken explained as Erik stopped to look at the thing. "We call it an ice box. We can pack it with ice and put meat or cheese or milk in there, and it will keep for much longer than it normally would."

From the kitchen, Ilken opened a door to their backyard. It consisted of two orange trees, a small patch of strawberry bushes, roses, and a fenced area for tomatoes and vegetables like beans and peppers. The latrine was there as well, and Ilken's shop.

"Come," Ilken said. "Let us have a look at what you have brought me."

They entered the smithy shop, familiar to Erik with its billow and anvil and cooling tank, and Turk motioned to Erik. Turk first gave Ilken Bryon's sword. The blacksmith took it with a slight bow and set it on a table, inspecting the scabbard. He then unsheathed the sword, and as a bright purple light bathed the dwarf's face, a wide smile spread and parted his lips into a toothy grin. He set the weapon down gently, and it hissed when it touched the wood of the table.

"Just as I thought," Ilken said, putting on two heavy, leather gloves.

"What is that?" Erik asked.

"If you were to touch the blade, it would burn you. Look at the mark it has made on my table." Ilken pointed to a black line of charred wood where the blade had touched.

The blacksmith ran his gloved hand over the blade, safe from burning with the thick leather protection. He leaned as close to the metal as he could.

"This is a fine blade indeed," Ilken said. "Good steel, despite its magic."

"Dwarf's Iron?" Erik said.

"No lad, just good steel," Ilken replied. "Elvish steel if my suspicions hold true."

"Elves?" Erik questioned.

"Aye," Ilken replied, a smile still on his face. "You'd never think the fancy little pricks, with all their dancing around and drinking too much, would be capable of making such a fine weapon, but they were, at one time, fairly good smiths."

"Have you seen an elf-made sword before?" Turk asked.

"Aye, but only one," Ilken said, looking at the dwarf over his spectacles before he pushed them back up his nose. "They are hard to come by any more, even ones not imbued with some sort of magic. This truly is a treasure. It is your cousin's you say?"

Erik nodded.

"Is elvish steel different, like Dwarf's Iron?" he asked.

"No lad, just steel worked by elvish hands. Well, let's have a closer look."

Ilken removed his spectacles and set them on the table before temporarily sheathing Bryon's blade. He then rooted through a box that was sitting on a short shelf behind him. He tossed aside wooden measuring tools and other trinkets when he grunted with satisfaction and held up another pair of spectacles, only these had lenses a pale shade of blue.

Ilken put on the new glasses and unsheathed the sword again. The purple light reflected brightly off those blue lenses. As the blacksmith mulled over the blade, he hemmed and hawed.

"These are certainly elvish runes," he said, still examining the sword. "They are old, predating even Middle Elvish. But I do not believe this sword is that old. These runes were old and outdated a thousand years ago. This is good steel with no impurities that I can see. That will keep the metal sturdy. The magic will help preserve the metal for even longer, but even then, after a thousand years, this blade should have begun to fade, lose its luster and essentially, fall apart."

"Can you read them?" Erik asked.

"A little," Ilken said with a shrug. "A dwarf is not supposed to know how to read any form of Elvish, but it can be very helpful to a blacksmith. I see a rune for fire, and that would make sense. I see another one for the elements. That leads me to believe this is elemental magic. And then, I think some of these are family names, perhaps. Where did your cousin get it?"

"He got it from a man, a mercenary, he killed," said Erik. "After the man tried to kill him, of course," Erik clarified.

"A lesser blacksmith might date it back to the Elvish Wars," Ilken said, a slight hint of haughtiness in his admission, "but that was a thousand years ago...too long. I would date it no more than four hundred years, to Evum Obscurium, the Age of Obscurity. Even with the elves retreating away from the world and into their hidey holes like the forests of Ul'Erel, there still would have been a good number of these weapons produced then. Some elvish knight probably owned it, and he died. A man who knew no better retrieved it, sold it, traded it, or died, and the rest is history."

Ilken looked it over more, turning it in his gloved hands.

"Elemental magic is such a fickle thing," Ilken said.

"How so?" Turk asked.

"Sometimes it works, sometimes it doesn't. One thing I do know is that most elemental magic is good."

"Good?" Erik muttered.

"Aye, magic can have alliances. It can be good or evil. In fact, in the hands of a man with a wicked, twisted heart, this sword probably won't even glow. Does it radiate its aura when your cousin holds it?"

Erik nodded.

"That is good," Ilken said. "At least you know your cousin isn't evil."

"You could fool me sometimes," Erik muttered.

Ilken laughed.

"Has he used it?"

"I don't think so."

"Well, let's try it," Ilken said. "What do you say?"

Erik just shrugged.

Ilken lifted the sword high over his head and, with a hefty grunt, struck the heel of his anvil. Erik closed his eyes, felt a puff of hot air hit his face, and heard a sound that sounded like metal scratching against metal and meat searing over a fire. When he opened his eyes, he saw Ilken Copper Head holding his cousin's blade, eyes wide and smile even wider. The heel of the anvil lay on the floor, the side once attached to the rest of the anvil glowing red.

"I would say it works," Ilken said with a hint of excitement.

When Ilken held the blade close to Erik's face, he could feel its heat. Sweat trickled down his face. It looked perfect, as if Ilken had just forged it.

"This is indeed a treasured blade," Ilken said as he slid the sword back into its scabbard. "Hopefully, your cousin keeps it, uses it well, and passes it to his son when that time comes. Is that all?"

Erik looked to Turk, and the dwarf nodded. He grabbed his jeweled dagger, stuck deep into his belt. His palm tingled as he grabbed the weapon. The tingle moved to his spine, and a jolt, like a hundred spiders crawling up his back, shot through his body. He shook.

"Are you okay?" Ilken asked.

"Yes. Just a shiver," Erik said. "Sorry."

Erik removed the dagger from his belt and handed it to Ilken. The dwarf reached out to the weapon, and when his fingers touched the handle, he quickly retracted his hand.

"What's wrong?" Turk asked.

"It stung me." Ilken rubbed his hand with furled eyebrows and a frown.

"Maybe I'm not going insane," Erik said.

"Perhaps," Ilken replied. "Or maybe we both are. Erik, set it on my table please."

Erik did, and the smith put his colored spectacles on and looked over the dagger.

"Can you unsheathe it, please?" Ilken asked.

Erik did. Ilken looked over the blade again, with his spectacles, making sure not to touch it.

"I have never seen anything with this type of aura."

The dwarf removed his spectacles and folded them, dropping them into one of the pockets of his apron.

"It is as if a thousand different types of magic are all working together. I can't even explain what I am seeing. There are no markings on the blade. These gems are clearly magical, but I can't tell how or why. The handle is magic. The blade itself is strong with a magical dweamor. This is something I have never seen. Where did you get it?"

"It was a gift," Erik replied. "From a gypsy friend."

"Gypsies, eh." Ilken continued to look over the weapon, making sure not to touch it. "This is certainly something that a gypsy might come across, in his dealings all over the world. Have you used this dagger?"

"Yes," Erik said.

"And what did it do?" Ilken asked.

"I threw it. I imagined it striking the back of the man I threw it at, but my throw was clearly off my mark," Erik explained. "However, as it wobbled through the air, the dagger glowed red and turned into an arrow and struck the man exactly where I thought I had aimed. When I went to remove it, it was a dagger once again."

Turk nodded in affirmation.

"I do not know what to say." Ilken scratched his bearded chin.

"I feel as if ..." Erik began to say, but then stopped.

"What, Erik?" Turk asked.

"Sometimes I feel as if it communicates with me," Erik finally said.

Ilken straightened his back and moaned. "Are you sure?"

"I don't know," Erik replied. read "I have a thought, but it's not my thought and I feel like it is this dagger communicating with me. I don't know how to explain it."

"If that is true," Ilken said, removing his regular spectacles once again from the pocket in his apron and putting them on, "then this is a powerful magic, a legendary magic, even."

"Elvish magic?" Erik asked.

"No," Ilken said, shaking his head. "Something much more powerful."

Erik's stomach twisted. "Should I be worried?"

Ilken shrugged. That was not the response Erik had wanted.

"I would be careful," Ilken said. "History has plenty of tales about magic weapons and items having a conscience. Some were good, some were evil. Those that were good helped make men heroes, saviors, warriors of justice and righteousness. Those that were evil normally took over their possessors, used them, twisted them, caused them to do great harm to the world and those around them, and then discarded them, looking for a new host like a disease."

"So, if it is evil, then I just throw it away?" Erik asked.

"That is easier said than done. The connection between master and weapon becomes addictive, more so than Black Root, Kokaina, Tomigus Root, or anything else you could think of," Ilken explained. "Some say Stone Axe's axe had such a conscience and, even though it was a weapon of goodness, the mighty king would spend nights away from his wife, talking to his axe. Carry this with great caution, Erik, if you choose to keep it."

Erik picked up the dagger and sheathed it, putting it back in his belt. He felt a familiar tingle at his hip and, for a quick moment, he smiled. It felt…good.

"Was he going to look at my sword as well?" Erik asked Turk.

"Was your blade made for you?" Ilken asked.

"I haven't even used it." Erik shook his head. "My cousin took it from the friend of his sword's owner."

"Interesting," Ilken said. "Hold it."

Turk offered the sword to Erik, handle first, and the young man took it, holding it as naturally as he could.

"May I?" Ilken reached out with his hands.

The young man nodded and handed the dwarf his sword, handle first.

"Yes, yes, this was clearly not made for you," Ilken said. "I am not sure who it could be made for. It is heavy, a blade that should be used with two hands, but the handle is only long enough to be used by one."

Ilken gave the sword back to Erik.

"Do not worry. It will do the job. You have strong arms and shoulders," Ilken said. "You have a strong back and strong hips. You will be able to effectively use this sword. Let me ask you a question. If you were to have a sword crafted for you, would you rather wield it with one hand or two?"

Erik scrunched his eyebrows and pursed his lips.

"I don't know," he replied. "I've never really been trained with a sword, or any weapon for that matter, other than a boar spear—and maybe the short bow. If I could choose something...Well, I think I've heard them called hand-and-a-half swords."

"Ah, yes, a bastard sword," Ilken said with a smile.

"Yes," Erik replied. "A bastard sword I heard too."

"A very popular sword among the peoples of Northern Háthgolthane," Ilken said. "I will keep an eye out for one."

Erik nodded with a smile.

Chapter 34

"I WILL JOIN YOU IN a moment," Turk said to Erik, suggesting he had private business to discuss.

"If you like tea," Ilken said, "Lita is brewing some."

"I do," Erik replied. "It has been a while since I've had tea."

"He's an extraordinary young man," Ilken said when Erik had walked into the house.

"Yes, he is," Turk replied. "He has a good heart. He gives me hope for the future of men—and for our future."

"Is he a capable fighter?" Ilken asked.

"He…he has, I believe, good potential," Turk replied, "and I should be more active in teaching him how to fight. A soldier from the east also travels with us, and I think, between he and I, we could turn Erik into quite a competent warrior. I fear I have failed him thus far in that."

"Do you think the King will let you go in search of Orvencrest?" Ilken questioned.

Turk looked at his blacksmith friend with raised eyebrows but should have known if any of the citizens of Thorakest would have heard of their arrival, the reason, and the King's decree, it would be the savvy Ilken Copper Head.

"We will see," Turk sighed. "I suppose I should have expected some disagreement. King Skella is a good king, but to let a group of mercenaries carrying a map to the lost city of Orvencrest go when you could send an army…"

"Be prepared," Ilken said.

"What do you mean?" Turk asked.

"As more people learn of your arrival and the reasons behind it," Ilken replied, "you might find yourself and your friends becoming increasingly unpopular."

"Even more so than we already are?" Turk said. "Arriving after so long, and with a retinue of men, seems to have rubbed many the wrong way."

"Frewin?" Ilken asked.

Turk nodded.

"He's a tick," Ilken said and spat. "A pest and a drain on the dwarvish people."

"I couldn't agree more," Turk said.

"Nonetheless, whatever happens, you should train that young man," Ilken said.

"I agree," Turk said, "whatever happens. An knows, if we are sent on our way, he will have to know how to fight, with Golgolithul's assassins on his tail."

Turk then suddenly looked at Ilken, a small smirk on his face.

"What is that look about, Turk?" Ilken asked.

"Well, my friend could use a better sword," Turk replied, "and you are an accomplished blacksmith."

"So are you," Ilken said.

Turk laughed.

"You jest," Turk said, "if you are truly comparing my skills with yours."

"Your skill will surpass mine when you are my age," Ilken said.

"That may be," Turk replied, "but right now, at this moment, you are a far superior blacksmith—a far superior blade smith."

"What are you getting at?" Ilken asked.

"Would you be willing to make Erik a sword?" Turk asked.

"That is a tall task to ask," Ilken replied.

"Aye, it is," Turk said, "but if there is a man in this world that I believe is worthy of such a gift, it would be Erik."

"If you are looking for a basic sword," Ilken said, but Turk cut him off.

"I am looking for a masterpiece," Turk replied. "I am looking for something that he can pass down to his son and grandson, something that will hail the hospitality of the dwarves in uncertain times."

"It is a lot you ask," Ilken said.

"I will pay," Turk said, "whatever the cost."

Ilken scoffed with an angry expression.

"I should whip you for saying such a thing," Ilken said with a frown. "To think I would ask money from you, even for a task such as this. But this will take time, and much effort. I will have to focus solely on this, which means I will not be able to fill orders that have already been placed. I will also not be able to take on new business, which will not set well with Lita."

Ilken looked at Turk with a smile.

"I will do them," Turk said.

"You?" Ilken asked with a smile on his face.

"You said I am a skilled blacksmith," Turk said. "I will fill your orders, as well as complete any new business you take on, if you agree to make a sword for Erik."

"And you will give that young man the training he needs and deserves?"

"Yes," Turk said. "Straight away."

Ilken smirked and nodded his head.

"I will do this then" Ilken said, "for you, and for your father, and for the legacy of the dwarves. I think I will need a fortnight to finish it. Come to my shop every day at dawn. You will work until noon. Then I will give you a break, so you might train young Erik. If there is anything else to do that day, you will come back and work until sundown. Is this agreeable?"

Turk nodded and shook Ilken's hand.

Turk retrieved Erik from inside Ilken's home and led him through the streets of Thorakest, back to the castle.

"Why would Ilken do such a thing?" Erik said, blushing slightly after Turk told him the blacksmith was making him a sword.

"Because he is kindhearted," Turk replied, "and because I have agreed to train you. And I volunteered Wrothgard to train you as well."

"Train me?" Erik asked.

"Aye," Turk replied.

"What if the King sends us home?" Erik asked.

"Then you will need training to survive the Lord of the East's assassins," Turk replied.

Erik didn't reply, and Turk didn't bother to look at the young man over his shoulder. He already knew what look was strewn across his face. It was the same one on his own.

Chapter 35

PATÛK AL'BANAN STOOD ON A tall cliff that overlooked the mining camp. Smoke rose into the sky, and the gray clouds it created covered the deep reds of the setting sun, giving the sky the look of blood. Patûk smiled.

"Does this please you, Princess?" She desired blood and death, and Patûk had given them to her, his Princess of Pain.

He thought he could see Cho's body—old and broken, and yet hard and defiant. He knew the miner would have never given over the camp. He was too proud. He was from an old stock. All Sorben Phurnan could say about the man was "old fool" and "worthless son of a whore." Cho may have been a son of a whore, but Lieutenant Phurnan was the fool. Cho was a man of principle. Perhaps if he could have talked to him, instead of that little, pompous ass Sorben, but, no. It was destined to end this way.

He looked to the horizon. They ran like ants into the Plains—two dozen of them—and Lieutenant Phurnan wanted to give chase.

"Shall we run them down, General?" Sorben had asked.

General Al'Banan just shook his head.

"But General," the Lieutenant had begun to plead.

That had brought on one of Patûk's steely stares, and the Lieutenant slinked back away from him. Perhaps that was the wrong thing to do. Perhaps the Princess would be upset. Maybe she wanted more sacrifice, more blood, more death. Perhaps she would retract the blessing she had bestowed on the General.

He denied her to spite Sorben. That fool would waste resources, time, men to chase, and kill two dozen peasant miners. From what Bu had said, Sorben Phurnan had wasted both men and trolls—Patûk's lip curled at the thought of those beasts—chasing the Lord of the East's mercenaries…and unsuccessfully. Fool. Fool indeed. Patûk's use for him had run its course. Besides, any man who dug through rock and rubble—who desired life that badly—deserved to live in Patûk's opinion.

"Bu."

His newly appointed Lieutenant stood just behind him. He stepped forward and knelt.

"Yes, sir."

"What word have you?" Patûk Al'Banan asked.

"Dwarves, sir," Bu replied.

Patûk heard the sound of meat slapping against the ground. He looked over his shoulder and saw the head of a dwarf—eyes half closed and tongue lolling out its mouth lazily—laying in front of the Lieutenant.

"They were tracking men. More mercenaries in the employ of Golgolithul, I suspect," Bu added.

"You killed them?" the General asked.

"Yes, sir," Bu replied. "Both the dwarves and the mercenaries."

"And how many men did this cost us?" Patûk asked.

Bu didn't reply. General Al'Banan half turned to look at his Lieutenant, still staring at the ground but with a cocked eyebrow.

"Lieutenant, I asked you a question," Patûk said. "I demand an answer."

"I am sorry sir," Bu said. "It's just…well, we lost none, sir."

Patûk turned back around. He didn't want Bu to see the smile on his face.

"Send for Bao Zi, Captain Kan," the General commanded, "and bring me the prisoners of note."

He didn't see the Lieutenant bow but knew he did. He could trust this man. But why? His ideas about trust and loyalty had changed over the last twenty years. When he had served in the Eastern Guard, his officers, society, taught him not to trust peasants, those of low birth, enlisted men, the commoners. The last score of years had taught him the exact opposite. He could trust those people. Men like Bu and Bao Zi, the common soldiers who came to serve him despite the usurper. And the others—men like Sorben Phurnan, this new prisoner, Andu—he couldn't trust these men. They had ulterior motives: self-advancement, personal glory, wealth, and riches. They didn't serve for honor. Especially men like this Andu—how does one give loyalty to one man and so easily change his allegiances? Fear of death?

"Weakness," Patûk whispered. He could hear Bu coming up behind him. The Lieutenant knelt again. Two other soldiers brought the prisoners. Bu looked over his shoulder and squinted his eyes, and the soldiers pushed the men to the ground. The General thought again how he needed to promote more men like Bu.

"Did you send for Bao Zi?" Patûk asked.

"Yes, sir."

"Introduce me to our guests," Patûk commanded.

Bu stood and looked over his shoulder again. His soldiers pulled the prisoners up to their feet. Patûk walked to the two men, facing first a young man with close-cropped, black hair and fair features. He'd arrived in Patûk's camp over a day and a half ago, and not a single whisker stood on his chin. He stood shorter than Patûk, but most easterners did. He wasn't soft, by Patûk's estimation. His shoulders and arms and chest looked well-muscled, a soldier's muscle.

"What is your name?"

The young man flinched at Patûk Al'Banan's voice, and at that, the General scowled.

When the man didn't respond right away, the corners of Patûk's mouth dipped low into a deep frown. He saw Bu move to his side and lift a gauntleted hand. The young easterner gasped and ducked, covering his head with one arm. The General thought he heard a whimper. He put a hand up.

"Stay your hand, Lieutenant."

Bu bowed and dropped his hand.

"Speak, quickly, before I let my Lieutenant beat you and then feed you to the mountain trolls."

"Andu, of House Gházjûka," the prisoner replied.

Patûk nodded to Bu. The Lieutenant struck Andu of House Gházjûka hard across the face. The prisoner fell to the ground, dazed, blood trickling down his cheek.

"When you address General Patûk Al'Banan, you will address him as sir." Bu reached down, grabbed the front of Andu's shirt, and pulled him to his feet. "Do you understand?"

"Yes," Andu replied.

Patûk looked at Lieutenant Bu again, and again, nodded. The Lieutenant struck the prisoner across the other cheek.

"He's crying," Patûk said with a muttering scowl.

Bu reached down and pulled him to his feet again.

"When you address me, you will address me as sir as well. Do you understand?"

"Yes." Andu, eyes wide, red rimmed, and wet, looked up at Bu. He started to shake, and Patûk thought he smelled piss. He put a hand up. "Yes, sir. Yes, sir."

Patûk Al'Banan saw a small smirk cross Bu's lips. That made Patûk smile.

"What were you doing at Aga Min?" Patûk Al'Banan asked.

"I... I w-was Sergeant of the camp g-guard," Andu replied, and when he saw Bu lift his fist again, he added, "sir."

"Little good your camp guard did. Wouldn't you agree?" the General asked. Before Andu could answer, Patûk added, "How did an inexperienced whelp such as yourself become the leader of Aga Min's guard? Did your father pay for your position?"

"I... I p-proved myself—"

Bu's gauntleted fist struck Andu across the face again. When the

Lieutenant pulled the man to his feet, the easterner's knees buckled, and he slouched just in front of the General. Bu pulled him up again.

"Stand. Be a man," the Lieutenant commanded.

"I don't like it when men lie to me, Andu of House Gházjûka. It greatly upsets me." The muscles of Patûk's hardened jaw rippled as he clenched his teeth.

"Y-yes, sir. M-my father p-paid for my p-position. We are a minor house—"

"Yes, I know of your house—and I know how minor it is," Patûk said with an element of disgust in his voice.

"W-we are wealthy, sir— extremely wealthy—and m-my father figured, if g-given the opportunity, I m-might prove myself a military leader and raise our house's status, but without paying for a position, I w-would not have that opportunity, sir."

"Why didn't your father do something to raise the status of your house?" Patûk asked. "And stop sniveling."

"He can't, sir," Andu replied, doing his best to straighten his back. "He is lame, sir. His left leg is crippled. He never had an opportunity to serve in the military. He never had an opportunity to prove our house's worth through combat."

"Much good you did for your family's honor" Patûk said. "Are you your father's only son?"

Andu nodded.

"Better you had stayed home and stayed a minor house, for now you may not have a house after your death," Patûk said.

Andu fell to his knees and clutched at the General's cloak. When the old soldier pulled his cloak away, the easterner groveled at his feet.

"Disgusting," Patûk hissed.

"W-we have money, sir. M-my father w-will pay whatever you ask." He looked up at the General. "I-I w-will serve you if y-you wish. I trained at the academy in Fen-Stévock. We really don't hold strong allegiances to the Stévockians."

"No, you hold allegiances to whoever helps your status. Your family has no honor, does it?" Patûk pulled his boot away from the man as he tried to kiss it. "What is your father's name?"

"Andu, sir." When Andu looked up, his face was still bloody, but tear-streaked as well. "He is the f-fourth of his name. I am the fifth, sir. I will do w-whatever you ask me, sir."

"Yes, I am sure you would." The General looked up at one of the soldiers. "Take him away."

"To the prison tent, sir?" the soldier asked, his head bowed.

"No," the General replied. "Take him to my tent. You may leave him unchained. He will go nowhere. Will you?"

"No, sir."

The soldier led Andu away, and Patûk walked to the other prisoner, a bald man with eyelids that hung only half-open.

"And you?"

"Li, sir." The bald man gave the General a half bow, hands folded and hidden under the sleeves of his robe.

"Who are you?" Patûk asked.

"My last employment was as Cho's seneschal, sir. I served him for three years. Before that, I served in the House of Mafu'Sûn, as Lûk Mafu'Sûn's manservant."

"You left a moderately-sized home, with decent political power, and employ of that house's heir, to serve the master of a mining camp?" Patûk asked, a level of disbelief rising.

"Cho paid better, sir. And I did not see myself rising above the level of a simple manservant with House Mafu'Sûn," Li said. "I must admit, I am an opportunist, sir."

"Clearly." General Patûk Al'Banan groaned loudly and frowned. "And where do your loyalties lie?"

"A man of my status can ill-afford loyalties, sir," Li replied. "I have no status, no family name, no wealth."

"So, what shall we do with you?" Patûk didn't like this man. He looked smug, pompous, and, worse, he had no reason to be.

The General saw the bald man, eyes still half-open, purse his lips. Was he thinking, trying to figure out some opportunity for himself?

"I could be your seneschal, sir," Li finally said.

Yes, indeed. Opportunity.

"I have no need for a seneschal," Patûk replied.

"You have no need for a seneschal until you actually have a seneschal, sir," Li said. "Then, suddenly, all the menial work you once did, I do, and you can attend to more urgent matters."

"We will see." Patûk looked at the soldier behind Li and nodded. The soldier grabbed the seneschal by the elbow and led him away.

"Sir." Li's voice was lazy, uncaring. Patûk didn't like it. But, the General thought him a man who didn't speak unless he had something important to say, so when he called for the General, Patûk Al'Banan stopped the soldier leading him away and let the seneschal speak.

"As you know, sir, mercenaries in the service of Golgolithul came to Aga Min."

"That is no mystery," Patûk replied.

"They were with dwarves," Li added.

Patûk Al'Banan looked to Bu. The Lieutenant nodded.

"Indeed," Patûk replied.

"They fed Cho some story about accompanying these dwarves to visit family," Li said. "In fact, they gave Cho little indication that they were mercenaries."

"You didn't believe them," Patûk replied.

"No, sir."

"Did you tell Cho that you didn't believe them?" Patûk asked.

"He is—was—a hard-headed man, sir. Once he set his mind to something, he rarely changed it. They convinced him they were simple travelers accompanying dwarvish friends into the mountain."

Patûk looked at the seneschal through squinted eyes. Could he trust this man? Telling Patûk this information served him how?

"We will talk later," Patûk said.

Li gave the General a simple bow.

The General turned to Bu.

"I am going to put Andu under you, as a sergeant," Patûk said.

"His nobility deserves that much, and perhaps giving him some status and rank will help convince his father to support us financially.

Bu bowed, "As you wish, sir."

"I do not trust him, but I feel he might prove useful. I will send word to his father," the General said. He didn't know why he felt he needed to explain himself to Bu, but Bu he trusted.

"His wealth may prove necessary. At the first sign of dissention, kill him. At the same time, I want you to give this Li an opportunity to prove his worth. I want you to set him to some tasks around my tent—transcribing letters, caring for my armor, charting those parts of the Southern Mountains we have explored thus far."

Bu bowed again. "Yes, sir."

Patûk turned back to the cliff and watched the sun setting. The sky looked more and more like blood, but now it was dried blood, old blood, the blood of an untended wound. The dusk disguised the smoke, but he knew it was still there.

Patûk saw his personal guard, Bao Zi, walk from behind a tree. The old man quickly knelt before Patûk and rose.

"You sent for me, sir."

"Yes." Bao Zi was loyal. He was loyal beyond question, and yet not a drop of noble blood flowed through his veins. He was so loyal, he had taken arrows for Patûk, lost his eye for Patûk, left his family for Patûk. "What are the known dwarvish cities in this area of the Southern Mountains?"

Patûk turned his eyes back to the smoldering camp, and the Plains beyond. Dusk was fully on them. He could hear the wild dogs howling to one another. His trolls had kept them away, but they were gone now, and they smelled blood, they smelled death and decay.

"Thorakest is their principal city, General. There is Strongbur also, just south of here," Bao Zi said. "Ghezwath is in the Western Tor. Gerburton is a fair number of leagues east of here."

"Do we know the whereabouts of their surface entrances?" Patûk asked.

Dwarvish cities, albeit underground, always had at least one surface entrance. They typically guarded them heavily and had them expertly hidden away, in Patûk's experience.

"I believe we have an idea, sir," Bao Zi said. "Lieutenant Bu thinks the dwarves he killed were from Strongbur."

"Good. Concentrate on Strongbur and Thorakest, but watch the others as well," Patûk commanded. "Watch any movement that might indicate interest in Orvencrest. Bu has recovered a map to Orvencrest for us, but I don't know if the dwarves know where the city is; it seems as if they do not. There were dwarves at the Messenger's meeting in Finlo, and there were dwarvish mercenaries traveling with men."

"Are we looking for these mercenaries," Bao Zi asked, "the ones traveling with dwarves?"

"Yes," Patûk replied. "We lost two trolls to dwarves working with men. And they were seen in Aga Min, as well. I think, if anyone has a chance to find this city and deal with the ancient mysteries of these mountains, it would be the dwarves."

"Do you expect them to surface, sir?" Bao Zi asked.

"If Orvencrest is where the usurper thinks it is, in the southern range, they will have to surface at some point," Patûk replied. "They will have to cross one of the many dwarvish land bridges that connects the two ranges."

"So, we are both looking for the usurpers mercenaries," Bao Zi said, "and the lost dwarvish city?"

"Yes," Patûk replied.

"Aye, sir. And when we find these mercenaries," Bao Zi asked, "or any other dwarves?"

"If these mercenaries have found a way, we will follow them as far as we can," Patûk replied. "Dwarves are cunning, and I expect we won't be able to follow them too long without being discovered. Any other dwarves... kill them."

"And when these dwarvish mercenaries discover us?" Bao Zi asked. For a man of such lowly birth, he always asked the most intelligent questions.

"Attack," the General replied. "Take the dwarves prisoner. Force them to show us the way."

"Do you think they will, sir," Bao Zi asked.

"It doesn't matter how prideful someone is," Patûk replied with a sinister smile, "they always start talking when you begin removing appendages."

Chapter 36

TURK WAITED A DAY BEFORE starting Erik's training, and they met in one of the castle's many training rooms. Watched relentlessly by guards, Erik could sense their disapproving stares even through the helms covering their faces. But he didn't care. He had learned to deal with disapproval, whether it was in the pig sties of Venton, the lumber yards of Waterton, or as a porter to the likes of Switch. Rather than worry about the watching eyes, he threw himself into Turk's instruction.

The first day, Turk simply put Erik through exercises of strength and calisthenics, and there were no weapons in sight. Erik was ready to swing a sword and axe, throw a spear, and shoot three arrows from a bow with one draw of the string. But, despite his disappointment, he listened and did as Turk commanded. That first session ended with meditation and balance training. And then the next day and the day after that continued in much the same way.

"I don't understand," Erik said.

"What is that?" Turk asked.

"I am already strong," Erik replied. "I am fast and agile. When am I going to learn to use a blade?"

"You are strong. You have endurance. You are agile," Turk agreed. "But your greatest attribute, my friend, is your brain and your willingness to listen."

Turk poked Erik in the side of the head.

"You are smart," Turk said. "Do you trust me?"

"Of course," Erik replied. He thought about his response for a moment. He didn't know if he really had a reason to trust Turk. He had known the dwarf for maybe a month. They had fought alongside one another, but so had he and Switch, and he didn't trust Switch. And now they were little more than prisoners in a dwarvish city. But there was something about Turk. Yes, he trusted the dwarf.

"Then do what you are told," the dwarf said.

Erik nodded and bowed.

The next day, Erik met both Turk and Wrothgard.

"I am well versed in many fighting techniques," Turk said, "but when it comes to the blade, there is none better to teach you than a former eastern soldier."

Wrothgard stepped forward and bowed to both Erik and Turk.

"I am honored," Wrothgard said. "I understand, Erik, that you have been promised a great gift, a blade that is made specifically for you. But for now, due to the King's decree, we must use practice weapons."

Erik could sense a bit of angst in the soldier's voice.

A week passed, and Erik learned moves like *Striking Snake, Falling Star, Rising Sun, Hawk in Flight,* and *Woodman's Axe,* simple names the soldier called different movements with the sword. After the first day, Wrothgard was so happy with Erik's progress, he commanded he meet with him twice a day. He taught Erik how to fight with and without a shield. He taught Erik how to fight with only a shield, and then with just his hands.

Turk then continued that unarmed context and taught the young man a different style of hand fighting, and grappling, before he introduced the intricacies of fighting with a battle-axe. All the while, more guards gathered and watched, some of them staring, some of them chattering silently, some of them cheering quietly when Erik mastered a movement, and some of them shaking their heads and cursing. After that week, Bryon showed up.

"You are behind, Bryon," Turk said.

"It's not my fault," he replied. "I didn't know you were training my cousin."

"If you wish me to train you," Turk said, "that is the last time you will speak back to me. Do you understand?"

Bryon nodded with an irritated expression.

"I will train you, from the beginning," Turk said, "while Wrothgard concentrates on Erik's more advanced training."

Erik couldn't help smiling, although he did try to hide it. It wasn't often he got the betterment of his cousin.

Their training continued, and in another week, Erik started learning to use a staff and a spear. He spent hours training, even on his own after Wrothgard and his cousin left, and Turk went to work for Ilken. He felt stronger. He felt accomplished. For the first time since his father had taught him to catch his first fish, or shoot his first deer, or plant his first grain of wheat, Erik felt as if he had done something worthwhile. Bruises and welts grew along his arms—Wrothgard carried a thin stick with which he would strike Bryon and Erik when they made mistakes—but he owned each one of those marks, and he wore them with pride. The soreness in his muscles felt good. The fading aches in his joints said he was improving. The burning in his lungs when he ran told him every day he could run a little farther.

As the watching crowd grew too big—now with noble and aristocratic onlookers as well as the guards—word of men training in the ways of dwarvish tactics spread throughout the city. Turk and Wrothgard now decided to move their training to a more obscure location, with the King's permission, of course.

Erik sat in the new room after their second day there. Wrothgard and Turk had since left, leaving Bryon and Erik and two guards to watch them.

"I am going back to the room," Bryon said.

"Alright," Erik replied.

"Are you coming?"

"No," Erik replied. "I think I'll stay here for a while."

He sat cross-legged, hugging his knees to his chest and looking at a giant tapestry that almost covered one wall. It was an intricate thing, with depictions of continents and oceans and lands and mountains and forests and armies. At the very top of the tapestry was a giant, winged lizard, sewn to span the entire width of the wall-hanging. A man—armored from head to toe—stood under the beast.

"I don't think you should stay here," Bryon said.

"Why not?" Erik asked, looking up at his cousin. Bryon had a genuine look of concern on his face. "I won't be long," Erik added, "I have to meet Demik soon for my language lessons."

Erik had been meeting with Demik to learn Dwarvish. If he was going to be trapped in the city of Thorakest, rather than wallow in misery and boredom like Switch, complain about injuries like Befel, or drink himself into oblivion like Vander Bim, Erik decided he would learn everything he could.

"I don't trust them," Bryon replied.

"The dwarves?" Erik asked.

"Yes," Bryon said.

Erik looked to the dwarves. They looked kind enough, but then again, he had been a poor judge of character in the past.

"I appreciate your concern," Erik said in a hushed voice, "but I think I will be alright."

"Suit yourself," Bryon said with a tone of finality as he turned and walked out of the room with heavy steps.

Erik just shook his head as he turned back to the tapestry.

"It is beautiful, isn't it?"

Erik thought he recognized the voice and turned to see King Skella walking into the room. Erik stood quickly and bowed as the guards snapped to attention.

"You have created quite a commotion, Erik Eleodum," said the King.

"I didn't mean to," Erik said.

"The fault is really not yours," the King said with a laugh. "But people can't help themselves. A man, in the castle, learning to fight using dwarvish tactics, but yet, eastern tactics at the same time. And then also learning our language. Who knows how the public hears of these things?"

"Gossip, I suppose," Erik replied.

The King nodded with a smile. Then, his eyes trailed to the tapestry.

"Drak Vurm," King Skella said, pointing to the giant winged lizard.

"A dragon," Erik said.

"Aye, a dragon in Westernese," the King replied. "They roamed the skies in the old days—some good, some bad. All terrible."

"How can something be good and terrible at the same time?" Erik asked.

"Indeed," the King said. "Those that were our allies were good, but still dangerous. Nonetheless, they are all gone now. The devastation of the Drak Vurm is legendary. The knight, however…"

"What of him, Your Majesty?" Erik asked.

"He is of your people, Erik Eleodum," the King replied. "The last of the dragon slayers, defender of free peoples, and foe to the Shadow. We don't know his name, but many suspect he was from the far west, from what is now known as Gongoreth, and ancestor to the people who now live in northwestern Háthgolthane."

The King stepped forward.

"You are a good man," the King said.

"Your Majesty," Erik replied with a bow.

"I have made many mistakes in my life," the King said, "and keeping you here, not letting you go off to find Orvencrest, may be one of them, but I have always been a good judge of character. I have always been good at reading a man's heart."

"I'm touched, Your Majesty," Erik said.

"I don't just say that as a frivolous thing," the King said. "You will do great things with your life, Erik Eleodum. They may not be here, but you come from strong blood. Remember that. Pay attention to Turk and Wrothgard and Demik. And keep an eye on your cousin and make sure he trains as hard as you, eh?"

"Yes, Your Majesty," Erik said with a bow.

"Get some rest," King Skella said. "Tomorrow is a new day, and that always brings new challenges."

Chapter 37

Erik stretched and yawned, sitting up in his bed and feeling refreshed. His brother and cousin were gone. His wash basin was empty. The closet was empty. His bags were gone. It was as if the room had never been used. He turned to look at his bed. It was undisturbed, sheets clean and pressed.

Erik opened the door and walked down to the bathroom. The heat of the room seeped from underneath the door. The smell of mint hit his nose when he entered, but behind that smell, though, was the stink of stale, wet clothes. The bathroom was empty, and a thick mist hung above the large, pond-sized bath.

As he walked towards the stone tub, the mist seemed to swirl around him, his ankles, and away from the water. It left clear spots so Erik could see the water, stale, deep and dark—almost black. Something moved and sent ripples towards the edge.

Erik knelt down at the bath's edge, waving the mist away. All he saw was deep, dark, black water. Small waves lapped against the side of the tub, and he saw something float to the surface. A face, mouth open in a silent scream, burst from the water.

Erik lurched backwards, his back and head slamming against the white deck.

"Damn dreams," he said.

He rubbed his head hard as pain shot through his neck and shoulders. He rolled to his stomach and pushed himself to his feet. He looked to the bath and a head, floating like an apple, bobbed along the water's surface. The head turned towards Erik, and he covered his mouth. Tears filled his eyes, and his hands shook, sweat collecting around his ears, and at the back of his neck.

"Turk."

His beard looked ragged and torn as his tongue lolled out of his mouth like a panting dog. His eyes were half-closed, barely revealing white pupils. His face looked pale, milky white like the moon. Now Erik saw more heads. Vander Bim and Demik. Wrothgard. Even Rory, Bo, and Del Alzon.

"It's a damn dream," Erik repeated, closing his eyes, and trying to make himself wake up.

Then he saw Bryon and Befel. Erik choked. He wanted to scream or cry or vomit but couldn't.

He looked at the deep, dark, black water.

"Blood."

He stood straight, staring at them as they stared back from across the pool.

Yessss.

It was a chorus of painful, ear-raking hissing. He saw their faces. Just a few days had rotted their flesh. Skin barely clung to their bones, and what skin remained had turned black. Maggots danced in and out of eye sockets, and they lumbered like slow golems.

Slavers. Murderers. Rapists. They jumped into the pool of blood and waded towards him. He could see the excitement in their rotting faces, in those vacant eye sockets. Erik crouched, like a cat, waiting to attack. They inched further. He pressed his fingers on the decking until they turned white.

"I told you," he said, "you have no power over me."

"We don't care what you say," they hissed together.

One made its way to his side of the pool, clawed at the edge, tried to pull itself out. Erik kicked its skull. Bone cracked under his boot, and the thing shrieked as it fell back into the pool of blood. Another came, and Erik kicked it. Its skull shattered into a thousand pieces.

The sharp, stinging smell of rotten meat struck Erik's nose. He looked to his right, and there was one of them, next to him, clawing at him. He stepped back, swung with a clenched fist, and hit it so hard, its jaw hung loosely to the rest of its skull by rotting ligament. Erik's foot slipped on the spilled blood, and he fell forwards. He reached out to grab the bath's edge, but it was no good, and he toppled in, the thick liquid washing over him as blood entered his mouth.

Erik burst upwards with a gasp and flailed about, trying to get to the bath's edge and pushing severed heads out of the way. He felt vulnerable as if the dead that haunted his dreams could hurt him there. They lurched towards him, moaning with malevolent groans.

As he scrambled to get out, severed heads snapped at him, cracking their teeth as their jaws crashed together. Teeth dug into his sides, into his legs. Blood poured from his body, teeth sticking into his flesh. The hot breath of the dead men flooded over him, but he continued to push himself through the blood; it was as if he were running on the spot. Finally, he reached the edge, almost jumping from the tub.

He felt the scratch of a bony finger on the back of his leg but did not look back as he heard the wicked laugh of the dead.

"You can never escape us."

He burst through the bathroom's door, but it was not the hallway that he ran into. Rather, it was a mountain ledge, the underground ledge on which they traveled in order to get to Thorakest. Before he could stop himself, he flew off the edge and into the dark ravine below. Down he fell, into the dark, falling, darkness, falling, darkness, falling…laughing, hissing, behind him.

Chapter 38

"WITH SUMMER CLOSE AT HAND, we have seen little movement in the Plains of Güdal, sir," Captain Kan explained, "and not a single ship has sailed east from Finlo this month."

"Why?" Patûk stood, his back popping as he leaned left and then right. He looked as stout as any young man, any soldier under his command, but many times, his body said otherwise. He could no longer stoop over maps and battle plans for hours on end and not feel it in his bones.

"Our sources tell us the usurper's efforts across the Giant's Vein have slowed as of late, sir," Kan expounded.

"And what have you learned, Lieutenant?" the General asked.

"Our spies," Lieutenant Bu replied, "have informed me that the resources in Antolika have been diverted. They tell me the garrisons along Golgolithul's northern borders have been strengthened, almost doubled, sir. The usurper is even strengthening his lands that border Gol-Nornor. He has also sent advisors to Hámon. I haven't found out why yet; nonetheless, he is giving the Dukes and the King of Hámon council on something, sir."

"If he sways Hámon to his banner, he could take the rest of the west." Kan poked at an outstretched map of Háthgolthane, almost jabbing his finger through the cloth.

"What could that fool be up to?" Patûk's utterances were only for him but loud enough for the Captain and Lieutenant to hear. They replied with a shrug. "Have you heard from General Abashar?"

General Pavin Abashar—Patûk was less than enthusiastic when he said his name. The taking over of the council by the Lord of the East—the title left the taste of sour milk in Patûk's mouth—left a number of resistance movements throughout the eastern kingdom and beyond. Patûk Al'Banan's proved the largest and most organized. Another deposed general, not from the Eastern Guard like General Al'Banan but from the regular army, named Pavin Abashar, led the second largest resistance movement—an army two-thirds the size of Patûk's. Patûk found him petty and disorganized, prone to misappropriation of resources for the simple show of strength and desire for battle. On more than one occasion, General Abashar had razed a town that could have easily been swayed to the *cause* just because they had entertained a Stévockian. Or, he might kill a noble prisoner because he didn't like the way he spoke, or the way he walked, when that noble's family could readily pay a hefty ransom.

Nonetheless, Patûk Al'Banan found himself in a position where he thought it advantageous to join forces. He had concentrated his men in the Southern Mountains and southwestern Háthgolthane. Pavin Abashar had concentrated his along the Yeryman Straits and southeastern Háthgolthane, even into Antolika and the Shadow Marshes. How many men did Pavin have under his command? He asked the question.

"Ten thousand in total, sir." Bu seemed unsure of his answer. His hesitation to the question, his crinkled eyebrows, his tight jaw all spoke to that. He was a man of integrity, however, so Patûk would trust his answer, even if it proved a best guess.

"Aye, General, I would agree with that—at least close to it," Kan said.

If Kan and Bu both said it, it must be close to true. That was a lot of men. Of course, they would be spread over a thousand miles. But still.

"And how many do we have?" Patûk asked.

"Just over thirteen thousand, sir." Bu seemed surer of that answer.

That proved less than Patûk Al'Banan had thought, less than what he had hoped.

"Your men are certainly better trained, more prepared for battle and combat, more willing to take your commands to the death, sir," Kan said.

"Yes, of course, Captain Kan. You need not entertain me with hyperbolic flattery in this tent."

The Captain bowed.

"Should we send envoys to Hámon?" Patûk Al'Banan rarely asked questions that revealed his uncertainties, even in his private councils.

"Personally, I do not like the men of Hámon." Kan stiffened as he spoke. His frown lengthened the crow's feet at the edges of his dark eyes. The thick, furled eyebrows above those eyes created lines along his forehead. His jaw clenched, and the gray hairs at his temple bristled. "I find them untrustworthy and petty."

"Better to deter them from allying with the usurper, sir," Bu said to Kan.

The Captain gave Bu a sidelong glance and then nodded.

"Captain Kan, I wish you to lead a small envoy to Hámon and meet with King Cedric," the General said. "You will explain to the King that if he chooses to ally himself with the usurper, there exists little in terms of eastern influence in the west. You must explain to him that many might be upset by an alliance between Hámon and Golgolithul. You must explain to him that this might create unwanted enemies and that the usurper has little to protect his kingdom in the west."

"Aye, sir," Kan replied with a bow.

"And Bu," Patûk continued, "you will position men across The Crack. Have Lieutenant Phurnan command them—and take the trolls. We will both search for this lost dwarvish city and the remaining mercenaries in the employ of the usurper."

Bu bowed low and then both he and Captain Kan left Patûk's tent. The General walked to a simple, wooden chair in the corner of his tent and took a seat. A pewter pitcher waited on a small wooden table next to the chair accompanied by a pewter cup. The General poured some of the pitcher's contents into the cup. He picked it up, swirled the cup, and the smell of spiced wine made him smile.

He took a drink and leaned back in his chair. Why couldn't things be as simple as they used to be? When he was a young man, things just seemed so easy. Take your orders, carry them out, and face the consequences. Success meant reward and life. Failure meant punishment and death. Simple.

He looked into his cup of mulled wine, at the streaks of cinnamon and nutmeg as they swirled around the edges of the cup. He sighed.

"The answer is simple. The world is changing. I am changing."

Chapter 39

CLOUDS ROLLED AWAY TO THE north, casting a shadow, a dark veil of rain below them. To the east, the new sun shooed away the mist that gathered just above the ground, wisps of gray running like scared ghosts. The west remained dark, and to the south, in the great distance, tall, white clouds loomed, speaking of more rains to come.

Bo flicked his reins, and one of his oxen replied with a deep groan and a quick snort as the wooden wheels rolled through wet grass.

"I know, boys."

He rubbed his face and reached between his legs, grabbing a ceramic bottle. He bit the cork, pulled it loose with a pop, and spit it into his lap. He put the bottle to his lips and took a quick drink. The muscles in his jaw tightened, and he clicked his tongue.

"That good?"

Bo looked to his left with a start. He saw Mardirru riding next to him, looking forward, watching the distant Gray Mountains flicker in and out of vision through the rain and the clouds.

Bo shook his head. "Aye."

"Are you all right?" Mardirru asked.

"Just tired, my friend," Bo replied.

"Let Dika drive. Get some rest. Sleep."

Bo smirked and chuckled under his breath. He looked over his shoulder. Dika slept soundly in the back of their carriage with their children, snoring softly as she always did even though she would never admit it.

"Dika drove all day yesterday. Besides, I can't sleep even if I try. I see them, Mardirru. Every time I close my eyes, I see them."

"The children? Those we've lost?" Mardirru asked.

"Aye, I see them," Bo replied. "But, when I close my eyes, I mostly see…"

"Erik and Befel. Bryon," Mardirru said. "That is who you see mostly."

Bo nodded his head.

"I see them too."

"I worry." Bo flicked the reins again and took another drink of the brandy in his ceramic bottle.

"As do I," Mardirru agreed. "They are safe, for now."

"How can you know that?" Bo asked. "And what do you mean by *for now*?"

"I don't know how I know." Mardirru always kept his eyes forward, always watched his people, his caravan, his children. "I just know. But they are about to encounter great danger. I had a dream about it last night. The visions I saw in my sleep were so vivid, so real, I was sure it had happened when I opened my eyes."

"What did you see?"

"Darkness, Bo, darkness. And in that darkness, I saw yellow eyes and white teeth. I felt fire burn my face and heard something like wings, but it was a hurricane, a tornado, and I felt it pick me up and whip me about like a doll. I heard a growl and a roar that, if I were awake, would have burst my ears and caused me to go deaf. Then I saw him—Erik. He was there, but he didn't look like himself. He looked as if he had aged ten years. He looked sad, angry, but strong. He—they—are about to be tested. Their faith is about to be tested. Their strength is about to be tested. Their will is about to be tested."

"I will pray for them," Bo said, "every day and every night."

"They will need it."

Bo noticed a small farm to his right, one that had the green shoots of—what would be growing this time of the year—corn and wheat in neat rows.

"We are near their homeland," Bo said.

"Who?" Mardirru asked.

"Erik and Bryon and Befel. I believe this is near their farmstead. North and east of Hámon. Land rich for farming. Yes, they are from here."

Bo saw a cart ahead of their caravan. It looked like a single horse pulled the cart, which looked simple with sides of slatted wood. It looked as if the man next to the cart had stopped his horse and he was on one knee, looking at either a cartwheel or perhaps the horse's hoof. When the front of the gypsy caravan started passing the man, he stopped what he was doing and stared.

As Bo's carriage came closer to the cart, he could see more of the man. He looked to be a short and broad-shouldered man, older with graying hair poking out the bottom of a wide-brimmed straw hat. He had no shoes, and his pants looked as if the man had cut them off just below the knee. When Bo was next to the man, he stopped. He could hear Dika stir in the back of the carriage.

"Is everything all right, my sweet?" Dika asked groggily.

"Aye, my dear," Bo replied. "Everything is fine. Go back to sleep."

The man looked up at Bo, standing straight. When he rubbed his chin, making a rough sound over the stubble as he did, the muscles in his forearms undulated and flexed. Even though his straw hat somewhat shadowed his face, the gypsy could see that the farmer had a rough face, not ugly, but worn from years of hard work. He had a squinty eye, and his chin bore a deep cleft, his mouth curved into a frown, and Bo could see a bulge in the left side of his lower lip.

"Can I help you?" He spit a black, inky stuff on the ground as he spoke.

"Black root," Bo muttered, then elevated the volume of his voice. "Perhaps."

"We don't see gypsies up in these parts much." The man spit

again and then slapped the flank of his horse as the animal snorted and stamped hard.

"What seems to be the problem?" Bo asked, nodding to the horse and the cart.

"None of your business." The farmer turned to the horse, stamping again, and groaned. "Stop that."

Bo stared for a while, and the farmer just stared back with that squinty look, spitting every once in a while.

"If there's something wrong with your horse, or your cart, we can help," Bo said.

"I don't much trust gypsies," the farmer replied. "I let you help and find myself with no seed, no cart, and no horse."

"I can assure you—"

"I don't care about your assurances," the farmer snapped.

"What seems to be the matter?" Mardirru asked, riding back to Bo.

"This farmer needs help of some sort, but he won't tell me what, so I am inclined to leave him here and let him suffer whatever trouble he is having."

"Nonsense," Mardirru replied. He looked to the farmer. "Good sir, what seems to be the matter? See that we do not need anything you have. We don't need your seed. We don't need your cart—we have plenty of those. And we don't need your horse. Let us help."

The farmer eyed them, spitting several more times.

"There's something wrong with my horse's shoe," he finally relented. "And because my horse started walking off the road, I have a broken wheel on the other side."

"We will fix them for you, both the shoe and the wheel," Mardirru said.

"And what do you want in return?" the farmer asked cautiously.

"Nothing," the gypsy leader replied.

Within moments, gypsy men were either shoeing the man's horse or working on the cart's wheel. The farmer eyed them suspiciously as they worked, but after a little while, he seemed to relax.

"What is your name?" Bo asked, who stayed up in his carriage.

"Jovek," the man replied.

"Are you familiar with all the farmsteads in these lands?" Bo asked.

"Aye," Jovek replied. "I've lived here my whole life. My family's farmed here for more than a hundred years. Why?"

"Do you know the Eleodums?" Bo asked again.

Jovek looked at Bo with a hard, steely look. The gypsy thought that perhaps this wasn't the land of the Eleodums. Or, perhaps their name struck a negative chord with Jovek.

"Aye, I know them," Jovek replied. "Rikard's got the largest farmstead 'round here, next to mine. His brother, Brant, not as big, but still decent."

"Rikard," Bo said to himself more than Jovek. "He must be the father of Erik and Befel."

"Aye," Jovek said. "He was... is."

"Can you show me where they live?" Bo asked.

Jovek just stared at Bo.

Chapter 40

"I THOUGHT WE WERE GOING to Waterton."

Kehl had grown weary of Len's questioning. He looked to A'Uthma. His Lieutenant seemed to understand what Kehl wanted.

"Shut your mouth, you worthless pig," A'Uthma said, "before I gut you."

Kehl hoped no one else could see his smile.

"Im'Ka'Da." A'Uthma spoke in Samanian. He always did when he didn't want the others to know, didn't want to question Kehl in front of the others. "Why are we going to Finlo?"

"As backwards a town as it is, we cannot attack Waterton with only six men. We must recruit more, and I know just the place in Finlo."

"Ah, I see, Im'Ka'Da. My apologies for questioning you."

Kehl, again, hoped none of his men saw his smile. "No apologies needed."

Kehl stuck to the western streets of Finlo for two reasons. Firstly, it hadn't been long since he and his men had burned down some fool's barbershop and left that fool in the street with one less finger. Finlo tolerated no crime—none. The crows' cages lining the road leading into the seaside city proved that. Most of the men that filled those cages were petty thieves, starving boys stealing bread. Secondly, the western streets of Finlo were the residence of Toth.

"Who be this Toth?" Albin asked.

Kehl turned sharply. He hated Albin's face. It was too thin, with a pointy chin and a thin nose that wheezed when he breathed hard. And in the shadows of the buildings of West Finlo, his sunken eyes looked almost black. Truth be told, he should have sacrificed Albin instead of Pierce. Not a day passed when Len didn't ask about the man. Truly, he had to have figured it out by now. What did he think, he just disappeared with four other men, just left? They all had to have figured it out.

"Hush. All of you. Shut your mouths. Look at no one and say nothing, especially his name."

Kehl turned and continued to walk.

"He is the guild master of the largest thieves' guild in Finlo. When I still lived in Saman, he was my smuggling contact. And when I moved to Háthgolthane with my brothers…" Kehl stopped for a moment. Something caught in his throat as if a piece of bread was stuck there. "When I moved to Háthgolthane, it was he who was the only one brave enough to receive and ship slaves."

He stopped at a windowless, two-story building whose frontage belied its depth complexity. A single, wooden door stood in the center of the building. It looked thick and worn, splintered and cracked. It was dark with moisture, and Kehl's nose curled at the smell of mold and stale wetness. He really hated the ocean and its scents.

Kehl's knock sounded muffled. He would have to hit that door with a mallet to make any significant noise. However, the sound of iron scratching iron resonated from behind the door, and it cracked open, just enough for the whisper of a voice to escape.

"Tehel klun?"

"Kehl, the Samanian."

"Tehel fen?" said the voice from within the darkness behind the thick, wooden door.

"What do you mean, who do I want to speak with?" Kehl hissed. "Who else would I want to bloody speak with?"

A hiss escaped the darkness, and the door quickly shut. Perhaps he should have been a little more cordial. These thieves did have a rather inflated view of themselves, being the largest guild in south-western Háthgolthane.

"These heathens," A'Uthma spat. "They would shut the door on us like dogs."

"They will be back," Kehl said, hoping he was right. "They need us as much as we need them."

They waited for a while then the scratching of iron on iron came from behind the door again and it cracked open, this time a little wider, wide enough for a man to pass into the darkness.

"Follow me," said the doorkeeper. Kehl could barely see the cloaked man in the dim light.

They walked down a winding staircase with a fading torch spaced at every thirty paces or so, just enough to cast a faint light on the steps, so people wouldn't miss a step and fall and break their neck. It seemed that every time Kehl visited this thieves' guild, his guide led him down a different set of stairs, a different hallway, through different doors into different rooms.

The stairs finally opened to a large room, well-lit and spacious.

"What is on their faces?" A'Uthma asked in Samanian, referring to the two dozen men and women who stood or sat around the room.

"A thief's mask," Kehl answered in the same language.

"No talking," a deep voice said, hard and rough. His voice sounded muffled from behind the white, long-nosed mask. "In any language."

Kehl looked to the man who spoke, a large, broad-shouldered man underneath the long, thick, black cloak and disguising mask. He was no thief. Too big. A tough. A guild guard. Perhaps a bodyguard. Kehl bowed slightly and hoped the big man could see the insincere smirk on his face.

"Kehl, my friend."

Dogs. They threw the word *friend* around like it meant nothing. A cloaked man at the end of the room walked towards Kehl. He was a slight man, even under the cloak, and as soon as he got closer, he threw off his mask to reveal a soft face with round cheeks and blue eyes.

"Kehl, it has been entirely too long." When he came face to face with Kehl—truly, this cloaked man stood a half a head shorter than Kehl—he threw his arms around him and squeezed him hard.

"Just so." Kehl tried to make his voice sound as indifferent as possible. He only came to Toth when he needed something, and the guild master knew it.

"Come now, my Samanian friend, let us drink a cup of wine together and discuss business. I always enjoy doing business with you."

Toth's wine always tastes sweet... with poison, Kehl thought.

"You are too kind," Kehl said. He jerked his head forward, motioning for his men to follow.

"And your men, shall they want wine as well?" Toth asked.

"No, they are fine."

"So few this time," Toth said with too much frivolity in his voice. "You typically visit with at least a dozen men. Is something the matter?"

Kehl followed Toth to a table at the other end of the room. On it sat a silver platter with bread and cheese and a silver pitcher and half a dozen silver cups. Toth poured one cup for himself and one for Kehl.

"Quite an entourage you have here," Kehl said, sniffing his cup of wine, "and in such interesting attire. Are you having a party?"

"Have we known each other for such a short period of time that we cannot trust one another?" Toth asked, a hurt look on his face that was clearly pretense.

He must've seen Kehl sniffing his wine. He smiled and took a hearty draught of his wine. Sweet? Yes. Poisoned? Kehl let it sit in his mouth for a moment. No.

"Good, yes?" Toth didn't wait for Kehl to answer. "A party. Yes. Of sorts. We are celebrating the end of spring and offering up prayers to Hymur, for a plentiful summer season."

"Any chance for drinking and orgies," Kehl said.

"Ha! Too true, my friend." Toth laughed, slapping Kehl on the shoulder. "So, is your visit pleasure or business?"

"Business," Kehl replied.

"Ah, pity," Toth said.

As they drank, Kehl noticed Toth's thieves removing their cloaks and masks. They passed jugs of, presumably, some type of liquor and took hearty draughts while female thieves began to snuggle up close to their menfolk.

"Is your party over?" Kehl asked.

Toth shook his head as a pretty, little, dark-haired woman walked up next to him, brushed his cheek with a slender finger and slid her other hand inside his cloak. A wide smile spread across the thief's face.

"It's just begun."

"Then, shall we speak our business before your party gets going?" Kehl asked.

"Indeed," Toth said. He snapped a finger, and the table of wine disappeared. Another snap and a slender door appeared in the wall where the table had been. Toth opened the door to a dark room, but another snap lit the torches, illuminating a small office with a desk, four chairs, a table, and a wall of bookshelves and books.

Kehl could feel the frown on his face. Magic irritated him. Thieves' magic infuriated him. All trickery and treachery. Toth walked to the desk, his woman following, and sat. She stood just behind him.

"Please, sit." The guild master opened his hand, presenting the four chairs sitting in front of the desk.

Kehl walked into the office and sat.

"Would your men like to sit? I can get more chairs."

"No," Kehl said. "They can stand."

As he sat, six large men walked in behind his own. Toughs. Toth's guards.

"So, what is your business?" Toth asked.

"What has my business always been? Slaves," Kehl answered, "and men. I need more men."

Toth cocked an eyebrow, and Kehl realized his admission.

"Business is growing. I don't have enough men," Kehl said, trying to cover his mistake. He cursed himself inwardly. Fool.

"Right. Well," Toth said, his fingers steepled in front of his face, "I have been thinking about getting out of the slave business."

Kehl felt his stomach twist. The vein in his neck thumped harder and quickened.

"Prices in your homeland have gone up. And the Finnish authorities have become increasingly aware of the underground here. It is a recipe that has ended many guilds and guild masters. I think I might just stick to pickpocketing and prostitution for a while. I have even considered postponing my smuggling trips to Crom."

"You can't." Kehl immediately cursed himself for his outburst.

"Oh, I can, and I will," Toth said, placing his hands on the desk and leaning forward.

"Im'Ka'Da." A'Uthma spoke Samanian in a whispered voice. "We should leave. This man seems false."

Kehl put a hand up. "It would be a bad financial decision to end our business agreement."

Toth laughed. "As if you are my only customer? As if it is your business that keeps me afloat? Pittance."

Kehl sat back. His face grew hot.

"And as for men, well, I think it might be a cold day in the seven hells before any of the thieves of Finlo would work for some Samanian pimp."

Now Kehl knew his face was red, and he heard a hissing curse come from A'Uthma. He heard the slightest sound of iron sliding against leather.

Toth now leaned forward on his elbows, a crooked, malicious smile on his face. "However, I might be able to find room in my employ for you and your men. Some of my men enjoy the company of other men. I am sure you might fit the bill."

"Hold your tongue, Fin, before I cut it out," Kehl spat.

"With what army, Kehl." Toth sat back. His woman had placed

a hand on his shoulder, and he rubbed it gently. "No, I believe this is it. I believe these five men are your entourage. You wouldn't have waited for so long to threaten me if it wasn't. I believe this is the end of your road, Samanian."

Len was the first to fall. Kehl knew it was he by the whining whimper he let out. He turned to see Ret falling, half his dark-bearded face gone, a bloody mess of skin and flesh. Ret was the last to fall. A'Uthma slid his scimitar across one tough's throat while the dagger in his other hand jabbed into the soft flesh just below another's chin. Flemming lifted another guard over his head, throwing him into the wall with a loud crunch. Albin ran another through.

Kehl turned to Toth. "I told you, a bad business decision."

"Samanian filth," Toth spat. "I'm going to cut your balls off, throw you in one of my pleasure houses for a month, and then slit your throat."

"The threats of a dead man," Kehl said with a smile. "They never cease to amuse me."

Kehl drew his scimitar. Toth tried to jump over the desk, knife in each hand, but Kehl kicked the guild master's desk forward. It caught Toth's shins, and he fell forward, face smacking the desk hard. Kehl heard the air escape the man's lungs, and he brought his scimitar down hard on Toth's shoulder. His blade punched through the man and stuck into the wood of the desk. He left it there.

Toth's woman screamed and retrieved her own dagger. She jumped over the desk, bringing her blade down hard at Kehl. He stepped out of the way, bringing his fist to her face. She fell backwards, the back of her head hitting the desk. She crumbled to the floor, motionless.

"You should've kept our business arrangement, Toth." The guild master squirmed as he tried to free himself from Kehl's sword. "Greed, the bane of every thief. We could've made each other rich, you Háthgolthanian dog."

"My men will kill you. Whatever you do to me, they will kill you."

Kehl laughed.

"Are you so foolish? How have you made it this far? How have you stayed alive this long? You know as well as any that thieves have no allegiances."

A knock came at the office door.

"Toth, you all right?"

"See," Toth seethed.

"An opportunist," Kehl said. "I am sure he would sooner see you dead so he might take your place. Now, where are your books?"

Kehl leaned on the scimitar pinning Toth to the table. Another knock came.

"What... books? I... don't... know... what..."

"Stop," Kehl said. "Don't attempt to lie to me. Your books of business, with your contacts and your whorehouses and your smugglers. Where are they?"

"Boss, what's going on in there?" came from the other side of the door as Toth shook his head.

Kehl covered Toth's mouth as he slid a dagger across the back of his left ear, removing it from his head. He felt the man's scream, a combination of sound and blood and drool, against his palm. When it finally stopped, he unclasped his mouth.

"Your books?"

"Piss off." Kehl could tell Toth forced the curse. He wanted to tell him. Perhaps one more body part. A finger. One that mattered. Not the little finger. No one cared about their little finger. A thumb.

He felt the scream against his hand again. Toth felt underneath the lip of his desk, squeezed something, and with a click, a panel in the office wall slid sideways, revealing a neatly stacked pile of books.

"Good boy." Kehl patted the man's head. "Now, your Thieves' Cants."

That took considerably more effort. Perhaps there was a little honor amongst thieves. Toth truly did not want to give up his book of thieves' incantations and spells. Kehl really did hate magic but couldn't help recognizing it might come in handy. Another thumb, a nose, another ear, two more fingers, and the flesh off one cheek.

That is what it took. Another button. Another panel in the wall. The Thieves' Cant now belonged to Kehl.

"This could've gone much differently, Toth," Kehl said.

"Im'Ka'Da," A'Uthma said at another knock at the office door. Kehl could tell a crowd grew at the door, a restless crowd. He nodded to his Lieutenant.

"I wish it had. I wish it hadn't come to this." Kehl retrieved his sword and looked at the bloody mess of a man, groaning and moaning as he lay on his desk. "No, I think that is a lie. This is much better for me. I will replenish my ranks with your men—and perhaps women. I will become wealthier than I had ever hoped to. And I will avenge my brothers."

Toth tried pushing himself up. Fool. Kehl brought his scimitar down hard, removing the head from the body. He looked to his three remaining men.

"Flemming and Albin, you now hold a special place. As we build this empire, you will be second only to A'Uthma."

He picked up the head of Toth and nodded to A'Uthma.

Kehl walked through the door, Toth's head lifted high in his clutched fingers. Many of Toth's thieves were naked, engaged in their festivities. As he emerged from the office, gasps rippled through the crowd of thieves, and some woman in the back of the crowd screamed.

"You are now mine," Kehl cried.

"The hell I am," spat one thief.

A second later, a thin knife appeared in the thief's eye, and he fell back, dead. Kehl looked over his shoulder. Albin gave him a quick wink.

There must've been forty thieves in that room, but as Kehl walked about them, showing each one the head of Toth, they cowered.

Weak. Dogs. Fools. Things would change. All who resisted would die. He would build an empire, and the first to face his wrath would be the men of Waterton.

Chapter 41

"It's been years since I've visited Dûrn Tor," Del Alzon said. The city came into view, half-hidden by the rolling hills of the Western Tor.

"I hope it was a pleasant visit," Maktus said.

"Aye, it was." Del could feel himself smiling. He remembered a tall pint of beer, a long pipe with cherry-flavored pipe weed, and a beautiful dark-haired girl with big...eyes. "Dûrn Tor has always been a pleasant place, a good place to visit. Good drink. Good women. Peaceful."

"Aye, fer sure. Peaceful. That's what I love about this place," Yager added. "They used to have this place—*The Hill Giant*—good beef."

"And there it is," Del Alzon said. "I'll never forget those antlers. It had to have been a hill giant to bring down such a creature."

Del Alzon paid a young boy to stable their horses. When he opened the door, he took a deep breath.

"Beef," he muttered. "Spiced wine."

He pulled at his pants. Through their travels to the Blue Forest, to Finlo, and then to Dûrn Tor, Del Alzon found himself tightening his girdle until he couldn't tighten it anymore. Looking down, he still had a belly that blocked any vision of his feet, and he still waddled when he walked, but his horse did seem to groan and complain less when he mounted the beast.

"I'll have to make a new hole," he whispered to himself.

"And what do we have here?" The voice sounded harsh and scratchy, and Del thought he remembered it. "What do you need?"

"Has this place always been so hospitable?" Maktus asked.

"You don't like my table manners?" The short woman walked up to Maktus, face red and eyebrows curled into a frown. The bun pulled tightly atop her head seemed to quiver, and even though her eyes only reached Maktus' chest, she seemed to tower over him. "You can just see your way out. Don't let the door hit you in the ass."

"No, no, Ms. Minx. Your table manners are just fine." Del Alzon bowed to the woman. "There are no better in all of Southland. We would like a table please, some of your world-renowned roasted beef, and a cup of your fine spiced wine for each one of my men."

She whirled on Del Alzon. "Flattery will get you nowhere in here, son. If you know my name, you ought to know that already."

"Indeed." Del straightened. "So, how about that beef and wine?"

She looked him up and down. Her glare seemed to burn him and freeze him all at the same time. She jerked her head to the side.

"Follow me," said Elena Minx as she led them to their seats.

"Do I look like that when I walk?" Del muttered, watching the way her arms swung outward to the side and the way her hips juggled as she waddled. For such a short woman, she was quite large, larger than the last time he saw her.

"Here's your table." Elena Minx turned and presented a large, round table to Del.

"This'll be just fine. Thanks."

"It'll have to be. It's all we have."

Del looked around the room. The dining area of *The Hill Giant* looked to be built for a hundred men and not even a dozen sat there now. He nodded.

"Maktus, Danitus, Gregory, Yager, spiced wine and roast beef for you?" Del asked.

"It'll have to be, 'cause that's all you're getting."

Del Alzon looked at the chunky hostess. He hoped his smile didn't look too facetious.

"Very well."

"If you've been here before, you know the rules," Elena Minx said, "but I'll go over them again. There are no whores here. If you offer a woman money for her services, she'll probably slap you, and you right deserve it."

"We've no interest in whores," Danitus said.

"Oh, well, look at you. And it's a good thing, 'cause I'm sure no whore would want you. Now, can I finish, or are you going to continue to interrupt me?"

Del Alzon looked to Danitus, whose face bespoke a little boy whose mother had just scolded him.

"There'll be no fighting. Tuc and Boz'll see to that. Kitchen closes at midnight, not a minute later. We serve good drink—"

"The best in Southland," Del Alzon interrupted.

Elena Minx squinted and pursed her lips but said nothing. He thought she might have even smiled.

"But if you can't lift your head off the table, you've drunk too much, and you'll find yourself waking up in the stables."

"Just like I remember," Del said.

Elena Minx gave him a harrumph but said nothing more. She turned and left them, and only a moment later, a younger woman came by to serve them roasted beef and spiced wine.

"What are we doing here, Del?" Danitus asked.

Del stared into his cup of wine. It swirled about as he tilted the cup this way and that. He could see brown flakes, cinnamon maybe, floating about. Expensive anywhere else. Not in Southland, so close to the sea. How many people even knew what cinnamon was? Would a poor boy from Golgolithul ever have known what cinnamon was if it wasn't for the army?

"How many lives did it take so I could know what bloody cinnamon is? How much blood is spilt in this cup? Son of a whore. Indeed, what are we doing here?"

"What are you saying?" Yager asked. "Yer making no sense."

"No, I suppose I'm not," admitted Del.

"You wanted to save the slaves," Maktus said, "and we did that.

What more is there to do? You want to find these boys. They could be anywhere. They could be dead for all we know."

"Don't say that!" Del hadn't meant to yell. Over his shoulder, he saw a bald man, large and broad and mean looking, eyeing him. He couldn't remember which one he was, Tuc or Boz. Either one, catching their attention normally proved bad. He looked down and realized he had grabbed Maktus' wrist. He squeezed so hard the man's hand started turning white. He let go.

"Sorry. Sorry. I overreacted. I'm sorry."

"What is the matter with you?" Maktus asked, rubbing his wrist. "What are you trying to do here?"

Del stared at his cup again. "Clear my conscience."

He motioned for the serving girl.

"Yes."

"Can you get Elena for me please?"

A moment later, the fat, old woman came waddling, flat lips and flared nostrils showing displeasure.

"What?" She placed her hands on the table and leaned forward. The wood creaked under her weight.

"I—we are looking for three boys."

"No girls. No boys. Your best bet is Finlo if you're looking for that kind of fun."

"Please, let me finish." Del Alzon, against better judgment, put a hand up to the woman, showing her his palm. Her cheek quivered, and Del could hear the air she breathed through her nose quicken. "They are friends. Three boys, young men really."

"We get more young men through here than I can count."

"They might have been with others. Sell-swords, I think."

"I told you…No wait. Mercenaries. A while back, we did get quite a few sell-swords through here. Have no liking for gutless wonders who'll sell their fighting skills to the highest bidder, but they did spend quite a bit of coin."

"Too many to recognize three young men, I suppose," Del said. He looked back at his cup of wine.

"Perhaps, you would be right, but not a few days after they left, maybe a week, another fellow came looking for them," Elena Minx explained. "A westerner, from Wüsten Sahil. Samanian if I had to guess. Exceedingly unpleasant and his entourage looked dirty. Had to deny him service."

"So, they are alive?"

"I don't know if they are still alive. That Samanian seemed like he had other notions. What I can tell you is that the young men you're looking for were with three other men, and when they left, they were with three dwarves."

"Dwarves?" Del Alzon asked.

"Aye, that's what I said. You think I'm lying?"

Del shook his head. He smiled. *Dwarves. Gypsies then dwarves. Oh, Erik, what have you gotten yourself into? What have I gotten you into?*

"I thank you, Ms. Minx, for your time and courtesy," Del Alzon said.

She looked at him as if she didn't know what to say. She gave him a quick smile.

"It's Mrs. Minx. Don't be thinking I'm available or anything. And you're welcome."

Elena Minx turned and left. Del sat back and finished the last bit of wine in his cup.

"Dwarves," he muttered.

"So," Yager said, "now that you know, what do we do now?"

Del shrugged. "Go home, I guess."

"Good. I miss my wife," Yager added with a smile.

"We'll stay here tonight. Leave in the morning," Del said.

"Sounds good," Danitus added.

The serving girl refilled Del's cup three times before he found himself to be the only one left in *The Hill Giant's* bar. His legs felt a little weak. His cheeks felt hot.

"Where are you, Erik? Where are you, with mercenaries and dwarves and who knows what else? Wherever you are, I hope you are safe. I pray you are safe. For my sake and yours, stay safe."

Chapter 42

Erik was back in the large bath tub but also back to reality, and he was reveling in what felt like a pool of warm water. Washing away a week of dirt made him feel both refreshed and revitalized. When he returned, he found his room empty and, for many reasons, he preferred it that way. A clean pair of soft wool pants and a clean cotton shirt lay, folded, on his bed. He dropped his dirty clothes, threw his towel to the floor, and pulled on the clean ones. They were warm. A smile swept across his face, and he turned around and sat at the side of the bed.

He rolled the sleeves of his clean, white shirt to his elbows and slipped on his boots. His eyes wandered to his pillow.

A tingle pricked the back of his head. A sting, almost painful, ran through his arms and back and chest and shoulders. He reached under the pillow and grabbed the dagger.

"It seems that, perhaps, I should always take you with me," Erik said, stuffing the golden dagger into his belt.

I agree.

"Am I bound to you?" Erik asked. "Are you going to try and control me?"

He thought he heard the faint sound of laughter in the distance.

Are you so easily controlled?

"I don't think so," Erik replied. "But, I would like to know. Are you a good conscience, like Steel Axe's axe, or are you malevolent, waiting to twist me and turn me into something wretched and then discard me?"

Erik waited a moment and felt nothing, heard nothing, and then said nothing.

The King's dining room was all in an uproar of dwarvish arguing. Turk argued with Demik and Nafer. He argued with several noble looking dwarves that sat next to the King. They argued back and then argued with the King. But everything took a turn for the worse when Turk stood and pointed a finger at King Skella.

Erik couldn't understand what any of them were saying. Turk and Demik had been teaching Erik some of their language as of late, but they were all basic words and phrases, and this was all too fast and complicated. And when Turk spoke to the King, he actually sounded like he was pleading. But then the moment he pointed his finger, the points of two spears waited just a hair-length away from the dwarf's throat. It was at that same moment that another dwarf, one sitting right next to King Skella—with bright red hair, a bright red beard, and a golden circlet centered with a ruby around his head—stood quickly, shouting angrily and giving commands.

Erik watched Wrothgard and Vander Bim and Switch. They looked uneasy. No one—at least none of the men—quite knew what was going on. They had started in on breakfast pleasantly. It was good food and reminded Erik of home. The red-haired dwarf had just sat there until the King introduced him. It was all in Dwarvish, but the dwarf stood and bowed, and Turk and Demik and Nafer did the same. The introduction was brief, the dwarf guest barely said ten words, and then the yelling started.

Turk sat back down in his chair, hands up in the hair submissively.

"Turk, what is going on?" Erik asked.

"Halt der mût!" the red-haired dwarf shouted, now pointing a finger at Erik, the veins in his neck pulsing against his high-collared jacket.

Wrothgard stood.

"What is the meaning of this?" the soldier asked as politely as possible but was met with spears now pointed at his throat.

"Is this what it's come down to?" Switch said, kicking his chair back, knocking it over, and grabbing a knife and a fork from the table. "Come at me, and I'll gut you with a damned fork, tunnel diggers."

The red-haired dwarf stepped back and moved from behind the table, just as two more guards pointed spears at the thief. Everyone was shouting. Erik couldn't hear a thing, and it looked like, at any moment, blood would be shed.

"That is enough!" King Skella shouted. He was old and white haired and looked almost frail, but at that moment, he stood quickly, and his voice boomed louder than Erik would have ever expected. Silence consumed the room. "General, that is enough. These are my guests, and you will treat them as such."

Without hesitation, the red-haired dwarf—the General—bowed to King Skella and sat.

"Your Majesty," he said, then turned to the mercenaries, looked at them with hard eyes, bowed, and added, "my apologies."

"Everyone, sit down," the King commanded, taking his seat as well. "Guards, stand down. For the love of the Almighty, just leave us all together."

The guards all stepped back, resting their weapons, but didn't leave, rather looking at one another with confusion.

"Did you not hear me?" King Skella asked, again raising his voice. "Leave us. Now."

Finally, the guards all bowed to the King and left, slowly and hesitantly.

"I am sorry, Skull Crusher," King Skella said, his tone somber, "but this is the way it has to be."

"A King owes his subjects no apologies," Turk replied, and Erik was surprised by the callousness in his friend's voice.

"What is going on, Turk?" Vander Bim asked.

"Perhaps I should explain," the King said, standing and leaning his hands on the dining table. He looked to the red-haired dwarf. "General Balzarak, please."

General Balzarak stood.

"I am sorry," the King began. "You all have been honorable guests here in Thorakest and, even if you didn't know of Turk's intentions, you have willingly placed your map—the key to your agreement with the Lord of the East—in my hands. General Balzarak is a cousin of mine, from the northern dwarvish kingdom of Thrak Baldüukr. Balzarak Steel Fist is the general of the Eastern Fortresses and Commander at Fornhig. He has come here at my request and at the request of the Dukes of Gerburton and Strongbur."

"And what does this bloody have to do with us?" Switch asked.

General Balzarak growled, but the King put up a hand.

"The discovery of Orvencrest would be monumental," King Skella said, "not just for we southern dwarves, but for our cousins in the north, as well. And the fact that Golgolithul somehow knows of its location, and we do not, is problematic. That, along with the reason I have invited General Balzarak to Thorakest—something I will not discuss with you—has given us great concern. General."

"Despite your allegiance to Golgolithul," the General said, his Westernese rough and accented. He looked to each one of the mercenaries, his eyes resting mostly on the three dwarves with a disapproving glare. "I thank you for coming to us with this map—this information—but I must inform you, however, that you cannot continue on with your journey. I will oversee the expedition to Orvencrest with a group of handpicked warriors."

The commotion that rose from the mercenaries after the General spoke was so loud, Erik couldn't even hear his own thoughts. He didn't think much anyway. He felt suddenly numb, as Switch and Vander Bim shouted obscenities, and as Wrothgard pleaded with the King. It was all for naught. Befel's shoulder. Drake. Even Wrothgard's companion Samus.

"This is hog piss, mate," Vander Bim cried.

"You're damn right it is," Switch yelled. "Tunnel digger trickery. What have you done, Turk? Was this your plan all along?"

"No, no!" Turk replied. Then he turned to the King. "Your Majesty, please."

King Skella put his hand up, and that calmed things down, but only a bit.

"I am sorry," he replied. "After long thought and several sleepless nights, this is the way it has to be."

"We will just leave then," Wrothgard said with finality. "We will continue on our journey and see who gets there first."

"No," General Balzarak said. "You will stay here… at least for a while."

"Now truly prisoners," Wrothgard said.

"I am sorry," King Skella said.

"No you're bloody not!" Switch yelled.

"You will watch your tone," the General hissed.

"Or what?" Switch replied. "You'll kill me? Execute me? Better now than later. Better a dwarf's axe and a clean cut to the neck than being skinned alive by the Lord of the East's bloody inquisitors."

The arguing raised up again, this time Demik and Nafer joining in. Erik looked to Turk. The dwarf looked as numb as Erik felt. He just stared at nothing.

"I know you don't believe me," King Skella said, "but I am truly sorry. You will be kept here, in the city, for some time. I know it is not true freedom, but you will be cared for, and my personal escorts will go with you whenever you wish to go into the city proper, to keep you safe."

"More like to keep an eye on us," Switch huffed, sitting back hard into his seat and throwing the kitchen knife he was holding on the table. "Make sure we don't escape."

"Take it however you wish," the King said. "When your time here is complete, I will have an escort see you safely home."

"Only to find a knife in my back," Erik heard Switch mutter.

"There are other mercenaries on this expedition, you know," Wrothgard said.

"We are aware of the others," Balzarak said. "My scouts tell me they are either dead or dispersed. Let me congratulate you on being the sole survivors of this mission from Golgolithul."

The General's face showed no signs of mirth or joy, and Erik suspected his compliment of being feigned.

"You already knew of the others?" Wrothgard said, crinkling his eyebrows.

"Yes," the General replied. "We knew of the meeting in Finlo. Let me say that if we did let you continue on your journey, you would end up like the others. We have saved your lives."

"You've prolonged them," Vander Bim replied. "You know we'll be wanted men, always looking over our shoulders."

General Balzarak just shrugged.

"And what of General Al'Banan?" Wrothgard asked.

"Let me worry about the General," Balzarak replied. "I have dealt with him before."

Turk tried speaking with the General in their native language, but Balzarak would barely look at the dwarf. He then pleaded again with the King, but King Skella just offered up his open hands and shook his head with sad eyes.

"We willingly gave you the map," Wrothgard said. "We could have lied, but we didn't. And when our friend Turk told us of his plan, we could have tried to stop him, but, again, we didn't. This does not seem just."

"As one soldier to another," the General said, the tone in his voice softening, "I do wish this could be different. I wish we could have discussed it more. I have nothing against your people. But there is more going on here than you know, and this is the safest way to do things. I am sorry, but there is nothing more to discuss. We have no choice."

"I am sorry," the King said. "I wish we could discuss this more. After you are allowed to leave my city, your involvement in our political dealings will be forgotten, of that, I can assure you. The Lord of the East would have to either have spies close to me or read my mind to know you helped the dwarvish people."

"Coerced by, is more like it," Switch whispered.

Erik felt his stomach knot even more. He looked down at a plate of half-eaten eggs and bread. When he had arrived in the dining room, he was ravenously hungry. Now, the simple sight of food made him want to retch.

"Will our weapons be returned to us?" Wrothgard asked as the King stood and called for his servants to help him back to his quarters.

"No," the King replied. "I am sorry about that as well. They will be returned to you when you leave Thorakest. And Turk, I will need those swords back."

Turk bowed slowly.

"Damn the gods," Switch hissed.

As the King's servants followed him out of the room, he stopped and turned.

"Befel, I understand you are in need of a surgeon."

"Yes, Your Majesty," Befel said, standing.

"When you return to your room," King Skella said, "Enfberg, my personal surgeon will be waiting for you."

Befel bowed as the King turned and left. General Balzarak bowed to the mercenaries and followed after the King.

"What a rat turd," Bryon said.

"That is my King you are speaking of," Demik replied with a red face.

"Oh, you mean the King that just imprisoned you in your own city and condemned you to a painful death?" Switch asked with a raised eyebrow.

Demik went to reply, but just sat back in his chair.

"We are doomed, mates" Vander Bim said. "I think I'll go home, buy a little boat, and sail as far away as I can."

"I'll go with you," Switch said and then spat on the table.

"Back to the farm," Befel muttered.

"Shit," Bryon added.

"If the Lord of the East is after us," Erik asked, "won't going home put our family in danger?"

"It's them he's after," Bryon said, nodding to the other mercenaries. "They're the ones who accepted the job, not us. We're just stupid porters, right thief?"

"Oh no," Switch said with a crooked smile. "We're dealing with the Lord of the East, my son. You truly think he doesn't know you are now a part of our little merry band? He'll skin you up and serve you to the pigs or the dogs or the poor just like he will us."

Erik felt sick.

"What do we do now?" he asked.

Befel just shook his head, and Bryon put his face in his hands.

"I cannot guarantee it will be the same." Enfberg put a soft hand on Befel's good shoulder after the surgeon had finished his work. "It will work mostly as it should, but its movement may be less than that of your right. Your strength may be a little less. It will be a while before it completely heals, and when I say a while, I mean longer than just a few weeks. Will you be able to raise a shield over your head, plow a field, chop wood, carry a child? Yes, I believe so. Not tomorrow, certainly, and not next week. Perhaps not even next month, but a year or two from now, your shoulder may be a simple annoyance at times, on a cold morning or after a restless sleep. A year after that, not even an annoyance, and five or six years from now, the only thing that would remind you of your wound would be a nasty scar and a vivid memory."

"Five or six years," Befel muttered. He didn't know if he had five or six years. Would the Lord of the East have him assassinated before then? Did the ruler of the most powerful kingdom in Háthgolthane actually care about him?

"Aye. I know it seems like a long time, but you are young. In two weeks, you might already feel better. Who knows? You seem to heal fast. I will leave several bottles of sweet wine for you. It is strong and will bring on sleep, so only drink it if you are in an uncomfortable amount of pain."

"Yethan," Befel said.

"Ir wolkom," Enfberg replied.

Enfberg motioned to his assistant to follow him out of the room and leave, but as he got to the door, he turned.

"Be careful with the sweet wine," Enfberg said. "You will sleep better than you ever have, and it will dull the pain. Many have grown dependent on its use. Use it sparingly."

Once they closed the room's door, leaving Befel alone, he lay down on Erik's bed, as his sheets were stained with blood and puss. He stared at the room's ceiling for a few more moments, and then, not meaning to, fell asleep.

Chapter 43

BRYON WALKED THROUGH THE COURTYARD, wishing he could hold his sword for only a moment longer. Erik had told him it was elvish—so said some blacksmith friend of Turk—but Bryon didn't really feel like he could trust any dwarf at the moment. Nonetheless, the thought of not only owning a magic blade, but one crafted by the mythical elvish race was exciting.

When the guards came to collect it—it had only been loaned to Turk so that he might have his friend inspect it—Bryon felt as if he were a woman whose child was being stripped away from her arms. He hoped he would hold it again. Could he even hope that the dwarves would return it? The King said he would return their weapons, but he had already betrayed them once, like all so-called noble-blooded people.

A field of statues lay to one side of the castle, all lined in neat rows. Bryon went from one effigy of a dwarf to the next, inspecting the intricacies of the stonework, the attention to detail. They looked real. He remembered the statue of Stone Axe in the tunnels leading to Thorakest, and a shiver crawled up his spine.

Bryon stared at one statue—a mean looking dwarf with a spear in one hand and a patch over his right eye—when something caught his attention, just in his periphery. His hand went to where his sword handle should have been as he crouched and, for a moment, he sighed in lament. He saw it again—the shadow of a man—going from one statue to the next. He trained his eyes on the statue behind which the shadow hid, hiding behind his own sculpture, and waited. There it was again…there he was. Switch.

Bryon followed the thief through the side courtyard of the castle, to an even more secluded area, with no guards and eerie shadows being reflected off the tall cavern cliffs and castle walls. Switch hopped in and out of the shadows, moving from one to the other like a cat. Bryon could see the dim glimmer of a blade in Switch's hand. He watched the thief's gaunt face stretch out of a shadow. The man stared at something intently, and Bryon followed Switch's gaze to another statue—the face of a statue.

This one was a little different than most of the others. The scepter the effigy of the dwarf held was made of gold, the crown on his head looked to be silver. It was accented with many different colors and precious metals, but that wasn't what Switch stared at. He stared at the eyes. Each eye was a large cluster of blue sapphires, centered by a diamond, and all attached to a gold disk.

Switch looked all around. Bryon slinked back deeper into the shadow of his statue. The thief raced towards the figure, jumping onto it like a cat, climbing up the tall statue and carefully jabbing his blade into the right eye of the stone dwarf, working around its edges. Within moments, the cluster of jewels popped away from the gold disk, and Switch caught it as it fell. It was bigger than the thief's hand, and Bryon could see Switch's lips glisten as he licked them. He was like a dog drooling uncontrollably over a piece of fresh meat.

He turned to the left eye, almost dropping the first jewel as he wrapped his legs tight around the statue's neck and grasped his quarry with both hands. He shoved the first jewel into a large pouch hanging from his belt, grasped the statue's head with one hand, and turned on Bryon, knife in the other. He hissed.

"What, by the Shadow, are you doing?" Switch furled his eyebrows and pursed his lips. Face red and jaw clenched, he looked like he might leap at Bryon. But then his look of indignation turned to a crooked smile. "I didn't even see you. You might make a fine thief someday. Now piss off."

Switch turned back to the left eye of the stone dwarf.

"Stop it." Bryon stepped towards Switch. "You're going to get us into trouble."

"Blood and guts and stone statues, boy." Switch turned back around to face Bryon. "We only get in trouble if I get caught. No one comes over to this courtyard. I know—I've watched it for the last two days now. Look at the dust on these statues. Not like the ones by the rose bushes. They haven't been cleaned in days, months, maybe even years. By the Shadow, it looks like it's been so long since someone has been over here, they may chalk up the missing gems to time and neglect."

"And what if someone does see the statue? What if someone connects our appearance with a missing jewel?" Bryon asked. "What about then, you fool thief?"

"You think I haven't thought of that?" Switch asked. "It's a risk I'm willing to take. Hell, it's less risky than handing over a mission given to us by the Lord of the East to damned dwarves. With this, maybe I can live the rest of my life in comfort somewhere in Wüsten Sahil or on the Feran Islands, away from assassins and imperial inquisitors."

"You're a bloody fool," Bryon said.

"Probably," Switch replied. "Smarter than you, though. At least I'm thinking about what happens after I leave this damned prison. Where do you go? Back to your farm and your drunkard father to wait for some eastern rat turd to show up at your doorstep and murder you and your family?"

Bryon didn't know why, but the thief's words twisted his gut, made his face burn, and his vision redden. He found a small rock next to his foot, picked it up, and threw it at Switch.

The rock struck the thief square in the back. Switch snapped around, face red. He clutched his knife with white knuckles. Any reminiscence of the sly, slippery, cynical Switch had vanished, replaced with rage.

Switch leapt from the statue, taking a few heavy, angry, purposeful steps towards Bryon. The young man took a few steps back, balling his hands into fists.

"You itching to die, boy?" Switch asked, pointing his knife at Bryon.

"Don't you care about what happens to us?" Bryon asked. "Don't you care about Turk and Demik and Nafer? Piss on the King and that General, but what about our friends?"

"Friends?" Switch said with a hint of both sarcasm and confusion. "You think…you believe they are your friends? What…do you think they would give their lives for you?"

Switch laughed, and it twisted Bryon's stomach even more.

"Troll shit," Switch said and then spat, his spittle striking the toe of Bryon's boot. "Erik might give his life for you—because he's an idiot. Befel, perhaps, out of duty. But even they aren't your friends. The dwarves would sooner leave you. The soldier, the sailor…come now. And me, well, you're lucky I haven't already stuck a knife in your back."

Then, Switch gave Bryon a half-smile.

"People say there's no honor amongst thieves. Boy, there's no honor among men, among anyone. You know that better than any of these other fools. Understanding that is what has kept me alive this long. You start fooling with what's kept you alive, well, you might as well kiss your ass goodbye. In my world, it's all about me. I don't have family and don't care to have family. By all the gods of the underworld, I bloody killed my own father when I found out who he was. Killed his wife too—slit her throat from ear to ear. I don't care about or love anyone but myself. It's bloody cruel, I know, but it's just the way it is."

"I don't totally believe that," Bryon said, taking a chance to step forward. "What about at Cho's camp? What about that mercenary that was about to…well, you know, what about that?" Bryon asked. "You could've waited until they killed me, and then killed them."

"Don't read into it," said Switch. "Didn't do me much good to kill you right before entering the mountain."

"You're a liar," Bryon accused, pointing a finger at Switch who was now only a few paces away. "I feel sorry for you."

"What about you, mate?" Switch said, pointing his blade at Bryon's chest.

"What do you mean?" Bryon asked, taking a step back.

"What about all your self-glory and honor? Taking the world by its goods and being your own master? Not caring about anyone but you?" Switch gently poked Bryon in the chest with his blade to make a point. Bryon flinched and swatted Switch's hand away. He jabbed his own finger into Switch's chest.

"I care about my family, and I won't let you hurt them," Bryon spat.

Switch shook his head. "You're different than them. It's too bad the dwarves bent us over and double crossed us with this treasure deal, because I think—as much as I hate you—that you got what it takes to make it in this world. Your cousins…no. But you…you're more like me than you think."

"I'm nothing like you."

"Sure you are," Switch chided, his smile growing.

Bryon punched Switch. The thief fell to his back. Bryon kicked Switch's blade out of his hand, grabbed him by the shirt, and pulled him up so that they were face to face.

"I'll kill you with my bare hands you piece of shit—you fucking waste of breath." Bryon seethed so hard that spit flew from his mouth and spattered Switch's face. The thief blinked as the saliva dribbled on his cheeks or his forehead, but nothing more. "How dare you talk about my family? How dare you put us in danger? You are filth, dirt, shit on a boot heel. I would do the world a favor by killing you, snuffing out your memory."

He shook Switch, whose feet were dangling off the ground, as he spoke.

"Do it then," Switch whispered so softly Bryon almost did not hear him. His voice sounded almost enchanted, hypnotic. A sickening glee entered his voice, and a cruel smile invaded his face.

"I should," Bryon hissed back. "I should. I could. I will."

He shook Switch every time he spoke. His grip around Switch's shirt collar tightened. His grip closer to Switch's neck tightened.

"I will. They'll thank me later," Bryon whispered silently.

Bryon blinked a few times, regaining some of his wits. He shook his head slightly, so slightly Switch did not see. Switch only smiled and wiped a trickle of blood away from his lip.

"Go ahead. Bloody kill me. Murder me in cold blood with your bare hands. Then we'll see who the scum is."

Bryon's hands loosened, and he dropped Switch. The thief got to his feet and brushed himself off.

"I didn't realize it at first either, but face it, you and I, we want the same thing."

Switch's words pierced Bryon. He knew they were true, but he did not want them to be. He wanted to be nothing like Switch, but that was what he had become.

"You are filth," Bryon said, but knew he was talking to himself. Worthless. Nobody. A waste. Those words rang through his head. The voice, though…it wasn't his voice. His father's voice. Worthless.

"You're a bloody survivor." Switch laughed. He chuckled at Bryon's hurt look. "Don't look so pained, my son. I'm the one with the sore jaw."

He hopped back onto the statue and continued to work at the left eye. Bryon backed away, his eyes fixed in a gaze, staring blankly at Switch, staring blankly at nothing. He turned around and walked back to the castle, his head down, tears filling his eyes, his face burning, and his hands shaking.

Chapter 44

"WE NEED TO GET OUT of here," Switch said in a hushed voice.

They had all congregated in Wrothgard's room. It was a secret meeting, and in the castle, they didn't need to worry about guards following their every step, but still, the tension was palpable.

"Then leave," Bryon said. "What's stopping you?"

"Guards following my every movement," Switch replied, glaring at Bryon as he spoke.

"Why can't we just wait?" Erik asked.

"Wait for what?" Wrothgard asked. "Wait for this General to leave? Wait to go home only to find it burnt to the ground? Wait for a dwarvish knife in my back?"

"A dwarvish knife..." Erik began. "You truly think the dwarves would assassinate us?"

Turk just shrugged.

"I don't know anymore," he said.

"I mean to continue on," Wrothgard said.

"Continue on?" Vander Bim asked.

"Aye," the soldier replied. "I am going to Orvencrest."

"And how do you plan on finding it?" Vander Bim asked.

"Each group had a map," Wrothgard said. "I still have mine."

"We are men," Vander Bim said, "and unfamiliar with these mountains."

"Turk?" Wrothgard asked.

The dwarf looked at Demik and Nafer, and all three nodded.

"It is folly," the sailor added.

"This whole mission is folly," Wrothgard said, "but I have lost too much already to quit. What honor do I bring Tedish and Samus if I simply lie down like a beaten dog and return home? What honor do you bring Drake?"

"Piss on you," Vander Bim said, standing.

"You're drunk," Wrothgard said. "That's all you've been doing since we've been here."

"Aye," Vander Bim replied. "What would you have me do? Learn the dwarves' language and train with a play sword like these two idiots."

"Who are you calling an idiot," Bryon said.

"Piss off," Vander Bim spat.

"I'm in," the thief said. Bryon looked at Switch, surprised. He nodded.

"Me too," Bryon added.

"Without talking to us?" Befel asked.

"What is there to talk about?" Bryon replied.

Befel looked at Erik. Erik truly didn't know. He was as upset as everyone else when the King forbade them from continuing on with their journey, but a part of him was happy to be returning home, to see his mother and father, his sisters... Simone.

"I don't know," Erik replied.

"You would actually consider going?" Befel asked.

There was something about his brother's tone that upset him. Erik felt his face grow hot.

"Home," Befel said.

"You're the one that wanted to leave!" Erik yelled.

"Oi, quiet down," Switch hissed.

"You stupid lubberwort," Erik accused. Then, he pointed to Bryon. "We would still be home if it wasn't for you and this rat turd."

"This is what we've come to," Vander Bim said before Bryon could retort. "Boys arguing about home? Dwarves considering treason? Shove a wooden leg up my arse. I'm going to get a drink."

The sailor walked out of the room, shaking his head and cursing under his breath.

Erik looked to his brother, then to Bryon—who scowled back—then to the dwarves, the thief, and then, finally, Wrothgard.

"I'm in," he said with a nod of finality. "I'll go."

Before Befel could say anything, Erik stood and left the room.

Erik looked over his shoulder, the two dwarvish soldiers eyeing him as he walked through the farmlands of Thorakest. Despite the constant reminder of imprisonment—guards following him whenever he left the walls of the castle—the low moans of cattle, the rows of wheat, the orange and apple orchards all made Erik think of home, and he smiled when he saw cherry trees.

He remembered Farmer Elgin trying to grow cherries, and he remembered his father buying cherries for his mother at the market. The little pink blossoms covered the trees so much you couldn't see the branches, and the buzz of bees flying from flower to flower created a loud, constant humming.

As he looked at the trees in the dwarvish fields, one blossom shook loose and twirled to the ground, landing at Erik's feet.

"No," one of the soldiers said when he reached up to pluck another blossom.

The two dwarves glared at him with hateful eyes.

"Why?" Erik asked.

"No," was the soldier's only reply.

Erik wondered if that was the only word in his language they knew.

"Are you a giant rat turd?" Erik asked with a smile.

"No," the dwarf replied.

That was definitely the only word they knew. He could have spoken to them in their own language. He knew enough now. But he figured there would be no point.

As he listened to the familiar constant hum of bees and looked at the pink covered trees, and then to the floor, carpeted by those same blossoms, wilting and turning brown, Erik was struck with the sudden realization that nothing could remain the same. The blossoms were beautiful. They gave life to the bees, but in order for the cherries to grow, the flowers had to die.

"Things change," Erik muttered. He turned to face his dwarvish guards. "Let's go."

He led his escorts—his captors, he thought—back through the farmlands and into the city. As they passed by homes and shops, the stares that the citizens of Thorakest gave him seemed different. Dwarves huddled in little groups, whispering, and the normal commotion of a city seemed gone, and Erik found it odd. The mayor stood out in front of the entrance to his keep, scowling at Erik, and when he approached the castle walls, Befel rushed out to meet him.

"Erik!" Befel yelled.

Before Erik could say anything, the two guards stepped in front of him, blocking Befel.

"Are you serious?" Erik asked, pushing one of the guards away. "He's my brother. Don't you know that?"

"Erik!" Befel cried again as he reached Erik. He looked upset. "The King has summoned us."

"What is going on?" Erik asked.

"It's Vander Bim," Befel replied.

"What about him?" Erik asked.

"He's dead."

Erik felt numb, standing in the throne room as Switch and Wrothgard and the dwarves argued with General Balzarak and King Skella. Their words sounded distant.

"You were supposed to bloody protect us," Switch hissed. "Or was this your plan all along?"

"Watch your tongue," General Balzarak said.

"Or what?" Switch asked cynically. "Will I also end up with an assassin's knife in my back, lying face down in some stinking dwarvish alley? Or would you have the balls to do the deed yourself?"

Another dwarf standing to the right of Balzarak stepped forward and yelled. Erik, even though he had started to learn the dwarves' language, didn't know what he said, but it didn't sound nice. The dwarf's hand went to the handle of his sword.

"Thormok," King Skella said, "stand down."

The dwarf bowed and stepped back, his scowl ever present.

"Just wait, Thormok," Switch mocked, "he'll sick you on us all in due time."

"That is enough from you as well," King Skella commanded, pointing a finger at Switch. "You have about exhausted my patience for your runaway mouth."

"With all due respect, Your Majesty," Wrothgard said. He tried sounding as cordial as possible, even though the look on his face said that he was just as angry as Switch. "You ensured our safety. Vander Bim was under the watch of your own personal guard when he was murdered."

Another dwarf, some other dignitary like Balzarak by his looks, pointed at Wrothgard, also speaking in Dwarvish.

"How is it not murder, Captain Gôdruk?" Turk asked. "This is no accidental death. He was stabbed…in the back…while under the protection of castle guards."

Gôdruk replied, again in Dwarvish.

"My allegiances are to my friends and those who I would feel are my people," Turk replied, "which, at the moment, seems to be these adventurers I stand next to."

That brought on more arguing, each person trying to speak over the next until no one could hear anyone else.

"A knife in his back?" Erik asked in a whisper.

"Aye," Befel replied. "Apparently, he had been drinking in some bar along Thorakest's main street. When the guards led him out the back door into an alleyway, someone stabbed him."

"The guards?" Erik questioned.

"They said they didn't see it happen," Befel replied. "They said Vander Bim ran from them, and when they caught up, he was lying face down with a knife in his back."

"A drunk sailor ran away from two well-trained guards?" Erik asked.

"Exactly," Befel said.

"If we aren't careful," Bryon said, "the same will happen to us... each one of us. We need to leave."

"How?" Erik asked.

"I don't know," Bryon said with a shrug.

Erik saw King Skella sit down in his throne, rubbing his temples with a thumb and forefinger.

"Quiet!" the King yelled. His voice, normally kind and somewhat feeble, had the uncanny ability to boom when he yelled.

The commotion in the throne room came to a stop as everyone waited on the King, sighing and groaning and rubbing his temples.

"This is my fault," King Skella finally said. "I cannot bring back your friend, but his death is on my hands. The Creator knows, I have had to bear the death of many good people. The dwarves who were supposed to be guarding him will see justice. A life for a life. That being said, I cannot let you stay here, in my city."

"Your Majesty..." Wrothgard began, but a firm hand ceased his voice.

"Let me finish," the King said. "You will go with General Balzarak and Gôdruk and Thormok here. I have assembled a small retinue of warriors that I trust to go with them, to find the lost city of Orven-crest. You will go with them."

"My King..." Balzarak said, and again, a firm hand stopped him from saying anything further.

"This is my decree, and my decision is final," King Skella said.

"These friends of Turk Skull Crusher will go with you, and they will help you find the lost city. They will retrieve this lost artifact of the Stévockians. As they expected to, they will also take with them whatever treasure they can carry."

The King now turned away from his General to address the men and the dwarves who traveled with them.

"I know that it cannot replace the life of your friend—and he seemed like a good man—but perhaps it can do a little to right a wrong. Hopefully, you will not have to watch your backs for assassins the rest of your life. Your weapons will be returned to you. Clearly, I cannot protect you, so you should have the right to protect yourselves within my city. And I have ordered my armorers to open the royal armory to you, so that you may take anything that you feel might help you on your journey."

The look Balzarak gave the King was disapproving, and the look he gave the company of mercenaries was downright malicious, but, nonetheless, he bowed.

"Are you agreeable to this?" the King asked.

"Yes, Your Majesty," Wrothgard replied.

"Who made you bloody leader?" Switch whispered.

"Shut up," Turk hissed.

"On this journey," the King continued, "General Balzarak will be your commander. I know he does not agree with my decree, but he is a good leader—the best—and a fair and just leader. Normally Captain Gôdruk and Commander Thormok are his seconds, but on this journey, I order that Wrothgard be his second. That way, both parties are represented. Are you agreeable to this?"

"Bloody..." Switch began.

"Yes, Your Majesty," Wrothgard replied, looking over his shoulder and glaring at the thief.

"General Balzarak?" the King asked.

"Of course, Your Majesty," General Balzarak said with a bow, but the look on his face said anything but agreement.

"Very well then," the King said, "you will leave for the city of

Orvencrest soon. I figure the sooner the better. We dwarves typically bury our dead, and you are certainly welcome to have the body of Vander Bim buried in one of our graveyards, but I will let you do as you wish with his body, whether it be cremating or whatever else…aside from cannibalism. I have heard that some of the tribes from Antolika do such a thing. That, I cannot allow."

Wrothgard looked to Switch. The thief just shrugged as did the dwarves.

"We would like to see his body, Your Majesty," Erik said. "Then, we can decide what to do."

"Very well," the King said with a bow.

"Bloody pig shit," Switch said as guards led them through a narrow hallway to a small room that held the sailor's body. Turk and Demik and Nafer had decided not to join them.

He lay on a simple table, naked save for a loin cloth. The four torches in the room cast eerie shadows across the man's body, but otherwise, he looked serene.

"Why are we here?" Wrothgard asked.

"I don't know," Erik replied. "I just thought I'd like to see him one last time before we decide what to do with him."

Wrothgard nodded quickly.

"I didn't know the man well, but he seemed like a right fellow," Wrothgard said. "I don't know what gods he prayed to, but I will pray to my family's patron goddess that he meets the afterlife well."

"I always thought I'd be the first to go," Switch said, looking down into the sailor's peaceful face, "but here you are. Seems funny, out of the three of us, the miner seemed like the one most worthy of living, then you, then me, and you two died first. Fate certainly is a dirty whore, isn't she?"

Switch pulled two rusted coins from his purse and placed them over Vander Bim's eyes. Wrothgard bowed to the dead man and then placed one more coin over the man's mouth. They both left, and Bryon followed shortly.

"Are you staying?" Befel asked.

"Yeah, for a little bit," Erik replied.

"Why?"

"I don't know," Erik said. "If it wasn't for him, we would still be in Finlo, or who knows where else. Maybe we'd be on some boat heading east or dead in Aga Kona, a pile of troll shit somewhere in the mountains."

Befel put his hand on Erik's shoulder and then also left.

When Erik was alone, he let a few tears escape his eyes but didn't know why he was afraid to let them fall in front of the others. He wasn't much concerned about looking weak. He figured in the last few weeks he had proven himself anything but feeble.

"You deserved better," Erik said to Vander Bim's body. "I suppose I didn't know you that well, and you could have been trouble before we met, but you were kind to me and my kin and for that, I thank you. I don't know what you believed, but I pray the Creator welcomes you, and I pray I will see you again. Hopefully, Drake is there to welcome you with open arms."

Erik put his hand on Vander Bim's shoulder. The man was cold and pale. It was different when his grandfather had passed. Even though he was gone, he felt warm, his old skin soft. His face had looked serene, happy almost. Without the coins, the sailor looked troubled and sad, and that look knotted Erik's stomach.

Erik felt a tingle in his back and knew it was time to go. Something inside his head—his dagger—told him that. It was time to move on and move forward.

Chapter 45

Erik held Beth and Tia's hands as they stared at their mother's roses. Tia giggled every time a petal tickled her nose, and Beth scolded her for getting too close; she always liked to enjoy them from a distance. Beth liked to enjoy everything from a distance, never getting too close, never taking too much risk. Erik's grandfather, before he passed away, had said Beth would make a farmer happy—loyal, hard-working, attentive. Tia, on the other hand, she might drive several husbands to their grave. Rikard Eleodum had scolded his father for saying such a thing, but Karita Eleodum just laughed, and Erik had no clue what that meant until he'd aged a few more years.

The roses were extra fragrant that day. His sisters couldn't stop talking about smelling them, watching the ladybugs dance about on their petals, watching the butterflies flutter as if they were applauding. They had asked Befel at first. He was the eldest, and Erik didn't feel hurt that they would ask their oldest brother to hold their hands while they inspected Mother's roses. But, as always, he was too busy, so they'd asked Erik and, of course, Erik could never say no to his sisters. He knew Befel would admonish him later and complain about how he always got saddled with all the hard work and his younger brother never had to do anything, but it was worth seeing his sisters smile.

"Erik, take us to the apple orchards," Tia had begged.

"I have to get back to work."

"But Erik." Tia was so good at pouting, surely she practiced it.

"Leave him alone," Beth had said.

Erik could see, from the corner of his eye, Tia sticking her tongue out at Beth. He squeezed her hand and shook his head ever so slightly.

"Girls." Erik's mother's voice always sounded so gentle, even when he knew she was upset. "Girls, your brother has work to do. He can't play with you and take you all over the Creator's world. You're going to get him into trouble. Come help me in the kitchen."

Beth hopped to obediently, but little Tia dragged her feet and drooped her arms to her sides as if she was a rag doll.

"Come on, Tia," Erik whispered, "you're going to get into trouble."

She looked back at him over her shoulder, smiled, and then stuck her tongue out before running into the house.

Erik stared at the roses. He held his hands out as if holding his sisters' hands, but they weren't there. His mother wasn't there. His father wasn't there. His house or his farm. He played his mother's voice over and over again in his head. He tried to remember it, exactly the way it sounded. Was that right? He might have forgotten it.

You'll never forget the sound of your mother's voice. He reached to his side and touched the golden handle of his dagger, knowing that's where the thought came from.

Erik heard the clearing of a throat behind him, several footsteps, and the heavy breathing of a dwarf. He turned and saw General Balzarak Steel Fist standing behind him. The dwarf bowed. Erik returned the favor.

"Erik Eleodum."

His command of Westernese seemed good, but his voice was so rough, one with the texture of bark and bare sharp edges.

"Yes," Erik replied.

Balzarak nodded with an affirmative grunt.

"I have spent many hours looking at these roses as well. We have them at Isen also, but they do not grow like this."

"They remind me of my mother's roses." Erik turned back and

thought he saw the golden hair of Tia bouncing between each bush, and then turned back to the General.

"Isn't it funny how certain things remind us of our mothers, no matter how far away we find ourselves?" Balzarak asked.

"Funny, indeed," Erik replied.

"You hail from the north, yes?" Balzarak asked.

"Yes," Erik replied. "Our lands are west of Nordeth and south of the Pass of Dundolyothum."

"Those are strong bloodlines," Balzarak said. "Those bloodlines belong to men who have been warriors, heroes, and friends of dwarves."

"I suppose," Erik said with a shrug. "That's what the King says, at least. I guess I don't know that much about our history."

"Yes, well, you should be proud of your heritage," Balzarak said. He extended his hand to Erik. "I think we got off on the wrong foot, as you men say."

Erik looked at the dwarf with a raised eyebrow and cautiously took his hand, shaking it.

"I cannot say that I much agree with the King's decree," Balzarak continued, "but if we are to travel together, we should try to be amicable. We need to work together."

"I agree," Erik replied, "but why tell me? Why not speak with Wrothgard or Switch…or the dwarves even?"

"I have," Balzarak said with a smile that looked a little forced. "But I think it is appropriate that I say this to all of you, not just your leader. I have already spoken with your brother and cousin."

"Very well then," Erik said. "As my grandfather used to say, the past is the past until we repeat it."

"Very good," Balzarak said with a smile. "The King, in preparation for our journey, has given you access to the royal armory. May I show you there?"

Erik nodded and followed the General.

Erik looked at the shield Bryon had picked up. It was round, with brown cowhide stretched over it. He slid it over his left forearm and lifted it up. It looked a good fit, and by the smile on Bryon's face, he assumed his cousin thought the same thing. Erik had found one almost just like it, only black.

Erik patted the mail shirt of iron scales he had found. It was heavy, and he wondered how an untrained soldier could have moved with such a thing, but he had grown stronger over the last few weeks.

What if I had sailed east on a Golgolithulian ship? Erik wondered. Wearing armor he couldn't handle and carrying a sword he didn't know how to use, he knew the answer would have been death.

His brother and cousin found mail shirts as well.

"Is it odd, that a dwarvish armory has shirts made for men?" Erik asked.

"You must remember," Turk replied, "Thorakest is large and trades frequently with the world of men."

Erik grabbed a scabbard that seemed to fit his sword well enough, a small hand axe that he slid through a loop on his belt, and a tall spear—at least a head taller than him butted with a thick iron shod and tipped with a broad, gleaming iron blade.

"What are you going to do with that?" Befel asked.

"Kill someone," Erik replied matter-of-factly.

"You don't know how to use it," Befel said.

"Truth be told, I prefer the sword," Erik replied, "but Wrothgard has taught me how to use a spear, and Turk has taught me how to use an axe."

"Just more to carry," Befel said, irritation rising in his voice.

"You should have been training with Bryon and me," Erik said.

"With one arm?" Befel asked.

"Then why don't you stay here?" Erik asked. "We will go on this journey and, Creator willing, when we return, we will pick you up and head to Fen-Stévock, and then back home."

"Are you crazy?" Befel asked. "Stay here? Leave you and Bryon to who knows what?"

"Is it such a crazy idea?" Erik asked in return. His own irritation was pushing aside his genuine concern for his brother.

"Out of the question," Befel said.

"What good are you?" Erik asked. He didn't mean for it to come out like that.

"Apparently none," Befel said, turning and storming away.

"Very tactful, cousin," Bryon said.

"Bugger off," Erik said.

"Gladly," Bryon replied with a quick laugh, "if there was someone here to bugger."

As his cousin walked away, and most everyone—save for Wrothgard, inspecting a long bow he meant to take—left the armory, Erik stood and waited, thinking. He looked down at himself, armor, sword, axe, dagger, spear, bracers covering his forearms and greaves covering his shins. What did he look like? He couldn't find a mirror. He didn't feel different, but, then again, he did. What would his parents say? His sisters? Simone?

He closed his eyes and tried to think of home. He had just held his sisters' hands, pretending they were there with him, and now he couldn't picture them. The faces of his father and mother faded. His grandmother and uncle. His grandfather, long gone to the Creator, even more so.

He tried to picture Simone. He tried to smell her, that subtle scent of fresh roses. He tried to feel her soft skin and her hands on his face and hear her voice—her gentle voice that could soften any man's heart. He tried to taste her honeyed lips. He couldn't. They were so long ago, so far away.

"Are you alright?" one of the dwarvish armorers asked in his own language.

Erik, for a moment, was surprised he understood the dwarf. He nodded. He didn't know how long he had stood there, eyes shut, thinking of home. Even Wrothgard was gone now.

The dwarf nodded back with a quick smile.

"Will I ever be who I once was?" Erik asked as he stared out the front of the armory. He squinted. "Do I want to be?"

Chapter 46

"ARE YOU HAPPY TO BE leaving,Thorakest?" King Skella asked as Erik passed through the throne room.

The voice startled Erik. He'd walked this way countless times as a shortcut to his quarters and had never seen the King sitting there alone.

"I…I suppose," Erik he replied, getting over the surprise. "I don't know, really, Your Majesty."

"Have you felt like a prisoner, here in my city?" the King asked.

"No," Erik said, and realized it was a quick response.

"Good," King Skella said. "That wasn't my intention. I realize I have put you and your companions in a very precarious situation. That wasn't my intention either."

Erik didn't understand why the King was explaining himself. Certainly, it wasn't necessary. After all, a King could do as he wished.

"Things happen for a reason, Your Majesty," he said as he shrugged.

"Yes, I suppose they do," King Skella said, rubbing his eyes with thumb and forefinger.

"Are you alright, Your Majesty?" Erik asked.

"Just tired, young Eleodum," King Skella replied. "My wife is not well. It keeps me up at night. And, to be honest, this situation with your map has been a worry as well."

"I am sorry to hear about the Queen," Erik said.

"Thank you," the King replied.

"And thank you," Erik said, "for allowing us access to your armory. That was a most generous gift."

"It was nothing. The least I could do," the King said with a smile and a dismissive wave of his hand.

"May I return to my quarters, Your Majesty?" Erik asked.

"Yes, of course," the King said.

Erik began to walk through the throne room, but then he stopped and turned to the King, who had gone back to rubbing his eyes.

"Your Majesty," Erik said.

"Yes," he replied.

"Speaking of getting little sleep," Erik continued, "I have had trouble sleeping myself lately. I know your surgeon gave my cousin something that helps him sleep—sweet wine he calls it. I was wondering if he might have some for me as well. I find myself tired every morning and less than enthusiastic to go to bed."

King Skella cocked an eyebrow and sat up straighter.

"My brother also had trouble sleeping," Erik added, "but it seems he is having the best sleep he has had in months."

King Skella pensively pursed his lips.

"I will have Tifur, my castellan, send for Enfberg. I am sure he can help you, either with sweet wine or dream milk. One must be careful, though. You can become too dependent on them and may not be able to sleep without them."

Erik bowed. "Your Majesty is too kind."

Erik threw himself into his training, his language lessons with Demik, and even lessons on history with the King himself, who willingly sat for hours talking about things that would have driven Switch mad and bored Bryon to death. He reveled in the knowledge—hand to hand combat, fighting, education, culture—and their restrictions within the city had been lifted. They were now allowed to roam freely, with weapons in hand and without guards watching them. But Erik still felt like a prisoner, and he couldn't wait to leave.

The thought of Vander Bim, since placed in a dwarvish cemetery, weighed heavy on Erik's mind, as did Drake and Samus and the dreams of his dead parents and tortured sisters. Even if they were no longer captives, he still felt no freer. The fake sun, casting its warmth and light into the cavern with mirrors, became almost mind-numbingly foolish. The way the dwarvish people bustled about their daily lives as if nothing was wrong with the world was infuriating.

"Let me smell the fresh air," Erik said to himself. "Let me feel the sun on my face."

Another week came and passed when Erik and his companions were sitting in the small dining room. Erik had met with the King almost daily, but since releasing them from their bondage within the city, he had not met with the whole group and could not understand the reasons for the delay in their departure.

"The King commands your presence," the guard said, walking into the room and stamping the butt of his spear on the floor.

Erik understood him, but the others hadn't a clue what he said.

"The King wants us," Turk interpreted.

"It's about flaming time," Switch exclaimed, throwing a chicken bone across the room, downing the contents of his wine glass in one gulp, and slamming that down hard against the table. "The sooner we can get out of this filthy city, the better."

Demik and Nafer both groaned, but they didn't say anything. Erik suspected, much to their chagrin, that they actually agreed with the thief.

King Skella wasn't actually in the room to which they had been summoned. It was small, and Erik suspected away from crowds of nobles and aristocrats, who seemed to grow every time the company gathered, watching them like caged animals.

"We're a damned spectacle," Wrothgard had once said.

General Balzarak was there, standing among six other dwarves.

They spoke freely, and, from what Erik could understand as he entered the room, it was about anything—small talk. They quieted as they saw the men.

"Where is the King, General?" Wrothgard asked.

One of the dwarves groaned when Wrothgard spoke Westernese.

"Tending to his wife," Balzarak answered with a quick bow. "She is not well these days."

"And Thormok and Gôdruk?" Turk asked.

That same dwarf groaned even louder when Turk spoke Westernese.

"Preparing," was Balzarak's simple reply.

"Well, you summoned us here," Switch said, "and here we are."

General Balzarak bowed again.

"We have been, how do you say, recruiting. These are the warriors who have agreed to travel with us," Balzarak said.

"This is the *retinue*?" Wrothgard asked with a hint of disdain.

Another of the dwarves said something in his native language, almost in a whisper, but Erik understood him.

"We were the only ones willing to travel with you," he said.

"Then the Creator smile on you for that," Erik replied, also in Dwarvish, without thinking.

The dwarves looked at him with surprise, and a few grumbled angrily until Balzarak put up his hand with the slightest smile.

"These are veteran warriors," Balzarak said, "and though they be few, each one is worth a retinue of warriors in his own right. Bim, Bofim, Beldar, Mortin, Threhof, and Dwain have all brought honor to their families, their clans, Thorakest, and Drüum Balmdüukr."

Each dwarf bowed, some deeper than others.

"We leave in two days," Balzarak said. "We will meet at the main passage in Gröde Handenhall. Prepare your things. This is a treacherous journey. Dwain, lead us in prayer please before we leave."

Switch grumbled as a dwarf with a beard and hair full of gray stepped forward and bowed his head. Erik understood some of what he said, but then, there were words that sounded completely foreign, and he wondered if it was some heightened Dwarvish language, or maybe an older Dwarvish language.

"Lasz'so Zine," Dwain finished with.

"Let it be so," Erik repeated quietly.

Chapter 47

ILKEN TAPPED HIS PIPE INTO a simple pewter tray, expelling whatever weed he was smoking, reached into his pocket, rustled around, and retrieved a handful of more, stuffing it into his pipe. It was brown and moist and clung together so that Ilken only had to pinch a bit to grab enough for his pipe.

"Where is Turk?" Erik asked, expecting to see his friend working diligently for the blacksmith.

"I have released him," Ilken said with a smile, "lest I lose all my business to that young dwarf. He worked so diligently, I found him just twiddling his thumbs half the time. My wife feared I would lose business to him."

Ilken laughed and then continued, "Nonetheless, I know you are leaving on the morrow. Turk needed time to collect his thoughts... and courage."

Erik took a sip of his sun tea and closed his eyes.

"It's good," he said, almost to himself.

"Remind you of something?" Ilken asked.

Erik opened his eyes.

"Home."

"Good," Ilken replied.

"Yes," Erik said. "Very good."

Suddenly, he felt a knot in his stomach as memories of home

flooded his mind—Mother and Father, orange brandy, rose bushes, his sisters... Simone.

"I'm a fool," Erik muttered. "I'm the most foolish man who has ever lived."

Ilken laughed at that.

"Oh, my young friend, I am afraid there have been plenty of men far more foolish than you. Take Silas, the Durathnan, for instance. He thought he fell in love with an elvish maiden and followed her into the forbidden forests of Ul'Erel. When he got there, he realized that his good looks and manners could not charm his maiden into bed for a night, at which moment he pledged his undying love to her and asked for her hand in marriage. Little did he know an elvish engagement lasted ten years, by which time he was graying and feeling the pains and aches of age. Not to mention, he had been quite unfaithful to his elvish beauty. If he had only realized that, on their wedding night, if he had remained faithful, the magic within that maiden's lips would have healed all the damage time had caused, but because of his infidelity, her kiss caused instant death."

"I suppose that taught him a lesson," suggested Erik, and Ilken laughed before he continued with his next tale.

"Even more foolish was Castor, who ruled the lands that would one day become Gol-Durathna. His people loved him so, for he seemed a most pious man, always giving riches to the poor, housing to the homeless, and power to the weak. An, however, knew his heart, and when he offered Castor anything he wanted, rather than asking for wisdom or a kinder heart, or a just heart, or the strength to do An's will, he asked for all the riches in the world. An was faithful and honored Castor's wish by giving him all the riches in the world, most of which belonged to other men. The very next day, an angry mob broke down the door to Castor's keep and stoned him to death."

Ilken tugged on his pipe and took a drink of his own cup of tea.

"How about Anish and Nisha, the first beings on our world, the first male and female, who An created and gave all things to?"

"Were they humans, or elves, or dwarves?" Erik asked.

"They were the first," Ilken replied. "They were all of us and then, none of us. An had given them a vast land, a garden west of Nothgolthane, beyond the Forbidden Hills, between the Namer and Nesher Rivers. It was anything anyone could ever want. They had no need to farm, hunt, fish. The land freely gave to them anything they wanted, and An often walked with them through their garden, talking with them, laughing with them. Can you imagine, the Creator walking with you and talking with you?"

"I don't think I could," Erik replied. "I think I would be too afraid."

"Aye." Ilken laughed. "Their only command was to never drink the waters from a certain well, the Well of Yada Hu Kock."

"And so, they drank from the well," Erik said. He was familiar with this story.

"Aye." Ilken nodded with a smile. "They did. Perhaps the most foolish thing anyone has ever done. So, you see, in comparison, you are not so foolish."

"I see," replied Erik, but he wasn't sure he was convinced. "Turk said you wanted to see me."

"I am done."

Ilken led Erik to his workspace. Lying on the same table on which he once inspected Erik's dagger and Bryon's sword was a long, broad blade. The blade itself looked simple, but upon closer inspection, Erik could see wavy patterns through the steel, along either side of the fuller.

"I am quite proud of this blade I have made for you. I don't know if I've ever made something so magnificent. Those markings are from hammering and folding pure steel," Ilken said. "It makes the steep durable, strong, and flexible."

The steel was a dull gray, rather than gleaming bright like the fables Erik had heard as a boy of great swords. The cross guard was also simple, slightly sweeping forward and wide enough to protect Erik's hand. Black leather wrapped the handle, and Erik could see a single undulation in the middle of it.

"You can use both hands," Ilken explained, "or only one if you wish."

And the pommel was also simple—round and large to counter-balance the weight of the blade. On one side of the pommel, Erik saw that it was studded with a small ruby, and on the other side, a sapphire. And on the cross guard, he saw a purplish stone—amethyst.

"The ruby stands for courage," Ilken explained, "and the sapphire for loyalty. These are both traits which I believe you possess. The amethyst is for clear headedness and wittiness, things you will need on your journeys."

"And these," Erik said, running his index finger over several runes neatly carved into the blade as it met the cross guard.

"Marks of the maker," Ilken replied with a deep smile. "They are my name, in Old Dwarvish, and the symbol of my clan, the Raven."

Erik picked up the sword and swung it, using the techniques Wrothgard had taught him. It felt like nothing he had held before.

"It feels like it is a part of me," Erik said.

"Good," Ilken replied, "that is the way it is supposed to feel."

Erik lowered his sword, taking the scabbard that Ilken had made to go with it and sheathing the blade.

"I can't ever thank you enough," Erik said.

Ilken put up a hand.

"I did this as a favor to Turk," Ilken replied, "and to you. I hope this is a sword that you can pass down to your son, and him to his. I hope this is a sword that speaks to the unity of men and dwarves and to the unity of all the peoples of our vast world."

Erik bowed.

"I only pray that this sword keeps you safe on your journey," Ilken added. "This is a perilous thing you are doing. It will take more than a well-crafted sword, or training, to keep you alive. These are the moments that test us, Erik Eleodum. These are the moments that try our hearts and minds and souls."

Erik stayed only a bit longer, talking with Ilken and just reveling in his company and hospitality. When he eventually left, the blacksmith looked almost sad.

"I do hope I see you again," Ilken said in his native language as Erik left. He didn't think the dwarf meant for him to hear him, but he did.

"Me too," Erik whispered.

Chapter 48

ERIK WALKED THROUGH THE CITY, Turk, Wrothgard, and Nafer in front of him, Demik to his side, and Switch, Befel, and Bryon to his rear.

They neared the mayor's keep. Erik saw Fréden Fréwin and a small entourage of militia and aristocrats standing just outside the building. The mayor eyed them coldly. He muttered to his administrators and followers as they approached him and then looked down and away when Erik made eye contact. Erik saw him give frowning, sidelong glances to the company, and then he thought he heard the mayor growl.

Erik looked over his shoulder, watching as Fréden Fréwin stared at the company, hands clenched, lips flat and curved to a deep frown.

You had better watch that one. Erik felt a tingle at his hip.

"Oh, so you decide to speak again. I still don't know if I should trust you," Erik whispered.

Trust or don't trust. You know he bodes you ill will. Be on guard for him.

"Who are you talking to?"

Erik saw Befel walking next to him.

"No one," Erik said. "Just myself."

"About what?" Befel asked.

"We should be cautious of the mayor," Erik said. "I don't trust him."

"We will never see him again," Befel said with a slight, condescending chuckle.

"Maybe," Erik replied. "Nonetheless, he doesn't like us, and he has agents loyal to him."

"Who are you, now," Befel asked, "an expert in political espionage."

"Joke all you want," Erik replied. "He is evil, he wishes us harm, and he hates what we are doing."

"Thormok," Balzarak said as he and the other dwarvish warriors came into view, waiting at the mouth of a large passage in the Gröde Handenhall.

The General's first cousin bowed.

"Threhof," Thormok said, waiting just a moment for the company to gather with them and take a breath.

Another of the escorts—an older dwarf, although, not as old as Dwain—bowed. He wore plate mail like Balzarak and his kin and, after bowing to Thormok, turned and slammed the butt of his spear into the ground three times.

"Dwain is the oldest," Turk explained to Erik, "but Threhof is the highest ranking, having once served as the captain of the city guard. He will lead us out of Thorakest."

The dwarves lined up behind Threhof, and once Erik jumped in behind Turk, they were moving.

"Will we travel through underground tunnels the whole way?" Erik asked.

"No," Turk said with a shake of his head. "There is a giant ravine that separates the northern and southern ranges of the Southern Mountains. It is too deep. We will travel along the surface. This is the main road to the rest of Drüum Balmdüukr. We will take it to another road that will lead us to the surface."

"Back to the bloody grand adventure, eh," Switch said.

"And back to sleeping in the open, under the stars," Wrothgard responded.

"Soon enough," Turk added.

"Just more steps farther from home, farther from anything I know, farther from Beth and Tia, Mother and Father, Simone."

Erik's utterance was so soft, no one heard him, but as he watched the shoulders of his brother slump, he knew he thought the same thing.

"You know what that will do to you," Erik said.

Befel looked at him, momentarily stopping the search through his bag for sweet wine. The main road to Thorakest was very large, well lit, and well-traveled. But they had turned away from it, onto this road towards the surface, more than a day ago. This one was dark and steep and, much to Bryon's constant complaining, low. Erik was glad for his recent training. He felt tired, but just slightly. His legs and shoulders were strong and well accustomed to the work. Befel, on the other hand, seemed worn down, and Erik knew it wasn't just his shoulder that hurt.

"I just need a little," Befel replied, continuing his search. He found it, smiled cautiously, and popped the cork.

"You'll be even slower," Erik said.

"Thanks," Befel replied facetiously.

Erik just shrugged and wandered away, beginning to talk to Bofim. Turk caught Befel's hand before he could put the bottle to his mouth.

"No," the dwarf said. "We can ill afford a sluggish trek right now. Fight through the aches and pains. We are going too slow as it is, and these dwarvish warriors with us are growing restless. You must have your wits about you, even if it brings discomfort. Do you understand?"

Befel nodded dejectedly.

"And can I trust you will not drink any tonight?" Turk asked.

Befel nodded again.

"You see Beldar?" Turk asked.

Befel followed the direction of Turk's pointing finger to look at one of the dwarvish escorts who was speaking to Erik, seemingly doing his best to speak Westernese. He was very broad-shouldered and fiery-haired with an upper lip—which he kept shaved—that looked mangled with a massive scar.

"He drank too much sweet wine and lost an ear. In a training accident. Think about what might have happened had it been in a battle."

Chapter 49

"We should be at the surface by now," Threhof said as they stopped.

"I agree with Threhof. This is not a good start," Balzarak said. "We are at least a day behind."

"What would you have us do?" Wrothgard straightened his back and put up his hands. "We're travel weary. Two months now, we've been on this journey."

"You no argue Threhof," Bofim whispered creeping up to Erik. The young man cocked an eyebrow and tilted his head. "No win."

Erik understood.

"Two months," Threhof scoffed. "Half of that was spent in the hospitality of the dwarves. Any warrior worth his axe could go double that and still move faster."

"Hospitality," Wrothgard grumbled. "As prisoners."

"All this talk about a warrior could do this, and a flaming warrior could do that, and a tunnel digger can walk a thousand leagues without food or water. Do you ever stop talking about how bloody great you all are?" Switch asked. His face was red, and Erik could see a murderous look growing in the thief's eyes. "A bunch of bloody bearded monkeys if you ask me."

Threhof's back stiffened, his lips pursed, and his gray eyes glared at Switch. Erik saw Switch lick his lips and tap the scabbard of one of his daggers with a thumb. That crooked smile crept across the thief's thin lips, one that spoke of blood and murder and the sickening satisfaction it brought. Switch inched his way towards Threhof.

Turk stepped in between the thief and the dwarf, putting his hand on Threhof's chest. The older warrior gave Turk's hand a sour look and slapped it away. Turk just shook his head at Threhof.

"I won't let a bearded midget come between our bloody fun, tunnel digger, if you won't," Switch chided.

Turk turned to Switch and grabbed him by the collar of his shirt. That clearly took Switch by surprise as he stepped back and almost slipped.

"Listen thief, if you really want to see what a dwarf warrior can do," Turk hissed, "keep on taunting him, and he'll show you. I won't step in between you two again."

With that, he pushed Switch away, sending him back so hard, if Bryon was not there to catch him he would have tumbled backwards. Switch quickly straightened and slapped Bryon's hands away from him. He clenched his hands with white knuckled fists and bit his lip hard but said and did nothing else.

"Is this what happens when you spend too many years with surface dwellers?" Condescension hung heavy and thick on Threhof's words, deliberately spoken Westernese.

Turk turned hard on Threhof and said something to the older warrior in their own tongue, something Erik didn't understand. Threhof went red-faced.

"Stop this!" Balzarak yelled. "This is foolishness. Turk Skull Crusher, stand down."

"Don't tell me I have no honor as a warrior," Threhof spat. "What would you know of a warrior's life?"

"I've been baptized." Turk touched a hand to his left breast. "So have my friends, Demik and Nafer. We are, by all the rights of our people, warriors."

Erik had no idea what they were talking about, but what he did notice was the apprehension leave the other dwarves—most of them dropping hands from their weapons and loosening the stern looks they had been wearing on their faces—all save Threhof.

"As I told Switch," Turk said, "I will not step in between you two again, and you might be surprised at what happens if you are foolish enough to fight him."

"Threhof, stand down," Balzarak commanded.

The older dwarf was not so quick to obey the General's command. Balzarak said something in Dwarvish, twice, which was repeated by Thormok. With his face still blazing with anger, Threhof finally turned from Turk and walked towards the front of the company.

"We must push our pace," Balzarak said, "regardless of how tired you are."

Erik felt his shoulders slump and heard his brother groan.

"This is going to be a long trip," Erik muttered.

"Aye," Bofim agreed.

"Halgüth," Erik said as they passed the single dwarvish guard.

Erik looked up at a fading night sky. That meant a full day of travel before they made camp, and, despite his training, he was tired. To his left, the mountain wall rose and to his right stood a stone wall a head taller than him, all covered in vines and creepers. He shivered.

Just as the pinks and purples of a coming morning began to stretch across an ensuing morning sky, clumps of clouds crept up from the south and covered the rising sun. Distant thunder rumbled through the mountains, echoing and shaking the earth. For a brief moment, the clouds actually warmed the air, but then Erik felt the first thick drop of rain on his head and the water felt freezing as it ran down his back. In moments, the rain fell in a heavy sheet.

As several cold and rainy days passed, along with freezing nights that required man and dwarf to huddle much too close together for comfort, the wall to Erik's right lowered until it was only waist high. It was then that they could see the great ravine that separated the northern and southern ranges of the Southern Mountains that they would have to eventually cross. And as the wall shortened, the path on which they walked narrowed, so much so that they had to walk in a single file line and, even then, Erik felt like his shoulders were rubbing against the undulations of the mountain slope.

When the rain stopped, Erik could hear the sound of water washing off the mountain somewhere and into the gorge, falling seemingly into an endless void, even though they could barely see it, until the protective wall disappeared. Then, the ravine was exposed in all its terror. A giant gaping crevice that slowly descended into darkness, so large that, as Erik looked to the other side of the gulley, the rest of the mountain looked faint, covered by a blue haze and fog. When that range pushed closer, and the rain lessened, and the haze lifted, he could see tall, white-barked pines and ashy-barked cottonwoods covering every foot of solid earth, the redness of new growth sprouting from their branches like a butterfly emerging from its chrysalis. Beyond that, Erik could see great, red-barked pines, so large they could be seen from leagues away, their tops scratching the bottoms of the clouds

That afternoon, Beldar found a cave—deep and wide, large enough to hold the whole company with room for comfort. Balzarak held up a fist.

"We will stop here," the General said.

Erik spoke with Bofim for a while—he and Beldar always interested in talking with him—and when they stopped, he closed his eyes and pretended to sleep. When he realized sleep would not come, he saw Wrothgard and Switch, Turk and Balzarak sitting at the cave's entrance, staring out into the blackness of a cloud-covered night. He crawled over to them, climbing over his sleeping companions. Wrothgard inspected the bow—etched with bone and silver—he had retrieved from Thorakest's armory while Switch played with one of his knives and the dwarves just sat.

"Aren't you tired?" Turk asked.

"Exhausted, really," Erik replied with a nod.

His muscles ached. It felt as if someone drove a rusted nail into his temples. Half the time, he saw double, his eyelids felt so heavy. But the alternative was darkness, death, screaming, shrieking, a night of fighting the dead.

"Do your dreams terrify you that much?" Turk replied.

"No, not my dreams," Erik replied, "but what is in them, what awaits me when I close my eyes, what it means."

"Get some rest, my friend," Turk finally said, patting Erik on the shoulder and walking to the back of the cave.

Erik looked out at the dark mountain. He could see shadows of pines, far away. He could hear the scurrying and pitter-pattering of small feet. He could hear the distant howls of wolves. He could smell a skunk. He could feel the fire dying.

Finally, he looked to the sky. Amidst breaks in the clouds, he saw stars and the faint outline of the moon.

"An, Almighty, Creator, God, whatever you might prefer to be called, please let me sleep tonight. Please." He breathed slowly as fatigue weighed on him so heavily that he wanted to cry. "I pray to you, please let me sleep. Give me this one night of rest. Please."

Erik awoke, still at the mouth of the cave. He must've curled up in his sleep. His night had not been dreamless. But the dead did not meet him. He had seen a distant hill, a quick sunrise, and a clear morning. It was a cool day, comfortable enough for a thin, stitched shirt. On that hill stood a single tree, tall and wide with branches that hung and dipped low to the ground, brushing the tall grass that grew about its base if a breeze caught them just right. He saw a man under that tree, a single man. He knew him in his dream, but now he couldn't see his face. Who was he? He knew him. He had run to him, embraced him, cried on the man's shoulder. And now he couldn't remember.

He closed his eyes and breathed deep.

"Thank you, An. Thank you."

Chapter 50

LIEUTENANT SORBEN PHURNAN LED HIS men, several dozen soldiers following him, through the heavily forested area of the mountain's southern range. He grumbled and ground his teeth before he touched his cheek and winced when he found the still slightly swollen spot. A gift from Lieutenant Bu. That bastard had chastised Sorben about his men, about their lack of training, and even ventured to say that it was his men's fault they had lost a troll.

"Maybe it's because you're a stupid cunt with not an ounce of noble blood flowing through your veins and you don't know how to lead," Sorben muttered. It's the same thing he had said to Bu in the confines of the officer's tent. It's the same thing that had led to Bu's gift—a fist to the face, a swollen cheek, and a black eye.

When he had told the General of Bu's offense, Patûk Al'Banan just laughed and asked Sorben if he had hit Bu back.

"We are not in the back alleys of Goldum or Bard'Sturn," Sorben had replied.

That caused the General to laugh even louder.

"Grow some balls," the General had said.

"I have balls," Sorben hissed to himself, grabbing his crotch aggressively and then promptly letting go, realizing he had grabbed himself a little too hard.

Sorben Phurnan had been so deep in his own thoughts he hadn't seen one of his scouts emerge from the darkness of the underbrush.

"By the gods," Sorben said, "you smell like shit."

"Sorry, sir," the scout said, bowing. He was out of breath.

"What is the matter?" Sorben asked, the level of annoyance in his voice almost at its peak levels.

"I found a dead troll," the scout said.

Sorben hadn't bothered to stop walking as the scout spoke, but this gave him cause to halt, holding up a closed fist.

"One of ours?" the Lieutenant asked.

"No, sir," the scout replied. "It had been mauled... badly. And I have lost track of Carl."

"Who is that?" Sorben asked with derision.

"The other scout, sir," the scout said.

Sorben could have cared less about the other scout, but a dead troll... that was cause for alarm.

"By the gods," Sorben said, "why do you smell so badly?"

"I rubbed myself with bear scat, sir," the scout replied, "to hide my scent."

"There is no hiding that scent," Sorben replied. "How far away from here was the dead troll?"

"Not far," the scout replied.

"What could bring down a mountain troll?" Sorben asked.

"Only a few things, sir," the scout replied. "A pack of wolves. But only in desperation, and this was not wolves. An antegant maybe, some possibly live in these mountains, but I don't believe it was that either. It left claw markings, but bigger than a cougar or bear."

"Sergeant," Sorben called. He noticed his scout duck as he raised his voice. He thought he even saw the man tremble.

Sorben's Sergeant finally came to him, bowing.

"How many men do we have?" Sorben asked.

"Two score," the Sergeant replied.

"Take a dozen men and search the forest ahead of us," Sorben commanded.

"Sir, I would not advise..." the scout began to say.

"It will be a cold day in the nine hells when I take advice

from a scout," Sorben snapped. "Sergeant, do you understand my command?"

Sorben's Sergeant stared at the scout for a moment, and he looked scared. The scout shook his head, only slightly, but Sorben saw it. The Lieutenant could see it too now, the fear on the scout's face, and it had got to his Sergeant. Pathetic. He grabbed the Sergeant by the collar and pulled him close.

"Do you understand my command, Sergeant?" Sorben repeated.

The Sergeant turned his attention to Sorben.

"Yes, sir," he replied.

"You will go with them, scout," Sorben commanded.

Then, he saw the scout sniff the air. He moved back, towards the company of soldiers, hand going to the handle of his sword.

Sorben, in turn, gripped the handle of his own sword.

"Scout, did you hear me?" he asked.

"Do you smell it?" the scout asked.

"All I smell is the bear shit stink coming from you," Sorben said, drawing his sword. "Obey me, or I will run you through right here."

"Do you hear it?" the scout added, seemingly unaware that the Lieutenant was even talking to him.

Sorben had had enough.

"That is…"

The Sergeant grabbed Sorben's wrist.

"Wait," the Sergeant said.

"Get your hand off my…"

"Shut up," the Sergeant said. "Something is out there."

Sorben felt his face grow hot.

"How dare…" but then, he heard something too. The crunching of branches. A low groan. Heavy breathing. And then he smelled it, and the stench made him gag.

The fading light and the dense canopy of trees made the forest look almost like night. Sorben could barely see a dozen paces ahead of him, and then there was a thick copse of creepers, bushes, and pines in front of them.

There it was again. A snort and a low growl. The smell was heavy, pungent, and thick. Then, with a thundering roar, it burst from the trees before the company of soldiers, knocking younger pines over and uprooting them. As it stood to its full height, twice as tall as any man, it opened its giant maw and roared again, spittle flying from its mouth.

"Bear!" someone from behind Sorben shouted.

But this was unlike any bear Sorben had ever seen. It was a brown giant with thick, matted fur, a bony plate covering its forehead, and bony ridges and protrusions along both sides of its jaw.

The Sergeant still gripped Sorben's wrist. The Lieutenant jerked his arm forward, throwing the Sergeant into the path of the giant bear. With one paw swipe, the creature ripped the head from the Sergeant's body, and it bounced away across the forest floor. A unified chorus of cries rang out from the retinue of soldiers behind Sorben and several spears flew over his head. Two bounced harmlessly off the beast's thick hide as one stuck, but the bear didn't even seem to notice.

"Protect your officer!" Sorben yelled. Walking backwards he tripped over a root, and as he tumbled to the ground, he pissed himself.

All he could think of was that giant bear crushing his limbs between his huge jaws. Coming to his knees, he felt hot tears on his face. The beast had killed two more of his men. Archers came to stand in front of Sorben. They fired arrow after arrow even though they did nothing but annoy the bear. It stomped and roared, and Sorben froze. He couldn't move no matter how hard he tried. He felt his bowels empty, and vomit rose in his throat as the creature roared, its stinking hot breath on his face, and the terror the sound created threw one of his archers back into him.

Screams and cries, cursing and shouting told Sorben that his men were dying, even as he lay helpless on the ground. He saw a blur of brown and red as the beast tore through flesh. The Lieutenant felt a jerk at his collar and looked up to see the scout that smelled like bear shit dragging him. The soldier lifted Sorben and threw him over another man's shoulder, and they ran.

As they ran away, Sorben looked up and saw that the bear didn't bother to give chase; it was too busy feasting on the bodies of his men. There weren't as many dead as Sorben thought, and he saw a good number of his men running with him and the scout and the soldier carrying him.

Within moments, the thick brush and trees masked the apocalyptic scene, and Sorben's men slowed to a walk until they stopped in a small clearing. Sorben was lowered to the ground, and he just lay there, eyes closed, unable to believe he had gotten away unharmed.

"By the gods," he heard one man curse, "what is that bloody smell?"

"The Lieutenant," someone replied in a hushed tone.

"Did he shit himself?" someone else asked, also in a whisper.

They must have thought he had passed out, but Sorben lay there, listening.

"I guess he got scared," a soldier added.

"We was all scared," the first man said. "Doesn't mean I bloody shit myself."

"I think I might have pissed myself," a younger voice, said, "at least, a little."

"You dumb cunt," said the soldier on whose shoulder Sorben traveled, "you're supposed to piss yourself when you see a giant fucking bear. You're nothing but a whelp with naught but a single hair on your balls. You're not a seasoned officer."

"Seasoned," someone scoffed. Sorben recognized that voice. It was the scout's voice. "The only thing he's seasoned at is drinking sweet wine and bending over for big, burly men like yourself, Kenneth."

"Fuck you," the bearer of Sorben, Kenneth, replied.

"I'll tell you what, though," the scout added, quieting his voice even more, "do you think Bu would've shit himself?"

"Not a bloody chance," Kenneth replied. "That crazy cunt

would've ran his sword right up that bear's ass. That's a man worth following."

Sorben felt his stomach knot, felt the tears flowing freely from his eyes. They would all pay for those remarks, all of them. He didn't care how many he had to kill. They would pay for such treasonous ideas…and then he would take care of Bu once and for all.

Chapter 51

ERIK FELT HIS STOMACH KNOT. The bridge was wide enough for two men to walk side by side, but one misstep would lead only to darkness. As he looked down into the great chasm, his breath caught in his throat, and he felt his knees weaken. Once, on the other side, the company rested a moment, and Erik noticed one of the dwarves, taller than the others and with dark hair and beard, lifting his head and sniffing the air.

Erik looked to Bofim.

"Mortin smell something," the dwarf said.

"What does he smell?" Erik asked.

Bofim shrugged.

"Don't know," the dwarf replied, "but it enough to make General want to move away from here."

"We're not hiking into the mountain from here?" Erik asked.

Bofim shook his head as Erik saw Mortin look to Balzarak and shake his head ever so slightly before moving off again. As they walked, Bofim talked with Erik quietly, as much as he could in his broken Westernese and, in turn, Erik would speak to him in Dwarvish.

"I could use song," Bofim said.

"A dwarvish traveling song?" Erik asked with a smile.

"Aye. Bim," Bofim said with a nod to another dwarf, this one balding and with a great scar that ran from the back of his head, through a now useless left eye, and into his beard. Bim nodded back and smiled. "My cousin, Bim. Good voice."

"Quiet," the General hissed. "Thegthû. We can ill afford unnecessary noise right now."

Rain intensified the tension of the silent hike. At first, it was just a light drizzle, but as the clouds created a premature evening, they also unleashed a soaking furry upon the mountainside that gave Erik cause to constantly and cautiously watch the mountain path and the wall that rose up to the south, which promptly turned to mud.

"How long do we have to walk before we actually get to the forest?" Erik asked, eyeing both the ravine to his right and the ever-rising wall of mud to his left.

Bofim just shrugged while Mortin shot Erik a dirty look.

"Something has the General on edge," Turk said in a whisper.

"We will hike along this path as long as the General wants us to," Threhof growled over his shoulder. "Now, shut your mouths."

Erik heard Nafer whisper something to Turk in their native language. He saw Turk nod with a scowl on his face. He tried discerning what his dwarvish friends were saying, but in the numbing din of rain and the softness of their voices, the only word he understood was danger.

Erik lost track of time as he could not see the moon or stars. The dwarves had resigned to lighting torches in the darkness of the storm, the pitch-smeared sticks resisting the rain as much as they could hope. The mountain wall to his left rose and fell, and he hoped they would soon be away from the giant ravine that separated northern and southern ranges.

Occasionally, Erik caught Balzarak speaking with Mortin. Their conversations always seemed short and never pleasant.

They had walked a long time, and it seemed that they were slowing down, perhaps stopping for the night, when something strong and pungent caught Erik's nose.

"What is that smell?" Erik asked.

"I said shut your..." Threhof began to say, but Turk cut him off.

"I smell it too," Turk said.

"Befel, do you smell it?" Erik asked.

His brother nodded his head, crinkling his nose at the smell.

"It smells like a decaying deer carcass," Bryon added.

"Worse," Erik said.

Erik then heard a great sucking of air, a wind that brought with it an even stronger, more putrid scent and an unusual warmth. It continued, over and over, slowly, methodically, like something was…

"Breathing," Erik muttered.

"What?" Befel asked.

Mortin stopped, put his nose to the air again, and then turned to Balzarak.

"Sprüga!" the dwarf yelled.

"Run!" Turk translated.

Just as the dwarves yelled, Erik heard a great crash and then a loud growl. He looked up to see the giant head of a bear, one with bony ridges along its jaw and a bony plate along its forehead, burst between the trunks of two large pines above them, growing along the top of the mountain wall. The head uprooted the trees, and they tumbled over the wall and into the ravine, taking much of the mud and earth with them. Erik had never seen a beast so big. It roared and growled, eyeing the party, but it seemed weary to attack, perhaps sensing the instability of the ground below its massive body.

"Cave bear!" Turk yelled. "Run for your life! Run as fast as you can, and do not stop!"

The bear swiped a great claw out in front of it and bounced up and down shaking the earth. Then, surprisingly, it disappeared back into the forest.

Erik slowed, but a firm hand to the middle of his back spurred him on again.

"It is not gone," Turk said. "It is following us. Keep moving."

Just as Turk spoke, the creature burst from the forest again, sending more earth and trees and shrubbery into the ravine. Its swiping claws barely missed Switch's head.

"By the gods," the thief cursed, ducking and stumbling forward.

The bear pounded at the earth, sending rocks flying. Erik felt debris against his face as the creature continued to claw at the ground and growl, swinging its great paws at the men and dwarves running by. The muddy wall behind the creature began to give way underneath the weight of the beast, spilling across the pathway and prompting the bear to retreat back into the forest once more.

Erik felt his heart pound, running as fast as he could while jumping over piles of mud that had spilled into his way and dodging roots and branches blocking his path. He had forgotten about the chasm to his right, only worried about the gigantic bear that seemed intent on making them its next meal. Its smell subsided, and its growling and breathing were gone, but they still pressed on at a furious, even reckless pace.

Finally, Balzarak slowed, and everyone else followed suit until they all stood together to catch their breath. Erik wanted to collapse, but rather grabbed at his knees and sucked in large amounts of air.

"What was that?" Erik asked.

"Cave bear," Bofim said.

"Don't all bears live in caves?" Bryon gasped.

"Aye they do," Turk replied, pausing to gulp in air before continuing. "But cave bears are the giant ancestors of what we call a brown bear. The territory of a single cave bear might be leagues upon leagues. They normally live in the deepest forests, away from any civilization, so it is odd that we would see one so close to dwarvish settlements, and that it would attack us. Something is truly amiss for it to be so close to Thorakest and the surrounding habitation and I ..."

Turk suddenly stopped and spun around as Erik smelled decaying flesh, heard the sound of sucking air, and felt the ground shake underneath his feet. Then, it burst from the forest again, rock and trees tearing away from their centuries old resting places. With a deafening roar, the cave bear jumped onto the mountain path, and it was too much for the conditions.

The ground underneath began falling away, creating a mudslide, and Erik watched in horror as Threhof fell away from the beast, tumbling down with the mudslide and going over the edge. Balzarak yelled to the dwarves, and Beldar let out a concerned cry, but they were on the other side of the waterfall of mud.

Erik looked down and saw that a large rock had broken Threhof's fall. Erik's eyes frantically scanned the surrounding and saw a creeper, rooted and anchored deep in the mountain wall; he knew that was Threhof's lifeline if he could reach it. As the bear, now bold enough to brave the unstable path, swiped and clawed and roared, Erik rushed to the edge of the pathway to find Threhof dangling there, desperately clinging to the thick creeper and slipping amidst the mud and rain just as the rock that had stopped his fall fell away and descended into the ravine.

Smaller rocks raining down on top of Erik told him the bear was close. He lay on his belly and reached down to Threhof, but the dwarf was just out of reach. He tried pulling up on the creeper, but the slipperiness of rain and wet earth, along with the weight of the dwarf, made that impossible.

"Someone grab my feet!" Erik yelled.

"Why?" Wrothgard called back.

"So I can grab Threhof," Erik replied.

"Leave him," Switch said.

"Hurry," Erik called. "He's slipping, and the earth is giving way beneath me!"

Wrothgard knelt over Erik, firmly grabbing his legs and tucking them under his armpits. Erik risked a quick glance over his shoulder to see dwarves contending with the bear, axes and swords barely nicking the beast's thick hide and spears bouncing harmlessly away. He looked back down at the stricken dwarf.

"Grab my hand," Erik called.

Threhof started to reach up but then ducked as a clawed paw swung over Erik's head. He felt the wind break against the back of his head and heard Wrothgard curse.

"Hurry, Erik," the soldier said, "before we become bear shit."

Threhof slipped farther down the creeper.

"Lower me further," Erik said.

"Damn it, brother," Befel said, "leave him, or you'll both die. And you'll take Wrothgard down with you."

"Just a little more!" Erik screamed over the yelling and roaring and the din of the deluge.

Wrothgard lowered Erik a little more until he finally reached Threhof, first taking one hand, and then the other.

"By the Creator, you're heavy," Erik grunted, and Threhof groaned at that. "Pull me up."

It was slow, and his wet fingers kept slipping, but with his muscles burning, Erik finally reached the path, Threhof in tow. As they both thudded to the ground in an exhausted heap, Erik saw that not only Wrothgard, but Demik and Bryon had pulled him up as well, the others doing their best to fend off the bear as the beast was now almost fully onto the pathway.

"Our weapons can't hurt it!" Turk yelled, desperation clear in his eyes.

Erik looked over his shoulder to his cousin.

"Bryon!" Erik shouted. "Your sword!"

Bryon stared at him.

"It's the only thing that will pierce its hide," Erik said.

Bryon looked frozen for a moment, but then, his hand went to the handle of his elvish sword, and he drew it. Erik could hear the rain hiss as it struck the purple blade, and Bryon inched forward. The glare of the magic light must have caught the bear's eye, as it turned its attention to Erik's cousin. It snorted and growled, stamping the ground.

It lurched forward, roaring, hot breath and spittle splashing against Erik's face. Bryon was within range of one of its paws. The beast walked fully onto the pathway, and Erik could see the ground beneath it move, ready to give way. It reared up on its hind legs, and with another mighty roar, it swung at Bryon.

Bryon put his sword up and gripping it in both hands, he swiped diagonally, one of the strikes Wrothgard had taught them. Erik saw the end of a paw fly away into the darkness, and the scream that came from the beast was hideous. It brought down its other paw, hoping to crush Bryon, but he jabbed upwards with his sword, and the blade hissed as it passed through the bear's flesh.

It pushed Bryon to the ground but retracted its wounded paw immediately. The ground underneath the creature began to give way, and it looked as if the animal would fall with the earth, but its massive claws in the other paw dug into the mountain side, and it pulled itself up.

Erik could only watch and wonder at the show of strength. The bear pushed fervently with its hind legs, pushing it up and up until it reached the line of trees just above the heads of the company. It looked back at them and snorted before it disappeared into the forest.

Erik finally stood. He helped Threhof to his feet as well.

"Ic näa thu famannblôd," the dwarf said, adding in Westernese. "I owe you a blood debt."

"I appreciate that," Erik said, "but we can talk about that later. Right now, we have to get off this dangerous path."

They all walked carefully on until the path took them away from the ravine and into the forest. As he trudged along, his muscles aching more than ever, Erik sensed the dagger by his side.

"I suppose I could have used you against that bear," Erik whispered, patting the golden handle of his dagger.

You could have, but it was good to give your cousin that chance.

"Give him a chance?" Erik wondered.

A chance to prove himself among your companions. They watch him with questioning eyes.

"Truly?" Erik asked. He didn't get a reply.

Chapter 52

ERIK'S SLEEP HAD BEEN DREAMLESS, and that was always welcomed. Still yawning, he sat up, brushing pine needles out of his chest hair. The rain had stopped, but his shirt, lying on the ground next to the fire, was still wet.

"Did you sleep well?" Beldar asked.

"I guess as well as can be expected," Erik replied.

"Erik," Threhof said with a smile. "You are awake. Once again, let me say to you how thankful I am for your bravery. You saved my life. I can honestly say that that was the first time in one hundred and eighty-eight years that I owe my life to a man."

"One hundred and eighty-eight years old?" Erik asked, sitting forward with raised eyebrows.

Threhof laughed.

"Don't look at me like that," he said, still chuckling, "I am not the oldest one here."

Threhof pointed to Dwain. Dwain said something to Threhof in Dwarvish.

"I am two hundred and one years old," Dwain said, "but I don't feel a day over one hundred and fifty."

"Now that he's awake," Wrothgard said, nodding to Erik, "shouldn't we leave?"

"Cave bear gone," Bofim said. "Bim track it. No find. Gone. We can rest some more."

"We'll need it," Dwain added. "Not many, even dwarves, come around these parts much. We'll have to be alert."

As the others talked, Erik laid back down, hands behind his head and thinking of his betrothed—Simone—he felt a tickle on his hip.

I would have been there if you had needed me.

"Truly?" Erik thought.

Truly, b*ut wield me with care, Erik Eleodum.*

Erik furrowed his brow, not understanding what his dagger meant.

Heed what the dwarf Ilken said. Many warriors have become corrupt because of treasures like me.

Erik felt less than comforted.

It is not because their weapons were evil, but because of the power they gave their owners. Men tend to become drunk on power. And remember this, the more power I exert, the longer I have to rest. Yes, be very careful how you use me.

Lieutenant Sorben Phurnan stood watching the dense forest, hands on his waist. He clenched his jaw. He watched two of his soldiers, men of *pure blood*, talk and joke.

"Pure blood," he hissed. "Fools more like it."

He spat. He was pure blood, noble, born to lead. These men were born to die. And they had grown bold since they were attacked by that giant bear.

"What's so funny," he hissed.

"Nothing," one of the soldiers replied, straightening his back in a half attempt to stand at attention.

"Nothing what?" Sorben asked, stepping forward.

"Nothing, sir," the soldier replied, straightening a little more.

Sorben Phurnan rubbed a finger up the man's cheek. He heard the slightest scratch of stubble.

"Why is your face not shaven?"

"I shaved this morning, sir."

The Lieutenant heard insolence and irritation in his soldier's voice. His face went hot.

"Then shave again, if need be, to keep that rubbish off your face, you piece of pig shit."

"Yes, sir."

The man didn't move.

"I just told you to go shave," Sorben said.

"Right now, sir?" his soldier asked.

"Yes," Sorben said. He clenched his fists.

The soldier bowed, did an about face, and walked back towards the camp. Sorben Phurnan looked to the other man. His face looked soft, almost fat. The Lieutenant looked up at the top of the overlooking, forested hill, and motioned to another soldier standing there.

"You two will stand here, motionless, quiet, and at attention," Sorben Phurnan said when the other soldier reached him. "What good is an ambush if the ones we wish to ambush can hear us?"

Just a day before, one of Lieutenant Bu's scouts came with an order. A contingency of men and dwarves were headed their way. They were to stop them. Sorben had refused at first. He didn't take orders from Bu, that son of a whore. When he threatened the life of the scout, the man laughed at Sorben, told him it would be a cold day in the nine hells when a man who shits himself killed him, and said that this day, he did take orders from Bu.

The hair on the back of Sorben's neck stood on end just thinking about it. The look that scout gave him, the look his men gave him, the look—that stupid smirk—he knew Bu had as he handed the scout the orders. Nonetheless, there they were, waiting deep in the forests of the Southern Mountains for dwarves and men, supposedly in the employ of the Lord of the East. Sorben had insisted that they didn't need to follow these ragamuffins. They had confiscated a map from another mercenary, but as soon as General Patûk Al'Banan touched the map, it went up in flames. They were to force these ones, at least one of them, to lead the General to some lost dwarvish city.

Sorben Phurnan stood, back straight, surveying the forest. He didn't know what he was looking for, but he had to at least give pretense. His men's loyalty was already shaky at best. His trolls slouched to either side of him. One gave a quick grunt and, without thinking, he swatted its massive shoulder with the back of his hand. The creature could have pummeled him, but it just looked at him with irritation in its eyes and picked its nose.

"You are a disgusting creature, you know that, right?" Sorben asked. "You haven't a clue what I'm saying, do you? Mongrel. If it were up to me, I would have all of you exterminated. Why the General employs you, I will never understand."

He looked back at the sloping hill that rose just twenty paces from where he stood. He scanned the terrain, trying to find the two archers he knew knelt there, behind a copse of firs and tall bushes. He spotted one—the tip of his iron helmet. Seeing him, he then made out the outline of the soldier's longbow amidst the shrubbery. He saw he had an arrow nocked and half-drawn. The soldier's dark eyes met the Lieutenant's eyes. The archer nodded and bowed, and Sorben nodded back.

"They will not know what happened." Sorben smiled.

One of the trolls next to him stuck its nose in the air, sucking in deep breaths through its nose.

"Shut up you stinking…"

Sorben stopped then. The troll looked to the south. He followed the beast's gaze. He thought he something move, behind several low hanging branches and a tall, reddish bush. His hand went to the handle of his sword, and he slid the blade out halfway.

Lieutenant Sorben's hand dropped from his sword, and he closed his eyes, sighing. A man appeared from behind a tree—leather breastplate and soft, leather boots. One of the men from General Patûk's spy network. One of Lieutenant Bu's men. Sorben felt a frown dip the corners of his mouth, and he hissed.

"Stinking Bu," he muttered.

He walked to Sorben, not bothering to kneel, bow, even salute.

"Lieutenant Bu wants a word."

"You forget yourself," Sorben seethed. "You are addressing an officer."

"Lieutenant Bu wants a word, sir," the soldier-spy repeated.

"I do not answer to Bu."

"Lieutenant Bu answers to the General. Do you answer to the General, sir?"

"Y-you insolent bastard," Sorben spat. His hand went to his sword. "I should have my trolls eat you where you stand."

"Sir, we both know you won't," the spy said with a sigh of impatience. "I am short on time, sir. Do you have word to send to Lieutenant Bu?"

"You can tell that poor excuse of an officer to go piss on his mother's grave," Sorben spat, punching an index finger into the chest of the soldier.

"So, you have no news of the men traveling with dwarves?" the spy asked, ignoring the finger.

Just then, one of the trolls grunted, and Sorben turned on the beast hard. He was about to kick it when he saw it, its nose to the air taking in deep breaths of air. It looked to Lieutenant Phurnan, then to the spy, then to the Lieutenant again. It grunted twice, and the Lieutenant thought it might have nodded.

"You can tell Lieutenant Bu that we have just found them, and they will soon be in our hands. You can tell him that, and when I am a Captain, I will make sure to…" Sorben turned to face Bu's spy, but the man was gone.

Chapter 53

Erik lost track of the days. They all seemed to cram together in one long blur of waking, training, hiking, training, and disturbed, dream-filled nights. That hill and tree started appearing in his dreams more often. A tree with low hanging branches stood atop it, and a man, someone he knew, always sat under that tree. And the undead were nowhere to be seen.

After another short morning training session, Erik knew something was wrong. As he became more proficient with Dwarvish, he overheard the dwarves arguing about the map the Lord of the East had given them. Erik didn't say anything to the other men, but from what he gathered, they were lost. The map didn't make sense to any of the dwarves, and none of them were familiar with this range of the Southern Mountains.

Erik had confidence in them, at least Turk, Demik, and Nafer, but his stomach sank when he heard trail and time hardened dwarves such as Threhof and Dwain disagreeing about which way to go and which landmark this was and that was. And on top of them being lost, he overheard Balzarak and Gôdruk speaking of danger in the forest that was mostly overgrown and teeming with unchecked predators that had little to fear in the way of men or dwarves. But it was a different danger of which they spoke, something more serious, more sinister, more deadly. Something or someone was tracking them.

When Erik came back to camp with Wrothgard from training, Dwain, the old, experienced warrior, greeted him.

"Come," Dwain said in Westernese. His mastery of the language was as good as any man who had grown up in Western Háthgolthane. "Break fast with me this morning."

Erik nodded with a smile.

"Where are you going, brother?" Befel asked.

"With Dwain," Erik replied.

"He'd rather spend time with the dwarves than his own blood," Befel said. "I am beginning to think he wants to be a dwarf."

Erik heard his brother but pretended otherwise.

"It is time," Dwain said to Erik as they walked a ways into the forest.

"Time for what?" Erik asked.

"A troll has been tracking us," Dwain replied. "We need your help."

Erik thought for only a moment before nodding.

"All right," he said, "tell me what I need to do."

"It will rain today," the dwarf said. "That will help cover things up."

"And why does it have to be me?" Erik asked.

"Trolls are weary of dwarves," Dwain replied. "And they would be weary of the soldier. I am sorry, but you are the least suspecting looking, but, then again, well-trained enough to survive our scheme."

Erik knew a troll had been tracking them, for several days now. The dwarves could tell that the beast thought it was well hidden, but they knew it was there almost the moment it had started following them. They also suspected the creature hadn't attacked, even while they slept, because it was employed by men and instructed to just watch. However, the dwarves knew instinct would always overcome a troll. Given the opportunity for a quick and quiet meal, the troll would act. Erik nodded his understanding.

They walked back to the camp, where the rest of their companions were packing up.

"I have to piss," Erik said.

"Bloody great!" Switch cried. "I always want to know when you wish to relieve yourself. Tell me how it goes."

The thief had become increasingly temperamental among the dwarves.

Erik felt his stomach knot as he walked out into the forest alone. He patted his golden-handled dagger and the scabbard of his dwarf-crafted sword—his only consolations. He walked far enough so that his companions were out of sight. He knew Dwain and Bofim were following him, somewhere even though he couldn't see them. He laughed silently. They would make good thieves. That would make Switch smile and Demik grumble. When he felt like he was far enough away, he pretended to relieve himself. It began to rain, very softly, and the feeling of slight, cold drops tickled his skin. Then, he heard a sound, a twig snapping, leaves rustling, a bird fluttering away.

Erik's heart raced as his hand went to the handle of his sword. He meant to grab his dagger first, but then he remembered what it had told him. The more he used it, the more time it took to recover. What was more urgent than fighting a mountain troll? Erik had a feeling he would need the dagger in the coming days more than this day. Then he saw it—a black tailed fox, with a large brown rat hanging limply in its mouth. The small predator scurried behind a bushy, green brush and then into the hollowed part of a log.

Erik dropped his head back and sighed as he felt his face flush and his heart drop into his stomach. His shoulders slumped forward, and his hand dropped from the sword handle.

"Thank you An," he mouthed.

Then it hit him, the smell of decay and rotting flesh and worse than latrines, pigsties, or a butchered chicken that had sat for too long.

Erik swallowed hard and kept his eyes closed. He slowly lowered his head, and his hand went back to the handle of his sword. The mountain breeze was disturbed by a stream of hot air that hit his face and it carried with it that rotten smell, only tenfold worse. Erik felt his stomach knot and turn, and the acid taste of vomit filled his throat. He looked up again, and they stared at him. Those eyes. Yellow with black beady pupils, filled with hate and death.

If a cat's purr had an evil twin, a deep rumble that denoted wickedness and filth and malice, that is what Erik heard. It rolled through this small space in the forest like quiet thunder, and with it, Erik knew the troll was about to strike.

It moved forward, planting both feet firmly into the ground a pace from where Erik stood. If Erik blinked his eye, it would be on him. His eyes fixed on the troll as if he might mesmerize it, slowly drawing his sword until he felt the tip of the blade clear the scabbard.

It took only seconds for a dozen scenarios to flit through his head, just as Wrothgard had taught him. Fight a fight a thousand times before you actually fight it. But each one ended the same. His death. That wasn't what the soldier had taught.

"Always envision yourself winning," he had said.

"And if I don't end up winning?" Erik had asked.

Wrothgard had just shrugged.

Instead of charging him, the troll straightened its back and lifted its chin. It gave a quick huff. It knew they were there. It was too late, but it knew. It inhaled a chest full of air, but before it could bellow out, the broad blade of a spear thudded into its chest. Erik turned to see Threhof running towards them. Then he heard the sound of bone breaking. He turned to see the troll hunched over, grimacing and growling as Bofim's hammer smacked into the troll's shoulder once, twice, three times.

The troll reached up and ripped the spear from its chest, taking a good chunk of its flesh with it. Blood poured freely from the wound. It lifted its head, and Erik knew it was going to howl, seeking to warn its handlers. He knew there was no more time to wait, and he punched his blade forward, straight into the fleshy part just above the troll's collarbone. The dwarvish blade slid easily through muscle and tendon. It looked at him, wide-eyed. It swung an arm to swat the sword away, and Erik's blade came down hard where the beast's neck met its large, sloping shoulders. Blood seeped from the troll's nose and mouth.

Erik slid the blade out of the troll's shoulder again, making sure to drag the steel along its flesh, and then struck again. At the same time, Bofim brought his hammer down on the other shoulder. They attacked together, again, again, and again. Threhof joined them, bringing his broadsword hard across the troll's exposed chest.

Erik saw the troll's eyes roll, its lids half-close. It was almost dead. His heart fluttered as pride welled up, as he avenged the death of Drake and Samus. A growl, forced and labored, rolled from its mouth, and the beast opened that gaping hole as wide as it could.

Erik struck, a move Wrothgard called *Striking Viper*. His blade punched through the mouth and hit the back of the troll's thick skull. Blood and brain and bone exploded from the back of its head. When he retrieved his blade, the troll slumped to the side, limp and stinking.

Erik looked at Threhof, and the dwarf nodded before he looked back to Dwain, who had remained hidden behind a tree. Dwain nodded back and put his hands over his mouth, making the sound of a blue jay.

"They are brutal," Threhof said, "but they are stupid. A well-coordinated attack will end like this most times."

"Good job," Bofim said, slapping the man's shoulder. "Good sword."

"Ilken made it for me," Erik said. "It's the first time I've used it."

"Ilken Copper Head?" Bofim asked with a nod of approval. "It is very good then."

Erik heard another blue jay call, this one coming from the direction of their camp. Bofim jerked his head, telling Erik to follow him.

"It is done?" Wrothgard asked when they came into view.

"It is done," Threhof said.

"What is done?" Befel asked.

"All thanks to Erik," Threhof added, presenting the young man with open arms.

"What are you talking about?" Befel asked.

"Good job, Erik," Balzarak said. "You seem to amaze me more and more each day."

"What are you talking about?" Befel asked again.

Erik explained what had happened, how he had agreed to be a decoy for a troll that was following them.

"And that seemed like a good idea to you?" Befel asked.

"It was the only option," Erik replied.

"Bull piss," Befel said. "I'm going to talk to Wrothgard right now."

"About what?" Erik asked. He felt his face growing hot. "Are you going to take up a grievance with the elders? We are in the middle of nowhere being followed by creatures we never knew existed a year ago. What exactly do you think you would do? Stop trying to be father."

He knew his words had hurt Befel, the look his brother gave him said that much. Erik waited for his brother to respond, but when he didn't, Erik just walked away.

"He only worries for you," Wrothgard said.

"It gets annoying," Erik replied.

"I know," Wrothgard said, "but it is only because he loves you."

"I know," Erik said more quietly.

"Clean your blade," Wrothgard said. "It saved your life today."

"Your training saved my life," Erik said.

"Also true," Wrothgard said. "But that sword had a lot to do with it. What will you name it, now that it has drawn blood?"

Erik looked at the grayish steel, deep with waves and still stained with blood.

"Ilken's Blade," Erik said with a smile.

Chapter 54

In his dream that night, Erik had Ilken's Blade. The dead were there, just like before, but there was no hill, no swooping willow tree, and no man he knew. He was in a large pasture with rolling hills and ankle high grass, dead and brown but still trying to pretend to be alive. The sky was red, the sun a distant point of light, and the moon was faintly showing orange when the dead came at him. But Ilken's Blade made little work of them. With every strike, he blasted the skeletal remains of someone out of existence. It was almost fun, but as he awoke, a tingle at his hip told him there was nothing to laugh about in his dreams.

"It seems I can will things into existence in that world," Erik thought as he patted his dagger. "Maybe tonight, I will dream of you."

But then the thought crept into his head as the tingle at his hip became a pinch. The dagger was not made for that world. It could not happen. And if it could... the thought trailed off.

"These are no simple dreams, then," Erik decided, but he felt no response.

As the sun rose higher, the company of dwarves and men walked along in single file, Bofim in front of Erik, and Demik behind him. Erik had been thinking of a number of things—his training, movements with his spear and sword, his language lessons, the troll—and didn't realize Bofim had stopped. The dwarf turned and put a finger to his lips. Switch and Beldar spoke with Balzarak, and then they gathered.

"Beldar and Switch scouted ahead," Balzarak said. "There are two archers sitting behind a cropping of firs, up on a hill. Two more men with spears and swords, and another with a plumed helmet. Two trolls as well."

"Perhaps we were wrong about the ambush," Threhof said. "That's not much of a force."

"There are more, hidden somewhere," Wrothgard said. "Eastern tactics. Feign weakness. Their main force will be hidden."

"We are close," Balzarak said. "We must continue slowly with caution. Be on the ready."

They crouched, then tiptoed a few paces, then stopped. Dwain and Threhof disappeared only to reappear a few moments later. After whispering to Balzarak, they looked to the rest of the party and motioned for them to resume, all at a crouch, bent low, weapons at the ready. Then they stopped again after just a handful of steps. This continued for the whole day, inching along, crouching, stepping carefully, sometimes crawling, stopping frequently until it grew dark.

"No sleep," Bofim whispered, looking over his shoulder at Erik.

Erik nodded.

"We attack, first daylight," the dwarf added, and Erik nodded his understanding.

Erik might have dozed off a few times. Night without a campfire in the deep forests of the Southern Mountains seemed to stand still, under the darkness of a canopy of trees. Their adversaries hadn't built a fire either, so there was no way of telling time until the sky overhead brightened.

Bofim gave a low whistle and then pointed to both his eyes, and then forward. Erik saw Switch and Wrothgard, duck walking at a good pace, bows in hand.

As Bofim pushed himself to his knees, Erik followed suit and followed the dwarf until they reached the General, around whom everyone began to gather.

"Switch and Wrothgard will take the archers," Balzarak explained. "There are only two of them. There are three more men and two trolls. We know there are more elsewhere, but this is what we can see as of now."

"We will split into two groups," Balzarak continued. "My group will go right. Dwain's will go straight on. Wait for my signal."

"What is your signal?" Bryon asked.

"Dwain will know it," Balzarak replied with a smile.

They continued to inch forward, this time crouched and only slightly faster. Bofim tapped Erik's shoulder.

"Look," the dwarf whispered.

Erik followed the dwarf's pointing finger and saw Wrothgard. Then he saw an iron helm with a small, purple plume.

"The archers," Erik muttered.

Then, the plume disappeared. Erik heard the call of a meadowlark off in the distance.

"Do meadowlarks live in the mountains?" Bryon asked.

Erik shook his head.

"It's a signal," Bofim whispered with a smile.

They stayed crouched but moved even faster. It wasn't long before Erik heard a voice, and the familiar grunting of mountain trolls. And then there was the smell. The language being spoken was foreign to Erik, but he had heard it before.

"Isn't that Shengu?" Erik asked.

Bofim nodded.

Erik heard the sucking of air. The troll was sniffing, and as it did, the man talking grew louder, his voice filled with anger and annoyance.

"They know we are here," Erik whispered.

"Man no listen," Bofim said.

The man, the one who controlled these beasts and commanded these men, wasn't listening. The trolls knew they were there. They could smell them. But that idiot of a soldier wasn't listening. It was evident in his voice.

"He'll die because of his ignorance," Erik said to no one in particular.

"Be ready," Erik heard Dwain say.

And then there it was again, the call of a meadowlark.

"Do you see how these men wear tunics?" Dwain asked Erik.

Erik nodded.

"If you can, draw your blade along their inner thigh, upwards, and at an angle. Cut there, and they will die within minutes from the blood loss."

Erik nodded again.

One more meadowlark call came through the forest.

"We attack," Dwain said, slowing creeping closer to the men.

Just then, Erik heard shouting. It was a mixture of Shengu and Dwarvish. He lifted his head a little higher to see Balzarak and his group. The look on his face was one of irritation. There were three more men than they had anticipated. Balzarak was in plain view, but the others were still mostly hidden.

"Did you think you could ambush us?" the leader of these men said in Westernese. "We knew you were here all along."

A part of Erik said that was a lie, but he knew the trolls had smelled them. As the now half dozen soldiers moved to intercept Balzarak, an arrow thudded into one of their chests.

"Wrothgard and Switch," Erik said with a smile.

"Attack," Dwain said in a loud whisper.

"Woo Chi!" the leader shouted, his purple plumed helm quivering as he moved behind his soldiers and the two trolls.

Erik stood with Bofim and Dwain and Befel and Bryon. The soldiers' backs were to them. Erik held his spear in both hands, stepped forward a few paces, and before a troll could give an alarming howl, jammed the blade of his spear into a man's back. As more dwarves emerged from the forest, the leader of these soldiers gave a surprised look.

"Sha tamen! Kill them!" he shouted before he ran back up the hill on which they had been standing. He somehow dodged several of Switch's and Wrothgard's arrows.

"He's going to alert his main force!" Wrothgard's voice was

distinct, but they couldn't worry about that now. The men fell quickly, but they had to contend with two mountain trolls.

Erik's group moved forward to meet Balzarak's, but a troll blocked their way. He could see the other one engaging the General and his warriors. It swung at Erik, and he ducked and sidestepped before he thrust with his spear, catching flesh. The beast howled, and Dwain thrust with his own spear. It howled again as Nafer rushed its side, bringing his mace hard against its ribs. The troll groaned and brought the back of a hand along Nafer's shoulder, knocking him to the ground. Dwain threw his spear, and it thudded into the troll's chest, and the beast stumbled back. Erik followed suit, but his spear didn't sink as deep.

The troll pulled Erik's spear from its chest and angrily snapped the weapon in two. Erik drew his sword and readied his shield as it charged. Erik felt heat close to his cheek and saw a purple glow flash in front of him before a huge gray hand fell to the forest floor. A howling cry of pain erupted from the beast as Bryon swung his sword again, reveling in his attack. A throwing axe sunk into the creature's shoulder. Nafer, recovered, struck again, as did Bofim and Demik. Erik drew his sword along the troll's chest as it tried to rear up, then brought his blade up, hard—as Wrothgard had taught him—into the soft, fleshy under parts of its jaw.

Erik felt his blade bite through bone and the heaviness of a giant monster as the beast went slack and fell to its side. A lesser blade made of lesser steel would have snapped under such pressure, but not Ilken's Blade.

"We killed a half dozen men and two trolls with barely a scratch," Bryon said, a smile growing on his face. Balzarak's group had made short work of the other troll.

"Don't get too cocky," Wrothgard said as he and Switch joined them. "There are more men—about two dozen—and trolls over that hill. We may have surprised their officer, but they were certainly waiting for us."

"More easterners?" Balzarak asked.

"Aye," Wrothgard replied.

"What is your suggestion?" the General asked.

"Make it to the crest of the hill before they do," Wrothgard said. "Fight them from the high ground. Don't let them get there first."

"That is a good plan," Balzarak said. "Let's go. You lead, soldier."

As they made their way up the hill, Erik saw one of the enemy soldiers on the ground. They must have presumed him dead, but his legs still moved. On closer inspection, he saw the man was alive, bloodied and pale. As he looked up at Erik, he clutched his stomach. He spoke to Erik in Shengu, but Erik just shook his head.

"Please," the soldier finally said in Westernese. "The pain."

"What do you want me to do?" Erik asked, moving closer. This soldier was younger than he.

"End it," the soldier said.

"How?" Erik asked, but then a dark thought crossed his mind.

This man should suffer. What hurt has he caused in this world? Would he have mercifully ended Drake's pain, or Samus'? Or would he have watched them bleed to death, or even worse, tortured them and laughed while they lived their final moments? Erik could be compassionate and send him to his death quickly, or he could show the same malice these men did and let him agonize. Erik shook his head. He wasn't this man. Erik rested the point of his blade at the base of the man's neck, the fleshy part just above the collarbone, and the man smiled amidst sobs.

"Thank you. I will tell Yama of your mercy when I meet him at the Yellow River, and I will tell Ga'an Yû of your strength," the man said before he closed his eyes and swallowed.

"No," Erik said. "Pray to the Creator. Ask him for forgiveness in this short moment. If you do not, I will know. I will see you in my dreams."

The man opened his eyes, looked at Erik curiously, nodded slowly, and then closed them again. Erik waited a moment and then he pushed, hard and quick. He heard a gulp, a quick gurgle, then nothing. The man's eyes never opened.

Erik caught up with his companions as they crested the hill. Below, he could see more enemy soldiers getting into formation. In front of them were several more trolls and behind them was their purple-plumed leader, barking orders.

"Form up!" Balzarak yelled in Dwarvish, and the dwarves started interlocking their shields, forming a wall. "Come, men, join us."

"Bofim is hurt, sir," Bim said.

"I will stay with him," Erik said. Bofim had been a good friend as of late.

"No," Befel said. "Let me stay with him. My shoulder, you know."

Erik nodded.

Erik and Bryon joined the dwarvish shield wall while Switch and Wrothgard stayed behind them with their bows.

"If it wasn't filled with two dozen men who wanted to kill us, plus several mountain trolls who wanted to eat us, this might be a very pleasant place," said Bryon and him and Erik laughed until an arrow thudded into Erik's shield. He saw some of the soldiers holding taller shields, covering archers. More arrows came at them.

"Fire back!" Balzarak yelled.

Switch and Wrothgard obliged.

"Down," Wrothgard said to Erik as one bowman moved from behind his shield with a nocked arrow. Erik ducked. Wrothgard fired and struck the man right between the eyes.

Switch's arrow found a home as well, not a bowmen, but the exposed flesh of a soldier.

"Their leader definitely has no idea what he is doing," Wrothgard muttered. "What a fool. It makes me wonder how he serves Patûk Al'Banan. That man is a military genius. If he were leading these men, we would be better off running."

"Tighten up," Balzarak commanded. "Wrothgard, Switch, cover us."

Without another word, the line of dwarves and men tightened, pressing shoulder to shoulder, and the two bowmen rushed to respective trees, one on either flank of the company.

"For Guthreth!" Balzarak cried out, and the other dwarves echoed him. They began to bang their weapons against their shields, chanting, "For Guthreth! For Guthreth! For Guthreth!"

Erik watched the soldiers' leader. He looked nervous, wide eyed, and shaking. He took a step back.

"Attack!" he yelled.

The soldiers all looked at him, unmoving. Of course they didn't want to attack. They were fighting a force of seasoned dwarves uphill. Even Erik knew that was a disadvantage.

"Attack I said! Advance! Attack you fools!"

The leader kicked one of his three trolls. The beast jolted forward, and its gray-skinned comrades followed, slamming their fists into the ground and rushing the dwarves and men on all fours, snorting and howling as they went. The soldiers ran after them.

The soldiers were fifty paces away, but the trolls closed in fast, forty, thirty, twenty. Arrows dotted their chests, shoulders, arms.

"Graben se fersen!" Balzarak cried.

The march stopped, and every dwarf crouched, slammed the bottom of their shields into the ground along with the butt of their spear if they had one. Erik and Bryon followed suit. Before he anchored himself, Beldar lowered his shield and hurled a spear at one troll. It skimmed the beast's side. He threw another. This one, its broad tip, slammed into the troll's shoulder, and it stuttered for a moment, but only a moment. It ripped the spear from its flesh, threw it away like some simple thorn, howled and spat and hurled itself into the wall of shielded dwarves.

"Are they cheering?" Erik asked as he thought the eastern soldiers before them shouted in joy when the troll hit the shield wall.

"It will be a short cheer," Bryon replied, ducking behind his shield and pressing his shoulder into it, magic sword in the other hand, ready to strike. "Look."

It was as if the shield wall was a cushion as the troll reeled back from the dwarves, bloodied and cut, flesh hanging from its body by thin tendrils of tendon and muscle. But where it fell back, another one was there to hurl itself into the wall.

Beldar threw his last spear, and the troll stumbled backwards. Mortin, standing on the other side of Erik, looked to him and winked. He lowered his shield and readied his spear to throw. Erik moved to cover the dwarf, and it was a good thing since two arrows thudded into his shield and would have hit the dwarf's chest. The dwarf threw his spear, striking the troll in the throat. The beast tripped backwards and fell. Mortin cheered and slapped Erik on the shoulder only to have two more arrows thud into his chest.

"Mortin!" Erik cried. "Mortin has been hit!"

"Tighten down," Threhof grumbled.

"What about Mortin?" Erik asked as he pressed shoulder to shoulder with Threhof.

"We will worry about him later." Erik saw the old warrior look back, over his shoulder. "That is why you don't cheer and celebrate until the battle is over."

Another troll fell in a bloody lump, laying on top of Bim. The last troll howled, turned, and ran.

"It's running," Erik muttered.

"It sees strength," Threhof said. "Trolls will not fight something—or someone—that is clearly stronger."

One of the soldiers fell, an arrow sticking from his chest. Another fell. A spear struck another, splintering his shield and sticking into his belly despite it and the leather breastplate. Their enemy's advance seemed to slow.

"Fight them, damn it!" their leader cried.

"Vorwats!" Balzarak yelled. "Shnell!"

"He's telling us to run," Erik said to Bryon.

Erik felt his stomach flutter. They all starting jogging at first, shields still interlocked, but upon Balzarak's command, as they closed in on the soldiers, the shield wall broke, and the dwarves rushed out to meet the enemy, screaming.

Threhof was the first to reach the enemy. He left his spear sticking in the belly of one man and drew his broadsword, chasing after another. Erik reached a red-cheek man, stepped around a spear jab, and thrust his blade into the man's neck. Turning, he faced another man, but before he could react, purple light flashed across the enemy's face, leaving a burning, bloody, screaming mess. Bryon leapt into the midst of two other soldiers, blocking one sword attack with his shield and swiping his sword at the other man, singeing the stubble that grew on his face. Erik saw another soldier rushing his cousin—no shield, spear held in both hands. Erik ran, stepping up onto Bryon's right hip and pushing himself off, through the air. The soldier lifted his spear, but too late, and Erik caught the shaft with a foot, heard it crack under his boot when he hit the ground, and thrust his shoulder into the man's ribs.

As the man rose with his own long sword in hand, he moved to bring the blade down on Erik. Erik crouched and blocked with his shield, quickly jabbing, pushing the soldier back and then standing and bringing his blade down hard onto his shoulder.

The steel dug deep. The man stumbled back as another soldier charged him. He hit the man with the broadside of his blade and kicked his legs from underneath him. He heard the snapping of bone as the soldier fell, and the awkward way his leg lay told Erik he had broken it.

Erik looked around, the battle won. He looked back at his cousin who stood over two bodies, steam rising from their wounds. He watched two arrows thud into an enemy archer's chest. He watched Nafer's mace demolish the face of another archer. One of Turk's throwing axes sailed through the air and struck a man just at the base of the neck. Demik's broadsword to the chest finished him.

"There are only five of them left," Erik said, "including their leader."

The man with the broken leg cried when he tried to stand.

"Four, soon, perhaps," Bryon said.

"Maybe," Erik said with a shrug of his shoulders.

"Lieutenant Phurnan!" Wrothgard called out.

The fighting halted as Balzarak raised a fist. Gurgling and moaning arose from the dying, but those were the only sounds besides Wrothgard's voice. The leader crouched behind one of his men. Three soldiers stood firm, one with nothing but a dagger, one with half a spear and a wide gash pouring blood down the left side of his face, and the other with his sword in both hands and clearly favoring his right leg.

"Will you offer your sword to Lord General Balzarak, as a sign of respect in defeat?"

Lieutenant Phurnan immediately stood. He puffed out his chest and lifted his chin, half-closing his eyes in what Erik could only assume was an attempt at haughtiness. He said something in Shengu.

"He looks stupid," Bryon said.

"Aye," Erik replied. He looked down at the injured soldier, the one with the broken leg. "How do you follow a man like that?"

The man didn't understand the question, but Erik knew the answer. Orders.

"Speak in Westernese," Wrothgard replied.

"The language of dogs!" the Lieutenant spat.

Wrothgard said something in Shengu, and the Lieutenant's eyes went wide.

"You are a traitor to your people," the Lieutenant said.

"So are you," Wrothgard replied. "Now, admit defeat."

"Defeat?" The questioning nature of the word was evident in the Lieutenant's voice.

"Come now, Lieutenant," Wrothgard said. He now stood next to Balzarak. Erik saw that he had strung his bow across his back and stood there, unarmed, hands spread as if offering something. "Look around you."

"Defeat is when the last drop of blood falls," the Lieutenant replied.

"The look on his men's faces says otherwise," Bryon suggested.

"Would you slovenly waste the lives of your men?" Balzarak asked, stepping forward, also unarmed. "Your men who are dead fought bravely, but look at these soldiers. There is no honor in killing them and, to speak truth, I would rather not."

"Who are you, tunnel rat?" the Lieutenant said.

"You are speaking to the Lord of Fornhig, Lord General Balzarak Stone Axe, Commander of the Dwarvish Armies of Thrak Baldüukr. But what does it matter who I am? I could have you killed with a single word. If I were but a lowly warrior, would it matter?"

"I do not treat with stinking tunnel diggers," the Lieutenant hissed.

"Oh, that's not good," Erik said when he heard a low grumble come from several of their dwarvish companions.

"What about your men?" Balzarak asked. "Would they treat with a stinking tunnel digger if I offered them their lives?"

"That is not their choice," Lieutenant Phurnan replied.

"Oh, I beg to differ," Wrothgard said.

Wrothgard spoke to the soldiers in their native tongue of Shengu. Slowly, they dropped their weapons and backed away from their leader.

"Don't forget this one," Erik called to them, pointing at the lame soldier at his feet.

The least injured of the three surviving soldiers came and propped the man up, draping his arm around a shoulder and half carrying him.

"What are you doing?" Lieutenant Phurnan cried. "You cowards! The General will hear of this, and he will have you flayed, skinned, fed to the trolls."

He started yelling in Shengu again and, from the smirk growing on Wrothgard's face, Erik could only imagine what colorful phrases the Lieutenant used. Despite the berating, the four soldiers walked out of the glade and into the nearby forest, never looking back at the Lieutenant.

"I have never known General Al'Banan to blame his regular soldiers for a defeat in battle," Wrothgard said, daring to take a few steps forward. "However, I have known him to hold his officers very accountable. And flaying, no, that is not his style. No, if I remember correctly, he prefers burning to other forms of torture and execution."

The Lieutenant's face suddenly went white. Erik could see him tremble as the dwarves surrounded him. He fell to his knees, clasped his hands together, and began to cry.

"No, please. Mercy. Don't kill me."

"Don't you wish for an honorable death?" Wrothgard asked.

The Lieutenant looked around, the dwarves closing in tightly around him. He dropped his chin to his chest and sobbed.

"No," he said. "I wish for life."

"Do not worry," Balzarak said. "Lowly dwarves such as ourselves have no business in giving you the honor of death in battle."

"Do they mean to take him prisoner?" Bryon asked, to which Erik simply shrugged.

"No."

Dwain's voice startled him, but Erik turned to see the eldest dwarf standing there, watching as Turk and Wrothgard dragged the Lieutenant to the middle of the glade and tied his hands behind his back.

"We seldom take prisoners," Dwain explained, "and certainly, now, that would be impossible. They will bind his hands, as you can see, and make sure he leaves into the forest. We will wait, make sure he doesn't follow or spy where we go. Perhaps even send scouts out to make sure he has truly left. And then we will move on."

"Why not just kill him?" Erik asked, but he knew the answer before Dwain could give it.

"Honor. His men have left him, surrendering to a stronger foe, living to fight another day, and, so, now he asks for mercy."

"Isn't there dishonor in surrendering?" Erik asked.

"No, young man," Dwain explained with a smile on his face. "If it is the prudent decision, if it is the decision that gives life rather than meaningless death, if it is the wise decision that leads to peace, there is no dishonor in surrendering."

Dwain broke his gaze from the binding of the Lieutenant and turned to Erik and his cousin.

"You two fought very well today." He smiled, and that made Erik smile. "Perhaps it makes things a little easier, having a magical sword. But, nonetheless, you fought bravely—like two well-seasoned warriors. A well-earned victory today, if not a costly one."

Dwain looked to the hill, as did Erik, and he saw Befel escorting a limping Bofim. When the dwarf came to the limp body of Mortin, arrows still sticking from his chest, he collapsed next to him and began to weep.

Chapter 55

Wrothgard looked on as Bofim, nose bloodied, and eyes bruised, sat by Mortin's body. Bofim whispered to the dead dwarf, hand placed firmly on his shoulder.

"They were good friends," Threhof said. "They went through much together in service in the tunnels. Their families are close. Bofim's son is married to Mortin's daughter. Mortin's eldest son was a hearth-warden to Bofim, and Bofim was present for the baptism of all three of Mortin's sons."

"Baptism?" Wrothgard questioned, but Threhof shook his head, and Wrothgard didn't press his question any further.

He looked on as Bofim held Mortin's hand.

"It is the great misunderstanding of the rest of the world in regard to dwarves," Threhof continued. "They think the only emotion we bear is anger and that we all yearn for death on the battlefield, that there is no other goal for a dwarf. The world thinks we beat our sons for crying, shun them for showing fear, cast out our daughters for bearing weaklings, and divorce our wives for bearing us only daughters."

"But, you do hail death in battle as an honor," Wrothgard said, almost questioning, "more so than other people."

"Yes." Threhof nodded. "Death in a righteous battle, death in a duel for a justifiable cause. But death is final. And even though I do believe our brother will be dining in the halls of An tonight, with his ancestors and all others who have gone before him—men and women—we will not see him again in this lifetime, and that is a very sad thing."

"I miss you so much, my brothers," Wrothgard whispered as Bofim cried over his dead friend. "How I wish you were here, with me. Are you dining in the halls of heaven with your ancestors? Which heaven? Or is it all rubbish, foolishness our mothers used to tell us at night to calm our nerves?"

He looked down at his open hands, his palms, and in that moment, they looked old. Worn, dirty, and bloody, cracked and splintered. They looked used.

"Tedish. Samus. I don't know who to pray to, but I do hope you are in a good place. I do hope you are laughing and joking, and I think I would give anything to see you again."

Bofim stood as best he could. He bowed his head, and the other dwarves joined him as Bofim chanted something in dwarvish and, even though Wrothgard had no idea what it was he said, the words sounded sad and joyful all at the same time, and they sent goose pimples up his arm. He decided he would bow his head as well and close his eyes and try to imagine what it was Bofim could be saying.

When Bofim had finished speaking, Wrothgard walked over to the Lieutenant, hands bound behind his back and on his knees, crying at the feet of Balzarak.

"Please," Lieutenant Phurnan pleaded. "You cannot leave me here with my hands tied behind my back. The trolls . . . they will come back . . . they will . . ."

He began to cry so heavily he could not speak.

"And what of your men?" Balzarak asked. "Do you not have the same concern for them? Do you not care that it could be them the trolls attack, kill, eat?"

"Uh . . . yes . . . of course. I must run to help them. Yes, help them. I cannot help them with my hands tied behind my back. Think of my men."

"You care nothing for your men," said Wrothgard before he spat on the Lieutenant and kicked him in the face.

He saw Balzarak give him a disconcerted look, but Wrothgard ignored it.

"Who are you?" Wrothgard grabbed Lieutenant Phurnan by the collar of his breastplate and pulled him up, so they were face to face. "Some nobleman's son who was forgotten when the Stévockians took over? Some lady's bastard child who could find no position in the new political machine of Golgolithul? The third son of a lowly family whose name has been forgotten by time? You are nothing."

Wrothgard threw Phurnan to the ground.

"You are no Lieutenant, no officer. You don't even know what that means."

"Enough." Balzarak stepped forward. "We have three options. I could kill you here—a fate you probably deserve."

Phurnan began to cry again.

"We could let you go or, we could send you back to Thorakest with two of my warriors."

Phurnan smiled at that, inching forward on his knees.

"Do not be so happy about that last option," Balzarak said. "You would most certainly be kept in the dungeons until you were either taken to the quarries to break rock for the rest of your days or executed."

"My lord," Wrothgard said, "we cannot afford to send warriors back. Especially with Mortin's death."

Balzarak nodded.

"You have the power to stand as this man's judge," Wrothgard said. "If he is let go, I fear we will see him again. Think of the men he has killed. Think of the dwarves he has surely killed."

Balzarak thought for a moment then shook his head.

"This man, as despicable as he is, eventually surrendered. I would not feel well standing judge over him without a trial. We will bind his hands and leave him. That is my decision."

Just then, Wrothgard made eye contact with Switch. The thief winked to him. Wrothgard felt himself smile, and he gave the fellow easterner a quick nod. Switch eyed the man as a wolf might eye a newborn calf, cornered and helpless. He licked his lips and gave a rictus smile, walking behind Phurnan—who paid no attention to the thief—gripping one his knives with white knuckles.

Balzarak turned to Thormok and Gôdruk.

"Lass se he."

"He's telling them to let him go," Wrothgard said to himself, "I know it."

Wrothgard looked to Switch. He nodded again. The thief wrapped his arm around the Lieutenant's throat, pulled him in tight, and plunged his knife into the back of the man's leg. Wrothgard felt himself grimace at the ripping and tearing sounds the blade made as Switch jerked it sideways and up and down. Phurnan screamed, and Switch let him go. He clutched at his leg, tried to step, and crumpled to the ground. The look Balzarak gave Switch was a hard look, filled with anger and distaste.

"Slipped." Switch nonchalantly shrugged his shoulder. "Sorry."

"Come," Balzarak said to his warriors. "Let us prepare Mortin."

Wrothgard let them go and waited behind with Switch. The thief knelt by the crying Lieutenant.

"I know what you look like," said Switch as he leaned in, close to the Lieutenant's ear. "You look like a little rabbit whose foot is caught in a bloody trap. Have you ever seen that? The way they whimper and squeal when they can smell the fox get closer."

"Of course he hasn't," Wrothgard said. "He's probably never hunted. He's never done the work for himself. He's no hunter. No fox. He's the pack master—the dirty, cowardly bastard who stays in the den and sends out the foxes for fear of getting blood on his new hunting boots."

The Lieutenant rolled onto his back.

"At least leave me my sword."

"Oh no," Switch sneered. "Little, fluffy bunny rabbits don't have weapons."

"If you truly want your sword, it's over there." Wrothgard pointed to the spot where the Lieutenant finally surrendered, his sword lying among the tall grass. "You can crawl over there and get it. Come on Switch. Let's go."

"Too bad I can't be around for lunch," Wrothgard heard Switch say, and he hated that it made him smile. "I would so like to see what's on the menu."

Wrothgard saw Bofim and Beldar putting Mortin's body, wrapped head to foot in furs, on a litter made of two spears, more furs, and leather breastplates from the dead easterners.

"Are we taking him with us?" Wrothgard asked.

Turk nodded.

"We will bury him in the forest, away from here."

"Why not here?" Wrothgard asked. "Or why not send him back to Thorakest with Bofim?"

"We cannot afford to lose any more warriors," Turk replied, "and if we bury him here, the trolls would certainly dig up his body—and it would take too long to bury him deep enough to stop them from it."

"You don't think something else will dig him up, out there in the forest?"

"Perhaps," Turk said. "It is an aspect of life. Our soul leaves our earthly body, and that body returns to the earth as dust. We know this. We accept this. In a way, it makes me laugh and think those silly that try and preserve the earthly bodies of their loved ones. We just don't want Mortin's remains to feed trolls, that is all. And we want time to pay our respects to our fallen friend, and this doesn't seem the place to do so."

"We all turn to shit when we die," Switch muttered. "What's it matter? Who cares where our dust eventually settles?"

Once the men and dwarves were out of sight, Sorben Phurnan crawled to the nearest dead body and grabbed the man's sword. He would have preferred his sword, given to him by his father, but this would do.

Sorben stuck the sword in the ground and tried to pull himself up, but the back of his leg burned, and he fell. He looked to the forest and saw those eyes. They were gone, but he could still see them. Dull. Gray. Evil. The man who cut his leg had waved and blown him a kiss before he disappeared into the trees.

"You will be the first one I deal with when I catch up to you."

He tried pulling himself up again, to no avail. His men had fled in that direction as well.

"Cowards." He spat on the dead soldier. "I hope the trolls find you. It will at least satiate them for a while. Give me more time."

He tried pulling himself up, one more time. This time, he stood, albeit wobbly and uncertain. His leg was on fire, from his heel to his hip, and when he tried to put weight on it, he found himself on his face again. He tried standing yet again but felt woozy, tired, worn. He thought he was bleeding to death and began to panic, but feeling the back of his leg, Sorben realized there was very little blood. He was just…scared.

Wind rustled through the high branches of the trees surrounding the meadow, and with the wind came a putrid smell. It made Sorben gag before he saw those yellow eyes and gray skin.

"Oh, you are disgusting." He put an arm to his nose. "You cowards. Come help me."

Mountain trolls were stupid, barbaric, and primitive, but they did have a language, and he knew they understood Shengu.

The troll just stared at him, leaning forward on its hands.

"Did you hear me, you stupid beast? Help me!"

He felt his face grow hot as his hands shook. His leg hurt more than he had ever hurt before, and he was tired.

The beast stood, put its nose to the air and sniffed, long, sucking breaths. It grunted several times, made a clicking sound, and then barked.

"Are you some sort of dog, you piece of shit? I know you know what I'm saying."

Two more trolls walked into the meadow. He recognized one of them, with a wide scar along its forehead and a left hand with only three fingers. They barked and growled back. They were talking.

"What is this?" Sorben muttered.

Two more trolls appeared. They barked and growled and grunted and then one of them howled, loud and long. The first one ran at him.

"You son of a—"

Sorben struggled to his feet again, trying to lift his sword and stand at the same time, but the troll's foot rammed into his stomach, and Sorben Phurnan felt himself flying.

He landed hard and felt the air leave his lungs as he heard cracking, felt more pain in his leg, felt new pain in his right elbow and back. He looked up, and a troll stood over him, its saliva dripping over his face. It reached down and grabbed the collar of his steel breastplate. With a single jerk, the creature ripped the armor from Sorben's body. He heard the leather straps snap, and a pinpointed heat seared through his back. The troll then grabbed his shirt, lifted him, and threw him as if he was a pebble. He landed hard again, this time face down and felt ribs crack and knew his left wrist hung limply, wrongly, twisted and broken. A thick hand grabbed his shoulder and turned him over.

He saw another troll, the one with the wide scar along his brow.

"You will regret this," Sorben hissed, his whole body racked with pain.

The troll seemed to laugh.

"I will watch as they skin you alive. I will make your hide into a rug."

It shook its massive head.

"No." Its voice was a gruff gurgle as it tried to voice words in Sorben's language. "You die."

"Die." Sorben laughed. "I think not. Any minute, General Patûk's troops will appear and kill you."

It shook its head again.

"You die. You food. I eat."

The troll looked down at him, its yellow eyes fixed on him, its teeth bare. It grabbed Sorben and picked him up over its head. He screamed as his whole body shook and the trolls howled. The troll bit into Sorben's shoulder hard, and with a single jerk, the troll ripped the man's arm off.

Sorben looked to where his right arm should've been, and he felt nothing. Shock and being so close to death seemed to have shut down his senses. Another troll ran over to him and bit into his side, tearing off a chunk of flesh, and this time Sorben screamed. Then another troll ran over to him, and the last thing he saw was the opened maw of a mountain troll that once cowered in fear of him.

Chapter 56

"THAT FOOL!" PATÛK AL'BANAN SLAMMED his fist on the table in front of him.

"I'm sorry, my lord." The soldier cowered, kneeling and head down. "He had us charge uphill. They slaughtered us. Then, they gave us a chance to surrender, but Lieutenant Phurnan wanted us to keep fighting, sir. But there was no point. I'm sorry."

The man started to cry. Weakness. It made Patûk sick to his stomach. Then again, this man was barely more than a boy.

"Stand, Corporal," Patûk said.

The man obeyed, sobbing quietly and head still hung.

"Lieutenant Phurnan's mistake should not be yours," the General said. "I will not hold you responsible for his follies. I have never surrendered in my life; then again, I have never charged a powerful foe uphill."

Lieutenant Bu walked into Patûk's tent.

"Report, Lieutenant."

The Lieutenant bowed and saluted.

"We were following them," Bu replied, "and then we lost them."

Patûk Al'Banan felt his teeth grind. Lieutenant Bu had proven himself, but he couldn't take any more failure this day.

"Why?" Patûk asked.

"It is as if they disappeared, sir," Bu replied.

"Are we following ghosts?" The General's voice rose.

"No, sir," Bu said, backing up a step and bowing low, "although, they act like ghosts in these forests."

"And what of Phurnan?"

"Sir." Bu looked to the Corporal who still stood before the General.

"Yes. Corporal, you are dismissed. Tend to your men. You need not fear punishment, for none will come."

The Corporal bowed and left the tent.

"I hope I am not getting soft in my older years, Lieutenant."

"Soft, sir?" Bu asked.

"In the past, I am quite certain I would have had those men who surrendered burned. If the men think I am growing soft…"

"Do not confuse wisdom for weakness, sir," Bu said.

"I do not know if I like your tone, Lieutenant," Patûk said. He heard the steel in his own voice.

"I do not mean disrespect." Lieutenant Bu bowed. "You are a wise leader. It would be ill advised to punish men for the stupidity of an officer. I do believe that your men would lose trust in you more if you did punish these soldiers for simply following orders over executing them for surrendering."

Patûk crossed his hands behind his back and turned to walk to his sitting chair. Andu stood there, pitcher in hand. Patûk nodded, and the Sergeant poured two cups of spiced wine.

"Where is Li?" Patûk Al'Banan asked.

"Here, my lord." The lazy-eyed man walked from out of a shadow in the corner of the tent.

"I do not like it when you do that," Patûk grumbled. "I feel as if you are spying on me."

"Me, my lord," Li replied, his voice the epitome of indifference. "No. I loathe spies and secrecy."

Patûk saw Bu's stare as he took a draught of his wine.

"Calm yourself, Lieutenant." Patûk laughed. "What of Lieutenant Phurnan?"

"Dead, sir," Bu replied.

"Really? Are you sure?" the General asked.

"Quite, General. My spies," Bu hung on the word and stared at Li, "reported that mountain trolls killed him. Ate him."

"Pity," Patûk said with a scoffing laugh.

He saw the look the Lieutenant gave him.

"He was a stupid man, Lieutenant, and a terrible officer, for sure. But he was of pure blood. He deserved a better death than that."

"I beg your pardon, my lord," Li said, "but does the purity of his blood make him an honorable man?"

"I think you forget your place, Li," Patûk said.

"My apologies, my lord." Li bowed. "But would Lieutenant Bu deserve less of a death because he is not of pure blood?"

Patûk's jaw tightened.

"Truly, you forget your place."

"My apologies again, my lord, but you did ask me to advise you. This would be my advice. You have men, such as Lieutenant Bu, who are loyal to you, despite not being of *pure blood.* Would you sacrifice their loyalty because of the circumstances of their birth?"

"No, of course not," Patûk replied. "That is something the Stévockians do. What is your point?"

"You have many in service to you who serve loyally, despite their birth, and they come not from wealthy families. And yet, you have men such as this Lieutenant Phurnan as your leaders. If Lieutenant Bu had been in command of these men, would the outcome have been the same? You have many men who are incompetent as officers. This is a thorn in your heel. Would it not be prudent to start elevating those loyal to you to places of importance?"

"And do what with the men who are already officers?"

Li just shrugged.

"Their families support our cause. Killing a wealthy man's son would certainly stop the inflow of his money," the General explained.

"You do not have to kill them, my lord," Li said. "Besides, in my experience, men will support opportunity and power."

Patûk crossed his arms in front of his chest and lowered his chin to his chest.

"So, should we forget about this map, the city of Orvencrest?"

Patûk saw Li smile.

"My lord, I would not forget about the dwarvish city. Nor would I forget about those trying to find it. But perhaps your efforts are a little misplaced."

"I need to start showing our power," Patûk said, lifting his head and crossing his hands behind his back again. "We need to make ourselves known."

"I believe that will cause conflict, my lord," Li said. Patûk groaned and felt his jaw tighten. "But, yes, I do believe it will also rally men to your cause."

Patûk smiled.

"And what is it, my lord?"

"What is what, my secretive advisor?" Patûk asked.

"What is your cause?"

The General looked at Lieutenant Bu, and the look he gave Patûk asked the same question.

"To depose the usurper, of course," Patûk replied.

"Yes, my lord," Li said. "And then what?"

"What?" the General asked.

"What do you plan on doing after you have deposed the usurper?" Li questioned. "Do you wish to be Lord of the East, or High Lord Chancellor, or King—Emperor, perhaps?"

"My loyalties are to the Aztûkians."

"And how have they supported you, my lord?" Li asked. "Do they give you money, men, information?"

How long had it been since he had received money from Martûk, patron of the Aztûkians, or Bartûk, his son? How long had it been since he received information about the usurper from them? When was the last time a large influx of men had come into his camp, into his service?

"Are they willing to risk all, as you have, as much as men such as Lieutenant Bu has," Li continued, "for if you lose, you will give all—and more. Your *pure blood* followers will most likely find their lives, wealth, position in politics spared for loyalty. You and any who are not *pure* will certainly become acquainted with the horrors of Stévockian wrath. What do you offer these men who serve you? What does their future hold?"

Patûk lifted his chin up, stared at the ceiling of his tent for a moment. He looked to Li, his half-closed eyes, that haughty half-smile that always crossed his lips. He looked to Bu.

"Li, you have given me much to think about. For that, I thank you. But you would be wise to remember your place as advisor."

"Yes, my lord." Li bowed.

"Leave me," Patûk commanded.

Bu, Andu, and Li all bowed and left. Patûk sat and drained the contents of his wine cup in one swallow. He poured himself more and drank again.

"How many of my officers would cringe at the thought of serving themselves wine?" he muttered.

He stood and paced his tent. He looked down at his hands. Worn. He looked at his boots. Worn. His pants. Worn. He felt his face. Worn. If he could see his soul, feel his soul. Worn.

"What has it all been for?"

That was a question he had never asked. He had always just acted.

"Bao Zi."

His personal guardsman walked out from the shadows of his tent, from the opposite corner in which Li had stood. They had never known he was there. That's what he was good at—secrecy. Perhaps he should've been his Officer of Spies.

"Do you wish to be an officer, Bao Zi? Do you wish to be my Master of Spies?"

"No, my lord." Bao Zi shook his head.

A man of few words. Patûk felt himself smile.

"If I may, my lord," Bao Zi added.

"Yes, of course."

"Perhaps, if you had asked me that question twenty years ago, I would have said yes. But today…no. I am thankful for the lot I have drawn in life—and I am thankful for the position you have given me, my lord."

"Very well, my old friend. I need you to take word to the Stévockians, Martûk—and his son Bartûk. It is time they supported us again, more so than they have in the past. It is time to make a move."

"Yes, my lord."

"And send some of your men to meet Pavin Abashar. It is time we joined our forces."

"Yes, my lord." Bao Zi bowed and turned to leave but then turned back to face Patûk. "And if he asks, who should lead your combined forces?"

"Me, of course," Patûk replied.

"Yes, of course, my lord."

Bu turned to Li.

"What are you about, seneschal?"

"What do you mean, sir?" Li asked.

Bu grabbed the seneschal's arm and pulled him close. He could smell perfume and spiced wine on the man.

"You know what I mean, servant."

"I am afraid I do not," Li said.

"I'll run my sword through your belly right now."

"And General Patûk Al'Banan will take no offense at you killing his seneschal?" Li asked.

Bu hated losing his temper. It didn't happen often. He released Li's arm, knowing he wouldn't kill the man. The General favored Bu, he knew that, but he also favored this snake.

"Why were you singing my praises in there, after defaming my position in the General's army?"

"Ah, what was that about?" Li said.

"Yes."

"I was not singing your praises, Lieutenant," Li said. "I was singing the praises of all the common, ignoble, non-pure blooded men that serve my lord. But...the General does favor you."

"So?"

"I am an opportunist, Lieutenant. You will continue to rise in the General's favor. I suspect that, given the right direction, the General will succeed. When he does, those close to him will be placed in positions of importance. And when the General passes on, who will take his place?"

"Certainly not me," Bu said.

Li shrugged.

"He is a wise man. He rewards those who serve him well. And he is working to bring about change," Li said.

"Well, one good turn deserves another," Bu said. "You keep an eye out for me, watch my back, and I will do the same for you. I suspect some of the officers, when they find out they are no longer officers, will be quite unhappy. When that happens, it won't take long for them to realize it was you who suggested their demotions."

Li nodded and bowed, turned, and walked into the camp without looking back. Bu watched him. Even with his back turned, he didn't trust that snake.

Chapter 57

THE FOREST SEEMED TO GET denser as they walked. As evening crept upon them, the atmosphere already dark because of the canopy overhead, the dwarves continued to argue about the map and what direction they should be traveling.

"What are they arguing about?" Bryon had asked.

Erik just shrugged. The last thing Bryon or Switch needed to hear was that the dwarves were lost. It seemed as if they were never meant to find the lost city of Orvencrest. Even more disheartening was the fact that the map was filled with ancient runes that even Threhof and Balzarak had problems deciphering. When Erik first saw the map, he simply assumed they were just decorations, a cartographer's embellishments.

As night overcame them, the argument went from the map to whether or not they should build a fire. Finally, they agreed to do so, and as they sat there, barely moving or talking, Erik heard a distant howl.

"That's a big wolf," Bryon said.

"That's no wolf," Erik replied. "That's a troll."

Bryon sat up.

"I wouldn't worry too much," Demik said.

"Oh, and why not?" Bryon asked. "Are they afraid of dwarves?"

"Aye, they are," Demik replied.

The night was quiet, save for the dwarves whispering to each other. Erik understood most of what they all said, arguments about the map and where to go. It seemed they had a better idea and had come to a conclusion and a compromise, but that still didn't ease Erik's mind. Then Turk asked a question. It seemed to come from out of nowhere, and it was an odd question, Erik thought, one about runes he found when they were traveling through the tunnels towards Thorakest and about some young dwarf that had been executed for treason in another dwarvish city.

It almost seemed a secret question, filled with cryptic meanings and carefully chosen words, even though they were the only ones there. Threhof looked angry when Turk spoke, and even chastised him, while Beldar gasped and Dwain just shook his head and clicked his tongue disappointedly. Even Nafer hissed at his friend, pointing an accusatory finger and saying something so fast, Erik couldn't catch the meaning. Turk kept saying something about *them*. But when Balzarak nodded and, from what Erik could gather, affirmed Turk's questions, the camp fell silent, and the dwarves said no more. The hush was so noticeable, that Bryon nudged Erik with his elbow.

"What's going on?" Bryon whispered.

"How should I know?" Erik replied with a shrug.

"Don't give me that," Bryon said. "I know you understand them."

"Why don't you learn their language if you're so intrigued?" Erik asked, taking a sip from his waterskin.

"Maybe I will," Bryon said, "but right now, instead of being an ass, maybe you could just tell me what came over them so suddenly. They were arguing so intently and then stopped."

"I honestly don't know," Erik replied. A darkness came over him, an ill feeling, as he watched the dwarves from across the fire. It danced off their faces and cast eerie shadows and, for a moment, Erik wondered if the shadows were some external symbol of the gloom in their minds.

"Whatever it is," Erik said, "it's not good.

A gentle breeze blew against Erik's face as he sat on that hill, under the great tree with low hanging branches. The grass, raising almost chest high as Erik sat there, was damp, even in the comforting warmth of the sun. He saw him out there, the Lieutenant that had led his men in a foolish attack. It was as Erik had suspected. He looked chewed upon, bite marks along his ribs and even his face, maggots crawling in and out of his festering wounds.

When the Lieutenant saw Erik, he wailed and cursed, but it only made Erik laugh. He had learned that the dead could not climb the hill, so as he entered this world of dreams every night, in this field of grass, he made his way to the hill and the tree and the man whom he knew, but still couldn't remember from where, although he wasn't here in this dream. He almost felt pity for the easterner, but then he remembered his folly, and the way he spoke of his men, and the way his men spoke of him.

"Fool," Erik mouthed.

When Erik awoke, he couldn't feel the breeze anymore, and the warmth faded. The wetness of the grass went away, and the cursing voices of dead men faded to a distant echo. He sat up to see his brother wiping sweat away from his brow.

"Are you all right, brother?" Erik asked, crouching next to Befel.

"Yeah," Befel replied. "Just had a hard time sleeping."

"Bad dreams?"

Befel shook his head.

"I think it's partly my shoulder, the air, yesterday's battle," Befel said. "I don't think I have ever seen that much blood. So much blood."

"You can't drink sweet wine right now," Erik said, "but maybe Turk can take a look at you."

"No." Befel shook his head. "He's busy with Bofim. And this is an old wound."

Befel rubbed his shoulder while Erik watched Turk tend to Bofim's nose and eyes, seemingly bruised even more a day later, even though the dwarvish warrior that had befriended Erik first seemed in better spirits today.

"This forest looks old," Erik said to Turk when the dwarf was alone.

"How does old look?" Turk asked.

"I don't know," Erik said with a shrug, "but if I were to imagine an ancient forest untouched by men or dwarves, this would be it."

"Good observation," Turk replied. "Dwarves don't come here much. All of the cities exist in the northern part of these mountains."

"What does that mean?" Erik asked.

"This part of the mountain is wild," Turk replied.

"Wild?" Erik asked.

"Unchecked, unmanaged," Turk replied, "at least, more so than the lands around Thorakest. Ancient creatures—giant cougars and bears and wolves and badgers—live here as well as mountain trolls and horned antegants."

Erik pondered for a moment, remembering the cave bear that attacked them. He couldn't imagine cougars and wolves and badgers that size.

"Does this forest scare you?" Erik asked.

"A little," Turk replied after pausing for a moment. "I think you would be a fool if it didn't."

"So, are we still lost?" Erik asked. "In this ancient forest."

"Lost?" Turk questioned with a smile. "You've been eavesdropping on dwarvish conversations. A dwarf is never lost."

Erik returned the smile and gave a short chuckle.

"I don't know, honestly," Turk added. "I think General Balzarak has a general idea of where we are going. This map is full of ancient riddles and runes that I didn't recognize—that even the General is having a hard time deciphering."

"Do you think the city even exists?" Erik asked. "Or have we been sent on a fool's errand with some ulterior motive?"

"Have we...? Most certainly," Turk replied, again with that smile. "But rest assured, the city or Orvencrest exists... or at least did exist. This map is a fickle thing. When was the cartographer here? A generation ago? A hundred years? Did the Lord of the East use his dark magic? How have things changed? Does the forest want us to find the city?"

"Does the forest... how can a forest want anything?" Erik asked.

"Remember, this forest is ancient," Turk replied. "In the old days, the forests talked, moved."

Erik looked up at a giant red pine, one so tall he couldn't even begin to see the top. He supposed if a dagger could speak, then certainly a tree or a forest could as well. He felt a tingle at his hip.

"And what of *them*?" Erik asked.

Turk didn't move, nor did he look at Erik. He seemed irritated and upset all at the same time.

"Your eavesdropping is going to get you into trouble, Erik," Turk said, his voice hard.

"I'm sorry," Erik said. "I didn't mean..."

"It is something we dwarves do not talk about," Turk said, "a darkness in our past. And it is something we certainly do not talk about in mixed company while camping in ancient forests. I am sure you saw or heard how upset the others were with me."

"Yes," Erik said.

"It is something that we will talk about at another time," Turk said, facing Erik and his tone softer. "It is something that could affect our mission, though. Do not speak of it again. At least, until I speak to you about it."

Erik nodded.

Erik had dreamed about his parents and his sisters and Simone. It had been a long while since he had had that dream. Part of him felt glad, lucky even, that he didn't dream of the dead, even though he had grown accustomed to just sitting on that hill. And part of him was glad that he still remembered the faces of his parents and sisters, of Simone. But then another part of him was sad as he watched his mother and father dangle from a tree, neck broken and noosed, and his sisters bound and crying in a cell. He hadn't seen Simone in this dream before, but in this one, some Hámonian knight raped her and then he saw her begging on the streets of Bull's Run, bastard child swaddled next to her breast.

"More bad dreams?" Befel asked. Apparently, Erik's face betrayed him.

"I dreamt of Mother and Father, Tia and Beth," Erik replied. "And Simone."

"And that's a bad dream?" Befel asked.

"They were dead," Erik replied, his voice flat. "Imprisoned. Raped. Homeless."

"Why?" Befel asked. "How?"

"Hámonian nobles," Erik replied, rising and gathering his things into his haversack. "They wanted our land. They killed Mother and Father. Imprisoned Beth and Tia. And raped Simone. They slaughtered our animals. Enslaved the men who work for Father."

"They're just dreams, Erik," Befel said.

He didn't know Erik's dreams. Maybe he had dreams that were similar, maybe not. But Erik's dreams were vivid, real. A part of him wondered if this dream was just his imagination. Or had this come to pass.

"Maybe," Erik said. "But Hámonian nobles are encroaching on our lands. This will come to pass eventually."

"Father would never let that happen," Befel replied.

"How would he stop them?" Erik asked. "How would Father stop some count or lord, with a small army at their disposal, from taking our lands."

"There are many loyal to the Eleodums," Befel offered.

"Farmers, Befel," Erik replied. "Not fighters. We understand that all too well and firsthand. And there are plenty of farmers who are jealous of Father and our success and would love to see him gone."

"Like who?" Befel asked.

"Jovek," Erik said.

"He wouldn't just stand by," Befel said.

Erik just shrugged.

"I fear that if we return home," Erik said, "home won't be there anymore."

Chapter 58

"Do you ever get the feeling that we're bloody lost?" Switch asked as they trudged slowly through the thick and ancient forest, shoulder high bushes and thick creepers crowding their path as much as wide-trunked pines.

"I am sorry to say, yes," Wrothgard replied.

"You speak their ugly language now," Switch said to Erik. "What do you think?"

Erik just shrugged.

"Don't give me that troll shit," Switch spat.

"I don't speak it that well and only understand it a little better," Erik said. No one knew he was lying. "And I am certainly not going to eavesdrop on their conversations."

"I wish you would," Switch said, that malevolent tone in his voice. "I would love to hear what those tunnel diggers say in secret."

"Hey! Tunnel diggers! Where are we going?" Switch asked.

"This way," Threhof replied.

"Why, thank you, revealer of secrets. So, we are just supposed to keep following you, without any hint of where we are going?"

"Yes," was Threhof's simple reply, and for once, Switch seemed lost for words.

"General Balzarak thinks he has figured out the way," Turk whispered to Erik in Dwarvish. Erik just nodded slightly as the thief watched him.

Erik felt better about their journey, now that the dwarves were more confident about their path, until they came to a wall of pines, bushes, and creepers. The forest wall looked impenetrable as if no living creature had ever passed that way. The wall was so thick, everything grown so close together, that hacking through was not an option. Wrothgard mentioned burning the wall away, but then the fear of starting a forest fire ended that idea.

"What, by the shadow, is this?" Switch cursed.

"The forest is speaking," Erik said to no one in particular.

"What does that mean?" Switch asked. "You've been traveling with these dwarves too long."

Switch turned to Threhof.

"Did you bloody bring us out here to kill us?" the thief asked.

"Why would we bring you all the way out here," Threhof asked, "sacrificing one of our own, when we could have killed you in Thorakest?"

"Well, you killed Vander Bim," Switch said.

"Calm down, Switch," Wrothgard said.

"Don't tell me to calm down," Switch replied. "I am tired of this mission. I am tired of dwarves. I am tired of you. Damn it!"

Switch clenched his fists and spat.

"You look like a little child," Bryon said with a smile, "throwing a tantrum."

"I'll show you what kind of tantrum I can throw," Switch seethed, walking up to Bryon.

Wrothgard moved behind the thief.

"I know you're there, soldier," Switch said. "As soon as I kill this gutter shite, I'm going to kill you."

"Stop this," Wrothgard said. "This is lunacy."

"Come now, Switch," Turk said.

"Stuff it, tunnel digger," Switch replied.

"I've had enough of you," Demik said, pulling his broadsword and stepping forward.

"Fine," Switch said. "I'll do you after the soldier."

Wrothgard's hand moved, as did Switch's, as did Bryon's, as did Demik's. Erik drew his sword and, in one motion, blocked Demik's blade and slapped the back of Switch's hand with the broad side of his weapon.

It was so unexpected that both Demik and Switch dropped their blades. Wrothgard stepped back, sheathing his own sword, and Erik stepped between Bryon and the thief, even as Switch swung, striking Erik's chin instead of his cousin's. Erik pushed Switch away, and the thief fell backwards. Erik put his foot on the thief's chest.

"Get off me," Switch hissed.

Erik put the tip of his sword at the base of Switch's throat and pressed just hard enough to break the skin. He watched the thief's eyes go wide.

"Are you truly that stupid?" Erik said. "We have come this far, only to end it all here?"

He lifted his foot from Switch's chest, withdrew his blade from the man's throat, and stepped away, shaking his head.

"We found it," Balzarak said as if completely oblivious to the near mutiny that almost consumed his company. "A small path. It will be tight, but it will suffice."

"Bloody great," Switch said, jumping up and brushing himself off as if nothing had happened. "I'll go first."

"No," Erik said. "Balzarak, you go first, and I will follow."

"Why?" Switch asked, almost pouting.

"I don't trust you," Erik replied.

Balzarak crawled through the gap he had discovered on hands and knees, and Erik followed. Low branches created a haphazard roof to the forest tunnel, and more than once, some twig or broken stub caught the top of Erik's head, and he felt blood trickle from his scalp and down his temple. Eventually, the path opened up allowing them to walk, and within fifty paces, they were standing in a heavily forested area that looked much like the area from which they had just come.

"This forest looks even older," Erik said.

"Dwarves do not come here, I think," Balzarak said. "Nor do mountain men, or trolls. My guess is that this is an area of the mountain that is primordial. Forgotten."

"A good area for a lost city then," Erik said.

Balzarak nodded.

"Do you know where we are going from here?" Erik asked.

Balzarak smiled.

"You understand our conversations," Balzarak said.

Erik nodded.

"Yes, I am fairly certain I know where we are going from here."

"Does the forest speak here?" Erik asked Turk as he emerged from the deer path.

"Oh, most certainly," Turk replied. He looked around. "This is the oldest of forests."

"This part of the forest is older than the other parts?" Bryon asked with a hint of cynicism.

"Actual years do not always explain something's age," Turk said. "This place is untouched, untraveled, unwatched."

"Untouched, yes," Balzarak said "but unwatched…no, there are eyes that watch this place."

The night was dark, despite the fire burning high in the small, circular clearing, ringed by tall, giant trees.

"The sounds are different here," Erik said as he looked up. There were no stars, and all was darkness and shadows.

"I don't hear anything," Bryon said.

"Exactly," Erik replied.

As if on cue, the long, moaning howl of a distant wolf broke the silence, and Erik saw Balzarak sit up. They had heard many distant wolf howls and troll growls in these mountains at night, but he had never seen the General act that way, alert and hand going to his sword. Something was wrong with that howl.

The General spoke to Gôdruk. Be ready. That is what he said. Be aware. And then he remembered what Balzarak had said. There were eyes that watched this place.

A chill crawled up Erik's spine. He watched the fire, trying not to stare at the darkness beyond. He closed his eyes and rubbed them with his thumb and index finger. In the darkness of his closed eyes, with the subtle glow of oranges and yellows from the fire, he saw them, the Fox and the slavers, dead soldiers he had killed, rotting, walking corpses. His eyes shot open, and he stood.

Erik looked to the darkness again. His eyes narrowed as his chest tightened. His stomach knotted, and his pulse quickened. Sweat beaded down his face, even in the chill of the night. How were they there? Outside of his dreams?

"What are you doing?" Bryon asked.

"Shut up."

"What's wrong with you, brother?" Befel asked.

"I said shut up," Erik hissed.

Through a sidelong glance, Erik saw Balzarak stand. He saw the dwarf follow his gaze.

A gust of freezing wind picked up, blew through the campsite and caused the fire to sputter. Erik's hand went to the handle of his sword.

"No one else heard that?" Erik asked.

"Heard what?" Befel asked.

"Laughter. Hissing," Erik replied.

Erik drew his sword, stepping around the fire and closer to the darkness of the forest.

"I know you're there," he whispered. "I know you see and hear me.

"Yes, yes, yes, yes," was the response that came with a small gust of wind.

"How are you here?"

Erik took another step forward. He gripped his sword tighter in both hands.

"Come, come, come, come," the wind said, "into the darkness, darkness, darkness, darkness."

Erik stepped forward again and felt a chill on his face.

"Are you with me?" he said aloud, looking down at the dagger at his hip.

He felt a tingle and took another step. They became louder, and he could smell them, just beyond the darkness. Another step. He said a silent prayer, and in the shadows, he could see...

A hand clamped down on Erik's shoulder, and he spun around to see Balzarak.

"Do not go into the darkness," Balzarak said. "It is seldom safe, especially in an ancient place like this."

"They are there," Erik said softly.

"Maybe. Maybe not," Balzarak replied. "This is a magical place where reality and imagination collide. Come, sit by the safety of the fire."

"Coward!" they screamed when Erik turned his back to them.

The wind picked up and swirled about the encampment as the howl came again, louder than before. The wind seemed to attempt to extinguish the campfire, and Dwain rushed to pile more wood on it. But it didn't matter how much fuel the dwarf added, the flames sputtered and diminished, and Erik saw their faces again, saw their shadows. And then...they stopped. The wind. The howling. The voices. And the fire regained its fervor.

A speck of white dust, almost glowing, floated by Erik's face. He felt a flutter of air on his face as something buzzed by him, and he wondered if it was one of the large butterflies they had back home. No. It was too cold here.

Another speck floated by, and this one touched his hand. It was warm, and Erik wiped it away. But then there was another one and another and another. He looked up.

"What by the Creator?" Erik gasped.

All around them, all around the clearing to the very tops of the trees, white dust floated by, like snow in the dead of winter.

"Is that snow?" Wrothgard asked, standing.

The specks of white fell on Erik's face as he looked skyward.

Again, it was warm and, in a way, comforting. And among the white, warm dust, he saw things flutter by, leaving streaks of light behind them. They weren't insects.

"What are they?" Wrothgard asked.

"Moon fairies," Balzarak said.

"Fairies?" Bryon asked.

"Is this some fable?" Wrothgard asked.

"This is a primitive place," Balzarak replied, "with primitive creatures, beings that are older than ancient, as old as the world. We have them back home, in the northernmost reaches of the Gray Mountains. One could just sit and watch them dance . . . perfect."

Balzarak extended a hand, and a glowing ball of light came to rest on his palm. Erik leaned closer and saw, as the bright light sputtered, that it was a tiny being, no taller than the width of his hand . . . a woman with dragonfly-like wings. She sat cross-legged on the dwarf's hand and stared at him, and he just stared back. Erik leaned even closer.

"It's a woman," he said.

"Be gentle around her," Balzarak said with a smile. "They are skittish. And, yes, this fairy is a woman. All moon fairies are."

"How is that possible?" Erik asked.

"They are born in the trees," Balzarak said. "Fairies. They are some of the first creations of An. It is from them the elves and all other Fairy Folk get their name. They are beautiful."

"I wouldn't say beautiful," Bryon said, staring at the fairy from over Balzarak's shoulder.

Erik had to agree with his cousin. The fairy's face was hard and angular, with a pointed chin and pronounced cheekbones. Her shoulders were narrow, and her hips were bony. Her eyes were black, void of any pupils, and her ears were tall and pointed.

"It is not her appearance that makes her beautiful, Bryon," Balzarak said, "but her very being. She is simple and pure. She harkens back to a time of creation."

More fairies appeared and, as they flew around the encampment, brightening the space with their white light, Erik heard buzzing and tinkling, whizzing and whistling. One fairy came to flutter just in front of his face, her light almost blinding, she almost touching his nose.

"Are those sounds their language?" Erik asked.

"No," Balzarak replied. "They don't speak. They communicate with their minds and thoughts."

"That's weird," Bryon said.

"Not so weird," Erik muttered, patting his golden-handled dagger.

Another fairy fluttered in front of Bryon, seemingly whistling as she floated about him, inspecting him. He went to touch her, but as his finger grew closer, she gave off a high pitched squeal, and her brightness grew to a blinding glare. The air around Bryon rippled and, with a loud bang, he flew backwards and thudded hard on his back. Switch and Wrothgard drew their weapons.

"Put your weapons down," Balzarak said, "they are ancient, primitive and powerful. They can be cruel if they feel threatened."

The fairies had dispersed, just for a moment, but when Wrothgard and Switch sheathed their weapons, they returned. The one that had fluttered in front of Erik's face returned. They all looked the same, but somehow, Erik knew it was the same one.

"Beautiful," Erik muttered with a smile.

She inspected him, flying around his head, tilting her own head this way and that. Erik felt the urge to sit, and so he did. The fairy floated so that she rested, cross-legged, on one of his knees. He felt warm, and any thought or memory of the undead in the darkness disappeared. He instantly thought of his wooden flute and retrieved it from his haversack. He put it to his lips and played.

Erik had no idea what he played. It wasn't like before, where he played his thoughts and imagination. He had no thoughts or imagination at that moment. He just played, and the fairies danced in the air and his companions all sat and relaxed, even the anxiety-riddled Switch.

The fairy dust rained over Erik as he played, alighting him almost as brightly as the fairies, and he looked to Balzarak. The dwarf just sat, smiling as he watched the fairy sitting in his hand. What was he thinking about? Home. It had to be home. With that smile, it was the only thing he could have been thinking about.

Suddenly, Erik thought of home as well, but it wasn't thoughts of his parents hanging from a tree, or his sisters' imprisonment, or of Simone's disgrace. He thought of his mother's roses, and his sisters' giggling, and his father smiling, and Simone's lips. He thought of Befel and Bryon rough housing, and his Uncle Brent coming over for a visit, not drunk on orange brandy, but happy, his wife and five daughters trailing behind him singing songs.

Erik eventually stopped playing, and his companions—all save for Balzarak—had fallen asleep. He looked to the dark forest, beyond the campfire and the light of the moon fairies and remembered the undead and the evil that awaited there. Would they be waiting in his dreams as well? Would he find his tree and hill and the man whom he knew but couldn't remember? He leaned back and closed his eyes.

Do not worry. You will not dream tonight. You will sleep, and you will rest, and you will wake renewed.

The voice wasn't his dagger, but soft and calm and feminine. He opened his eyes again to see the moon fairy that had been sitting on his knee. She now stood on his chest, although he didn't feel a thing. She tilted her head and smiled.

Sleep, Erik Eleodum. Sleep.

When Erik opened his eyes, brief arrows of sunlight sought to push through the roof of the forest. It was morning, and there had been no dreams. He stood and yawned and rubbed his face.

"Are you all right, brother?" Befel asked.

"Yes," Erik replied with a nod. "In fact, I feel great. I haven't felt this good in a while."

"Probably because you slept in while the rest of us packed up," Bryon huffed as he passed by.

"My back is loose. My arms and legs feel strong. My head is clear," Erik continued, ignoring his cousin. "Yes, I feel excellent."

Erik rolled up his bed blanket and stuffed it into his haversack. As he opened the pack, he saw a pouch, one that might hold coin or berries or nuts, closed tightly by a drawstring and bulging. It sat atop a change of clothes. He picked it up. It might as well had been filled with air. He squeezed it.

"Sand?" he whispered to himself.

When all hope seems lost, when darkness closes in, when your dreams whisper to you in the dead of the night, and you have nowhere to turn, you will know what to do with our gift.

Erik looked to the forest and saw the faintest glow of white behind a tree.

"Is that..." he leaned forward and squinted, tilted his head towards the glow, "giggling?"

"Come," Balzarak said as he passed Erik, "we must move."

Erik nodded and stood, slinging his shield and his haversack over his shoulders.

"I trust you had a restful sleep last night," Balzarak added, looking at Erik over his shoulder.

"Yes," Erik said. "How would you...?"

Balzarak winked at him.

Chapter 59

ERIK SHOOK HIS HEAD, SCRAPING away bits of thick moss and flicking it to the ground. The green stuff seemed to cover everything, any space not invaded by green creepers or yellow flowered vines. He looked up, trying to peer at the sky through the cracks made by the tallest branches of the red-barked pines. The dimness of dusk began to settle in the distant sky, and the forest darkened once more.

"No moon fairies to protect us this time," Erik muttered.

"There should be something," Balzarak muttered. "Some sign."

"He's been wandering around, from tree to tree, for…well, I don't know how long," Bryon said.

"A long time," Erik replied. "He's frustrated. The entrance should be here."

"Should we split up, maybe," Befel said. "Go in groups of two, look for signs, cover more ground?"

"No," Turk said. "Not here. We are safe together."

"As safe as we can be," Dwain added.

"This place worries me," Threhof said. "I'd prefer not camp here another night."

"That's concerning," Befel said.

"What?" Erik asked.

"When he says *worries*," Befel replied, "I hear scared. Threhof being scared of something is concerning."

"Aye," Erik agreed.

The forest darkened further, and the sounds of nighttime began to fill the air. Erik heard them, in the distance, a faint echo. The undead were there again. He was nervous and didn't want to spend another night there either.

"By the…" Switch said. Standing in between two giant roots of a large tree, he picked his foot up, something sticky and gooey clinging to his boot.

"What is that?" Bryon asked.

"Probably troll shit," Switch said, crouching down. But he quickly covered his nose with his arm and fell backwards. The thief gagged. "Blood and guts and…"

"Yes, it is," Demik said, walking to where the thief lay. "It is the intestines of something… someone. Here is their sword."

Demik picked up a long sword and threw it towards Balzarak, the blade landing at the General's feet.

"This was a man," Demik said, "once."

"One of Patûk's men?" Wrothgard asked.

"I thought no one ever ventured into these parts of the mountains," Bryon said.

"He doesn't look—at least what is left of him—like one of those soldiers we fought," Demik said. "I think his skin is dark, perhaps a Samanian."

"There was an ebony-skinned man at the meeting in Finlo," Erik said. "Maybe he's a mercenary."

"They made it this far?" Threhof asked, surprised. "And without the help of dwarves."

"I wonder…" Turk began to say and then joined Demik.

He ignored the remains of the man, lying between the roots of the tree. Rather, Turk began feeling about the tree trunk, under the roots, among the tall grass and creepers and bushes that grew about the base of the gigantic pine.

"What are you doing?" Erik asked.

"Ha!" Turk yelled. "I found it."

"Praise An!" Balzarak exclaimed.

"Help me," Turk said.

It took four dwarves to lift the door, a piece of thick iron and oak covered by years of soil and foliage. Stairs, covered by ancient dust, descended from the opening.

"It has been years since anyone has used this tunnel," Turk said, a small smile on his face.

"And yet," Demik said, "there's a speck of blood."

Looking at the first step, a single red drop lay there.

"Maybe it seeped through a crack," Switch said, "from this poor bastard."

"There are no cracks in this door," Turk said, "and it was covered by years of soil."

"Maybe it's old blood," Bryon said.

"No," Demik replied, "it's fresh."

"What do we do?" Erik asked, standing next to Balzarak.

"Tread carefully," the General replied.

"What magic is this?" Switch asked.

"A deep, dark magic," Turk replied, daring to move onto the first step.

"Like the Messenger?" Befel asked.

"Deeper," Balzarak replied, giving Turk and the rest of the dwarves a concerned look. "Darker."

The torch flame licked at the ceiling, so low they had to stoop as they descended the steps. Finally, at the bottom, they gathered around another body, a man armored in mail, his throat slit.

"Seems very odd in a tunnel that hasn't been traveled for a thousand years," Wrothgard said.

"Odd indeed," Balzarak said.

The hallway at the bottom was barely wider and taller than the stairway, and when Erik looked behind them, he saw only a wall. The stairs were gone, yet the body remained.

"By the Creator," he gasped.

"What the bloody Shadow is this?" Switch asked. "More dwarvish tricks?"

"I fear not," Balzarak replied. "No. This is some other magic."

"What do we do, General?" Threhof asked.

"Keep going," Balzarak said. "It's the only thing we can do."

They walked only a short distance when they came to another wall. Two more men lay in front of the wall, both dead, both recently disemboweled, their corpses putrid.

"From Finlo?" Erik asked as Turk knelt next to one of the bodies to inspect it.

"What's it bloody matter?" Switch replied. "We are trapped underground with nowhere to go."

"I don't know," Turk said, picking up a broken sword, "but they certainly were fighters, adventurers."

"It's the only explanation," Demik added. "It's the only way they could have found this place.

"I still don't see how they could have found it without the help of dwarves," Threhof said.

"Bring your light closer to the wall, Erik," Balzarak said.

Erik did as he was told. His torch revealed script.

"What is it?" Erik asked.

"Blood," Balzarak replied. "It's written in blood."

"Their blood?" Erik asked, pointing to the dead men.

"I suspect so," Balzarak replied.

"Can you read what it says?" Erik asked.

"It's in Old Elvish and Old Dwarvish," Balzarak said, "that much I know."

"Look at the stone at the foot of the wall," Dwain said. "It's clear that this wall was erected after the fact. The tunnel continues."

"Let's knock it down then," Threhof said. "It can't be a load bearing wall if that's the case. Beldar."

Beldar charged the wall, even as Balzarak commanded him to stop. When Beldar's axe blade struck the stone, the steel exploded into a thousand pieces, and the dwarf flew back a dozen paces, unconscious and breathing shallowly.

"Does anyone here read Old Dwarvish and Old Elvish?" Befel asked.

"Old Dwarvish, yes," Balzarak replied. "At least a little. Old Elvish?"

The dwarf shook his head.

Befel leaned in closer to look at the script written in blood. When he touched the wall, he stood straight instantly, and his body went stiff.

"Brother are you alright?" Erik asked.

Befel's eyes turned a bright white, void of any pupils, and his mouth began to move even though no words came out.

"Brother!" Erik yelled, running to Befel, but as soon as he touched him, his skin cold as ice, a force threw him back against the wall.

Erik blacked out for only a moment, but when he came to, his head throbbing and his back aching where he struck the wall, his brother—body still stiff and eyes still glowing white orbs—was speaking, but it wasn't his voice. It was a low, booming voice, one that shook the walls and caused the floor to move. He spoke a language Erik didn't recognize, but it sounded like Dwarvish.

"What is he saying?" Wrothgard asked, trying to yell over the din of Befel's possessed voice.

Balzarak shook his head, but then, as if something had also possessed Erik, he understood what his brother was saying. He said it over and over, the same phrase. Erik felt his heart stop and his stomach churn as he heard his brother's words. He looked around and, seemingly, no one else understood Befel. He began to voice the words, at first silently, but then louder and louder, until he shouted them in unison with Befel.

"Woe to those who enter here, for their fate will be met with blood and fire! Woe to those who enter here, for their fate will be met with blood and fire! Woe to those who enter here, for their fate will be met with blood and fire!"

Then, suddenly, Befel's voice stopped, and he collapsed. The hallways stood still, and the air suddenly tasted stale. The torches began to sputter. Erik could see the panic in his companions' eyes. Turk tried to wake Befel while Switch cursed and Demik began to pray.

"Woe to those who enter here, for their fate will be met with blood and fire," Erik said to himself, and then he heard them, in the distance, beyond the wall. The dead. Their laughing. Their hissing. He could smell them. Then he heard another voice, a bolder voice, one that cut through the chorus of the undead.

"Your chains of bondage are not made of iron, but of flame," the voice said, determined and emboldened with a hint of pleasure. "You cannot break the flame."

Just then the torchlight fluttered out, and complete darkness consumed Erik and his companions. He heard *them* coming.

Christopher Patterson lives in Tucson, Arizona with his wife, Kellie, and children. A Tucson native, Christopher studied literature and creative writing at the University of Arizona and currently teaches in Tucson. He gained a love for adventure and fantasy at a young age and started writing fantasy-adventure stories using his grandmother's typewriter. She would title all of his stories "The Next Great American Novel." His family has always been encouraging and supportive of his craft and it was in college when he discovered he desired a career as an author and began seriously writing. He has also played the guitar for over 20 years and is active in both the music and youth ministries at church. Christopher is also involved in sports, coaching both wrestling and football, and competing in power lifting.

Made in the USA
Coppell, TX
24 April 2020

22299237R00247